NAPOLEON

A remarkable figure in French public life, MAX GALLO is the author of eighty books – biographies, novels, historical novels, memoirs – which have sold in their hundreds of thousands. Formerly Professor of History at Nice University, he has been or continues to be an MEP, newspaper editor and éminence grise in the last French elections. He lives in Paris.

Also by Max Gallo in Macmillan

NAPOLEON: THE SONG OF DEPARTURE

NAPOLEON: THE EMPEROR OF KINGS

MAX GALLO

NAPOLEON

The Sun of Austerlitz

Translated from the French by William Hobson

PAN BOOKS

First published 2004 by Macmillan

This edition published 2004 by Pan Books
an imprint of Pan Macmillan Ltd
Pan Macmillan, 20 New Wharf Road, London N1 9RR
Basingstoke and Oxford
Associated companies throughout the world
www.panmacmillan.com

ISBN 0 330 49003 6

First published in French 1997 as *Napoléon: le soleil d'Austerlitz*
by Editions Robert Laffont, Paris

1 3 5 7 9 8 6 4 2

A CIP catalogue record for this book is available from
the British Library.

Typeset by SetSystems Ltd, Saffron Walden, Essex
Printed and bound in Great Britain by
Mackays of Chatham plc, Chatham, Kent

For Anne and Antoine Ottavi

My mistress is power. I have given too much to its conquest to let it be taken from me, or even suffer anyone to covet it.

Napoleon Bonaparte to Roederer, 4 November 1804

I am not a king. I do not want to be insulted by being called a king. People treat me like a royal monkey. Me a royal monkey? I am a soldier who has come from the people and risen by my own efforts. Can I be compared to Louis XVI?

Napoleon Bonaparte, 1 February 1801

PART ONE

Neither red cap nor red heel, I represent the nation

11 NOVEMBER 1799 (20 Brumaire Year VIII) TO 7 SEPTEMBER 1800

I

NAPOLEON IS THIRTY YEARS and four months old.

He hears the shouts of 'Long live Bonaparte! Long live peace!'

He goes up to the French windows that line one side of the drawing room in the rotunda, the largest room in his house in Paris. At the end of the garden, beyond the hedge, he can see the little crowd that has invaded the rue de la Victoire. It appeared the moment people learnt from newspapers and posters that yesterday, 19 Brumaire, he had been elected one of the three provisional consuls of the Republic, and that he had sworn an oath in the middle of the night before the deputies in the château of St Cloud.

Curious onlookers walk up and down the railings, hoping to catch a glimpse of Bonaparte and Josephine de Beauharnais, and mill around the carriage drawn by four black horses that stands in front of the gate. The horses of the escort of dragoons paw the ground and whinny, their nostrils veiled in steam which, after a few moments, merges into the fog. It is cold and damp, normal weather for the time of year, on 11 November 1799, 20 Brumaire Year VIII, a little after eleven o'clock in the morning.

Bourrienne, Bonaparte's secretary, opens the drawing-room door. The other two provisional consuls, Sieyès and Roger Ducos, are waiting at the Luxembourg Palace, which yesterday was the seat of the Directory, and today is that of the Consulate which has been born overnight.

Napoleon turns and faces the mirror hanging above the fireplace.

Twenty-five days ago he entered this room on his return from Egypt. It was dawn. The house was empty. Josephine wasn't there; he wanted to disown her. Now, here she is, in that long diaphanous tunic which shows off her body, leaning nonchalantly on the mantelpiece, beautifully made-up already, as she is at every moment of the day. A blue silk ribbon holds up the curls that frame her powdered face.

Twenty-five days have passed. He has given up the idea of divorce. He has not forgotten what he found out – that she had been frivolous and adulterous and had taken him for a fool – but in the preparations for 18 and 19 Brumaire she has been a useful ally and a tender and attentive wife.

Everything has indeed changed in these twenty-five days. On the morning of the 16th, the day of his return, he was only a general who had left his army abandoned in Egypt, and who, although he enjoyed public support, could be about to be accused of desertion and discharged by the government.

He has played his hand.

Yesterday, 10 November, in the *orangerie* at St Cloud, when the members of the Council of the Five Hundred rushed at him shouting, 'Outlaw! Death to the dictator! Outlaw!' he had thought for a few minutes that he was lost. He had started to panic. The marks of it are still there on his ashen face which, when he was surrounded by that yelling, menacing pack, he had clawed at with his fingernails, gouging open the spots dotting it and tearing at the dry skin until he drew blood.

The deputies had attacked a grenadier who stepped in to help him, but what in heaven's name could they have been hoping for, that band of lawyers who had violated the Constitution time and again, only now to invoke it as a sacred text? Last night he had castigated their attitude, their hatred, 'the savage cry of assassins raised against a force destined to crush them'. He had dictated the proclamation which Bourrienne has just brought him a copy of, in poster form, and which Fouché, the efficient Minister of Police, has had posted all over Paris.

Twenty-five days ago he was only a general with ambitions of power.

Yesterday afternoon, he was only a man under threat.

This morning, 20 Brumaire, he is one of the three provisional Consuls of the Republic.

One?

He must be the first of three. That is what must be decided this morning. That is his goal.

He heads towards the door. Josephine puts her arms around

him. He smiles and extricates himself. He is a different man to the one he was twenty-five days ago.

Victory is always a coronation.

HE STRIDES briskly across the garden with Bourrienne, but does not look at him as he thinks out loud.

'A new government needs to dazzle and amaze,' he says. 'The moment its splendour fades, it falls.'

Shouts ring out. He must have been seen from the street. He hears the alert shouted by an officer: 'The General-in-Chief, Consul of the Republic.'

That is what he is now.

Nothing has been said, but he knows he will be first of the three consuls. Who will dare challenge his ascendancy?

But then where will he steer? Towards what? Already this question haunts him. He does not know the answer. He must reflect, but he senses that whatever happens, he cannot stop; the only way he can keep his balance is by moving forwards.

He gets into the carriage; the shouting becomes twice as loud. 'A great reputation,' he says as the carriage moves off, 'is a great noise. The more noise one makes, the further it carries. Laws, institutions, monuments, nations – all these disappear – but the noise remains and echoes down through the generations.'

The horses have broken into a trot and Napoleon waves the dragoons of the escort away from the sides of the carriage. He wants to see and be seen. He can hear the shouts of 'Peace' in the distance as he leans out of the window. The streets are almost empty on this *décadi*, the day of rest.

'My power rests on my glory,' murmurs Napoleon as he leans back into the corner, 'and my glory on my victories. My power will vanish if I do not give it a foundation of greater glory and fresh victories.'

As they approach the Seine, in the faubourg St Honoré, the streets become more crowded. People are clustered around posters with titles in big black letters which he can read as he drives past:

PROCLAMATION OF GENERAL-IN-CHIEF BONAPARTE
19 Brumaire 11 o'clock in the evening

Fouché has performed his mission.

The carriage turns into the place de la Concorde and the horses break into a gallop. The fog has grown thicker, making the square look like a ruined, abandoned amphitheatre.

'Conquest has made me what I am,' Napoleon muses. 'Only conquest can preserve me.'

II

NAPOLEON WALKS THROUGH the galleries of the Luxembourg Palace to drum rolls as the guard salute his arrival. It is the inaugural session of the Consulate.

He knows this palace, he came here as an anonymous petitioner, but yesterday the man he used to solicit, Barras, became a man without power, fading into obscurity to work his way through the fortune he accumulated in the highest office of state. Only hours ago, Barras was one of the directors to whom everyone was answerable, whose orders everybody awaited in a fever of expectation. That time is over. He enters the room with frescoed ceilings. Sieyès and Roger Ducos are standing waiting for him.

These two men share power with him. Ducos is a cipher, with just a walk-on part, but Sieyès is a skilful strategist, a man of ideas, a figure of the Revolution. He is the one to be reckoned with. Napoleon observes him. Sieyès seems old, without any real energy. If it came to a fight between the two of them, Sieyès couldn't win, he must know that, but, as in the last twenty-five days, he will still try to lay traps and use all the weapons of his political skill.

Perhaps he thinks that one can box in a man like me with a jurist's quibbling and articles of the Constitution.

Sieyès pulls the doors to and carefully checks that they are shut.

'There is absolutely no need to vote on the Presidency,' Ducos says as he sits down. 'It is yours by right, General.'

Napoleon looks at Sieyès, who says nothing but his face tenses too obviously for him to be able to hide it. Napoleon takes his seat in the armchair in the middle, and then declares that he refuses to accept a permanent presidency. He knows he must wait and let Sieyès expose himself. It is only provisional, this period starting now. When the new Constitution is drawn up, that is when everyone's positions will be decided definitively.

If Sieyès thinks he can bury me with honours, he is mistaken.

Sieyès has stood up. He is checking the doors are shut again. Then he points to a chest of drawers.

'You see this beautiful piece of furniture,' he says to Napoleon. 'You probably have no idea how much it is worth.' At the end of their term of office, the directors planned to divide up a sum of money that is hidden in the chest of drawers. 'Now there are no more directors. So we are the owners of what's left. What shall we do with it?'

Ah, he's as greedy as Barras, this fellow. People who crave gold want power for the riches it brings them. So one only needs to glut them with gold and they will abandon their power, since it is not their genuine passion.

'I did not know this money existed,' Napoleon says, looking away, 'so you and Ducos can share it out amongst yourselves – you're former directors – but hurry, because tomorrow it will be too late.'

They open the chest of drawers, and, after a while, start whispering and arguing about how to divide up the eight hundred thousand francs they have counted out. They ask Napoleon to arbitrate.

'Settle it amongst yourselves,' he says. 'If I get wind of it, you'll have to give it all up.'

They fall silent and look at one another. Sieyès has taken six hundred thousand francs for himself.

Yet the treasury hasn't enough to pay couriers to take dispatches to the provinces or to General Championnet, Commander-in-Chief of the Army of Italy! How can that be?

NAPOLEON CONSULTS former ministers, examines the files. The army is not being paid or fed or clothed. He summons a former higher civil servant under the monarchy, Gaudin, who is also Sieyès's candidate for minister of finance. The man seems efficient and discreet. 'Have you worked in finance for a long time?' Napoleon asks him.

'For twenty years, General.'

'We need your assistance, I am counting on it. Go and take an oath. We are in a hurry.'

He feels the same sense of urgency all that day and appoints ministers at the double. Talleyrand returns to Foreign Affairs, Laplace, the scholar who examined him at Military School, becomes minister of the interior, but the main thing is the work of the commissions which have been set up to write the new Constitution.

Sieyès has a clever plan which involves a grand elector for life at the top of a pyramid of assemblies – a Senate, Legislative Corps and Tribunate. He will be a figure without real power elected by politicians, thereby creating the appearance of universal suffrage when in fact the people who elect him will themselves be appointed from above.

Napoleon quickly familiarizes himself with Sieyès's projects. He is not averse to rendering universal suffrage an illusion in this way. Trust should come from below, authority from above – and anyway, what is that, the people?

He questions the ideologues and thinkers who dream of an enlightened despotism at the receptions he gives at the Little Luxembourg, where he has installed himself with Josephine. He listens to Cabanis, who tells him, 'The ignorant classes must no longer exercise their influence on the legislature or the government. Everything must be done for the people and in the name of the people, but nothing must be done *by* them or under their thoughtless dictation.'

He appoints commissions which work directly with him. Then, one evening, Roederer comes up and whispers a proposition that Sieyès has for him: this post of grand elector for life he has come up with – would Napoleon take it?

Don't react, listen.

'It would carry,' Roederer continues, 'an income of six million and a guard of three thousand. The grand elector would take up residence in Versailles and his job would be to appoint the two consuls.'

So here it is, the trap. Might as well write off anyone who accepts that office without power.

'Am I hearing you correctly, Roederer? I am being offered a position where I will appoint all those who have something to do and where I will be unable to take a part in anything . . .' He moves away from Roederer, raising his voice so that the members of the commission can hear. 'The grand elector,' he continues, 'will be a shadow, an utterly disembodied shadow of a shiftless king. Do you know a man whose character is so base that he could take pleasure in such a monkey trick? I will not play a ridiculous role. I'd rather play none at all than be ridiculous.'

WHEN SIEYÈS appears before the commission, Napoleon instantly challenges him warmly: 'How could you have thought, Citizen Sieyès, that a man of honour, a man of talent and some capability in public affairs, would ever agree to being nothing but a pig put out to graze on a few million in Versailles?'

'So you want to be king,' murmurs Sieyès, but already he speaks like a bitter, defeated man. He has exposed himself. He has lost.

Now Napoleon must lead the charge, day after day, night after night: he inspires, steers, fires up the meetings of the commissions. He overcomes resistance. He convinces the doubtful, confounds the antagonistic.

He watches Sieyès as, little by little, he loses interest.

They submit it to the vote: to the three assemblies will be added a Council of State and, at the top of the edifice, a first consul, who will be the corner stone of the executive, elected for ten years and overriding the two other consuls, who are only present in an advisory capacity. Cleverly, and ironically, Napoleon turns to Sieyès and calmly asks him to put forward his candidates for the three Consuls.

Sieyès hesitates, and then wearily says the names Napoleon expects: Napoleon Bonaparte, Cambacérès – who voted for a suspended death penalty for the king – and Lebrun, an associate of the royalists.

Napoleon is pleased with this choice. 'Neither red cap nor red heel, I represent the nation,' he says. 'I like decent people of every stripe.'

The Constitution will be submitted to the popular vote. Napoleon dictates the preface: 'Citizens, the revolution is hereby established on the principles with which it began. IT IS FINISHED.'

IT IS THE END of the year 1799, the end of the century. Napoleon is in his thirtieth year. He is entering the nineteenth century as a conqueror.

He does not remember his reversals, the fruitless assaults on

St Jean d'Acre. He feels as if it is enough for him doggedly to want something for him to be able to get it. Does that mean the men who have opposed him have been short of intelligence or will or courage? He observes them, those servile, greedy courtiers. He gives instructions for Sieyès to be granted national land, the Crosnes estate, as a 'reward from the nation'. Cambacérès? 'Of anybody, he is the man most likely to bestow gravity on baseness.' Talleyrand, the former Bishop of Autun? 'I know the only thing that ties him to the Revolution is his misconduct. Jacobin and deserter of his order in the Constituent Assembly, his interest will answer for him for our purposes.'

With a fixed stare, Napoleon listens to Talleyrand repeating, 'I only want to work with you. That is no vain pride on my part. I speak only in France's interest.'

How could I not dominate this swarming mass of men?

EVERYONE FLOCKS to the receptions he gives as First Consul in the rooms of the Luxembourg Palace. They vie for a look during performances at the Opera. When he is alone with Josephine she tells him what they are saying in the salons. Has he heard the poem Parisians are whispering amongst themselves? He listens to her.

Sieyès gave Bonaparte a sumptuous throne
Thinking to bury him under a pompous charade
Bonaparte gave Sieyès the estate of Crosnes
Him to demean and degrade

She laughs. Does he know that people are also saying that Cambacérès and Lebrun, the other two consuls, are like the two arms of his armchair?

She wants to lead him off to the bedroom, but he leaves her. He must think.

In his study, he reads the police reports. Public opinion is enthusiastic. In one theatre, when one of the actors was eulogizing a character in the play, 'By his courage, he has saved us all from death and pillage,' the spectators stood up and applauded for a long time, some of them crying, 'Long live the first consul!'

He must maintain and nurture this mood.

ONE MORNING, when he comes back slightly intoxicated by the cheering that has accompanied him all the way through Paris, Roederer tentatively reminds him, 'The acclaim you are witnessing is nothing compared to that La Fayette inspired in 1789 and 1790.' A few months after which, La Fayette was forced into exile.

A victory must always be exploited and consolidated.

On 16 January 1800, he summons a secret council. They have to talk about newspapers, he says; they form the opinions of thousands of people.

'What is a newspaper?' he asks. 'It is a dispersed club. A newspaper influences its subscribers the way a club demagogue influences his audience.' What would be the point of banning speeches, which only affect hundreds of people, if daily newspapers can be sold which influence a hundred times more? Intractable newspapers must be suppressed, he argues. Editors must be 'party men'. The council agrees and drafts a decree which suppresses sixty out of seventy-three newspapers.

As he is leaving, he takes Bourrienne by the arm and murmurs, 'If I give the press free rein, I shall not be in power for three months!' Then what would be the point of all the battles he has fought? What would be the good of having won?

OFTEN WHEN they entertain at the Luxembourg or Malmaison and Josephine moves amongst the guests, polished and attentive to all, whether regicides or émigrés, he listens to stories from the Revolution and realizes that he only experienced a few episodes of it. For most of those ten years, from 1789 to 1799, he lived outside France. What he hears confirms him in his belief that, if he wants to underpin his power, he must be the one who incarnates a return to order, security and peace after the decade of revolution. When he hears that Washington has died on 14 December 1799, he siezes the opportunity. 'When I die,' he says to Talleyrand, 'I want a period of national mourning for ten days, and a state cremation at the Temple of Mars [the former Church of the Invalides].' In the public mind, he must become his country's Washington, the one who reunites the people. Jacobins? Émigrés? 'I make use of all those who have the ability to march with me . . . Places will be open to Frenchmen of every opinion, as long as they have intelligence, talent and courage.'

He knows repressive measures and proscriptions are not enough; he has to win people over as well, captivate them. He writes to General Jourdan, 'Were you affronted by the proceedings of 19 Brumaire? Now the first moments are over and I desire most earnestly to see the victor of Fleurus embark upon the road that leads to organization, true liberty and happiness.' To a member of the Five Hundred who was proscribed after 18 Brumaire, he says, 'Join me, mine will be the government of youth and lively intellect.'

It would be so simple if the country had the unity and discipline of an army. That is his firm belief, and also the reason why he is so skilful. 'The simple title of French citizen is undoubtedly worth that of royalist, Clichien, Jacobin, Feuillant or any of the other thousand-and-one denominations engendered by the spirit of faction which for the last ten years have sought to hurl the nation into that abyss from which at last the time has come to rescue it, once and for all.'

He knows that Josephine sees émigrés' relatives every day who are petitioning to have their names struck off the list which was closed on 25 December 1799. To be able to return to France after that date, an émigré must have his or her name removed. He is aware of the overtures she makes to the various ministries. She is spinning a web for him that stretches a long way, to families such as the Montmorency, the de Ségur and the Clermont-Tonnerre. Let her continue receiving them every morning in her salon. People say she is a royalist, do they? No matter. He holds the reins of the country, and he is not afraid of any criticism 'anarchists' or 'exclusives', those implacable Jacobins, may level at him. Their time has passed, he thinks. France has been through the Committee of Public Safety, the *enragés*, Robespierre. It may be useful to brandish every now and again, but the Jacobin threat is only a spectre.

THE ROYALIST threat is the serious one.

The Chouans are still fighting in Vendée. He promises them an amnesty if they lay down their arms. He allows mass to be celebrated on Sundays, even though it is a day that has been removed from the calendar since the *décadi* replaced it. How else should one treat royalists except as other men? Captivate them, buy them, threaten them and crush them. When Talleyrand announces in the middle of December that Hyde de Neuville, a royalist living in Paris, and Fortuné d'Andigné, one of the Chouan leaders, want to meet him, why should he hesitate to grant their request?

Talleyrand shows the two men in with his typical, ancien régime courtesy; Napoleon is polite and understanding. He sees surprise in d'Andigné and de Neuville's eyes. The two men have the well-groomed appearance of aristocrats, whereas he has purposefully chosen to dress carelessly in a greenish tunic. After a few minutes he brings his mordant irony, and cynicism to bear.

'You are always talking to me about the king. Are you royalists?' He is amazed. How can one follow a prince who has not had the courage to get in a fisherman's boat and go and join his loyal followers fighting in his name? What is the worth of a king who has never drawn his sword? 'But then I am not a royalist,' he concludes.

He walks over to the fireplace, and then swings round towards d'Andigné. 'What do you want to be?' he asks. 'Do you want to be a general? A prefect? You and your men will be whatever you want to be.'

Once the hook is baited, one must wait, but these two men don't seem tempted. He must flatter them, tell them he understands their struggle, say he is prepared to restore religious freedom.

'I want good priests too. I will re-establish the clergy. Not for your sake, but for mine . . .' He glances at Hyde de Neuville, who looks slyer than d'Andigné. He must try and create a sense of complicity between them. 'It is not that nobles such as us are particularly religious, but the people need it.'

They stay silent. One must threaten them, then.

'If you do not make peace, I will march on you with a hundred thousand men. I will set fire to your towns; I will burn your cottages.'

He stops and changes tone. 'Too much French blood has been spilled in the last ten years.' He turns his back. The audience is over.

Now, since persuasion and threats have not succeeded, he must take action. He must demand the rebels' surrender.

'Those that remain in arms against France can only be men without faith or country, treacherous instruments of a hostile foreign power.' He must send reinforcements to back up these words.

IN JANUARY 1800 the surrenders begin, and in February one of the Chouans' most determined leaders, Georges Cadoudal, gives up the struggle.

Napoleon does not show any joy, as if he knows that his work has no end. He needs to organize the administration of the departments, see bankers, obtain a loan of three million. He needs to take the armies in hand again, flatter the generals, keep an eye on Augereau and especially Moreau, the cleverest and proudest of them all. He should write to him, intimating that of the two of them, Moreau is having the better time: 'These days I am a sort of puppet that has lost its freedom and happiness. I envy you your good fortune: you go and do fine things with brave men. I would gladly exchange my consular purple for a brigade-major's epaulette under my command.'

Moreau probably won't be fooled; these are only cunning words, the sort of thing a fox says to a crow.

In his study on the ground floor where he saw Hyde de Neuville and d'Andigné – and where Fouché has reported that General Moreau is suspected of having royalist connections, perhaps even with Georges Cadoudal – Napoleon has a sense of emptiness. He feels nostalgic for the intensity of the eve of a battle, for the way men fuse together, soldiers and officers alike, and feel they are an invincible force as they sweep forward and charge as one. He would like to feel that again. He has been searching for this emotion in vain since becoming first consul because, in the administration of men and organization of things demanded by his position, 'fusion' is merely a mirage that one chases after.

So, he often returns to military questions. In any case, who can seriously think that peace is going to be secured without new victories? 'Long live Bonaparte! Long live peace!' they shout whenever he passes, and each time he hears the crowd shouting like that, Napoleon tenses. That is what they want! And so does he! But without illusions.

He has written to the King of Prussia, Frederick William III, who is not an enemy, assuring him of his 'sincere wishes for Your Majesty's prosperity and glory'.

He has written to the Emperor of Austria, Francis II, 'Being foreign to every sentiment of vain glory, the first of my desires is to prevent the shedding of blood.'

He has written to George III, King of England, 'Must the war which for eight years has ravaged the four corners of the world be eternal? Is there no way to understand one another? By abusing their powers France and England can carry on for a long time avoiding exhaustion, to the wretchedness of all; but I dare to say that the fate of all civilized nations depends on an end to a war that is setting fire to the whole world.'

PEACE!

He puts on his desk dispatches from the network of agents Talleyrand and Fouché are running both in Europe and in Paris's royalist circles. In London and Vienna his desire for peace is treated as a joke. Pitt claims the surest way to achieve that would be to restore the monarchy in Paris, adding that the First Consul is 'the son and champion of all the atrocities of the Revolution'!

So what should he do?

Reorganize the army, create a reserve army which can move rapidly from one front to another and, above all, think of the soldiers, because everything depends on them. Victory is only possible if they agree to die. For that they must believe in their leader, who they see at their side, and they must be rewarded when they perform exploits of valour. Napoleon creates honours – muskets, trumpets, honorary batons – for the grenadiers, cavalry and drummers. He is furious when a member of the Institute speaks derisively of these 'baubles of vanity'.

'It is with baubles that men are led,' he replies. 'Do you think you could make men fight by analytical argument? Never. That is only good for the scholar in his study. The soldier must have glory, honours, and rewards.'

Josephine has given lunch to the two grenadiers who stepped in and protected Napoleon from the deputies of the Five Hundred at the palace of St Cloud, on 19 Brumaire. At the end of the meal, she slipped onto the finger of the one whose uniform was slashed by daggers, Private Thomé, a diamond worth two thousand écus! And she kissed him.

That is how one must treat men. Reward and flatter them.

The Consular Guard has new, richly coloured and brocaded uniforms; they are commanded by Murat who has just married Caroline Bonaparte, and it is they who parade on the day the results of the referendum on the Constitution are declared: 3,011,007 citizens in favour, 1,562 against. In some places there were so many abstentions that the ballot boxes had to be stuffed with Ayes. This is how one governs!

He tells Bourrienne, who reports these figures to him, 'One must appeal to the eye, it does the people good.' Stepping up to the window and looking out at the gardens around the Luxembourg, he adds, 'Simplicity has its place in the army, but in a great city, the head of a government must draw attention to himself by all means possible.' He has made his decision: he will move into the Tuileries.

On 19 February 1800, a procession of carriages sets out from the Luxembourg Palace to go to the Tuileries, which has been renovated. The artillery salvoes ring out. Three thousand men, a regimental band, a towering drum-major juggling his cane, and a troop of cavalry precede the Consul's coach which is drawn by six white horses, a gift from the Emperor of Austria at the signing of the Treaty of Campo Formio. Napoleon is wearing a red uniform with gold braid.

The route along the embankments of the Seine to the wicket gate of the Louvre is lined with vast crowds, shouting, 'Long live Bonaparte!' On the place du Carrousel, the troops are drawn up in rows and Napoleon mounts a horse to review them. He lifts his head and sees inscribed on one of the guardhouses built during the Revolution: '10 August 1792, the monarchy in France was abolished and will never rise again.'

He gives the signal for the march-past to begin and as the demi-brigades with torn flags pass in front of him, he doffs his hat. The crowds covering every part of the square, some even perched on the rooftops, erupt into cheers.

Then he enters the Tuileries Palace. He goes up to the first floor, which he has decided will be his, into what were the apartments of Louis XVI and his family. Josephine will be on the ground floor.

He and Roederer walk through the rooms. They are enormous and funereal.

'They are melancholy, sir,' says Roederer.

'Yes, like glory.'

Napoleon turns his back on him and walks away. Once again, he has a sense of emptiness. He goes into Josephine's room and feels a flash of merriment, at the sight of her standing at the foot of the bed.

'Come on, my little Creole, into your master's bed!' he calls jokingly, but Josephine does not smile. She wants to talk. He stops her. He does not need to hear about her fears when she thinks about the monarchy; he does not want to be told about her forebodings. He is here, in the Tuileries, in these same rooms which he walked through on 10 August 1792, when they were full of a frenzied rabble.

That was less than eight years ago.

EARLY THE NEXT morning he goes to the Diana Gallery which he has had lined with the busts of the great men he most admires – from Demosthenes to Brutus, Caesar to Washington, Frederick II to Mirabeau. He walks slowly, stopping in front of each face, and he remembers the previous day's procession, the crowds' wild cheering when he bared his head in front of the flags.

'The people's joy was genuine,' he tells Bourrienne who is at his side. 'Besides, look at the best thermometer of public opinion, the value of stocks: eleven francs on 17 Brumaire, now twenty-one! At this rate, I can let the Jacobins prattle on. So long as they don't talk too loud.'

He retraces his steps and stops in front of the bust of Alexander, then Hannibal and again in front of Caesar.

'Bourrienne, being in the Tuileries is not everything. Now we must stay here.' He looks out at the place du Carrousel and again sees the inscription celebrating 10 August. 'Who hasn't lived in this palace?' he murmurs. 'Brigands, members of the Convention.' He stretches out his arm. Over there is the window of Bourrienne's brother's house, from where he saw the Tuileries being besieged and the capitulation of Louis XVI.

'Let them come!' he cries.

III

TOWARDS NOON, AFTER reading the police reports, answering his correspondence and dictating directives and other instructions, he goes to the topographical office which is reserved for maps. He wants to know the movements of all the armies and their supply lines. The English and Austrian spies must believe that the reserve army at Dijon is only a decoy designed to make them think that a field force is being formed. So there must be a great deal of emphatic talk about it, to confirm their belief that it is propaganda, whilst he continues to assemble it. He has said nothing of this to the other two consuls, or to the council of state, which he has attended. Cambacérès, who does not like the assemblies, is afraid that the council of state will grow too important or become a seat of opposition. He definitely does not know men, even if he does like them young and well-built. But it is true, it is their bodies more than their minds that he is attracted to.

To subjugate men, it is enough to spoil them. The saying's a valid one, isn't it? 'I will treat those men I have put into the council of state so well that in no time this distinction will become the ambition of all men of talent who wish to make their way.'

NAPOLEON LIKES the middle of the night. Time seems to expand. In the silence and darkness that enfold his apartments he feels as if the hand that has been squeezing him since dawn has relaxed its grip.

He gets into the bath and lies down, and his Mameluke puts more logs on the fire. He needs this heat. All day he tries to shake off a feeling of cold that seeps into him. When he goes outside, he is chilled and pulls the lapels of his grey woollen frock coat together. Perhaps it is his thinness that makes it hard for him to resist the cold. That morning in his study his teeth were chattering when he was getting ready to listen to articles from the English and German press. The French papers hardly matter. Sometimes he dictates their articles himself. He had interrupted Bourrienne for a moment and exclaimed, 'I am cold. You see how sober and thin I am. Well, nothing will rid me of the idea that at forty I will become a great eater and put on lots of weight. I sense that my constitution will change and yet I take plenty of exercise. But what can you do? It is a foreboding, it is bound to happen.'

He shuts his eyes and immerses himself in the hot water. All his muscles gradually relax, even his right shoulder which tenses when he feels angry or agitated, and shoots up in a sort of nervous twitch which he cannot control. The water also soothes the smarting, itchy skin that often afflicts him in the daytime. Sometimes all it takes for it to flare up is a piece of correspondence from abroad, with another instance of Pitt's or the Austrians' stubbornness, or a dispatch from General Moreau deploring, in the name of prudence, the plan to attack through Switzerland and hence outflank the Austrians, and intending instead to cross the Rhine frontally. But he must not criticize or break with Moreau, not yet. His reputation is too established. He is in touch with too many officers. When one is dealing with those who have power over armed men, caution is the rule.

There are still some babblers in the Tribunate, deputies who say, 'Within these walls, if someone should dare speak of an idol of fifteen days, we will remind them that we have seen the fall of an idol of fifteen centuries,' or, like Benjamin Constant, who speak of a 'regime of servitude and silence'. The memory of these words, though they were quickly drowned out by protests and their authors' apologies, is enough to shatter the calm that has gradually been building up in him.

'I am going to cut off those lawyers' ears,' he tells the aide-de-camp, but then restrains himself. This is not the way to act.

He gets out of the bath and his Mameluke dries him, with the help of two young Abyssinians who also serve him at table. He will go downstairs and see Josephine.

He must talk to her about money, the insane debts she has been running up on her jewels, her finery, her hats, her furniture, her *objets d'art*. She is good at entertaining, it is true. He approves of Malmaison, the property near Rueil which she has bought and elegantly done up. He spends weekends there, from noon on

Saturday to noon on Monday. They are usually at least twenty at every meal, and sometimes there are over a hundred guests. However, he has learnt from police reports and Bourrienne and gossip that Josephine owes more than a million francs, perhaps even double that! He must get Bourrienne to settle her debts, with six hundred thousand francs – he can threaten her creditors, if need be; they're bound to have exaggerated her bills – but once they have been paid, Josephine will start spending again, he is sure. He needs money for her and for the future. Besides, what would be the sense of being in power and lacking money? Power is money too.

The first consul's salary is five hundred thousand francs; the other two consuls are only entitled to one hundred and fifty thousand; and then there is an expenditure allowance for the 'consular household' to the tune of six hundred thousand francs. When a uniform – coat and breeches – only costs thirty-two francs, a horse three francs and a day's wages are between one and two francs, the fact that a major-general is paid forty thousand francs may seem exorbitant, but there can be no equality between men who command and those who obey.

Am I to be the only one not to enjoy a fortune when everyone else has made themselves rich?

Of his family, Lucien, the minister of the interior, is embroiled in so many questionable financial undertakings and is the object of so many rumours that he is going to have to send him away. Joseph, who is a member of the council of state and in charge of the family's affairs, has taken up residence in the sumptuous château and estate of Mortefontaine – Murat and Caroline were married there – and also has an elegant townhouse built by Gabriel in rue du Rocher. Pauline and her husband, General Leclerc, have moved into a house on rue de la Victoire. Letizia Bonaparte, his mother, is always surrounded by financiers giving her advice about her investments.

They are my family; this is what I owe them. It is the nature of things, just like poverty and destitution. Intelligence and stupidity. The right to command and the duty to obey. Is that an aristocrat's way of thinking? Well, what is wrong with that? So long as the nobility is open to talent and one can join the elite by effort, courage and knowledge. There must be a fusion – that is my word for it – between the France of before, that of the ancien régime, and the new France, the one born of the Revolution. And I am this fusion, I represent the nation.

IT IS 25 FEBRUARY, at Talleyrand's country house in Neuilly. Napoleon, thin, eyes glinting, moves among the throng of aristocrats from the faubourg St Germain whom the former Bishop of Autun, the minister of foreign affairs, has gathered for a lavish party. Laharpe, the critic and translator, recites poetry; Garat, the former leader of the *Incroyables*, the royalist dandies, sings, accompanied by Madame Walbonne, the most fashionable singer of the moment. The rooms are lit by hundreds of candles. The gold and silver gleam. Napoleon recognizes relatives of the late Louis XVI, Barbé-Marbois, the chevalier de Coigny, La Rochefoucauld-Liancourt and even Abbé Bernier, who is negotiating with the Chouans to try to secure their surrender.

THESE ROYALISTS mustn't labour under any illusions! They are the ones coming over to the government's side, not the government coming over to them!

When Frotté, one of the Chouan leaders, falls into the hands of General Brune's men, his safe conduct offers him no protection. 'That wretched Frotté,' writes Napoleon. 'He has preferred capture to laying down his arms.'

His hand does not hesitate as he writes, 'He should be shot immediately. In this manner the tranquillity of former Normandy will be much strengthened.'

Almost every day five or six Chouans are executed: the iron fist for those who will not submit, especially because Fouché reports that attacks and kidnappings are planned on the road to Malmaison.

This is not the moment of my death.

In the evening Napoleon often goes out walking through the streets of Paris, just with Bourrienne, in his grey frock coat and with a round hat pulled down on his brow. He makes small purchases and talks to people as if he were an ordinary citizen, critical of the first consul. The responses he gets give him pleasure.

One evening in March he goes to the Italian Theatre without

his carriage. *The Sabine Women* is being performed. The consular guard is there, armed. As if he were just an ordinary passer-by, he asks why all these troops are out.

'That's a big to-do about nothing,' he says, when he is told they are waiting for the first consul, and only reveals who is when someone cries, 'That man should be arrested.'

He is not afraid for his life.

In one of the reception rooms in the Tuileries, he receives Georges Cadoudal, a giant figure of a man, a royalist and implacable fighter for the Chouan cause. It is their second interview, but this time they are alone, whereas their first meeting was with other Vendéean leaders whom he hoped to win over. Cadoudal? A coarse Breton, a fanatic, he thinks, perfectly capable of strangling him or blowing his brains out – but he wants to lure him, disarm him and, why not, make him a general. That would be better than carrying on with this Vendéean dagger buried up to the hilt in the country's side as the Austrian armies mass on the Danube and march towards Italy and the Rhine.

Cadoudal appears furious, pacing up and down the room. Napoleon's aides-de-camp have left the door ajar, to come running at any sign of danger. But why should he be afraid of this giant? The lion tamer should mistrust the lion, not tremble before him. He must touch every nerve to see if the man is hungry for power, or blinded by passion.

No, it is as he thought – an irreparable enemy. So be it. 'You take a wrong view of things,' concludes Napoleon, 'and you are mistaken in not wanting to hear of an agreement. But . . .'

He must still leave an opening.

'But,' continues Napoleon, 'if you insist on returning to your country, you will be as free to go as you were to come to Paris.'

Fouché can follow the man, keep these royalists under surveillance and stifle the plots they are hatching with the English.

To assassinate me? Or attempt to make me restore the king?

Every day Josephine and her daughter Hortense talk to him about émigrés. They are still helping a whole host of people who want to be struck off the list.

'Those women are mad!' Napoleon says heatedly. 'The faubourg St Germain has turned their heads; they have become the royalists' guardian angels. Still, it doesn't matter; I don't hold it against them.'

One day in March, Talleyrand hands him a letter he has received which has been delivered, he says, by hand. He shows no indignation, only smiling indifference.

Napoleon unseals the letter and glances through it. It is signed Louis XVIII. He feels a surge of pride. He's the one who is in the Tuileries Palace, and the king is in exile. The king entreats and flatters him like a courtier. 'Whatever their apparent conduct,' he writes, 'men such as you, sir, never inspire anxiety.'

Napoleon lifts his head and looks at Talleyrand. Has he read this letter, despite the seals? Does he know its contents?

'You have accepted an eminent office, and I am grateful to you for doing so,' continues Louis XVI's brother. 'You know better than anyone the strength and power that are needed to secure the happiness of a great nation.'

Napoleon takes in the following lines at a glance. 'Save France from her own rages and you will answer the foremost wish of my heart. Restore her king to her and future generations will bless your memory. You will always be too necessary to the State for me ever to be able to discharge, by important appointments, the debt of my family and myself.'

Napoleon wants to smile. Why should he give up his position to become the second-in-command of a king whose only weapon is a fallen dynasty's history?

He hands the letter to Talleyrand. He may answer, but not now. Now he must wage war in order to bring peace.

IT IS 17 MARCH, and the map of Italy is unrolled in the topographical office, which is next to his study. He kneels, almost lies on it, studying every detail and sticking in pins with black and red heads.

The Austrian general, Melas, has set up his headquarters in Alexandria. He is besieging Genoa where Masséna is holding out. With his finger, Napoleon traces a line on the map between several pins. They must cross the Alps with the reserve army assembled in Dijon by the Great St Bernard Pass, he says, and then fight Melas in the plains, 'Here, at San Giuliano.'

Bourrienne bends down and reads the name of a nearby city: Marengo.

They must act fast. Time is short enough as it is. They must take advantage of Masséna's resistance in Genoa and the victories of General Moreau who has just crossed the Rhine, although with excessive caution.

ON 5 MAY, as he walks round his study, Napoleon dictates a letter for Moreau to his secretary whose desk is placed against the window.

> I was starting for Geneva when the telegraph brought news of your victory over the Austrian army. Glory, and three times more glory!
>
> The position of the Army of Italy is critical. Hemmed in in Genoa, Masséna has provisions that will last until the 5 or 6 Prairial. Although much weakened, Melas's army seems considerable.
>
> With my affectionate greetings,
>
> Bonaparte.

He gives his final orders. It will be a new challenge: if he brings it off, his power will be consolidated, but leaving Paris will allow the teeming ambitions there to run rife. If he is defeated . . .

He sends for Joseph and entrusts him with the management of his finances during the campaign. Joseph starts to say something. He would like . . .

He has to interrupt him. Is there anyone who does not know what Joseph would like? To be his appointed successor. It is too soon.

Fouché enters his study in turn, speaks of the English plot and then reports on a Jacobin conspiracy which he has broken up. Paris will be calm in his absence, he assures him.

How can these men be trusted, who for ten years have survived by desertions, reversals, betrayal and cowardice? They are loyal only to the victor. Once again everything depends on the fate of war. So everything depends on me and Fortune.

ON THE evening of 5 May, Napoleon goes to the Opera, and the bulletin announcing Moreau's victory at Stockach is read out. The spectators get to their feet and applaud for a long time. Napoleon leaves soon afterwards.

At two o'clock in the morning, 6 May, he gets into the post-chaise that will take him to Dijon, where the reserve army awaits him.

IV

THE ROAD IS DESERTED as they speed towards Sens and Avallon. The window is open, and Napoleon often leans out. He loves the air with its smells of the forest. The weather is mild and the light soft as it falls through the pale green leaves. Bourrienne and Duroc, who are sitting opposite him, have tried to give him letters to read or sign, but he has waved them away. The start of a journey is a time for reverie. He looks at the cultivated fields, the villages, the rides that stretch away through the forests of Fontainebleau, and when they enter Sens, where they are going to dine at Bourrienne's house, he gazes at the majesty and power of the cathedral, the solid beauty of its bourgeois residences.

'Beautiful France,' he says.

During the meal, which lasts barely half an hour, he repeats, 'Ah, beautiful France, how much pleasure it will give me to see it again.'

Then they set off in bright, almost hot, sunshine for Avallon, where they are to spend the night. 'The sun that shines on us is the same as the one that shone on us at Lodi and Arcola,' he murmurs.

Italy, land of his first victories. How could he fail to do better than then? 'Four years ago, didn't I drive hordes of Sardinians and Austrians before me with a feeble army?' He dozes as it grows dark. He is like Alexander who gave everything to Greece, he says in a low voice, just as he gives everything to France. 'Though he died at thirty-three, what a name he has left behind him!' Napoleon has conquered Milan, Cairo and Paris. He is the First Consul, but what would posterity remember of him if he were beaten tomorrow in Italy?

In Avallon, which they reach at seven thirty, he goes through his mail until almost midnight, gives his orders for the following stages and then sets off for Dijon at dawn. The roads are choked with troops marching to the town. The soldiers recognize him and start cheering.

At Dijon, he speaks to the men and then presses on to Auxonne. He feels as if he is revisiting his past as a second lieutenant: figures from back then step forward; he visits the directorate of artillery. 'This is a room where I've played a game or two of lotto!' So few years have passed since then and so much has happened; he feels dizzy and makes haste to leave.

As they climb towards the Jura plateaux, the night grows colder and denser. They overtake columns of troops on the march. In Morez all the houses are lit up. How can he ignore the mayor who, when his carriage stops in the square, exclaims, 'Citizen First Consul, do us the pleasure of showing yourself!' A little crowd has gathered and it repeats, 'Bonaparte, show yourself to the good inhabitants of the Jura! Is it really you? Are you bringing us peace?'

Answer, 'Yes, yes,' and continue on my way.

HE IS IN Geneva on 10 May and there meets Necker. So this is the man who held a share of the power in France in 1789! Napoleon observes him, listens to him talk. Is this all he was? An ideologue, a banker. How could men like that have saved the monarchy?

How far can I go, I who am of a different calibre?

He feels bolstered in his ambitions and certainties.

When the interview is over, he spells out his orders: General Lannes is to start on the Great St Bernard Pass and take Fort Bard, on the other side, in the Dora Baltea valley, then the fortress of Ivrea beyond that. The pass must be crossed before 15 May.

He has made his choice. Now to take up the challenge.

The pass is 2,472 metres high and snow fell only a few days ago. The paths are narrow and run alongside precipices and glaciers; the guns have to be dismounted, put on sledges and pulled up by ropes – but, if the army can get across, they will fall like Hannibal on the rear of the Austrian General Melas, who is still immobilized by Genoa's resistance, and Piedmont, including Milan, will be taken.

He needs to write to General Moreau, requesting he block the rest of the Alpine passes with fifteen thousand men, but as he does so, his hand hesitates. How can he accept depending on someone like Moreau whose jealousy and ambiguity he suspects? How can one admit that one has to put oneself in his hands? A leader needs subordinates who will carry out his orders promptly and devotedly, not prominent figures who think of their own interests. Nonetheless, he writes, 'If the manoeuvre is executed promptly and decisively and is close to your heart, Italy and peace are ours. But no doubt I have already laboured the point. Your zeal for the prosperity of the Republic and your friendship for me will speak to you enough.'

NAPOLEON REACHES Martigny on 20 May. With bands playing and drummers beating the charge at the hardest parts, Lannes's troops have crossed the pass in fog and snow, tearing their shoes on the icy ground and nibbling on the biscuits which hang round their necks in garlands. However, Lannes says the fortress of Bard is impregnable, built on a peak dominating a valley. They will have to work their way round it, and there's a danger it will threaten the advance of the troops with its cannon.

At eight o'clock, his hat covered with oilskin, wearing a grey greatcoat, white breeches and waistcoat and a blue coat, Napoleon mounts his horse. He is carrying a sword and a whip and rides as far as the village of St Pierre. A guide leads forward the mule on which he will cross the pass. The sky is overcast.

The mule climbs so slowly; time is so precious. What is happening in Paris? How many days will Masséna hold out in Genoa? And this fortress of Bard – will he have to leave it as a threat in his rear?

The mule's hooves have slipped. Napoleon is careering towards the Dranse gorge. The guide grabs hold of him.

Death has brushed me again.

Here is the hospice, with its tall arches, its sombre grey stone, its morgue where the desiccated bodies have been waiting for centuries to be buried in holy ground, its chapel and library. It is cold. Napoleon leafs through a copy of Livy, looking for the passage on Hannibal crossing the Alps. Then the prior invites him to dine on boiled salt beef, mutton stew, dried vegetables, goat's cheese and Gruyère, accompanied by an old white wine from Aosta. But how can he stay there for more than a few minutes? A courier brings news of Fort Bard's resistance – impregnable, says

Berthier. They must leave it, it will fall later, like an overripe fruit. Night descends. They have to set off, slide down the ice and snow on a reverse slope and sleep on hay in the village of Étroubles.

Napoleon feels surrounded by the ghosts of history in these valleys. He stops at Aosta. He wants to visit Augustus's triumphal arch and the Roman fortifications. He is treading in the footsteps of conquerors and emperors, just as in Egypt.

On 25 May, he has galloped ahead of his escort with Duroc when suddenly he finds himself face to face with an Austrian cavalry patrol which demands they surrender. Luckily his escort catches him up.

Fortune, once again, has protected me.

HE GIVES instructions for six white horses to be harnessed to the carriage in which he will enter Milan. It is 2 June, but the weather is stormy and the rain, when it comes, is torrential; Milan's streets are deserted. He has grown used to cheering crowds and triumphal processions and the city's silence irritates him. He becomes furious and calls for Bourrienne. All this must change: they shall liberate the political prisoners locked up by the Austrians, revive the Cisalpine Republic. At one o'clock in the morning he composes a letter to the consuls. Who in Paris will see the difference between the facts and his words? Words acquire a truth of their own. 'Milan,' he begins to dictate in a clipped voice, 'has offered me a spontaneous and touching show of affection.' In Paris all the coveters, plotters, rivals, cowards and greedy, cunning survivors of so many ages of terror are just waiting for a sign of weakness. They must not be given any grounds for hope.

As he dictates a letter to Fouché, he walks up and down the great rooms of the palace. 'I counsel you again, strike vigorously the first to step out of line, whoever he may be. This is the wish of the entire nation.' He stops. Fouché badly needs to be reassured, flattered. That man is clever, but he fears for his position, just like any man. He thinks that he is threatened himself, the victim of slanders. 'The best answer to every intrigue, cabal, and denunciation,' Napoleon continues, 'will always be this: in the month since I have gone, Paris has been perfectly quiet. Anyone who has performed such services is above calumny . . .' Perhaps this is the way to maintain one's hold over Fouché. The people need to be addressed differently.

Napoleon has just been informed, a few hours previously, of the capitulation of the Army of Egypt. 'Let Citizen Lebrun compose an article in person to let Europe know that if I had stayed in Egypt, it would still belong to France.'

One piece of good news has emerged from this Egyptian affair – the return of General Desaix. He must write to him as well. 'I feel for you all the esteem that is due to men of your talents, coupled with a friendship which my heart, now old and having too deep a knowledge of men, feels for no one else.'

That is the truth: men disappoint me every day! Enemies keep emerging, such as Georges Cadoudal who the police say is organizing a plot with fifty former chevaliers of the king's household to assassinate or kidnap me.

'Take that rogue Georges dead or alive,' he dictates. 'If you catch him, have him shot within twenty-four hours . . .'

Georges: one can expect nothing from him but hatred! But his brothers, Joseph and Lucien Bonaparte, are already anticipating defeat, and conducting preliminary discussions amongst themselves. Napoleon waves the letter he has just received from Joseph at Bourrienne. In a few awkward sentences, his elder brother reminds him that he is a candidate for the succession. 'You cannot have forgotten saying to me more than once . . .' he writes.

Oh yes, my heart is old!

WHEN, ON THE evening of 4 June, Napoleon enters the Scala in Milan and the gilt gleams under the chandeliers and the audience stands and cheers, his bitterness subsides. This admiring crowd is a balm, their uplifted voices a caress that transports him.

He recognizes the young singer with a dark complexion and hard features, slightly heavy cheeks and jet-black hair down to her shoulders, who is standing a few paces in front of the choir, about to perform the baroque opera, *The Virgins of the Sun*. It is Giuseppina Grassini whom he has met before, and rebuffed, in 1796.

He remembers his passion for Josephine, how blind he was then.

The times have changed.

Giuseppina Grassini may have put on a little weight, but she seems as captivated as ever as she walks across the stage towards Napoleon's box without taking her eyes off him. She is there to be taken, like a country that offers itself up, and there is nothing now that can hold Napoleon back. The only criterion he has now is that of his desire, of his will. He is what he is and what he wants to be.

At the end of the performance he strides purposefully towards the performers' dressing rooms. They clap and bow and take him to Giuseppina Grassini, who blushes with pleasure and takes his arm. She will follow him wherever he wants to take her, she murmurs.

She abandons herself to passion all night. She is in ecstasies, swooning, grateful, and it delights him.

When Berthier enters the salon next morning, Napoleon laughs with pleasure at the general's surprise at finding the singer having breakfast.

'She shall sing in Paris,' says Napoleon.

Then he thinks of Josephine. He will have to invite other singers along with Giuseppina because Josephine is jealous – but she will accept the situation. What else can she do?

I control people now. The time when I was dependent on her is over. I am only subject to Fortune.

FORTUNE SEEMS to be in two minds. A courier announces that Masséna has surrendered in Genoa on 4 June, which means that Field-Marshal Melas will now be able to turn on Lombardy.

Napoleon must be in the field. He leaves Milan and crosses the Po to join Lannes's troops, which have already engaged the Austrian army under General Ott that has come up from Genoa, but by the time Napoleon reaches the battlefield at Montebello, Lannes has won. 'Bones were cracking in my division like hail falling on a skylight,' Lannes tells him.

Napoleon passes among the men. They are exhausted but joyful. Victory transfigures everyone. He must give each of them a sign, pinch this man's ear, ask that man a question: 'How many years' service have you?'

'This is the first day I have come under fire,' replies Grenadier Coignet, who has distinguished himself.

Put him down for a musket of honour.

'Well then, when you've been on four campaigns you'll join my Guard.'

That is how one forms a personal bond with each soldier.

Will Fortune smile on me?

HERE IS Desaix with his long hair tied back with a ribbon. He begins to speak of Egypt and the hours pass. 'I do not want rest,' Desaix says. 'Whatever rank you give me, I shall be content. To work to increase the Republic's glory and yours is all I wish.'

Napoleon listens.

The man is sincere. He could be my second. If I was king, I would make him prince. He is an old-fashioned character. He is disinterested and enthusiastic. I have no knowledge of unselfishness.

Desaix is put in charge of a division.

THEN THEY have to wait for several days. The sky is heavy, stormy. There are violent downpours which leave the rivers swollen. The enemy may try to disappear, slip out of the net they are caught in. A decision must be taken, troops sent to look for them.

At seven o'clock in the morning of 14 June, the Austrians attack, and for more than seven hours they fight on irrigated land between canals and hedges. General Victor's men buckle, the units break up, and Napoleon hears the soldiers shouting 'All is lost.' Marengo's plain is covered with fugitives.

Napoleon is sitting on an embankment beside the road. He is holding his horse by the bridle, scattering pebbles with his whip. He does not see the cannonballs that skid across the road, or the soldiers coming past. He has made a mistake. He has gone looking for the Austrian army, thinking it was melting away; he has divided up his forces to hunt it, and now Melas has attacked with his full strength: thirty thousand men and a hundred cannon.

He is the one applying my motto, 'Keep your forces together, do not leave yourself vulnerable at any point . . . never detach a part of an army: on the eve of an attack, a battalion can decide the day.'

Napoleon calls an aide-de-camp and, resting the paper on his knee, starts to write a note to Desaix, who at this moment should be marching towards Novi, away from Marengo: 'I thought I was going to attack the enemy. He has anticipated me. Return, in heaven's name, if you still can.'

Having smiled, shall Fortune now abandon me?

Napoleon leaps on his horse.

'Courage, men!' he cries. 'Reserves are coming. Hold fast.'

Hold on. Don't let oneself think that Fortune is frowning. Take one's place in the front rank of the consular guard that is going to Lannes's assistance. But the men continue to fall back. Here and there soldiers are shouting, 'Long live Bonaparte', but the plain is littered with dead and wounded, the sides are uneven, and there are only a few pieces of French artillery left. At three o'clock the battle is lost, and Napoleon feels his staff officers looking anxiously at him. Suddenly an aide-de-camp gallops up, shouting, 'Where is the first consul?' Desaix is arriving, he announces.

Will Fortune smile again?

Desaix's division looks like 'a forest swaying in the wind' with its batteries and cavalry.

Marmont assembles the remaining cannon and opens fire. Desaix's grenadiers are hidden behind hedges. Everything will be decided by this moment.

Napoleon gives the order to Kellermann on the left wing to charge. His six hundred horses break into a gallop; the ground trembles; Marmont's cannon rain grapeshot on the Austrians; Desaix's grenadiers fire a salvo, then launch themselves forward. Desaix falls among the innumerable dead, but the Austrians are taken by surprise just when they thought victory was won, and they flee or surrender at General Zach's command.

Napoleon remains alone for a long time.

Six thousand Frenchmen have fallen on the plain of Marengo, but this victory will drive everyone waiting and hoping for my death in Paris back into their burrow.

'General,' says Bourrienne enthusiastically, 'here is a fine victory, you must be satisfied?'

Satisfied? What a strange word. Desaix is dead. Ah, what a glorious day it would have been if I could have embraced him after the battle. Before blessing me, Fortune proved uncertain. Nevertheless I am satisfied. This victory is mine. Now I shall dictate an account of how it should have been.

On 15 June Napoleon is waiting at his headquarters. General Zach and Prince Lichtenstein enter, respectful, defeated. He is blunt: 'My terms are irrevocable. I could demand more and the position I am in would permit me to do so, but I shall temper my claims out of respect for the grey hairs of your general . . .'

Force makes the law. The armistice is concluded. The French are to occupy a large part of Lombardy; Genoa is to be given up. The fortresses are to be surrendered.

Now to take advantage of this victory by writing to the consuls, mentioning those Hungarian and German grenadiers who, when taken prisoner, shouted, 'Long Live Bonaparte!', and sign off with the words, 'I hope the French people will be pleased with their army. When one sees all these brave fellows suffer, one only has a sole regret: that one is not wounded like them so as to share their pain.'

Nothing must be left to chance. He must plan ceremonies for his return so that the victory of Marengo will be unforgettable. The Consular Guard must leave for Paris and arrive before 14 July. This time the festival must be more glorious than ever: 'A firework display would look well.'

However, he must also be modest. Napoleon dictates a letter to Lucien, minister of the interior: 'I shall arrive at Paris unexpectedly. My intention is to have neither triumphal arches, nor any sort of ceremony. I have too good an opinion of myself to set much store by such gewgaws. I know no other triumph than public esteem.'

This is how one wins over opinion. Milan bears him out. He rides through the streets thronged with enthusiastic crowds. He attends a Te Deum in the Duomo. What do 'the atheists in Paris' know of the people's feelings and how to govern them?

With brutal frankness, he tells the Italian clergy, 'No society can exist without morality; there is no good morality without religion. It is religion alone, therefore, that gives to the state a firm and durable support. A society without religion is like a ship without a compass; a ship in that state can neither be sure of its route nor hope to enter port.'

He is the first consul, the master of the ship. Since this is how one leads people, he must attend the Te Deum, and meet Cardinal Martiniana at Verceil and tell him of his desire for an agreement, a concordat with the new Pope, Pius VII.

Let the 'ideologues' complain, what does it matter? They should listen to the acclamations of the crowd that besieges the Hôtel des Celestins in Lyon, which Napoleon reaches on 28 June. The people shout, 'Long live Bonaparte!' At Dijon, on 30 June, the women of the city strew flowers in his path. At Sens, *Veni, Vidi, Vici* has been engraved on the frontispiece of a triumphal arch. Like Caesar.

Desaix died at Marengo. 'Go and tell the first consul that I die regretting not having done enough to live on in posterity,' he said before collapsing. Napoleon learns that on the same day, 14 June, Kléber was assassinated in Cairo by a Muslim fanatic.

Death for others, victory for me.

AT TWO o'clock in the morning of 2 July 1800, his carriage enters the courtyard of the Tuileries.

V

THOSE SHOUTS, DISTANT at first and then growing louder, those shouts that wake him are the crowd that has flocked from the faubourgs. Napoleon gets up and goes to the window. Women are pressed up against the gates of the Tuileries. They rush forward when they are opened, crying 'Long live the First Consul! Long live Bonaparte!'

Bourrienne enters. Since the announcement of the victory at Marengo, all of Paris is celebrating, he says. Napoleon must show himself. He goes to the window of his cabinet and the cries grow doubly loud and shrill.

He thinks back to that day in 1792, eight years ago. It was a beautiful morning, just like today, when the frenzied crowd burst into the Tuileries, armed and uttering deathly cries.

Napoleon looks around at Bourrienne.

'Do you hear those cheers?' he begins. Then, almost in a murmur, as if he dare not acknowledge it, he goes on, 'That sound is as sweet to me as Josephine's voice. How happy and proud I am to be loved by such a people.'

The cannon of the Invalides begin to fire at regular intervals. Between the deafening reports, the band of the Consular Guard can be heard playing in the gardens; the cheering of the crowd drowns out the sound of the drums and the cymbals.

ONE AFTER ANOTHER, the consuls, ministers, members of the Council of State, members of the Institute and delegations from the different assemblies are shown in. Napoleon scrutinizes them. They are admiring and servile. How many of them are up to their ears in intrigues? How many were thrilled when the first courier arrived declaring Marengo was lost? He must draw a hypocritical veil over those moments, although that is not to say he has no opinion.

'So here we are again, citizens!' he says. 'Well, have you done good work since I left you?'

'Not as much as you, General.'

He takes one or other of them by the arm and leads him aside. 'What would you have done if I had died?' he asks.

Some protest, others confess their anxiety in the hours when the battle's outcome was in doubt. They denounce one another. One thought of pushing Carnot, the minister of war, forward; Roederer says his thoughts went to Joseph Bonaparte.

The second day of July passes in this fashion.

As dusk slowly gives way to night, Napoleon sees the lit-up buildings from his window. Over the faubourg St Antoine the sky is aglow. People have lit bonfires; there's dancing in the squares. All of sudden, the sight of the bonfires fills him with melancholy. He wishes Giuseppina Grassini were already in Paris. He will see her here, in a little mezzanine apartment which he has had fitted out above his official apartments.

His conversation with Roederer has also irritated him. The man is pretentious and tactless. 'France would be more secure,' he'd said, 'if we could see an heir-at-law at your side.'

Once again, he has referred to my death.

He had to repeat, 'I have no child. I have no need or interest in having one. I have no family feeling. My heir-at-law is the French people. That is my child.'

But Roederer had not stopped talking about an heir, a child, a child again.

'You are not making sense,' Napoleon declared.

Roederer has no idea what a government is, any more than any of the ideologues. 'I am the only one who knows through experience. I believe at this moment that no one apart from me, be it Louis XVIII or Louis XIV, could govern France. My death would be a misfortune.'

THAT CONVERSATION comes back to him all evening, like a nagging ache. By the morning of 3 June, it has left its mark on Napoleon's face.

Mounted on a grey horse caparisoned in orange-red velvet with gold braid, he reviews the army. The painters Isabey and Vernet have set up their easels. Later in the day he sees Isabey's sketch.

'Is that me, that man in a washed out greatcoat, leaning over the neck of such a richly adorned horse? That sadness on the stone grey face, those sunken, glittering eyes – are they mine? Do I give off that feeling of exhaustion and melancholy?'

'I have drawn you as you are, Citizen First Consul,' is Isabey's reply.

HE DOES NOT like these ceremonies he is obliged to attend for days on end. They are necessary but they exhaust him. He opens a Desaix quay, then, in the heat of 14 July, walks across the Champ-de-Mars and the esplanade of the Tuileries as the crowd breaks through the barriers and swarms into the Invalides, acclaiming him.

Thankfully there is a moment of enchantment and promise when he sees Giuseppina Grassini walking along the nave of the Temple of Mars, as the church of the Invalides is still called. She sings under the flags captured from the enemy. Her voice portends that night's pleasures when she will appear, as agreed, at the little door of the mezzanine apartment and Roustam will let her in and show her to the bedchamber. A moment of peace.

But first he must attend a banquet for a hundred at the Tuileries.

He waits impatiently for the toasts. The president of the Tribunate raises his glass 'To philosophy and civil liberty!' Before he has sat down, Napoleon calls out in a loud voice, 'To the Fourteenth of July! To the French people, the sovereign of us all!'

The applause is deafening as he leaves the room.

Giuseppina Grassini is waiting for him already, he is sure.

What do they know of me, when I know everything about them, including that they would have applauded whatever I said?

NEXT MORNING, as he does every day, he sees the consuls, the Council of State and members of a commission he has established to draft a civil code.

Anger often wells up in him. What do they know of the country's needs? Their reasoning is often dictated by greed. Of course he accepts the fact that men, his own brothers included, want to enrich themselves – Bourrienne, whom he sees all day every day, thinks of nothing else – but there are courtiers who dream of marrying Hortense de Beauharnais; Duroc and Bourrienne have entertained that hope. And that does shock him.

'I am surrounded by rogues!' Napoleon exclaims. 'Everyone steals! What is to be done? This country is corrupt. It has always been. Whenever a man becomes a minister, he builds a château.'

He goes out into Malmaison's park, takes a quick turn and then immediately returns to work, not noticing when it is time for meals, only allowing them a quarter of an hour or so, and then shutting himself away again with the consuls, ministers, members of the Institute and generals who come from Paris. He observes them. These officers he has known for years have changed.

'When one has fought in so many wars,' he murmurs, 'whether one likes it or not, one must have a little luck.'

But what about the people? The people who only ten years ago rose up in the name of equality – how can one make them accept this situation where few are wealthy and most are poor?

Napoleon grows furious with the chatterers and ideologues who don't even think that this is a question. They shower him with useless compliments. One day in the Tribunate he admonishes them. 'I am not a king. I do not want to be insulted by being called a king. People treat me like a royal monkey.'

He looks at them, these prominent citizens, speechmakers and ideologues who have fought authority without understanding that authority is necessary, if only to resist revolutions. Theirs are vague, deceitful minds. They might be worth more if they had studied some geometry.

'Me, a royal monkey?' he continues. 'I am a soldier who has come from the people and risen by my own efforts. Can I be compared to Louis XVI? I listen to everybody, it is true, but my mind is my only counsel!'

He dictates imperiously, revises, and becomes a jurist. He loves this work of organization. He creates and models institutions. Here he builds roads; there he decrees a duty to establish record offices, or plans a Bank of France. Between taking decisions, he sometimes goes fox hunting around Malmaison, but without any real passion for it. He rides in a reverie, transported by his thoughts.

He has already made the south of France safe from the brigands who call themselves royalists; he is continuing to pacify the west. Now he must make peace abroad; this is what the people want, but Austria rejected his peace proposals at the end of July, and

England is as implacable as ever. Perhaps he will have to reopen hostilities.

First, however, one must secure what one has. Returning to his study he writes to Masséna, who is in command in Italy, 'Examples must be made. Pillage and burn the first village in Piedmont that rebels.'

The law of force: if Louis XVI had ordered cannon to fire on the people invading the Tuileries, he might still be king. But is force enough to keep men in line?

I have had distinctions shared out amongst the privates and officers who performed heroically in the battle of Marengo – swords, muskets, batons of honour. Their praises have been sung.

But the people?

This question haunts him. What will be the good of new laws if the institutions that have stood for centuries are overthrown – and he has experience of this – in a great wave of revolt?

I must talk about this, but even the people who witnessed it first hand cannot do so. Sieyès, who has seen everything, is nothing but a metaphysician. Roederer perhaps?

HE HAS talks with Roederer in the park at Malmaison.

'Society cannot exist without inequality of wealth,' Napoleon says, 'and inequality of wealth cannot exist without religion.'

He glances at Roederer.

He is an ideologue. He does not like my mathematical logic. My proofs disturb his hypocritical cavilling.

'When a man is dying of hunger beside someone who has abundance,' continues Napoleon, 'he cannot accept such a difference unless there is an authority telling him, "God wishes it thus. There must be poor and rich in this world, but afterwards, and for all eternity, the lots will be different."'

He smiles at Roederer's grimace. He remembers the time when he tried to win the prize set by the Academy of Lyon, dreaming of emulating Rousseau. In those days Rousseau was one of his mentors, but people change. He has changed.

'It would have been better for the peace of France,' Napoleon murmurs, 'if Rousseau had never existed.'

'Why, Citizen Consul?'

'He was the one who paved the way for the Revolution.'

'I would not have expected you to complain about the Revolution.'

Napoleon carries on walking in silence, then says, 'Perhaps it would have been better for the peace of the world if neither Rousseau nor I had ever existed!'

But I do exist, I have read Rousseau and I am a product of the Revolution.

JOSEPHINE SOMETIMES forgets this.

She welcomes envoys of Comte d'Artois and Louis XVIII. The Comtesse de Guiche, a friend of Comte d'Artois, assures him at lunch at Malmaison that when the Bourbons are restored they will make him their constable. Indeed, some of those close to Napoleon are starting to entertain the possibility of the king returning to guarantee the future. Bourrienne confesses to it himself.

'What will become of us?' he says. 'You have no children.'

Walking with his hands behind his back, across the little bridge that leads from his cabinet to the avenue in Malmaison's park where he likes to walk, Napoleon explains with a sort of weariness, his head bowed, 'The Bourbons would return to France no matter what they had to promise, because of their desire to recover their heritage – and the eighty thousand émigrés who would come with them would share their desire. What would be the fate of the regicides then, and of all the men who declared themselves with abandon during the Revolution? Of national land and the whole mass of transactions that have been performed in that last twelve years? Can you see how far the reaction would go, Bourrienne?'

Napoleon slowly returns to his study.

'I know how these women, Josephine and Hortense, plague you,' he says, 'but let us not talk about it any more. My decision is made. Let them leave me in peace and get on with their knitting.'

HE SHOWS a letter to Bourrienne on 7 September. This is what Louis XVIII has written this time: 'You are losing valuable time. We can assure the peace of France, I say we, because I need Bonaparte for that, and he could not do it without me.'

Napoleon gestures to Bourrienne. He will dictate his answer to the Bourbon.

Sir, I have received your letter and I thank you for the courteous things it contains.

You ought not to desire your return to France; you would be obliged to march over 100,000 dead bodies.

Sacrifice your interests to the repose and happiness of France . . . History will remember this.

I am not insensible to the misfortunes of your family. I shall contribute with pleasure to the pleasantness and tranquillity of your retreat.

Bonaparte

First Consul of the Republic

PART TWO

There must be a religion for the people

SEPTEMBER 1800 TO JULY 1801

VI

Napoleon often slips out at night. He goes down a dark staircase, pushes open a little door and there is the street, the smell of dead leaves, the wind heavy with rain. A hundred or so metres away, in the light of their lanterns, the sentries of the Consular Guard march up and down in front of the gates of the palace, but here everything is in shadow. The Tuileries are just a dark façade which every now and then a nondescript passer-by walks past.

After only a few paces, Napoleon becomes an anonymous silhouette who can merge into the crowd and not be recognized in his black frock coat and round hat pulled down over his eyebrows. He doesn't need to look at Berthier who has come with him to sense the general's anxiety, even fear. When he comes out like this without an escort and mingles with the citizens, whoever comes with him is gripped by the same dread; Duroc and the aides-de-camp keep their hands on their pistols the whole time.

He is the one people want to kill, but he is not afraid of dying. Death will choose its moment and he feels that it has not come yet, even though he knows Paris is seething with plots.

Napoleon turns towards Berthier and asks him about the latest conspiracy to be uncovered. Was it royalist or Jacobin? Since his reply to Louis XVIII's letter, the fanatics of the fleur-de-lys have only one hope – to kill him.

'If I were to believe Fouché . . .' Napoleon begins before Berthier can reply.

According to his Minister of Police, royalist plots to kidnap and assassinate him are multiplying, and English money is pouring into the country, but is Fouché to be trusted? Isn't he in league with the Jacobins? Isn't he protecting them because he fears more than anything else a return of the Bourbons, who would make him pay dearly for his past as a regicide and terrorist? 'Robespierre's tail' is definitely still wagging.

Napoleon can't help it: he loathes those fanatical, destructive men. He does not understand them. What is it they are hoping for? At least the royalists have a clear aim – to recover their privileges and property under a king – which is also why he is hostile to them. They would put France to fire and sword.

A revolution is not something you erase: you channel it, correct it; you build new institutions, 'masses of granite', on the rubble left in its wake. This is what he devotes his energies to every day, from dawn till late into the night – and it is to get away from this forced labour for a few hours that he slips out of the Tuileries. He wants to feel free, to gaze at the women, some of whose eyes light up with a come-hither look when they see him studying them.

He is seeing Giuseppina Grassini tonight, which is another reason he walks through the streets, so as not to have to wait for her. Soon the house he has chosen for her in rue de la Victoire will be ready. Then he will be able to see her there, perhaps every night. He won't have to worry about Josephine suddenly appearing and Constant, his chief valet, or Roustam, his Mameluke, warning him that 'la générale' is on her way, that she wants to come upstairs and pay a visit to the first consul. Josephine is jealous. The tables are turned! Giuseppina, in her house on rue de la Victoire, will sing just for him. Her voice is like her body – full, iridescent, as soft as velvet, languid. It envelops him.

'IT WAS A small explosive device,' Berthier is saying.

He must return to the death that is lying in wait for him, to these Jacobins who in their subversive pamphlets call for 'thousands of Brutuses' to rise up from the French people. They glorify 'tyrannicide'.

Me, a tyrant?

Napoleon turns to Berthier. 'I have been in power for almost a year now and I have not spilled a drop of blood.'

They want me dead. But why? What do they hope to gain? It will bring them nothing but chaos and defeat, since Austria is going to go back to war and England is as determined as ever; or they will pave the way for the restoration of the Bourbons, like sorcerer's apprentices. Unless they are looking for another First Consul, someone more docile, under their heel, who would practise their party politics rather than seek to represent the nation.

'What is General Moreau doing?' Napoleon asks, interrupting Berthier again. Moreau is the real danger. He is in Paris, on regular leave, entertaining many of the generals at his house: Burne, Augereau, Lecourbe. Word has it that he sees Sieyès, the mole, and Madame de Staël, who considers herself a man of politics, but he might just as well serve the royalists. Moreau is a genuine threat. He must be disarmed, won over, or crushed.

'A small explosive device . . .' resumes Berthier.

Fouché's men were alerted by an explosion in the Salpêtrière district, in the house of someone called Chevalier, a former employee of the Committee of Public Safety. They found a strange device, a barrel hooped with iron and filled with nails with big heads and splinters of glass and iron. The bomb had a detonating fuse. Following an investigation, a dozen Jacobins have been arrested.

'They were planning to blow up Malmaison,' Berthier reports.

Napoleon remains silent. This is a fight to the death between him and his enemies, whether they're the red cap or the red heel. Have they understood anything of what he wants? Of what he is trying to do for this country?

'I am the only one who can meet the French nation's expectations,' he murmurs. 'The only one . . .'

Berthier seems amazed.

'If I always seem prepared, ready for everything, it is because before I embark on a course of action, I spend a long time thinking, imagining everything that might happen.' He stops and looks Berthier in the eye. 'There is no genie who secretly reveals what I should say and do in circumstances that seem unexpected to others; it is all the result of my meditation.'

I want to bind the French together. And not deliver them up either to the vengeance of returning émigrés, or to the anarchists' blind fury.

THAT IS WHY he gives orders for Marshal Turenne's remains to be transferred to the Invalides on the Festival of the Republic, 23 September. He organizes a glorious cortège to follow the coach drawn by four white horses, comprising soldiers from the Army of Italy, all the old generals and an escort of Consular Guard; it winds its way through crowds gathered on the quays.

The following day, in place des Victoires, he lays the first stone for a monument to Desaix and Kléber, 'killed on the same day, within the same quarter of an hour', one at Marengo, the other in Cairo.

These French heroes must be grouped together.

'Do you know what the crowd were shouting, Berthier? "Long live Bonaparte! Long live the Republic!"'

It is the union of these two entities that his potential murderers want to destroy.

'Let us go back,' he says.

HE ASCENDS the concealed staircase. On the landing leading to the mezzanine apartment he sees Constant's silhouette.

'She is here,' the valet murmurs.

Napoleon roughly dismisses him and pushes open the door. Giuseppina Grassini is lying on the bed.

Let us forget death, forget it.

THE NEXT morning he spends a long time getting dressed. He examines his grey face which, since he has started wearing his hair short, looks even thinner than usual. Laid out on an armchair is a colonel of the Guard uniform that he has picked out. Constant helps him into it. He likes the austere dark blue coat with red and blue facings, the white waistcoat and breeches, the gold epaulettes and black boots, but for a moment he sees his artillery lieutenant's uniform. 'That was the most beautiful of all,' he murmurs as Bourrienne comes into the room.

Bourrienne is grave-faced; one cannot give way to nostalgia when one is at the top of the pyramid.

'Come on,' he says to Bourrienne.

A senator has been kidnapped, Clement de Ris. His captors are demanding a ransom, but it is not yet known whether they have other motives. Perhaps Clement de Rio has documents that would be compromising for certain important figures who became involved in intrigues when the first consul was in Italy, because they thought he would be defeated? Bourrienne does not need to say Fouché's name. This pale man with veiled eyes is privy to every political mystery. What does he want exactly?

Bourrienne is not finished. A group of Jacobins have been

denounced by one of their accomplices. They are planning to murder the first consul at a performance of an opera at the Theatre of the Republic in rue de la Loi on 10 October. What should they do with these men? He reads out the names, which include a painter, Topino-Lebrun, an Italian, Cerracchi, a former employee of the Committee of Public Safety, Demerville ... Bourrienne hesitates. With a nod, Napoleon urges him to continue. 'And Arena, a Corsican, the brother of a member of the Five Hundred who threatened you with a dagger on 19 Brumaire.'

The old island hatreds are never laid to rest.

Ought he to arrest the conspirators?

Napoleon thinks it over. He needs to turn the tables and use this plot to mobilize opinion and perhaps unmask Fouché.

'We have to nurture the conspiracy and see it through.'

In war, as in politics, one must fight one's adversaries by uncovering their intentions, letting them reveal themselves as one feigns weakness or ignorance, and then strike at the desired moment.

IN THE theatre's brightly lit passages, Arena and his accomplices are arrested on 10 October. They are carrying daggers. Now one can just denounce these 'ghosts of September' publicly, those spillers of blood whom the people have rejected because they remember the massacres of September 1792.

The next day at a military parade on the Carrousel, the crowd cheer Bonaparte with unprecedented enthusiasm. Now he can show his strength and contempt for 'these seven or eight wretches who had the desire but not the ability to commit the crimes they meditated'. He can reassure the people, and admit that 'governing France after ten years of such extraordinary upheaval is a difficult task'. But what of it? 'The thought of working for the best and most powerful people on earth' fills him with all the courage he could hope for.

What about you, Fouché?

Napoleon looks at the minister who is calmly sceptical, unconvinced by the seriousness of the conspiracy.

'Must I wait for a dagger in my heart to have proof?' exclaims Napoleon.

I AM THE target because I am the keystone of the whole edifice. There will be another 'night of the daggers' tomorrow. What if they kill me?

He must think of this and of whom his replacement will be.

'There is a gap in the social contract,' he says to Cabanis, one of the senators who is devoted to him. Cabanis says nothing. He is one of those who helped prepare for 18 Brumaire, but he is a prudent man. 'This gap must be filled,' continues Napoleon. 'If one wants to guarantee the peace of the State, a consul designate is indispensable.'

Napoleon stands by the window of his study. There is a large mirror with a sculpted frame facing him.

'I am the target of all of these royalists and Jacobins,' he says. 'Every day my life is threatened, and it will be even worse if I am to resume war and have to put myself at the head of the army again.' Cabanis has stayed dead still, as if he were afraid a movement might betray what he is thinking. 'What would be France's fate then? How can one fail to warn of the misfortunes that would inevitably succeed such an event?'

Death. Kings have created dynasties to fight against it.

And I?

VII

Napoleon paces about his study in the Tuileries. He kicks a pamphlet he has just thrown on the ground out of his way. It skids across the floor to the chair on which Bourrienne is sitting. 'Have you read that?' asks Napoleon.

No need to wait for an answer. Everyone has read that handful of pages.

This morning, Josephine came into his bedroom. As always, her silhouette and perfume both move and irritate Napoleon. What does she want? To discuss, with her usual bitter irony, his visits to Giuseppina Grassini? To ask him about the pleasure he takes with this woman? He does not like her trying to establish an unambiguous relationship with him in which everything is said. He doesn't want to live with his wife in such a fashion. He refuses to behave like a libertine who takes pleasure in the pleasure his partner takes with others. He detests vice and perversity. Josephine, however, knows how to play on the feelings she arouses in him.

She had sunk down, catlike, on her knees, stroked his hair, and then whispered, her lips touching his ear, 'I beg you, Bonaparte, do not make yourself a king. It is that nasty Lucien who is urging you to do it, don't listen to him.' He had sent her away, spent a long time dressing in his bathroom, and then had gone down to his study, where Bourrienne was reading that pamphlet. He had grabbed it and then thrown it on the ground.

'Well, Bourrienne, what do you think?'

Bourrienne hesitates. Napoleon holds out his hand and Bourrienne picks up the pamphlet. Napoleon takes it and leafs through it.

Does Bourrienne agree with this *Parallel between Caesar, Cromwell and Bonaparte*? Has he read what Louis de Fontanes says? 'Bonaparte should be compared to Martel or Charlemagne, not to Monk.'

Napoleon flings the pamphlet back down. He is seized with

rage. He knows this Fontanes, a marquis who returned from exile after 18 Brumaire; a man of letters who writes for the *Mercure de France*, a fine speaker. His homage to Washington at the Invalides showed great talent. The day he delivered it was also the day Elisa Bacciocchi let Napoleon know she was Fontanes's mistress. He could only accept it. How could he reproach his sister? Elisa had been married to a poor man, a lowly Corsican officer without talent or ambition, but she is a woman of character. He has seen Fontanes since, at Lucien's house. After Lucien Bonaparte was widowed, Elisa took her brother's social arrangements in hand. She organizes and hosts a literary salon which attracts La Harpe, Arnault and Roederer, and shines there in Fontanes's company. Lucien and she, no doubt with Joseph's complicity, must have thought it necessary, after the night of the daggers, to express publicly the idea that Napoleon should become king and hereditary ruler and that he is the founder of a dynasty.

Naturally, since that is what Lucien, Joseph, Elisa and the entire Bonaparte clan think and want, Josephine is against it. Which is why she was there this morning, deploying all her charms and talking of 'that nasty Lucien'.

They all hate each other. She is afraid if I become king I will need an heir, which she cannot give me. She is afraid of repudiation, divorce. I give everyone as much as I can and they fight like hungry dogs. They are impatient. I'm the one they tear apart. Imagine someone writing, 'Where is Pericles' successor? Nero, Caligula, Claudius – they are who replaced the greatest of mortals at Rome, when he was basely assassinated . . . People of France! You are sleeping on the edge of an abyss.'

'I think, General,' Bourrienne begins, 'that this pamphlet is calculated to produce an extremely unfavourable effect on the public mind. It strikes me as inopportune, since it prematurely reveals your plans.'

What does he know of my plans? And what are people saying about them?

Napoleon asks to see Fouché. He questions him and grows irritated with his replies.

'Your brother Lucien sponsors this pamphlet,' Fouché explains. 'It has been printed and published on his orders. Well, it comes from the Ministry of the Interior and has been sent to every prefect.'

Napoleon takes several pinches of snuff, but those quick movements and deep breaths and the acrid smell do not calm him as usual; they only irritate him more.

'That is of absolutely no consequence to me!' he cries. 'Your duty as minister of police was to have Lucien arrested and put in the Temple.'

He takes more snuff.

'All that imbecile can do is think up new ways of compromising me,' he says.

He remembers his childhood with Lucien, and his younger brother's manoeuvrings at the time of the confrontation with Paoli which changed the course of everything – but to cancel all that out, there was also 19 Brumaire and Lucien's courage and presence of mind. Mightn't the day have ended in disaster without him?

He is my brother. They are my family. I do what I should for them.

Joseph has been appointed to conduct negotiations with Austria at Lunéville; Lucien is a minister.

Napoleon loses his temper in front of Roederer.

Lucien is clever but headstrong, erratic. He cannot remain as Minister of the Interior. There are too many rumours flying around about this pamphlet and other affairs he is said to be mixed up in. Apparently he took commission on a sale of English wheat. Lucien must not be allowed to tarnish the Bonaparte name.

'Do you know what Fouché's spies are putting about? That Lucien may have been involved in the assassination attempt at the Opera!'

Now follows a moment of tension, more unbearable than those minutes when the outcome of a battle hangs in the balance. Napoleon sends for Lucien to announce that he is dismissing him from his post as minister of the interior and appointing him French ambassador in Madrid.

When the interview is finished, he has to brave the looks of those who have been waiting in the Tuileries salon for over two hours.

Josephine is sitting in a large armchair, hiding her elation. She loathes and fears Lucien, lest one day he should marry Hortense de Beauharnais and give Napoleon an heir. Although perhaps Hortense can be married to Louis Bonaparte, whom Napoleon keeps saying is 'an excellent sort'.

Elisa Bacciocchi stands in the shadows. She is on the verge of tears, shooting looks of hatred at Hortense de Beauharnais who, sitting near her mother, is not as discreet in her joy as Josephine.

Napoleon walks through the salon. The generals, Lannes, Murat and Lecourbe, the aides-de-camp, the state councillors and Chaptal, who knows that he is succeeding Lucien Bonaparte at the Ministry of the Interior, step aside. He hears laughing and turns round. Lucien is chatting gaily to Josephine, bending down towards her and whispering in her ear.

My family: ferocious rivalries masked by a smile.

I prefer war.

WAR IS THERE knocking on the gates of the east. In the negotiations at Lunéville, Joseph keeps coming up against Austria's reluctance, behind which lies England's money and determination. These two powers will only accept the Republic's conquests if they themselves have been defeated. They want France to return to its borders before 1789; London will keep urging Vienna not to settle for anything else. Will he have to leave Paris again and thereby expose himself to the intrigues and plots of a capital which will hang on every scrap of news and, in some cases, hope for Napoleon's defeat?

On 3 December 1800, at five o'clock in the evening, in his study in the Tuileries, Napoleon writes to Joseph himself, 'If I set out, the house of Austria will have good reason to remember it. So I must know by return of courier if all hope is lost, as Pitt's speech in London would lead one to believe.'

Napoleon begins to give orders for stages to be prepared along the route into Germany, but on that very day, 3 December, after some uncertainty, General Moreau takes Vienna's army by surprise and crushes it at Hohenlinden. The road to Salzburg is open. Almost ten thousand Austrian soldiers are in full retreat. Vienna may be threatened by a pincer movement since General Brune's men are advancing through Tuscany and can push on to the capital of the Empire.

Can the war be won without me?

Napoleon spreads out the maps of Germany on the floor. Moreau seems to be slow pursuing the Austrians, and through excessive caution renouncing this chance to destroy them, but he must keep any reproaches to himself. Moreau is sensitive, jealous and acclaimed in all quarters.

'I cannot convey all the interest I have taken in your fine and skilled manoeuvres,' Napoleon writes to him. 'Once again you have surpassed yourself in this campaign. These unfortunate Austrians are truly stubborn; they were counting on the ice and snow, they do not know you yet. I salute you affectionately.'

I can imagine what feelings this victory must awaken in Moreau. A glorious, ambitious general is always, whatever he may think himself, a danger – and there are too many men who want my downfall or death for one of them not to think of Moreau. Just as I do.

'If I were to die three or four years from now of a fever in my bed,' he says to Roederer, 'and to finish the novel of my life I made a will, I would tell the nation to be wary of military rule. I would tell it to appoint a civilian.'

Roederer is surprised. They were talking about Austria and Moreau's victory at Hohenlinden.

'There is no need for a general to fill the post of first consul,' Napoleon continues. 'It has to be a civilian. The army will obey a civilian rather than a soldier.' What are the generals amongst themselves? Jealous rivals who spy on each other and all think they're as good as the other and assume that it is enough to be victorious on a battlefield to be able to rule a country.

'In Egypt, when there was a revolt in Cairo, the whole army wanted me to burn the mosques and exterminate the clerics,' he says in a low voice. 'I didn't listen to a word of it. I had the leaders of the revolt punished and everything calmed down. Three weeks later, the army was delighted.' He sighs. 'If I die in four or five years, everything will be in place and it will go fine. If I die before, anything might happen.'

He raises his arm to Roederer, stopping him replying.

'A military first consul with no knowledge of government would let everything be the way his lieutenants wanted it to be.' He pushes the map of Germany aside with his foot. 'Moreau only ever talks of military rule. That is all he understands.'

VIII

It is 24 December 1800. Napoleon is sitting by the fireplace in the salon at the Tuileries. He is wearing the blue coat with red and white facings of a colonel of the Guard and he has slipped his right hand into his white waistcoat. His bicorn is pulled down over his eyes which are shut. He hears a commotion: Josephine and Hortense and a few of the generals are coming to find him; he recognizes the voices of Lannes, Berthier, Lauriston and his aide-de-camp, Rapp. He does not move.

He is meant to be going to the Opera with them for a performance of Handel's *Creation*, but he would rather stay in the Tuileries and review the discussions he has been engaged in all day in his study. He is the one who has to make the decisions, he needs to analyse and make sense of the situation, and for that he needs to meditate on war. Will England ever want peace so long as France extends to the left bank of the Rhine and thereby absorbs Belgium and Holland? It was the Convention, not him, who started this expansion and these wars he has inherited. He is the heir to their ambitions. He may have replaced the Committee of Public Safety on the chessboard, but the game was afoot long before he appeared. What should he do? Renouncing these territories would be the equivalent of agreeing to a Bourbon taking up residence in the faubourg St Antoine. Keeping them would mean war.

Josephine whispers quickly in his ear, insisting he come to the Opera. He works too hard, she says. The music will divert him. He stands up and goes downstairs. The escort of mounted grenadiers is waiting, their horses pawing the ground. Napoleon walks to his carriage, looks up and sees his driver, César, who seems to be swaying on his box. Drunk, perhaps.

Napoleon gets into his carriage. The grenadiers swing off at a trot, the carriage briskly follows suit and soon they are turning into rue St Niçaise. The horses abruptly break into a gallop and the carriage picks up speed while Napoleon drowses. A grenadier orders a hackney carriage out of the way to let the first consul pass a cart that has stopped by the roadside. A little girl is holding the carthorse by its bridle. César whips up the horses as soon as the way is clear. The carriage grazes the cart and then turns left into rue de la Loi.

Suddenly Napoleon feels as if a cannon is firing next to him. Half-asleep, he thinks he is in battle and shakes himself awake; there's shouting, sounds of breaking glass and neighing. He leans out of the window; behind him the sky is lit up by a dark red glow. The carriage stops at the corner of rue des Boucheries and an officer runs up. Before he can even explain what has happened, Napoleon realizes it was an assassination attempt. That cart exploded a few moments after the first consul passed.

'Give orders to the consular guard to take up arms,' Napoleon cries.

So, they wanted to kill him. He is calm, serene. He turns towards a second officer.

'Go and tell Madame Bonaparte to meet me at the Opera.'

Then with a wave, he bids César drive on.

Once again death has brushed him, as if to remind him of the precariousness of his power and the necessity of never letting down his guard. Who are these people who have tried to kill him? Undoubtedly accomplices of the 'conspirators with daggers', those terrorists who perhaps have formed links with Jacobin generals, the envious 'old moustaches' of the Republic's campaigns who cannot accept a return of domestic peace and order and the fusion of all the French. Who knows if Moreau isn't behind them?

As he gets out of his carriage at the Opera, Napoleon sees generals and officers rushing towards him. The massive explosion has been heard all over Paris. Houses have been blown apart and the glass in all the buildings in that district and in the Tuileries has been shattered. There are several dead and mutilated. A woman has had both breasts torn off by a piece of iron. The scattered remains of a little girl have been found.

These terrorists must be crushed.

He goes into the Opera and pushes open the door of his box.

'Those rascals wanted to blow me up,' he tells Junot. Then he sits down. 'Bring me a copy of the oratorio,' he adds in a calm voice.

But the entire theatre is on its feet, shouting, 'Long live the first consul!' The applause is so loud it makes the walls shake. Several times Napoleon comes forward, and each time he sits back down the cheers force him to stand again. It is only after a long while that he can tell the orchestra to start playing.

He listens to the music for a few moments. Once again his enemy's actions can be useful to him if he can counter-attack and take advantage of this wave of emotion.

HE LEAVES THE Opera, and as he approaches the Tuileries the crowd grows denser. Cheers break out as soon as his carriage is recognized. In the Tuileries he is fussed over by his intimates.

He sees Fouché standing on his own; the minister of police's clean-shaven, emotionless face grates on his nerves.

'Well,' he calls out, 'are you going to say this is royalists again, Fouché?'

He doesn't like the way Fouché, remaining calm, replies that he will prove that it is them. Napoleon cannot accept this. Recently he has done more and more for émigrés. What sort of people were Ceracchi, Arena and Topino-Lebrun who tried, such a short time ago, to assassinate him at the Opera? 'Jacobins,' he repeats, 'terrorists, wretches in permanent revolt who are arrayed against every government.'

He strides up and down the salon. His intimates think like him; he is swept along by their murmurs of agreement and Fouché's isolation.

'I shall not be deceived. There are no Chouans in this, or émigrés, or former noblemen, or former priests,' he thunders. They are all Jacobins, Septembrizers. He advances towards Fouché.

'I shall mete out spectacular justice in their regard.'

He is irritated when Fouché again says it is Chouans and that he will prove it within a week. He turns his back on him.

HE REMAINS awake for part of the night.

Almost all his entourage have advised him to sack Fouché and Dubois, the prefect of police – the minister remembers having been a terrorist and the prefect is an incompetent – but he hesitates. He must strike at any Jacobins suspected of sympathizing with the night of the daggers, and he must not let himself be persuaded by Fouché, but that doesn't mean Fouché cannot be allowed to carry on.

Either way, popular sentiment must be exploited to show that he is a bulwark against a return of the guillotine. If there is one thing the French want no more part of, it is that.

His mind is made up. The assassination attempt in the rue St Niçaise must become a weapon to cut down his enemies and rally the French around him.

WHEN HE goes out into the courtyard of the Tuileries to attend a grand parade of the troops the crowd acclaims him and the officers in the palace's guard rooms do likewise. The president of the Tribunate and the municipal and departmental authorities come to assure him of their ardour. Then it's the turn of members of the Council of State and the Institute to pay him homage. Speeches follow one after the other; oaths of loyalty are sworn over and over again. He observes these men with their solicitous, emphatic declarations. He has no illusions. To them he is merely a convenient shield. They must be controlled by the fear that infects them.

'This gang of brigands attacked me directly,' he says. 'From now on these wretches who have libelled liberty by the crimes they committed in her name will no longer be permitted to do any harm . . . They are Septembrizers, the dregs of all those bloodthirsty villains who used the Revolution as a cloak for their crimes.'

Fouché is still the only person to remain sceptical and assures Napoleon that it is a royalist conspiracy. His opinion is the subject of discussion that evening in Josephine's salon, where generals' wives and public figures gather. Napoleon passes through the room, hectoring Dubois, the prefect of police: 'In your place I would indeed be ashamed of what has happened!' He raises his voice so everyone can hear him, 'Fouché has his reasons to keep silent. He is serving his own party. What could be more natural for him than to seek to screen a band of men covered with blood and crimes? Wasn't he one of their leaders? Don't I know what he did in Lyon and the Loire? Well, Lyon and the Loire are what explain Fouché's conduct.'

He looks around him.

Josephine is the only one who speaks up for Fouché, because she thinks that the minister of police is opposed to the Consulate being turned into a monarchy, which would entail an heir and the repudiation of her as Napoleon's spouse, but everyone else has chills up their spine when they remember the Terror. It is good they remember it. It is useful if France fears a return of the guillotine.

SOON A LIST is drawn up of one hundred and thirty Jacobins for deportation.

Napoleon addresses the Council of State in a voice thick with anger and determination. It does not matter if these Jacobins are not directly implicated in the attempt in rue St Niçaise, he says. 'A great example is needed to bind the intermediate class to the Republic. We cannot hope for this as long as they see themselves threatened by hundreds of rabid wolves who are just waiting for the moment to hurl themselves on their prey . . .'

As he speaks he looks hard at each member of the Council of State listening attentively. He sees the uncertainty in their eyes. They are afraid of the Jacobins and afraid of getting involved. Cowards!

'I am so certain of the necessity of making a great example that I am prepared to summon the scoundrels before me, try them in person and put my signature to their sentence. Besides, I am not speaking for myself. I have faced dangers before; my destiny protected me then and I count on it doing so again. What is at stake here is the social order, public morality and the glory of the nation.'

THE JACOBINS will be deported to the Seychelles.

Public life is a war. They fight me, I strike them down.

Are they responsible for the assassination attempt in rue St Niçaise?

Fouché asks to see the three consuls and Napoleon paces up and down as Fouché speaks in a steady voice.

'The police have been busy,' he says. 'I promised a reward of two thousand louis for any information.' He does not look them in the eye, but one only has to listen and look at him to know that he has succeeded in his pledge and that he will triumph.

The police, he explains, by means of the remains of the mare harnessed to the cart full of explosives in rue St Niçaise, have discovered who sold the horse, and consequently who bought it, a certain François Carbon. Again from the debris, they have identified the cooper who hooped the barrels of powder. The three culprits are Chouans, agents of Georges Cadoudal . . .

Fouché breaks off and stares at Napoleon, who continues pacing the room.

'They are,' Fouché resumes, 'the royalists François Carbon, Limoëlan and Saint-Réjeant. The latter was the leader of the Chouans in the Department of Ille-et-Vilaine. François Carbon was arrested on 18 January and Saint-Réjeant on the 28th. Limoëlan is still at large, but he is being hunted.' They are Chouans, Fouché repeats. The infernal machine was the handiwork of a royalist conspiracy under the leadership of Georges Cadoudal.

'Find him and arrest him,' Napoleon says simply.

Has he made a mistake? Should he now not proscribe those Jacobins who had nothing to do with this 'infernal machine'?

But they wanted to kill me as well, didn't they?

Aren't they just as dangerous, or even more destructive, than the royalists?

On 9 January 1801, the Jacobins implicated in the 'night of the daggers' had been sentenced to death, but their plot had barely passed its initial stages. This infernal machine on the rue St Niçaise had killed twenty-two people and wounded fifty more.

AT MIDNIGHT on the night of 29 January 1801, a secret council meets at the Tuileries. Napoleon presides, flanked by the two other consuls and various notables, such as Portalis, Talleyrand and Roederer. They debate the petitions for reprieve lodged by some of the men convicted of the 'night of the daggers'.

Reprieve is refused for all concerned.

When he had addressed the Council of State on 26 December, referring to 'the vengeance that should be striking for such an atrocious crime', Napoleon had declared, 'Blood must run.'

They are guillotined on 31 January.

IX

Napoleon stops in the doorway of the salon where Josephine, as she does every night at the Tuileries or Malmaison, is entertaining.

He studies Laure Junot. He has known her since she was a child, but he never paid any attention to her when she was just the daughter of Madame Pernon, a friend of the Bonapartes living in Montpellier. Madame Pernon had watched over his father Charles Bonaparte when he was on his death-bed in that town in 1785. Napoleon had expressed his thanks to her on several occasions and had even thought of marrying her, even though she was a fair amount older than he was.

Looking at Laure gives him pleasure. She is full of life; her whole body expresses verve and energy. Is she beautiful? What does that mean exactly? She is fresh-faced, no make-up, dark complexioned with quick movements, slightly heavy round the waist since she is pregnant, but so lovely to look at, like a vigorous, healthy plant.

He glances at Josephine and feels a twinge of despair and anger. She is so made-up, so full of artifice that sometimes he feels an involuntary welling of aggression, a desire to hurt this ageing woman he is deeply attached to; although she has given him pleasure and been useful to him, she has also deceived and humiliated him, and now she is incapable of giving birth to a son.

He looks away because she has seen him and he does not want her to guess what he is thinking. But she knows anyway.

A few days before he had persuaded her to go on a drive with him and Laure Junot in Malmaison's park. The estate now has over three hundred hectares.

He had noticed Josephine's sulky expression as she got into the caleche. Nonetheless he had ordered the driver to set off and leapt up on his horse like a young man. After all, he is not yet thirty-two. Josephine is older than him; he is so aware of that now. He had looked at Laure Junot sitting in the carriage: this young woman's vivaciousness simultaneously enchanted and exasperated him.

When the carriage came to a stream, Josephine had repeated that she didn't want to cross it, that she was afraid. He had taken Laure in his arms, crossed on foot and ordered the postillion to whip the horses. Josephine had started sobbing. He felt guilty and burdened by this woman. Why couldn't he have a wife like Laure Junot?

'You're mad,' he had grumbled, sensing that Josephine was jealous of Laure.

She knows that sometimes, early in the morning, when Laure is staying at Malmaison alone and Junot has remained at his headquarters in Paris, Napoleon goes to see her for the pleasure of looking at her and touching her, like a mischievous elder brother whose intentions and actions hover on the verge of ambiguity.

'You know I hate all these jealousies like poison,' he had said to Josephine. 'Come now, kiss me and be quiet. You are ugly when you cry. I have told you that before.'

She had dried her tears, but she has not stopped being jealous, either of Laure or Giuseppina Grassini.

HE IS GOING to send the Italian away from Paris. She cannot accept being his alone, and having to wait in that house he has chosen for her which he visits in the middle of the night when he can finally stop signing dispatches, writing, and working with the consuls, aides-de-camps and ministers.

Giuseppina tells him over and over again that she is bored. Fouché, with that incomparable cleverness of his, that combination of the policeman's and priest's arts, has also intimated that not only is it reckless to pay visits to the singer at night with only a servant as company, when there are so many attempts on his life, but also that Grassini has been seeking consolation in the arms of a violinist, a certain Ride.

He had to keep his calm in front of Fouché, but the minister was not fooled. What, or who, could fool him? That man is too wily and too intelligent to be trusted, which is exactly why he is indispensable – for the moment.

But la Grassini – she has to go. After all, she is only a woman.

He is still angry at himself for having been so submissive to Josephine when he was in love with her. He was so young then, so naïve. What did he know of women or power?

Now he only has to appear at the Opera or enter a salon in the Tuileries or Malmaison, or in Cambacérès' or Talleyrand's house at Neuilly, for them to offer themselves. Why should he reject them? They desire him – for himself, for money, for glory – and he needs them. After the arid council meetings, the debates on financial bona fides and the civil code, the constant presence of death and cruelty that is a part of power, they represent peace. The doors are closed; chandeliers and candles flood the room with a glittering light. The women are there, offered like open cities which he does not even need to lay siege to. He wouldn't have time, anyway. Luckily they guess this; they await an order. He loves their submissiveness and abandon and this swift game he plays with them as and when he pleases.

It is not very important. He takes what he wants, rewards them for it, and sometimes they come back again – Madame Branchu for instance, a singer with an ample figure in whose company he has passed a few hours. It all counts for so little in the end, that sometimes he prefers work to a woman. The actress Mademoiselle Duchesnois, for instance, came to the assignation he had made with her, undressed as his chief valet Constant instructed her, acting on his orders, waited in his bed and then, in the early hours of the morning, was given the order by the valet to get dressed again! That night he had been too preoccupied for even the slightest distraction.

Similarly with Mademoiselle Bourgoing, also an actress, who had arrived when her official lover, the good Chaptal, minister of the interior, was still in Napoleon's study because their discussion had gone on longer than expected. If Chaptal had had any illusions about the virtue of his mistress – and it is said he did – at that moment he received an education in the ways of the world. The minute he heard Mademoiselle Bourgoing's name being announced, he testily slammed his files shut, left the study and filed his letter of resignation.

And after all that, Napoleon did not even see Mademoiselle Bourgoing!

She has not forgiven him and speaks ill of him at every opportunity, telling stories and secrets and spreading gossip, a humiliated, outraged woman.

It is only one more hatred. Learning to be hated is part of being in power.

NAPOLEON ENTERS the salon. All heads turn towards him and conversations stop for a moment and then start up again, quieter. He goes over to Caroline Murat, but only exchanges a few words with his younger sister. She is like his brothers Lucien and Joseph and his sister Pauline – greedy, never satisfied with what she has. What does she think? That their father left the government of France as a legacy to be shared out amongst his children?

He, Napoleon, is the one who has won it.

However, this is his family, and he neither can nor wishes to renounce the ties of blood.

He turns away and sees Hortense de Beauharnais chatting to Duroc, an aide-de-camp. From the way she is talking, he guesses she is attracted to this officer. She has already dropped several hints that she wants to get married, but Josephine has other plans. She is contemplating marrying her to Lucien Bonaparte, even though they loathe each other; since becoming ambassador in Spain, he has been increasing the fortune he began to accumulate as minister of the interior. Josephine remembers even envisaging marrying Hortense and Louis at one point. That way the two families would be joined definitively, and Napoleon's heir – the question on everyone's lips – would be Hortense's son.

Napoleon walks away. He feels concerned and at the same time utterly removed from all these petty manoeuvres, convinced that his destiny will map out the future in an unforeseeable way. So why let himself be snared in these woman's schemes? Why dwell on these slanders that, as people blithely inform him, allege that he is Hortense's lover? That's right – him!

He wants to find Colonel Sébastiani, who with his soldiers from the Army of Italy was one of the officers to disperse the members of the Council of Five Hundred on 19 Brumaire, but first here is Roederer, talking about the financial system. Napoleon lets himself be drawn into the discussion.

'I don't get angry at all if someone contradicts me,' he says. 'I am looking for people to enlighten me, to express themselves boldly, to say what they are thinking – we are all friends here, this is family.' But once again, as when discussing the civil code with jurists, he feels sure he grasps the matter at hand quicker than anyone else. Perhaps all these experts have forgotten experience and plain common sense, or they haven't read the Justinian code, of which he remembers whole reams.

Suddenly he declares, 'Making laws is easier than enforcing them . . . It is as though you were giving me a hundred thousand men and asking me to make good soldiers out of them.'

He takes a few steps back and then looks round. A true leader must be able to shock, to take people by surprise. 'Well,' he continues, 'I would answer, "Give me time to send half of them to their deaths and the rest will be good."'

He likes to see the people he is talking to disconcerted and reduced to silence.

More and more often – but perhaps he has always thought this – he feels that he is the only one who is both clear and far-sighted; in any case, he is the one who makes the decisions. He does so for the Civil Code, the new financial legislation and the building of three new bridges in Paris, one of which will end at the Jardin des Plantes, another which will join the Île de la Cité and the Île St Louis, and one that will cross the Seine between the Louvre and the Institute.

Besides, when I'm not in command it ends in failure.

In Egypt, what remains of the army has been defeated by the British battalions that have landed. In Germany, Moreau – for what reason is not known – has not pursued and destroyed the Austrians he defeated.

I have to be the impulse at every moment, from building a road over the Simplon Pass to encouraging women to choose lawn rather than muslin, so that certain factories will be given a boost!

The exercise of power never stops.

AT NINE o'clock in the morning, Napoleon enters the room in the Tuileries where General Junot, his senior aide-de-camp and the commandant of Paris, reports to him. Junot has several officers with him. Napoleon walks up and down, taking pinch after pinch of snuff, and General Mortier, in command of the first military division, haltingly explains that there have been further attacks on stagecoaches by brigands.

Napoleon interrupts, exclaiming, 'More attacks on stagecoaches, more robbing of public funds? Is there no one who can take any measures to stop these crimes?'

Mortier lowers his head and says nothing.

Napoleon continues pacing. He talks loudly to the assembled company, clearly enunciating every word, and yet they have the feeling he is alone, swept along by his train of thought.

'The stagecoach roof should be made into a sort of miniature redoubt. Parapets should be constructed of narrow bolts of thick mattress, loopholes opened in them, and as many good marksmen placed at them as the roof can hold. Come along, General, see that these orders are executed speedily.'

He watches General Mortier leave the room.

'I myself love power; but I love it with an artist's love; I love it as a musician loves his violin, something from which to draw sounds, chords and harmonies.'

Do the people who set themselves against me understand that?

They make speeches in the Tribunate. They question the usefulness of special tribunals. They murmur amongst themselves. Who are they to take such a liberty? 'A handful of metaphysicians fit for drowning. They are like vermin in my clothes,' Napoleon says to Roederer. 'No one should think that I will let myself be attacked like Louis XVI. I will not tolerate it.'

Anyway, what can they do, so long as the people acclaim me and the army is loyal? To ensure that, I must have a victorious peace.

THAT STILL seems a difficult prospect at the start of 1801. Austria may have been defeated in Germany and Italy, but England is implacable. Nonetheless, with peace and fresh alliances on the continent, it could be isolated, intimidated and forced to make terms. Napoleon writes to Joseph who is negotiating at Lunéville with Cobenzl, Vienna's representative: 'Austria must make haste to be reasonable . . . Make it clear to Monsieur de Cobenzl that his position changes every day and if hostilities resume, my power may well stretch to the Julian Alps and Isonzo . . .'

So much for Vienna. That leaves his grand plan: to become the ally of Tsar Paul. Napoleon sends word to the Tsar's envoys, Kalitchef and General Sprengportern. He must receive them with every consideration at the Tuileries or Malmaison; they must be dazzled. An alliance with St Petersburg would open the way to his dream of sharing out the Turkish Empire between France and Russia, undertaking joint expeditions against India, and clamping the entire continent in the jaws of an alliance which would force England to yield and recognize those French acquisitions on the left bank of the Rhine which it has denied since 1792.

Napoleon goes up to General Sprengportern, whom he has invited to dine at the Tuileries. The Russian envoy is the centre of attraction; the Prussian ambassador to France, the Marquis de Lucchesini, is at his side. Prussia can be another ally on the continent. He must astonish these diplomats, display his wealth and power.

Napoleon has put on the first consul's red coat with gold embroidery, and is wearing a richly ornamented sword from a shoulder-belt. He unhooks it, hands it to General Sprengportern, and explains that he has had the weapon adorned with the finest diamonds from the crown: the Sancy diamond on the hilt and the Regent on the hand-guard. The sword passes from hand to hand until it returns to Napoleon who slowly fastens it back on. 'We have created everything by the sword,' he says.

A FEW DAYS LATER Louis XVIII, who has taken refuge in St Petersburg, is invited by Tsar Paul to leave the city, and Joseph can tell Napoleon that Austria has signed the peace treaty at Lunéville which, to all intents and purposes, repeats that of Campo Formio and so confirms the cession of the left bank of the Rhine to France. Anvers, 'that pistol aimed at the heart of England', remains under French control. The Cisalpine Republic is enlarged. France can intervene in German affairs.

Napoleon is the faithful heir of the politics of the Revolution.

In the south of Europe, Spain, taking note of the Treaty of

Lunéville, signs the Treaty of Aranjuez, by which it commits itself to waging war on Portugal, England's ally. In Italy, Parma and Piacenza are ceded to France.

AT THE announcement of the signing of the Treaty of Lunéville, Paris, which is already celebrating carnival, erupts with cries of joy.

Napoleon goes to the window of his study in the Tuileries and sees a crowd like that which formed the day after Marengo. He orders the bands of the Guard and the Paris garrison to play and turn the streets into a huge ballroom.

He prises himself away from the scenes of merrymaking for a moment, sits down at his desk and writes to Joseph, 'I have one more thing to tell you. The nation is pleased with the treaty and I am wholly satisfied with it. A thousand things to Julie.'

He sends for the prefect of police. He wishes him to go to each quarter with the mayors, proclaim peace to the people and read the declaration he has just written:

> People of France, a glorious peace has brought the war on the continent to an end. Your frontiers have been returned to the limits marked for them by nature. Peoples long separated from you rejoin your brothers and increase your population, your territory and your forces by a sixth. You owe this success above all to the courage of your warriors . . . but also to the fortunate restoration of concord in the nation, that union of feelings and interests which more than once has saved France from ruin.

HE REMAINS alone.

Peace? He wants it and he has almost achieved it. It now just has to be imposed on England. The game afoot is a simple one. He holds the European continent. The alliance with Russia is the key to its pacification which supposes an Austria reduced to obedience, as is happening, and a French presence in Germany and Italy.

Will it be possible to keep all the pawns together? Control the north and the south of the chessboard, the east and west?

How long will England set itself against him?

This is the situation. It is not in his power to change it, since it is what France wants and keeping the left bank of the Rhine is his legacy from the Revolution. It is impossible to give it up. It is the very heart of his inheritance.

When the delegations file through the vast salons of the Tuileries to congratulate him on having finally concluded peace, he is particularly attentive to the representatives from Brussels. 'The Belgians are French,' he says solemnly, 'like the Normans, the Alsatians, the Languedoc, Burgundy . . . Even if the enemy had established their headquarters in the faubourg St Antoine, the French people would never have relinquished their right or renounced their desire to be united with Belgium.'

The Belgian representatives are grateful and excited and Napoleon is cheered. He seems concerned. Is peace possible?

HE GOES TO the château of Neuilly where Talleyrand is hosting a lavish celebration to mark the signing of the treaty. The poet Esménard recites verses glorifying the First Consul. It seems as if he is being honoured more than the peace. Returned émigrés, ambassadors and Paris's most beautiful women throng around him, but he simply passes through them, smiling and distant.

'From triumph to failure is only a step.'

This occurs to him every time he has a success and the crowds cheer. He is not racked by the thought that glory is fleeting and that his power is precarious. It is simply there, like a reality he is aware of and must not forget because he knows where he has come from and what he has seen; as he says to Bourrienne on that 12 April 1801, 'At the most important moments a trifle has always decided the most important events in history.' Bourrienne hands him the dispatches the northern courier has just delivered to the Tuileries.

Napoleon reads them.

Tsar Paul has been strangled in his palace and his son Alexander, probably an accomplice of the assassins, has been crowned in his stead. The official explanation is that he died of apoplexy. Russian circles in favour of the alliance with England are ecstatic. London is triumphant.

Napoleon has come to a halt in the middle of the room.

He is crumpling up the dispatch when Fouché, who has just

obtained a detailed account of the murder from his own sources, enters the study. Paul was strangled with his scarf and his skull was shattered by a sword hilt in his own bedroom. The conspirators took three quarters of an hour to kill him.

There is a look of disgust on Napoleon's face.

'What!' he exclaims. 'An emperor isn't safe even in the midst of his guards?'

Fouché starts to explain that such events are usual in Russia, but Napoleon interrupts him. He wants to be alone with Bourrienne.

He walks up and down the room and thinks of what his fate will be in this palace. Whatever Fouché says, anyone who rules is always a target. Didn't they try to kill him only a few weeks ago in rue St Niçaise? Even if the courts have sentenced François Carbon and Saint-Réjeant to death, the police have still not found Limoëlan, the third of the men who devised 'the infernal machine', or the instigator of the whole plot, Georges Cadoudal. Some Jacobins must still be sharpening their daggers. And what about the generals – Moreau or Bernadotte, jealous and convinced they could be first consul?

But there is worse. One side of the chessboard has now slipped out of his grasp.

'I was certain that with the Tsar I could deliver a fatal blow to English power in India.' Napoleon curses. 'Now a palace revolution is throwing my plans into disarray!'

How can one fail to think that the English are hiding behind the Tsar's murderers, just as they are Cadoudal's sponsors and supporters? London wants, at all costs, to prevent peace in continental Europe. It has just delivered an ultimatum to the governments, including Denmark who have formed a neutral northern league. England wants their ports to be open to its merchandise and assumes the right to search all shipping. To impose its demands, Nelson's squadron has just entered the Baltic on its way to threaten Copenhagen.

'Write this down,' Napoleon says to Bourrienne.

The public must understand that England is setting obstacles in the path of peace, 'a peace the world needs'. Napoleon dictates a few lines which are to be published in the *Moniteur*: 'Paul died on the night of 24 March. The English squadron has passed the Sound.

History will reveal the connection that probably exists between these two events.'

Then he repeats to himself, 'An emperor . . . in the midst of his guards.'

ON 21 APRIL 1801, the day that François Carbon and Saint-Réjeant, two of the perpetrators of the attack in the rue St Niçaise, are guillotined, Napoleon receives Monge and Laplace, two scholars who are also senators.

He shows them the police report of the execution: as the two Chouans climbed onto the scaffold, they shouted 'Long live the king!'

Turning towards Monge and Laplace, Napoleon says slowly, as if he is thinking out loud, 'The French people must tolerate me with my faults, and find some advantages to me.' He stops, and then repeats what he has already said in the Tribunate: 'I am a soldier, a child of the Revolution who has emerged from the bosom of the people. My fault is that I cannot endure insults. I will not suffer anyone to insult me as a king.'

X

Napoleon looks at himself in the mirror Roustam the Mameluke is holding. Constant, his chief valet, approaches carrying his English razor, which is sharpened or replaced every morning, and his soap, also English-made, on a gilt tray.

Rather than, as usual, seizing the razor and shaving in a few swift strokes, cutting through the thin, barely lathered soap, Napoleon takes his time and continues to look hard at his reflection.

Late yesterday afternoon, in David's studio, he had pored over a sketch of the painting the artist had just started. So this is how he will be seen: swathed in a cape, under a forbidding sky, controlling a rearing horse, its mane and tail blowing in the wind, as the soldiers pass behind him on the edge of an Alpine precipice, pushing their cannon.

'Bonaparte crossing the St Bernard,' David had murmured.

The face David has given him bears very little resemblance to the one he sees in the mirror. The painter's is full, the skin smooth and white, its features harmonious. This morning his eyes are deep set, his skin almost dark yellow, and the chin seems too long for his thin face. Perhaps he is the only one who sees himself as he is? Perhaps the truth now is what David paints? Perhaps he is already seen as a hero, a king's son?

He looks around. Suddenly he feels as if he is suffocating, even though he asks Roustam to open the windows every morning. He cannot stand the stuffy atmosphere when he wakes up, the overpowering smells of the night and the body.

'Open it,' he calls to Roustam, 'so I can breathe the air God gave us.'

The sky is low and it's chilly. It is barely past seven and the sun cannot break through the layer of grey fog on this May morning.

Napoleon shaves in a few minutes. Constant was right to have convinced him to shave himself, because he cannot stand being in someone else's hands, unable to move. What does it matter if he does a patchy job? He splashes eau de Cologne over his face and then gets into the hot bath. The room is already full of steam. He loves painfully immersing himself in near-boiling water this way, getting the measure of his body and experiencing temporary relief from the almost endemic irritation of his skin.

He stays there for a long time. This is where he feels calmest, in his bath. Sometimes in the middle of the night he will get into this hot water to relax.

Yesterday evening Josephine had reproached him when – maliciously, admittedly – he had let her know that Lucien had received an offer from the Spanish court and Prince Godoy: Infanta Isabelle as a spouse for the First Consul if he finally decided to divorce. Josephine never gives way to anger, but she had assumed her holy mourner's expression.

He cannot stand these faces and lamentations. He had burst out that he wanted to organize a hunt, despite it becoming dark, and Josephine had finally given in to her resentment. 'You cannot be thinking of a hunt, Bonaparte, all our animals are pregnant,' she had protested.

He had replied that he would change his mind, adding, as a parting shot, 'Everything is prolific here, except Madame.'

Was that cruel? Wasn't he just telling the truth?

As for the Spanish marriage mooted by Lucien – *as if I was a royal heir* – Napoleon is unconvinced. He had said as much to Volney the previous evening: 'If I was in a position to marry again, I would not go looking for a wife in a house in ruins.' But what does Lucien understand? He must have been bought, since he has accepted the policies of Prince Godoy who, despite making a commitment, has only waged a ridiculous war with Portugal, a 'war of oranges', so that the treaty of Badajoz can be hastily concluded with Lisbon. According to Fouché, Lucien and Prince Godoy have divided thirty million francs between the two of them. After which Lucien has had the naivety or effrontery to ask for a portrait of the First Consul to give to the prince!

BOURRIENNE HAS come into the bathroom. Despite the steam, he prepares to read to Napoleon or take dictation.

Napoleon begins a letter to Lucien: 'I shall never send my portrait to a man who keeps his predecessor in a dungeon, and who adopts the customs of the Inquisition. I may make use of him, but I owe him nothing but contempt.'

Napoleon gets out of the bath. Roustam splashes his body with eau de Cologne, and then starts brushing him. 'Do it hard, like a donkey,' says Napoleon. Then he goes into his dressing room, where Constant stands, holding out his white kerseymere breeches. At the end of every day they are either blotched with ink, because of his tendency to wipe his pen on them, or stained by the coarse snuff he prefers.

Bourrienne begins to read the most recent letters to have arrived, two from Lucien who protests and apologizes simultaneously: 'I fully admit that I have certain deficiencies; I have known for a long time that I am too young for affairs of state.' Bourrienne hesitates, and then continues reading. 'I wish to retire in order to acquire what I lack . . . There is only one authority I know that can keep me in Spain, and that is death.'

Napoleon recognizes Lucien's extreme character, his energy and jealousy and hatred of Josephine when he rails against 'a fresh torrent of slurs and disgraces . . . I am torn to shreds in your salon, accused of rape, of premeditated murder and incest.'

Enough!

In Madrid Lucien has let himself be caught up by 'court cajolery'. He is the sort of man whom flatterers corrupt, who let themselves be bought.

So who can I really count on in this family? My family! Jérôme is serving under Admiral Ganteaume, whose squadron has just won a modest success in the Mediterranean, but is unable to go to the assistance of what remains of the army of Egypt – just when we need a daring and powerful navy, since England refuses to sign the treaty of peace and Nelson's fleet is bombarding Copenhagen. If only Jérôme could become my eye and arm at sea! I must encourage him, write to him.

'I learn with pleasure,' Napoleon dictates, 'that you are getting used to life at sea. This is the only place nowadays where glory is to be won. Go up aloft, study every part of the ship, and when you come back I hope to hear that you are as agile as any good ship's boy. Don't let anyone tell you your job. I hope you have already learnt to keep your watch and plot your position.'

Didn't I start off as a good artilleryman?

He has put on his colonel of the Guard uniform and before going to the orderly room, where General Junot and other officers are waiting for him, he reads the abstracts of all the newspapers and books published in the last ten days, compiled by his personal librarian, Ripault.

He does not want these newspapers and books to repeat the slanders that the English press and the pamphleteers in their pay are spreading across Europe. That is how institutions are destroyed and governments lose the trust they are owed. He has said this to Saint-Jean-d'Angely, himself a loyal supporter: 'Before railing against the government, people should first put themselves in its place . . .'

Then, sitting at his desk alone in his study, he reads the reports of his personal police who keep Fouché's police under surveillance. Who can one rely on? The Tsar was assassinated in his bedroom, in the heart of his palace, and his own son was complicit in his murder!

At the highest reaches of power everything can be done and everything can be forgotten. Duroc has been sent to St Petersburg to establish good relations with Alexander and accept the fable of Paul having died of an attack of apoplexy!

But I am not the son of a king. So I shall protect myself.

He takes his quill and writes to Fouché, 'Here, Citizen Minister, are some notes which I can vouch for as trustworthy.' He passes on to Fouché the information he has received concerning Georges Cadoudal, who is still in France, as well as those who he calls 'satellites of Georges and his usual emissaries'. They must be captured, dead or alive.

He stands up. He still has to hear General Junot's reports, and then he will have finished the preliminaries to his day.

That is when the matters of real importance will begin!

XI

TODAY, 22 MAY 1801, as the afternoon draws to a close, Napoleon is waiting for Monsignor Spina, the Archbishop of Corinth and the Pope's envoy.

He goes out into Malmaison's garden. It is a mild day. He turns and catches sight of Talleyrand and Abbé Bernier in the drawing room of the southern pavilion. He has put these two in charge of negotiating with Monsignor Spina, who arrived in Paris several months ago, a concordat with the Pope, but so far their discussions haven't made any headway.

He knows that Talleyrand, a former bishop who swore allegiance to the civil constitution of the clergy and who supports the right of priests to marry – reasonably enough, since he is planning to do so himself – has reservations about this agreement. As have many others: ideologues, scholars such as Monge or Laplace, generals who profess atheism, and a host of casual Voltaireans hostile to any reconciliation with the Pope.

What do they understand about my policies? To pacify and establish complete control over this country, there must be a return to religion.

He has explained this to a few people already – saying, 'After a victorious army, I know of no better allies than those men who guide individual consciences in God's name' – but he will have to say it again and, above all, take the negotiations in hand himself, as he does every time the stakes are high. And when are they not when one governs?

This is why the diplomat François Cacault has set off for Rome with specific instructions – 'Treat the sovereign pontiff as if he had two hundred thousand men,' Napoleon has told him – but just because one's adversary is powerful does not mean that one must treat him carefully or capitulate to him. After all, Henry VIII founded the Anglican Church, other monarchs are Protestants, and the kings of France were Gallicans!

Why must I bow to the Pope?

Abbé Bernier comes to find him. Napoleon trusts this former officer in the Vendéean army whose ambition and realism led him to join the Republicans. Bernier has the build of a peasant, but he speaks with the gentle persuasiveness of a parson and exhibits the intelligence and cunning of a Jesuit.

Bernier announces Monsignor Spina's arrival. He must be welcomed with every courtesy and at the same time unsettled and shown that there will be no concessions on any essential points. He must be left in no doubt that it will cost the papacy dear if it refuses to come to an agreement; it will lose the Legations, those territories it cares about so keenly.

As soon as they start talking, Napoleon sees a look of anxiety in Monsignor Spina's eyes. He must intimidate him further, abandon the honeyed, dissembling language of Roman diplomacy.

'I am the one you have to come to terms with,' Napoleon says, pacing about the salon, stopping occasionally to take a pinch of snuff. 'I am the one you have to trust, and I am the only one who can save you.'

He approaches the archbishop. 'Are you laying claim to the Legations? Do you wish to be rid of French troops? Everything will depend on your responses to my requests, in particular those concerning the bishops.'

Spina shrinks into his chair and stammers; it is as if every word Napoleon says strikes him like a blow. Now is the time to charge furiously, as one would if this were war.

'I was born a Catholic and there is nothing I would like more than to restore Catholicism,' Napoleon slowly begins. Then his voice becomes clipped. 'But the Pope is behaving in such a manner that I am tempted to become Lutheran or Calvinist and take all of France with me.'

He hammers out each sentence, gesturing with his hand. 'The Pope must change his attitude and listen to me!' he says. 'Otherwise I shall restore another religion; I shall furnish the people with some form of worship with bells and processions and dispense with the Holy Father. As far as I will be concerned, he won't exist anymore.'

He turns his back on the archbishop, sets off towards the park and calls out, 'Send a courier to Rome today to tell him that.'

HE IS SATISFIED. When he left Malmaison, Spina had been softly spoken, like someone who has already submitted.

'One can give matters an impetus,' Napoleon tells Talleyrand, 'and then they carry you along with them.' He is convinced that he has found the right tone, that of someone who won't be overawed by an adversary, even if it should be the Pope. He knows what he wants: a concordat which would give him the right to nominate bishops. The agreement would restore the papacy's authority over the Church of France, but only in exchange for the loss of its pre-eminence. Catholicism would merely be the religion practised by the first consul, and the Church would renounce all claims to former properties that had been sold as national land. He is sure he has the best cards in his hand, which he is not afraid to play. Can anyone, even the Pope, stop him?

Abbé Bernier has reported Spina saying in a whisper that the first consul is 'sending him off his head'. So much the better! That is how one prevails.

A FEW DAYS LATER, Napoleon sees Monsignor Spina again, in the illuminated gardens of the château of Neuilly. The archbishop finds him in the middle of the guests invited by Talleyrand to celebrate the visit of the King and Queen of Etruria, as Napoleon has decided to rename the Grand Duchy of Tuscany. The new king is Louis de Bourbon, the King of Spain's son-in-law. An attentive throng crowds around Napoleon as he observes the royal couple. They are the first Bourbons to enter France since the Revolution.

He feels a sense of intense satisfaction. He is the one in power, welcoming the descendant of that illustrious family, and even if it is Louis de Bourbon who is the guest of honour, it is the first consul on whom the poets shower praise. Italian arias are sung for him and it is for his benefit that a vast set has been built depicting the Palazzo Vecchio square in Florence.

Monsignor Spina informs him that Cardinal Consalvi, the Vatican's Secretary of State, has left Rome for Paris to conclude negotiations concerning the Concordat, and Napoleon smiles slightly as he listens to this piece of news which he already knows and which confirms that he handled Spina correctly.

Louis de Bourbon approaches and says to Napoleon, '*Ma in somma, siete Italiano, siete nostro.*'

What does he think, this Bourbon whom I have made a king? That I have something in common with him? Me, Italian? Me?

'I am French,' he replies curtly

He loves France. He remembers those first years at Autun and Brienne, how he was treated, the teasing, his accent, how he longed to return to Corsica and serve alongside Paoli, his people's liberator, but he no longer thinks of the island of his childhood. All that remains of it is his family – his brothers and sisters and his mother. He knows their faults, but like him they have torn themselves away from Corsica, or been driven from it.

Among the men of France, his soldiers in Italy and Egypt, he has become French. He knows this country; it was not given him but he has conquered it and he wants its greatness. In essence, he and the new nation that emerged in 1789 were born together, but that is not enough; France did not start with the Revolution, hence his desire for the different eras of its history to come together, to 'fuse', in him. He can do it on his own because he belongs to no political clan; he is from elsewhere and has absorbed this country's memories through history books. He does not rue the days before 1789; he knows that such a 'before' exists. Which is also why he wants internal peace, the Concordat, so that the re-establishment of religious harmony can bring genuine order both to society and men's souls.

He says to Bourrienne, 'I am convinced that a part of France would become Protestant, especially if I were to favour that disposition, but I am even more certain that the majority would remain Catholic . . .'

He muses, deep in thought.

'I dread the religious quarrels,' he continues, 'the conflicts within families, the inevitable upheaval. In reviving a religion which has always prevailed in the country, and which still prevails in the hearts of the people, and in giving the liberty of exercising their worship to the minority, I shall satisfy every one.'

He shows Bourrienne a book Elisa has brought him. The author, François Auguste René de Chateaubriand, is a returned émigré and regular visitor to her salon. His book, *Atala*, extols the genius of Christianity. This chimes exactly with the people's feelings and his own wishes for the present.

He often thinks of religion in that spring of 1801 as the negotiations with the Pope's envoys follow their course. More often than not he stays at Malmaison, where he convenes the Council and his ministers every day. In the evening, in the cool air that comes from the park and the woods, Josephine presides over their receptions. He receives the King and Queen of Etruria. He goes for long gallops and hunts, despite Josephine's objections. He takes walks in the park. One evening he invites Thibaudeau to accompany him. He likes this former member of the Convention who has become a state councillor; jokingly he calls him 'the powdered Jacobin', but he is a good person to talk to.

'That reminds me,' Napoleon says to him, walking slowly, 'I was here last Sunday, strolling in the solitude and silence of this country. Suddenly I heard the bell of Rueil and I was deeply moved, so strong are one's first habits and education.'

He glances at Thibaudeau, who is nodding in agreement.

'I thought then what an impression this must make on simple, credulous folk.' He stops and takes Thibaudeau by the arm. 'What would your philosophes and ideologues say to that? The people need a religion, and this religion must be in the hands of the government. As it is, fifty émigré bishops in the pay of England control the French clergy. Their hold must be broken. The Pope's authority is needed for that . . .'

He starts walking again, remaining silent for several minutes, and then he murmurs, 'They will say I am a Papist, but I am nothing. I was a Mahometan in Egypt. I will be a Catholic for the good of the people.'

He looks hard at Thibaudeau.

Can I say everything that is on my mind?

'I do not believe in religions,' he confides. 'But the concept of a God . . .!' He points to the sky. 'Who made all this?'

Head bowed, he listens to Thibaudeau arguing that, even if one believes in God, a clergy is not necessary. Napoleon shakes his head. Is Thibaudeau as naïve as that?

'The clergy still exists,' Napoleon says. 'It will exist as long as the people have a religious spirit, and that is innate . . . So the priests must be brought back into the Republic.'

He feels free, but he knows the strength of prejudice. It must be reckoned with if one wants to govern a people.

He puts on the first consul's scarlet coat with gold embroidery, and wears the consular sword studded with diamonds at his side to receive Cardinal Consalvi, who has finally reached Paris. He watches him walking towards him through the Tuileries great reception hall, which is crowded with ministers and delegates from the Assemblies, all of whom have donned their full regalia; it must be a solemn audience.

He goes to meet Cardinal Consalvi who is wearing the black robe, red stockings and tasselled hat of a cardinal of the Roman Curia.

A new game is beginning, and Napoleon must win it.

'I revere the Pope, who is a man of great kindness,' he begins in a low voice, 'and I wish to come to an agreement with him, but I cannot accept the changes you have been considering in Rome. You will be given another version of the agreement. It is absolutely imperative that you sign it within five days.'

Consalvi appears taken aback. He must consult with Rome, he says.

'That will not be possible.' Napoleon has barely raised his voice, but his gaze compels Consalvi to bow his head. 'I have very serious reasons why I cannot allow a moment's more delay. You will sign within five days, or everything will be broken off and I will adopt a national religion. Nothing will be easier for me to do than this.'

He has drawn up the plan of battle. Now Joseph Bonaparte must conduct the negotiations with Abbé Bernier.

When he sees Consalvi again on 12 July at Malmaison, it seems they are nearing agreement.

'You know,' Napoleon says smiling, 'that if one doesn't come to terms with the Good Lord, one comes to terms with the Devil.'

He does not listen to Consalvi's protestations, or pay any heed to his nervousness. He is not concerned. His plan must succeed.

He stays at Malmaison. He has a fever, is unwell. Sometimes he feels violent pains in his side. This is something he must live with, he thinks; it will be possible to temper its effects; he trusts his new doctor, Corvisart. He holds out his arm and Corvisart applies blisters. His skin puffs and swells, he feels a burning sensation. He does not feel like seeing anyone, but he can read and write. He does not want to be the slave of his body.

'Being sick is a good time to come to terms with the clergy,' he says.

DURING THE morning of 14 July, as he is preparing to preside over the Fête de la Concorde and is finishing his dictation of the proclamation in which he celebrates 'continental peace', the imminent end of 'religious divisions' and the disappearance of 'political dissensions', concluding with the exhortation, 'Rejoice in your position, people of France, rejoice, all the peoples envy your destiny,' Joseph enters his study.

He wears an expression that wavers between contrition, anxiety and satisfaction.

Napoleon is beside himself with impatience, telling Joseph to give him the document he and Consalvi have settled on. He takes the pieces of paper, glances through them and throws them into the fireplace where, despite the heat, he has had a fire lit. Why has Joseph accepted all these concessions? He will not bend.

That evening at a dinner he gives at the Tuileries, he addresses Cardinal Consalvi. His voice bristles with scorn; he wants to show all his strength and anger.

'So Monsieur le Cardinal, you wish to break everything off. Very well. I have no need of the Pope. If Henry the Eighth, who hadn't a twentieth of my power, could not only envisage changing his country's religion but also carry it through, I shall be all the more able to . . .'

Each of the two hundred and fifty guests has their eyes riveted on Napoleon and Consalvi. He must strike harder.

'By changing the religion of France, I shall change that of almost all Europe, wherever the influence of my power extends. Rome will see the losses it has incurred and it will mourn them, but there will be no remedy.' Napoleon moves away from Consalvi, adding in a loud voice so that all the guests can hear, 'You can go, that is the best option left you. You wanted to break everything off, well then, so be it, since you so wished.'

He must not give in, and yet, deep down, he feels doubt mounting. Is this the right way? He is surrounded by people urging him to give the negotiations one last chance.

'Very well,' he calls to Joseph and Monsignor Consalvi. 'To prove to you that I am not the one who wishes to break off, I approve the motion that tomorrow the commissioners shall meet again for the last time. Let them see if there is any possibility of arranging matters, but if they part without having come to any conclusion, relations will be considered definitively severed and the cardinal may leave.'

At two o'clock in the morning on 15 July, the Concordat is signed. The link between the royalists and the Church is broken. The clergy will be under the government's control, and he will be able to choose the bishops.

Napoleon savours the moment. He is the peacemaker. He has imposed his views on the millennial throne of the Pope. Only a few monarchs have ever done so in all history. Now he is one of their number.

He goes to the window. It is raining. He is alone. He writes to Josephine who is taking the waters at Plombières and Luxeuil with Hortense, 'It is such bad weather I have stayed in Paris. Malmaison without you is too sad. The festival was very fine, it tired me a little.'

PART THREE

Peace is the foremost of needs,
as it is the foremost of glories

JULY 1801 TO MARCH 1802

XII

NAPOLEON HAS BEEN galloping for more than two hours, changing course at random, jumping streams and hedges, plunging deep into the woods. He has recognized Butard's forest, which he has just bought to increase Malmaison's land still further. Sometimes he crosses one of his farms on the estate. The peasants step out of the way, surprised, but he does not stop. He likes taking long rides like this, only accompanied by Roustam or an aide-de-camp. It feels as if he were alone. He needs this physical exertion. He needs to feel the stamina and agility of his body. He cannot stay shut up, day in day out, in the salons or studies which some of his ministers never leave, shuttling from one to the next. They are alarmed, terrified even, whenever they hear that he has gone out into the countryside or woods. Is this fitting behaviour for a first consul who has just negotiated with a Cardinal, the Pope's secretary of state? What amazes them is his ability, moments after jumping down from his horse, to chair meetings of the committee working on a draft of the Civil Code and to point out errors, even errors by Portalis, a lawyer and state councillor who is learned, thoughtful and has a prodigious memory.

If he wishes to be pre-eminent, he must be everywhere and show those he governs that they belong to a system of thought and action which is their superior and of which he is the sole organizer.

'One must be a leader everywhere and in everything,' he says.

HE RIDES back to Malmaison. It is 15 August 1801. He is thirty-two today. He has mastered, and legislated to, one of the oldest ruling houses in Europe, the Hapsburgs of Austria; he has made the Pope yield to him. He, Napoleon Bonaparte, has done that.

He leaps off his horse.

If peace is finally established in Europe – and for that relations must be resumed with the Russia of the new Tsar, Alexander, and a treaty signed with England – then he shall have truly brought to an end the troubles that have steeped France and Europe in blood for more than ten years.

He enters the salon and sees Talleyrand, the Minister of Foreign Affairs, leaning on one of the chairs.

They say he has had a fine pair of boots made for him so that, despite his infirmity, he can keep up with me on horseback.

Napoleon beckons him over and Talleyrand approaches, limping heavily but as nonchalant as ever, a smile faintly lighting up his face. His calm and reserve irritate Napoleon. He would like to give him a good shake, this imperturbable man who, even when he is at his most servile, seems inaccessible. It is impossible to get any hold over him, but still, what has he to reproach him for? He makes the women of the salon laugh with his remarks, for he has a ready tongue. The consuls? he murmurs. He only refers to them in Latin, as *Hic, Haec, Hoc*: *Hic*, the masculine, is Napoleon; *Haec*, the feminine, is Cambacérès, whose tendencies are well known; and *Hoc*, the neuter, is Lebrun.

As he is going to his study, Napoleon gives instructions to Talleyrand who follows him a few paces behind. The new Russian ambassador, Markov, has just arrived in Paris.

'Ask him for passports for Russia, where I wish to send an officer, Citizen Caulaincourt, colonel of carabineers.'

Napoleon signals to Talleyrand that he can sit down, but the Foreign Minister simply rests a hand on the back of a chair.

'I want it made clear to Markov,' Napoleon says, 'that this officer must deal directly with His Majesty the Emperor Alexander.'

Talleyrand nods.

Always brush entourages aside and try to speak privately with the ones who decide.

I am certain that then I can convince him. I must speak frankly, as I did with Cardinal Consalvi. Markov has protested, in Russia's name, against France occupying Piedmont and doing injury to the kinglet of Sardinia; 'Well then, let him come and take it back!' I'll say.

Diplomats and monarchs are men just like anyone else.

HAS HE EVER thought otherwise, even when he was just a little second lieutenant aged sixteen? Perhaps at first, when he thought about Pascal Paoli, he felt Paoli was someone out of the ordinary, a superior being? But then he got close to him at Corte and his illusions disappeared. Since then he has seen so many men of every stripe that at thirty-two he feels that he can never be surprised again.

At such a young age, he has led thousands of men to death. He has ordered men to open fire on others. He has had people shot. He has refused petitions for the reprieve of men sentenced to death.

He remembers the camp at Jaffa, the chaos that reigned among the soldiers, the women everywhere, the order he gave to round up all those troublemaking females in the courtyard of the lazaret-house. They were taken there, where a company of light infantry was waiting and opened fire. On his orders.

He knows that that day he was called 'an inhuman monster shedding blood more for his own pleasure than through necessity'. He is unaffected either by the memory or by this verdict of him which he read at the time in an officer's letter.

What do they who judge me know of the necessity that grips one who commands? 'There are cases where expending lives means sparing bloodshed.'

IT IS FOR the sake of all these wars he has fought and won that he wants peace.

He repeats this to Talleyrand. England must be made to understand that he is sincere in his desire to conclude a treaty. 'Explain to them, Citizen Minster, that, in the position in which France finds itself, I am opening diplomatic relations with all the powers and have made it a rule never to show any hint of bad faith.'

Has his minister understood?

Napoleon raises his voice. Talleyrand must set a limit, as they had to in the unending negotiations with the Pope. 'If they want to push us further, I am resolved to break off negotiations and I want everything to be finished before 10 Vendémiaire [2 October].' He advances towards Talleyrand. 'Tell them this with some pride: they risk losing everything, like the Emperor of Austria, if they want to have more.'

BUT WHAT can words do if they are not backed up by weapons and force?

Napoleon summons the generals and prefects: from the Gironde to the mouths of the Escaut, he wants redoubts built, guns assembled, craft of all sizes armed and telegraph stations established. England must fear invasion and know that it is powerless to do anything against the Republic. Nelson's fleet has twice been driven out of Boulogne by Admiral Latouche-Tréville. That is the example to be followed. People listen to reason when it is backed up by cannonfire.

On 11 October 1801, at Malmaison, a courier brings word that the preliminaries of peace have been signed in London. England commits itself to restoring to France, Spain and Holland their respective colonies. Malta will be restored to the Knights of St John and the island of Elba will be under French sovereignty.

Napoleon ponders for several minutes, holding the dispatch in his hand. Nothing has been said about France's gains on the continent, nor is there any mention of Louisiana, San Domingo or maritime trade. The real issues have been avoided.

'Fire the cannon,' he says, 'and let the signing be proclaimed in Paris this evening with a torchlight procession.'

IN THE STREETS of the capital, the people cry, 'Long live the Republic! Long live Bonaparte!' In London, Napoleon's aide-de-camp Lauriston is welcomed enthusiastically when he comes to ratify the preliminaries. The horses of his coach are unharnessed so that the crowd can pull it themselves through the brilliantly lit city.

Napoleon smiles when he sees Talleyrand coming towards him. The minister is unable to hide his disappointment; his voice is slightly shrill; he says that he only learnt that the preliminaries of peace had been signed when he heard the Invalides' cannon.

'I am *Hic*, am I not?' says Napoleon.

HIC, MASCULINE! It suits him, Talleyrand's name for him. He feels wholly male. He does not deny himself either Madame Branchu or Mademoiselle Duchesnois or Josephine.

When he looks at the men gathered round him in the Council of State, some of whose sessions concerning the Civil Code he chairs, he is certain he dominates in vigour of mind and body these dignitaries who, in any case, depend on him. He listens to Portalis deliver his report on the Civil Code. The man reads slowly because, being nearly fifty years old, he is losing his sight. His memory and intelligence are as quick as ever, but his body is not keeping pace.

I am only thirty-two! I have just ratified the Concordat, which has finally been approved by the College of Cardinals in Rome.

A box of diamonds worth fifteen thousand francs has been given to Cardinal Consalvi, and one of eight thousand to Monsignor Spina, as well as twelve thousand francs to divide amongst the offices of the Chancery.

Men are men. 'And men are like numbers: their worth depends only on their position.'

HIC, MASCULINE!

Portalis is talking about the article in the Civil Code concerning marriage: he is in favour of keeping divorce, but, he explains, 'Infidelity on the part of the wife implies greater corruption and has more dangerous effects than on the part of the husband.' Divorce will therefore be the husband's right, if the wife is adulterous, but the man will only be considered at fault if he introduces his concubine into the family home.

Portalis leans towards Napoleon, seeking his approval.

Divorce: he had thought of it when he returned from Egypt, knowing Josephine's infidelities. Today his brothers Joseph and Lucien, his sisters Pauline and Elisa and perhaps even his mother wish he would divorce. They dream of it.

Napoleon starts to reply slowly, 'What is a broken family? What are children who no longer have a father? Who cannot enfold in the same embrace all fathers severed from their progeny? Ah, let us take care not to encourage divorce. Of all fashions, that would be the most pernicious. Let us not put the stamp of fault on the husband who resorts to it, but let us pity him as a man who has suffered a great misfortune. Let custom shun this sad recourse that the law cannot refuse unfortunate husbands.'

He stands up and says in a loud voice, 'The wife must know that in leaving the tutelage of her family she enters that of her husband.'

XIII

Two years already since 18 Brumaire!

Napoleon does not sleep on that night of 8 November. He is not trying to remember everything he has accomplished in these two years. He walks up and down his study in the Tuileries. He has not woken Roustam. He does not want to take a hot bath.

He goes to his desk and reads the proclamation he drew up last night that is to be read out this morning. As is his wont, he wrote it in one go: 'People of France, at last you have it, this peace you have deserved through such long and wholehearted efforts! The world now consists only of friendly nations . . . Let the glory of battle give way to a glory that is gentler on our citizens and less formidable to our neighbours.'

He says what he hopes and what the people wish for, but he knows that nothing is conclusive; even if he has had in places to extol what he has accomplished, he is convinced that everything is still to be done, because nothing is certain.

Peace? London has signed the preliminaries, but every passing day shows that it is on its guard and jealous of its rights. In all likelihood this is only an interlude.

A few days ago, Fox, one of the leading English Members of Parliament, came to Paris. They spoke, but everything seemed to make Fox anxious. When he visited an exhibition at the Louvre of products made in France, he had the concerned expression of a representative of a trading nation visiting a competitor. Someone was stupid enough, when they were giving a globe to the first consul, to declare as they pointed at England how small a nation it was! Fox had become impassioned. 'Yes,' he said, 'it is on this little island that the English are born and it is on this island that they all want to die.' Then he took the globe in his arms and added, 'But during their lives they fill this globe and encompass it with their might.'

I could only agree. I feel England's resistance at every moment, when peace still has not been concluded.

The announcement of the departure for San Domingo of an expedition led by General Leclerc to reconquer the island which the blacks have taken control of, with one of their own, Toussaint l'Ouverture, at their head, worries the English, but this is a French colony which they have not laid claim to. What do they find offensive? That Napoleon wrote to the inhabitants of San Domingo assuring them that, 'no matter what your origin and your colour', they are all 'Frenchmen, all free and equal before God and before the Republic'? Are the English afraid of the contagion of liberty, or of seeing San Domingo's sugar and coffee breaking their monopoly? Perhaps they think that, since Pauline Bonaparte is to accompany General Leclerc in March, a French empire is being envisaged over there in the Americas?

Napoleon stops in the middle of his study.

He is thinking of that, it is true. At the centre will be a reconquered and pacified San Domingo; to the east, Martinique and Guadeloupe; to the south, Guiana; and to the north Louisiana.

He daydreams for a few moments.

He must make sure the expedition leaves as soon as possible.

WHAT AN immense field of endeavour lies before him! The future is calling him. How could he look back to tally up what has been done in the last two years?

He reads a few lines of the proclamation again: 'People of France, two years ago, this very day saw an end to civil strife and the annihilation of all factions.'

But even that is not complete! In the three Assemblies, an opposition is trying to form itself. In the Council of State, the Legislative Corps and the Senate, people are lampooning and criticizing his signature of the Concordat. Factions! They are not dead yet! How many times has he said, 'Large assemblies lead to cliques, and cliques to hatred.'

Nothing is ever finished.

He sits down at his desk and begins to glance through the letters Bourrienne has sorted. His correspondents flatter, solicit, and overwhelm him with proposals.

He dwells for a moment on one from the General Council of the Seine which proposes to erect a triumphal arch in honour of the first consul of the Republic. Such is the lot of one who governs; certain assemblies snap at his heels, others shower him with praise. Has he ever known anything else? It feels as if he has always been a ruler. He finds it difficult to picture his life before. Perhaps he has always believed so strongly that he would attain supreme power that he forgot the actual present he was living through.

And now what is he doing except thinking of the future? He begins a reply to the General Council of the Siene. 'The idea of dedicating monuments to men who make themselves useful to the people is an honourable one for nations,' he writes. 'I accept the offer of a monument which you wish to build for me; let its place remain allocated, but let us leave the task of building it to the centuries to come, if they ratify the good opinion you have of me. I salute you affectionately.'

The superior man is imperturbable; he is blamed, he is praised, but he always goes his own way. Sometimes, however, he must feign anger or let it show.

When the men I have put in the heart of the Assemblies, or tolerated when I could have proscribed them, rise up against me, I can only say, 'They are dogs . . .'

Napoleon cannot stay still; he walks from one corner of his study to the other and glances out of the window, momentarily distracted by a movement amongst the sentries of the Consular Guard.

Why does he saddle himself with tribunes, legislators, senators and state councillors? 'The Assemblies have never combined prudence and drive, or sense and rigour,' he murmurs.

He turns towards Stanislas de Girardin. This member of the Tribunate, a friend of Joseph, is devoted to him, but his colleagues have been raising procedural objections for weeks. They chatter endlessly and reject articles of the Civil Code, which is their way of showing their antagonism towards the first consul and his policy of reconciliation with the Church. 'I run into these dogs everywhere,' Napoleon resumes. 'They put their spokes into the wheel everywhere. This is not how one organizes a great nation. The Tribunate is a barrier which delays the execution of the most salutary intentions . . .'

He barely listens to Girardin and shrugs his shoulders when Girardin stresses that in fact there is only a handful of opponents.

'No doubt, but they are always the dogs who besiege your tribune. They gang up, they have a pack leader.'

Perhaps Sieyès is one of those. One can never be wary enough of men's resentment and their dogged desire to wreak harm and recover what they have lost.

They have only just celebrated the anniversary of 18 Brumaire, and already here is Sieyès again.

Can he see himself winning against me, now, when he lost two years ago?

Men blind themselves about their strength and their position.

'And ambitious subordinates only ever have shabby ideas.' Napoleon is now speaking to Cambacérès. Each time he finds himself facing this man, he thinks of the way Talleyrand qualifies him: *Haec*, feminine. It is true that this powdered and perfumed consul, pink-skinned, graceful in his gestures and with a dancing gait, has something of a woman about him. He loves young people and surrounds himself with them. Very well, but he is a good jurist and loyal. He devises solutions that enable one to bypass obstacles. He has the adroitness, finesse and trickery that is often characteristic of those of his persuasion. He suggests that the mandate of those members of the Tribunate and Legislative Corps who oppose him should not be renewed, and that the Senate should be used to draw up the lists of the excluded.

'Let us seem as if we are using the Constitution,' says Cambacérès. 'We can do good with it.'

Napoleon purses his lips. This necessary detour grates on him. He remains silent for several minutes.

'Medusa's head must not reappear in our tribunals or our Assemblies,' he says. 'Let the dissidents be removed and the right-minded be put in their place. The nation's will is that the government is not prevented from doing good. There must be no opposition for twenty years.'

He grumbles to himself, 'Ten men talking make more noise than ten thousand who keep quiet; that is the secret of the babblers on the tribune. The sovereign government represents the sovereign people, and there can be no opposition to the sovereign.'

He goes over to Cambacérès and scrutinizes him. All opposition needs a pack leader. The second consul knows Sieyès well and will be able to pass on the message to him, because Sieyès might be tempted to play the role of the Grand Elector.

'Sieyès's conduct in these circumstances,' Napoleon begins, 'proves absolutely that after contributing to the destruction of all the constitutions since 1791, he wants to try again with this one.'

Cambacérès is all attention, his smooth face expressing no opinion.

'It is extraordinary,' Napoleon continues in a harsh staccato, 'that Sieyès does not sense the folly of his attitude. He should light a candle in Notre Dame for having got out of it so well and in such an unexpected fashion.'

He turns his back on Cambacérès and looks out of the window at the blue winter sky. 'But the older I get,' he says, 'the more I see that every man must fulfil his destiny.'

Where is mine leading me?

There is no time to wonder. He only knows that there is just one 'secret to ruling the world and that is to be strong, because there are no errors or illusions in strength: it is truth laid bare.' This applies to every act, when one has decided to command men.

WHEN LORD Cornwallis, the English negotiator who is finalizing the peace treaty at Amiens according to the preliminaries of London, comes to Paris, Napoleon orders displays of the greatest possible magnificence. 'These proud Britons must be shown that we have not been reduced to beggary.'

He summons General Duroc. He is fond of this aide-de-camp who has served him since Italy. Duroc was wounded at St Jean d'Acre, and returned with Napoleon from Egypt aboard the *Muiron* as one of the tiny band of faithful.

His nature pleases me. He is cold and hard, and he never cries.

He has Duroc sit down and observes him.

'The government must be a permanent representation,' he says – that is why he wants such splendour in the Englishman Cornwallis's reception – but the people are what they should concern themselves with first. 'Public opinion is an invisible, mysterious force which nothing can withstand; nothing is more mobile, more uncertain or more powerful.'

Duroc is attentive, serious, almost grave, as is his wont.

'Yet however capricious it may be,' Napoleon goes on, 'it is also true and accurate and reasonable much more often than one thinks.'

He sees a hint of surprise crossing Duroc's face.

Is it necessary to explain to him, apart from these generalities, that I want to put a stop to the disorder that reigns in the Tuileries?

Josephine has a very mixed circle, including women from his past, the time of Mesdames Tallien and Hamelin and all those whom public opinion calls the 'gauze-covered nudes', or the 'priestesses of the sans-chemises'. They are sullying the image of the first consul.

'I want you to be the grand marshal of the Tuileries Palace, assisted by four prefects of the palace,' he tells Duroc.

Times are changing. It does not matter if people think these appointments are creating something like a court around me. Why shouldn't I do this? There must be etiquette, and that is why Duroc must become Grand Marshal of the Palace.

There will be a military household with four generals. Napoleon hesitates a moment, and then names Lannes, Bessières, Davout and Soult. Eight aides-de-camp will assist them. The prefects of the palace will be responsible for the rules of etiquette and the supervision of entertainments.

'The first consul's wife should have lady companions,' he murmurs. 'Madame Lannes, Savary, Murat . . . especially ladies from the nobility, Madame de Rémusat, Madame de Lucay.'

He stops and gives Duroc an ironic look.

'Hortense de Beauharnais . . .' he starts.

The sordid rumours that cast his stepdaughter as his mistress don't affect him, but they are spreading and Hortense's marrying could put a stop to them. It is also said, in the Tuileries, that Hortense is in love with Duroc, but he has shown no reaction.

He must be aware, though, that I am not opposed to such a marriage, quite the opposite. I told Bourrienne, so that he would tell him, 'I will give Duroc 500,000 francs and name him commandant of the eighth military division. He will set out the day after his marriage with his wife for Toulon, and we shall live apart. I want no son-in-law in my home.'

Duroc does not respond. He must know Josephine's plans. She wants a prince or Louis Bonaparte for her daughter and not a General Duroc.

Napoleon feels a twinge of irritation and gently shakes his head. He has borne with this family marriage which he sees taking shape; he knows it is a clever tactic of Josephine to bind him to her even more closely.

Napoleon has brought up Louis since his brother's youth. Louis was his aide-de-camp in Italy and Egypt, ambassador, and then brigade-major. Napoleon would never abandon one of his brothers. How could he, especially if Louis were the husband of Hortense, to whom he feels a warm affection? How difficult it would then be to break with Josephine, since the two families would be thus interlinked.

Napoleon knows all this.

He even knows that Louis most probably suffers from venereal disease, that he is prone to attacks of melancholy and often imagines he is being persecuted.

But he is my brother. And since Duroc doesn't answer, either out of caution or because he is not attracted to Hortense, then let us yield to Josephine.

NAPOLEON IS present at their side for the signing of the marriage contract at the Tuileries on 3 January 1802. Then, the following day, he goes to rue de la Victoire, where, at eleven o'clock in the evening, Cardinal Caprara conducts the religious ceremony in the large salon where an altar has been set up.

Napoleon looks straight ahead as Josephine sniffs and sighs loudly beside him. She wishes her civil marriage to Napoleon could also be blessed by the cardinal on this occasion. Murat and Caroline, who have only had a civil wedding, are preparing to receive the cardinal's blessing after Hortense and Louis.

Josephine tries to take Napoleon's hand, but he pulls it away. He will not give in. Let her cry. He wants to keep a door open in his destiny for another marriage, to a different woman, that will take place in the bosom of the Church. Admittedly one can always dissolve a religious marriage, but why make things more difficult? Ending a civil marriage by divorce, if he should so choose, will be so easy.

He is one of the first to leave the salon.

Murat is swaggering about in a glittering uniform and Caroline seems satisfied for once. Talleyrand whispers to Napoleon, 'Caroline Murat has the head of Cromwell on a beautiful woman's shoulders.'

She is the one in charge of that couple. It is she who has decided to buy a large estate, La Motte Saint-Héraye, it is she who has acquired the Thélusson house for 500,000 francs, who has entreated and demanded that Murat be awarded, before he returns to Milan to his command, the sum of thirty thousand francs a month for his extraordinary expenses . . .

Napoleon has given in. Isn't she family?

THE NEXT DAY, at the Tuileries, he hosts the banquet in honour of the newly weds. Neither Hortense nor Louis look happy: Louis is pensive and distracted; Hortense seems not to see him. Josephine alone is radiant with happiness. She gives the impression of having forgotten her sadness of the previous day and her unconsecrated marriage. This union of Louis and Hortense is her first great victory. By contrast, Letizia Bonaparte and Napoleon's brothers and sisters appear sombre.

Is it then written that one can never unite men in one movement? Is the fusion of factions impossible, and must it be that, opposing and even hating each other, they only join together in their gratitude to a single leader? Can one only 'conquer necessity by having a single absolute power'?

He leans over to Josephine and tells her that he is going to Lyon for a few days where a State Council of Italian deputies will meet.

'People swear you are going to have yourself elected King of Italy,' Josephine says.

He laughs and remembers Voltaire's tragedy, *Oedipus*, which he read in his youth. He recites, 'I have made monarchs and never wanted to be one.'

THREE DAYS LATER, 8 January 1802, when he has just left the Tuileries for Lyon, he thinks of that marriage feast again, and those people gathered round him – brothers, sisters, officers, dignitaries.

In the hours immediately following it he had to reprove Louis who, like an ordinary citizen, had sent out wedding announcements.

When will they understand who I am? What they owe me? The respect for their situation, the name and titles they have? They have no gratitude.

He has offered Joseph the presidency of the Cisalpine Republic, who has refused it arrogantly, saying that he does not want to bear his brother's 'yoke' and be just a 'political puppet'. But if he were to accept, he would insist that the French troops be withdrawn, that Murat leave Milan and that Piedmont be joined to the Cisalpine Republic.

What does this elder brother think, that he conquered it himself?

His coach drives through the snow-covered countryside. It is two o'clock in the morning. Napoleon has decided to sleep at the relay at Lucy-le-Bois, in the Côte d'Or département, then lunch at Autun and stop overnight at Chalon. On the 11th, he will stop at Tournus and reach Lyon in the evening.

A short distance from Lucy-le-Bois he sees large fires lit at the side of the road, and when the coach comes closer, peasants rush forward, crying, 'Long live Bonaparte!' At the stop, a small crowd has formed in front of the coaching inn and is demonstrating enthusiastically. The same scenes recur throughout the journey.

Do they really love him? What is popularity? Easy temper? Who was more popular or easy-tempered than the unfortunate Louis XVI? And what was his destiny? He perished. And yet everything that is done without the people is illegitimate.

Napoleon huddles up in the corner of his coach which has sped off once again, leaving Tournus behind and drawing closer to Lyons.

How is one to trust?

Love is only a word: I do not love anyone. No, I do not love my brothers. Joseph perhaps a little, but if I do love him it is out of habit, because he is my elder brother. Duroc? Ah, yes, I love him . . . As for me, it is all indifferent to me; I know I have no real friends. As long as I am what I am, I shall make it seem as if I have as many as I want. One must let women snivel, that is their business, but I am not sensitive. One must be firm, have a firm heart; otherwise one shouldn't get involved in war or government.

He dozes off.

ON 11 JANUARY, at eight in the evening, he reaches Lyon.

He leans out of the window. The city is lit up. The coach moves at walking pace through the streets that lead to the town hall. He looks at the sleeping lion that has been put on top of a triumphal arch, under which the coach passes.

He immediately starts seeing the four hundred and fifty Italian delegates who constitute the State Council or *Consulta* of the Cisalpine Republic.

As the days pass he has the feeling that he is changing the lot of his people, of Italy and Europe. He speaks to them in Italian, in the deconsecrated church where the *Consulta* has met. He is acclaimed, and greeted as the president of the Italian Republic.

He is called 'the immortal Bonaparte, the hero of the century'. He is the liberator of a people. He feels borne along by a great force. The Italian Melzi is appointed Vice-President.

On 25 January, on the place Bellecour, he reviews the troops that have returned from Egypt.

The weather is superb, the sun glitters in a luminous sky. The dry, cold winter's day resounds to the enthusiastic shouts of the crowd and the soldiers who wave their helmets and caps on the tips of their muskets. Among them there are Mamelukes, Copts, Syrians and, above all, those old grenadiers whose faces he recognizes and whose names he sometimes remembers, campaigners from Italy and Egypt, survivors of St Jean d'Acre and Aboukir. He shakes their hands and pinches their ears.

What is more a part of the people than the army?

He stays with them for a long time and it is hard for him to leave these men in arms who cheer him.

What would he be without them?

So little.

XIV

On his return to Paris on 31 January, at six thirty in the evening, Napoleon starts to read the dispatches from Joseph, who is conducting the negotiations with Lord Cornwallis at Amiens.

He is irritated and cannot stay seated at his desk. Do these English really want peace or are they just feigning so that they can prolong the negotiations, reinforce themselves during this truce, and then break them off when it suits them?

He stops reading.

The journey from Lyon was tiring and vexing. The road had been lashed by rain and snow, and it was bitterly cold in the coaching inns at Roanne, Nevers and Nemours. He calls Roustam. He wants an even hotter bath than usual.

He stays in there a long time and then returns to his desk. He pushes Joseph's letters aside, he will read them later, and leafs through a handwritten pamphlet circulating in Paris which has been seized by police spies. People are talking about it, according to the report included with it, and passing it on. The author is unknown. Napoleon reads through it and feels as if his skin is burning. Who is this unknown who dares insult him and slander him like this in the handful of verses he calls 'La Napoléone'? He closes his eyes and tries to keep calm. This is the price one must pay for glory and success. He reads:

> He comes, this treacherous foreigner
> To trample insolently upon our laws
> Cowardly heir of a parricide
> He squabbles with executioners over the royal haul.
> Alexandria vomited forth this soul of sycophancy
> To cover our land in blackest infamy
> And plunge the world into bitter mourning;
> Our vessels and ports welcome the shuffler.
> From a deluded France he receives sanctuary
> And France in chains a new penitentiary.

What is Fouché doing? This piece of verse is by a royalist, probably a member of one of the secret societies, perhaps the Philadelphians, who are still conspiring and dreaming of his murder. He stands up. The bath and his anger have warmed him up. He no longer feels any tiredness from his four-day journey. He must take police matters in hand in a more exacting way than he has done thus far.

'Citizen Fouché,' he starts to write. 'The restoration of peace with the European powers allows me to take a more particular interest in the police, and I wish to be informed of everything in the greatest detail and to work with you at least once, and often twice a day, when it is necessary.'

He looks up and thinks for a few seconds, then he continues, 'The most suitable times are 11 in the morning and 11 at night.'

He cannot allow this type of publication to be in circulation. Its author must be discovered and imprisoned; the 'scribblers' cannot be allowed to poison public opinion. That is why he is going to order Fouché to be doubly vigilant and not allow émigré literature into France.

Most often it is from London. He searches through the files and finds the pamphlets which call him a 'brigand'. He rereads them as if they are a medicine he forces himself to take to make himself stronger; when he is discussing a peace treaty with England, he ought to know what Ivernois or Peletier are publishing about him in London. Both are émigrés, one from Geneva, the other from Paris, but they are not the only ones. Others go as far back as his childhood to concoct more vicious slanders. 'Bonaparte,' one scandal sheet claims, 'never exhibited the lovable openness of children; melancholic, dissembling, vindictive, he combined the vices common to the grimmest tyrants and, by a singular similarity of taste with Domitian, like him he spent hours killing flies, a worthy recreation for the man who one day would find his favourite pastime sending men to be exterminated.'

He must not be made to feel anything by these ridiculous, contemptible slurs; he must not hate these creatures who want to slaughter him and who accuse him of 'pinching Josephine so hard he draws blood, out of delight in hurting her', and of having had

Desaix assassinated on the battlefield of Marengo so as to rid himself of a rival!

'A true man never hates,' he repeats to himself. 'His anger and bad temper never go beyond the immediate moment.'

None the less, they have written the worst things imaginable about him. He finds a portrait, also published in London, which he reads again.

> People have claimed that this great statesman, soldier and philosopher was the enemy of debauchery, immune from those weaknesses with which one can reproach several great men, but in fact he has two preferences which are rarely combined in the same individual; he is dissolute with women and he has proved himself to be a practitioner of that vice of which Socrates was falsely accused. Cambacérès assists him wonderfully in this shameful pursuit. I would not be surprised if, to imitate Nero completely, he were to marry one of his pages one day, or one of his Mamelukes. Without respect for decency, to him not even incest seems to need to be covered up. He has lived publicly with his two sisters, Mesdames Caroline Murat and Pauline, the wife of General Leclerc. The former boasted about it high and low. It is well known that when Madame Louis Bonaparte, the daughter of Josephine, became pregnant by Napoleon, he forced his brother to marry her . . .

HE RECOILS, disgusted; it takes him a while to shake off this feeling, then he continues his letter to Fouché: 'I wish you to speak to Lord Cornwallis about the abominable piece of work you will find enclosed, and impress upon him how much it is against the dignity of the two states to let an émigré print such stupidities in London.'

Unless, he thinks, this flood of insults repeated by the London press, in which he is invariably called 'the poisoner', is proof that England is shying away from signing the peace treaty?

He sees Talleyrand. The minister is convinced that Addington's government wants peace, but that the prime minister is being put under pressure by committees of merchants and ship-owners. 'Public confidence in that country is not centred on St James but on London's Stock Exchange,' Talleyrand explains. 'Otto, our ambassador, writes as much.'

'Just a truce then,' murmurs Napoleon.

That would be painful, discouraging.

'If Lord Cornwallis is sincere,' Napoleon concludes, 'peace must be signed before the nineteenth of March.'

He hopes for this peace. He thinks it uncertain and it will still be fragile if it is sealed, but it will allow him to devote himself solely to the administration of France.

HE IS SO impatient that, during those days of waiting, he takes even more decisions than usual, constantly instigating new enterprises. He goes to the place des Invalides one morning and questions the navvies – he wants the square to be finished quickly; he is present at the start of the opening up of a new street which will connect the terrace of the Tuileries to the Place Vendôme; he visits the château of St Cloud, which is to become the consular palace.

On 26 March 1802, when he is returning from one of his inspections in Paris, he learns that the peace treaty has finally been signed in Amiens. London must evacuate Malta, and France the Neapolitan ports it occupies. No mention is made in the treaty of the French conquests on the European continent, or of the opening of its ports to English goods.

But still it is peace; so long awaited.

On 27 March, Napoleon asks Constant to put out a silk coat, white stockings and gold-buckled shoes. He wants to receive the ambassadors in civilian clothes to celebrate the signing of the treaty.

'It is the first time since 1792 that France is no longer at war with anyone,' Napoleon murmurs.

He has already asked the Admiralty a question which haunts him on the day that peace is celebrated: 'If, by ill fortune, peace does not last, what would be possible?'

PART FOUR

You judge that I owe the people a new sacrifice: I shall make it

APRIL 1802 TO AUGUST 1802

XV

Napoleon turns his back on Bourrienne and goes to the window. The sky on 3 April is a light, almost transparent blue.

Bourrienne is speaking in a strangled voice. How can he justify what he has done? He has just been caught red-handed, and yet even now this secretary is trying to explain that he was not involved in this bankruptcy, he barely knew the Coulon brothers – one of whom has just committed suicide – who, after receiving hundreds of thousands of francs, were unable to provide the equipment they were meant to supply to the cavalry. How much did Bourrienne get from the deal? Napoleon does not want to ask. He remembers him as his schoolfellow from Brienne; he is his oldest friend. Friend? They had met up again in 1792; they roamed about Paris together; they are the same age.

I got him out of prison when he was locked up as an émigré.

Since then Bourrienne has been at his side – Italy, Campo Formio, Egypt, 18 Brumaire. Not a day has passed without his taking dictation for dozens of letters.

He is Josephine's confidant.

He lied to me for her, I know. And he has made himself rich. I saw his magpie eye glinting covetously, and I accepted it.

But this is too much.

Bourrienne carries on trying to justify himself.

I am surrounded by men whom I have trusted and who have betrayed me.

He thinks of Saliceti who denounced him in 1794 – Saliceti whom he pardoned and sent away from Paris to Corsica and then to Italy. He thinks of all the people who have used him: Tallien, Barras . . . but ought he be surprised? One can only trust oneself.

Bourrienne is still talking, but in such a muffled, weak voice one cannot hear any more. In the end his lips are moving without him uttering a word. Napoleon waves him away. Let him go to Hamburg and represent France as a chargé d'affaires. He'll carry on stealing there, if he can.

But who can I count on?

HERE IS the new secretary, Méneval. Napoleon looks hard at him. According to Joseph, whom Méneval has served, this young man of twenty-four is discreet and efficient. Napoleon gives him his instructions. He must be available at every moment, day and night, and live in the Tuileries where four rooms have been allocated to him on the servants' floor. He must sit there – Napoleon stretches out an arm – between the inner and secret apartments, and he must not ask for any help with his work, either from a secretary or a copyist.

Napoleon immediately starts dictating the law of public worship that is to be included in the Concordat. These Organic articles will be an unpleasant surprise for the Pope but, after all, they are only a revival of the old Gallican tradition of independence of the Church of France in relation to Rome and of the principle by which the government polices religions.

I am the one who is going to choose the bishops.

To celebrate the Concordat, Napoleon has appointed Monsignor de Boisgelin to be cardinal archbishop, who twenty-five years before, gave the sermon at Louis XVI's coronation! He studies Méneval's face but his secretary continues to take his dictation. He is too young to have been a Jacobin or to be shocked by this desire to repair the links in the chain of time and restore the authority of the state and religious peace.

But some people are rebelling.

And some in the army would like me dead.

He knows them, Augereau, Moreau, Bernadotte, Lannes and so many other generals, the 'old moustaches' of 1792 who are starting to show their spurs around Paris now peace has been concluded. In conquered cities they have got into the habit of acting as they please. Now, with nothing to do, they dream of doing battle with him. He was one of them and so they imagine he is no different from them either.

They want to kill me! Fouché has had to admit that the information I have is correct. During a banquet for generals and officers, one of them, Major Donnadieu, said that my murder was to take place in Notre Dame if, as expected, a Te Deum was held at Easter, on 18 April, to promulgate the Concordat and the Organic articles.

A general who was once aide-de-camp to Augereau, Fournier-

Sarlovèse, has pledged to kill the first consul in the nave of the cathedral. He has bragged of being an excellent pistol shot.

Who not to suspect? One is only truly supported by one's inferiors when they know you are unbending.

He brutally sends Méneval away.

A FEW DAYS later, in the grand salon at Malmaison, he assembles Portalis, Cambacérès, Lebrun and Roederer for an extraordinary council.

What use is there talking to them about the plot? General Fourneir-Sarlovèse has been arrested, but what is to say he won't have a successor? Too many men and generals are seething with jealousy and ambition. They disguise it under impeccable Jacobin sentiment, those hypocrites' trappings that mask their yearning to be first and their resentment at not having been able to do so.

'Did you notice that when he was giving his speech at the reception, Cardinal Caprara was trembling like a leaf?' Roederer remarks.

Napoleon does not answer. The day before he had been struck by the fearfulness of the papal envoy in the Tuileries. One must be wary of priests. He walks a little in the garden and sees Josephine and Hortense. Can he even trust those closest to him? Besides, a police spy claims that Joseph – *my eldest brother* – is refusing to stand beside the first consul during the singing of the Te Deum at Notre Dame on 18 April, and he prefers not to be in amongst the state councillors! He must have got wind of the plot and is not too keen on being hit by a bullet or shell splinter.

Napoleon goes back into the salon.

'Will the first consul kiss the paten?' asks Portalis.

Napoleon imagines himself kneeling or bending forward, pressing his lips to the dish containing the host. His whole body recoils. 'Don't make me do ridiculous things,' he says.

He does not just fear the sniggering and threats from the Concordat's opponents. Even in the Council of State there was some laughter when Portalis read out certain passages of the agreement with the Pope. But opposition in the Assemblies has been quelled, thanks to Cambacérès's advice. Lots weren't drawn to see which delegates should be returned; instead, they simply identified his opponents and two hundred and forty of them, almost all, lost their seats.

No, the power of the priests is more worrying, really. Giving way to them would be a fool's bargain. The clergy intends to have exclusive hold over the intelligence, the noble part of man. 'They claim to reduce me to a point where I only have influence over the body,' Napoleon adds, incensed. 'They keep the soul and toss me the corpse.'

Do they think I will accept that?

He strides up and down the salon, occasionally stopping in front of the open French windows. He looks straight ahead. He knows what has to be done. In the weeks and months to come this is the task he will settle down to.

'There can be no stable political state unless there is a teaching body with fixed principles,' he says, turning back towards Portalis and the others. 'Until people are taught from childhood whether they should be republicans or monarchists, Catholics or irreligious, the state will never form a nation.'

He stretches out his hand towards Roederer.

'You, Roederer,' he says, and puts him in charge of everything concerned with public education.

Then he returns to Portalis. First the Concordat must be finished with and the power of the first consul affirmed. He smiles. The first consul will give each of the archbishops and bishops at their consecration a cross, a crook and a mitre.

'Citizen Portalis, make the necessary arrangements for these objects to be finished in time . . .' He stops and his smile grows broader. '. . . and with least claim on the public purse.'

He stays silent for a few minutes. He looks at each of these men in turn; their clothes proclaim the importance of their positions, but here, facing him in Malmaison's reception room, they are all equally subservient.

'One has to have accomplices in government,' he thinks, 'otherwise there will be no end, no boundaries.'

He goes up to Portalis. He wants, he says, the bathroom adjoining his study in the Tuileries to be converted into a chapel.

That is where bishops who have not yet sworn an oath will do so. It will be the first consul's chapel – and it will be consecrated by an Archbishop of Paris, who will hold mass there. As he leaves the room he calls out that he has chosen monsignor de Belloy as Archbishop of Paris. He stops and says, smiling, that he knows the former Bishop of Marseilles under the ancien régime is ninety-two years old, but that he will be an excellent pastor for Paris.

ON 18 APRIL, he gets up earlier than usual.

He wants this Easter Day to be a day of glory. He could have made do with a discreet promulgation of the Concordat, but, despite the generals' conspiracy, he has stayed with the Te Deum and Pontifical Mass at Notre Dame, with choirs from the Conservatory. There has to be brilliance and spectacle, for people to be aware of the change that has been wrought.

He calls his chief valet.

Constant helps him put on the first consul's official costume. He steps into the white silk knee breeches and dons the scarlet coat without facings but with a broad embroidery of palms in gold on all the seams and a black collar. He attaches his Egyptian sword to a narrow belt, and gathers up his French hat with tricolour plumes. At ten thirty, he goes down into the courtyard of the Carrousel. He is due to give flags to some new units.

He walks slowly. He feels as if he is on a battlefield, at the very start of the battle when everything is at stake. Suddenly he hears the crowd cheering: 'Long live Bonaparte! Long live the first consul.'

It will be a beautiful day.

He has given instructions that Louis XVI's ceremonial coaches be made as good as new. The coachman and lackeys are to wear green livery with gold braid.

At eleven thirty, he gets into the coach which is drawn by six greys. Josephine is sitting next to him. They are, as he wishes, like a royal couple.

A vast crowd cheers them all the way from the Tuileries to Notre Dame. The conspirators can dream all they wish. From informers he knows their plan, which is to kill him during the Te

Deum and then have the Army of the West under Bernadotte – Joseph Bonaparte's brother-in-law, Désirée Clary's husband (such are men!) – march on Paris.

However, Duroc and Junot have massed the light infantry of the Consular Guard at the Tuileries, and the units inspected less than an hour ago are made up of loyal men.

He enters the cathedral which is lit by hundreds of candles and filled with the crowd of notables.

He sees the generals' uniforms in the side-aisles. Leaning over he says to Cambacérès, 'Military government will never take root in France, unless the nation has been brutalized by fifty years of ignorance; all attempts to impose it will fail and their authors will be the victims.' He speaks without looking at Cambacérès; the rest of the cathedral might think he is praying. 'I do not govern as a general,' he continues, 'but because the nation thinks I have the civic qualities needed for government. If it didn't think so, my government would not last. I knew what I was doing when, as a general in the army, I accepted the title of member of the Institute. I felt sure of being understood by the smallest drummer.'

The mass ends. He appears on the square. Look, there is the enthusiastic crowd. The group of generals is hanging back. 'The distinctive characteristic of soldiers is to want everything despotically,' he continues. 'Whereas that of civilians is to submit everything to discussion, to the tests of truth and reason.'

Accompanied by Duroc and Cambacérès, he heads towards the generals. Duroc whispers that General Moreau did not attend the ceremony, but was seen instead ostentatiously smoking a cigar on the terrace of the Tuileries, surrounded by officers.

He will not forget Moreau.

'One must not relate centuries of barbarity to the present,' he says to Duroc. 'We are thirty million men united by the Enlightenment, property and commerce; three or four hundred thousand soldiers are nothing compared to our mass. The soldiers themselves are only the children of citizens. The army is the nation.'

The generals have dispersed. Most are afraid to confront him, but one of them, General Delmas, has stayed behind, striking a provocative pose, arms crossed, legs splayed.

Napoleon knows this heroic officer of infantry. So, what did he think of the ceremony, he asks him.

'A fine show of piety,' Delmas grumbles. 'All that's missing is the hundred thousand men who died to abolish all this.' He turns his back on Napoleon and strides off.

I shall never finish fighting.

XVI

NAPOLEON SPINS ROUND. He asks General Duroc to repeat what he has just reported in a matter-of-fact way. Duroc appears surprised and then, in a slow voice, outlines again the situation of the Consular Guard responsible for Tuileries security. Napoleon grows impatient. Duroc hesitates, trying to understand the reason.

'This suicide,' says Napoleon.

Duroc nods. For the second time within a month there has been a suicide in the corps. Both have been 'for love'. Grenadier Gobain, the most recent, was a very good fellow. What does that mean, 'for love'?

Napoleon seems to forget that Duroc is there. He speaks rapidly, as if he is clarifying something for himself. 'Josephine is always afraid I will fall seriously in love,' he says. 'She does not know that love is not made for me.'

He looks at Duroc, or rather realizes he is there again.

'For what is love? A passion which puts the whole world to one side so as only to see and contemplate the beloved. I can assure you I am not the sort to indulge in that kind of exclusion.'

He shakes his head. 'I have always loved analysis,' he says, 'and if I became seriously in love, I would dissect my love bit by bit.'

He inhales a pinch of snuff, and then folds his hands behind his back and changes tone, beginning to dictate, 'The first consul orders that it be put in the orders of the Guard, "That a soldier should know how to conquer the pain and the melancholy of his passions; that there is as much courage in suffering mental pain with constancy as there is in remaining firm under grapeshot from a battery. Giving oneself up to chagrin without resisting, and killing oneself as a means of escape, is abandoning the battlefield before being conquered."'

He sends Duroc away and remains alone.

THAT SPRING of 1802 is a special moment in his life. He has the feeling that everything is possible and at the same time that everything is still fragile and can be undone in a matter of minutes. After his death, the work he has undertaken could slip between the fingers of time like a handful of sand.

What would remain?

He summons Roederer and Cambacérès. They are level-headed men whose advice he sometimes listens to and who are particularly helpful in allowing him to refine his arguments, either for his own sake or before he presents them to the Council of State or the Senate.

They both approved of the Concordat and the *senatus consultus* permitting the last émigrés to return, so long as they did not attempt to recover their property. These aristocrats are sometimes his policies' staunchest supporters.

A few days ago, Napoleon showed Fouché a book that has just been dedicated to the first consul by the Viscount de Chateaubriand. What could be more supportive than a work entitled *The Genius of Christianity*?

Fouché smiled faintly. The author and publisher should have waited for the Te Deum in Notre Dame marking the Concordat before launching their book, in order to cause as great a stir as possible and the best sales!

Fouché! Fouché! A man who isn't content with fine words, who can't be bent to another's will, who will serve but only as long it serves him to do so.

At this moment the minister of police only has one concern: that the Assemblies will not grant the first consul the consulate for life. So he is intriguing for them to accept an extension of Napoleon's mandate for another ten years, when the ten years prescribed in the Constitution – which would take Napoleon to 1819 – are up. Fouché is putting it about everywhere that any other course of action would be perilous.

He has indoctrinated Josephine, who spies on me for him, I know, and is given a small monthly income in return! She thinks I don't know any of this. 'It would be dangerous,' she says, 'shocking the army's elite and the people from whom the First Consul has his temporary power . . . It would risk him losing the advantages of such a magnificent position, by putting him either in too steep a gorge or on too sheer a slope.'

Naturally Josephine adds her personal touch. How could a Bonaparte dream of attaining the supreme office of the Bourbons?

Does she not dream of it herself, involuntarily? Do I?

At Malmaison, when the future was being spoken of by Lucien, Talleyrand, Fontanes and Cambacérès, she had leaned closer to the First Consul and whispered, 'When are you going to make me Empress of Gaul?'

'What? Little Josephine, an empress?' he answered, so loud that everyone stopped talking. 'Absurd.'

IS IT REALLY absurd?

Cambacérès and Roederer are urging him to modify the Constitution and obtain the consulate for life, rather than just ten more years as Fouché is suggesting.

He listens to them and forces himself to think it through. How do you stabilize what is moving, pin down what is slipping away, stop or slow this onrush of time that has always led him on, this feeling of precariousness he still has?

He has learnt that in the procession going to Notre Dame the carriage Generals Bernadotte, Augereau, Masséna and Macdonald were in had been stopped on Bernadotte's orders, but the four officers had hesitated to get out and address the troops to rouse them against the first consul.

So his intuition had been right when he had seen the generals congregating in the nave. He is at the mercy of any one of these conspiracies.

'One of the things that contributes most to a monarchy's stability is the fact that the idea of the crown is invested with the idea of ownership. One says that such and such a king is the owner of his father's throne, just as a private citizen is the owner of his father's field. Because everyone has an interest in their own ownership being respected, they respect the monarch's.'

Common sense, surely?

But can he take the plunge?

HE SEES them all around him, like scavengers on a battlefield, pushing not only for the consulate for life, but also to appoint his successor. Lucien and Joseph each declare that they do not want to be his heirs, that there should be a man like Cambacérès to succeed Napoleon, and yet each is thinking of what is to come.

After my death!

He receives Cambacérès, who has come once again to advocate the idea that the first consul should be appointed for life and, perhaps, have the power to name his successor.

Napoleon walks around his study, his head bowed and, as always when he is debating something with himself, he takes pinch after pinch of snuff.

He stops, and has Roederer sent in, who was waiting for them in the antechamber.

'As long as I am here,' he suddenly bursts out, 'I will answer for the Republic, but it is true, one must plan for the future.'

Cambacérès and Roederer agree.

'We must fix some blocks of granite in the soil of France,' Napoleon adds.

He wants lycées to be created everywhere, in all the departments, so that public education can form the minds of those who will be the backbone of the nation. Also, for the best citizens, an order must be set up, a new knighthood, the Légion d'honneur.

'People will say it is a new aristocracy,' Roederer murmurs, after a moment's thought.

'There will be strong opposition in the Assemblies and the Legislative Corps,' Cambacérès adds.

Napoleon flies into a rage. 'I defy anyone to show me a Republic, ancient or modern, which has not had distinctions. People call them baubles, I know, they've said it before, and I have replied that it is with baubles that men are led.'

He gesticulates, hammering out the words, stamping on the ground. 'I do not believe that the French people love liberty and equality. They have not been changed at all by ten years of Revolution; they are just what the Gauls were, proud and fickle, so one must give their pride sustenance. They need distinctions. Do you think you can make men fight by analysis?'

He paces up and down for a long time in silence and then, in a resolute voice, he adds, 'Do you think one can rely on the people?

They shout with equal indifference "Long live the King! Long live the League!" You have to give them a direction and have the means to do that.'

'Exactly,' Roederer and Cambacérès insist. 'The consulate for life will reveal the path with complete certainty.'

He barely listens to their arguments. Has he ever done anything other than what he wants? Can he envisage giving up one day, after ten or even twenty years, the duties he exercises as first consul? This costume has become his body and skin.

'You think that I owe the people a new sacrifice: I shall make it if the will of the people demands what you suggest,' he says.

Roederer instantly presents the plebiscite that will be put to the vote of the French people, with registers set up in every commune on the government's initiative. Citizens will be asked to answer two questions, 'Shall Napoleon be consul for life?' and 'Shall the first consul have the faculty to designate his successor?'

Napoleon picks up the document, goes to his desk and, with a furious stroke of his pen, crosses out the second question.

'The will of Louis XVI was not respected!' he cries. 'Would mine be any the more?'

He takes a few jerky steps and then adds, 'A dead man, whoever he may be, is nothing.'

HE REPEATS this to himself all the way to Malmaison. He cannot imagine what will happen after him, and he cannot accept that his brothers will succeed him or argue among themselves to take his place, or else share power with someone like Moreau or Bernadotte.

He spends a restless night at Malmaison and the following morning, at six o'clock, he manoeuvres two battalions of the Guard in the barracks at Rueil and Malmaison. He loves the bracing air of the bright dawn, the measured steps, the order of the columns, the geometry of the battalions dividing space into hard-edged figures.

As he shouts commands, he thinks of the plebiscite. Will the French grant him the consulate for life? Why would they refuse? In the Tribunate only Carnot voted against, and in the Legislative Corps only three deputies opposed the plebiscite.

He brings the manoeuvres to an end and invites the officers of both battalions to lunch at Malmaison.

He likes these meetings. It is in and through the army, since childhood, that he has known men. He mentions a few memories of the siege of Toulon, then other campaigns. 'Courage cannot be feigned,' he says. 'It is a virtue that is immune to hypocrisy, but it is like love, hope is its nourishment.'

What do I hope today, as I am nearing my thirty-third year? That in all the communes, citizens in their hundreds of thousands are going to vote for or against the Consulate for life?

Since the registers have been opened in town halls and the offices of clerks of court and notaries, large crowds, according to first reports from prefects, have come to sign. He stands up and, before leaving the table around which the officers have also got to their feet, he says, 'Whatever my destiny shall be, consul or citizen, I shall live only for the greatness and happiness of France.'

THAT EVENING in the auditorium at Malmaison, its inauguration, he watches a performance of Paisiello's *La Serva Padrona* by a troupe of Italian burlesques. The farce makes him laugh and he feels the Italian language as his own. He has done a great deal to give that country independence, but the news reaching him from Milan shows that the government of the Cisalpine Republic is weak. Will it be that country's lot never to amount to anything?

France will always be a great nation.

He is proud to be French and at the head of this people and nation to whom he has given himself, and who, in exchange, have granted him everything. 'The finest title on earth is to be born French,' he says. 'It is a title bestowed by heaven, and no one on earth should be given the power to remove it.'

And I am the First Consul of this people!

THE FOLLOWING morning, Fouché asks to be seen, but Napoleon purposely keeps him waiting.

For several days he has been receiving reports from a host of informants. There has definitely been a generals' plot. They thought of deposing Napoleon on the grounds that, having been elected President of the Italian Republic, he could no longer exercise the duties of first consul. The generals wanted to form a deputation to threaten him with insurrection if he encroached upon freedoms. Bernadotte – Napoleon laughs mockingly – only asked his accomplices to abduct the first consul and not to kill him!

What more can Fouché say? Whatever new information he may bring, must they be dealt with ruthlessly? Even if Bernadotte deserves to be shot should they go that far? He is popular with the troops, like Moreau. Why take the risk of stirring up the army against the government? It will be enough to send Bernadotte away, along with the other generals. Lannes shall go to Lisbon, Brune to Constantinople, Macdonald to Copenhagen and why not Bernadotte to Louisiana, or as France's representative in the United States of America?

Napoleon has Fouché sent in. The minister of police is grave-faced, but Napoleon does not question him and instead watches and waits, as he slowly starts to speak. General Simon has had to be arrested in Rennes, he explains. Bernadotte's former chief of staff was sending scurrilous satires to all the garrisons in blue and red envelopes, those of the Army of the West.

Napoleon holds out his hand. He wants to read these pamphlets that Fouché's police have seized, notably in coaches heading to Paris.

The pamphlet is entitled, 'Appeal to the French Armies by a Comrade'. It consists of a few pages which Napoleon first flicks through quickly and then reads.

'It would seem,' the pamphlet runs, 'that the generals and armies which won in Italy, Helvetia and at Hohenlinden have disappeared and been scattered like smoke: first consul, Lunéville, Amiens – Amiens, Lunéville, first consul – this is all the French nation now consists of . . . Soldiers you have no motherland left, the Republic does not exist any more, your glory is sullied, your name is without brilliance or honour!'

Napoleon dashes the scandal sheet on the floor.

'Well?' he asks.

Fouché, calm as ever, answers that General Simon and several other officers have been arrested, notably Bernadotte's two former aides-de-camp, Captain Foucart and Captain Adolphe Marbot.

Then Fouché assures him that General Bernadotte was in complete ignorance of his subordinates' activities.

He does not lower his eyes when Napoleon looks at him.

'The general, Citizen Joseph Bonaparte's brother-in-law . . .' continues Fouché.

'I'll have that bugger shot on the place du Carrousel,' Napoleon snaps. He knows Fouché will report what he has said, and it will make people tremble.

One also rules by the fear one inspires.

XVII

WITH A LOOK NAPOLEON orders his secretary not to move. He does not like to be disturbed, especially when he is dictating. The sentences follow on, one after the other, his thought develops . . . and now someone has knocked on his study door, the one that gives onto the little staircase by which one reaches Josephine's apartments.

Napoleon continues dictating an article for the *Moniteur* to Méneval. He won't sign it, but people will be able to recognize his thinking, since everyone in France and abroad knows that this paper expresses the First Consul's views.

A job is not well done unless one does it oneself. The article is an important one. It is about the peace. The English press is launching more and more attacks against France. 'All the ills and scourges that can trouble mankind come from London,' Napoleon repeats several times. *The Times* exaggerates in its 'perpetual invective against France. Two of its pages are used every day to give substance to contemptible slanders. Everything the imagination can conceive of by way of baseness, vileness and malice, that wretched paper attributes to the French government. What is its aim? Who pays it? Whom does it want to influence? . . . The island of Jersey is full of brigands sentenced to death by our courts . . . Georges Cadoudal openly wears his red ribbon, as reward for the infernal machine that destroyed a whole quarter of Paris and killed thirty women, children and peaceful townsfolk. Doesn't this special protection justify one in thinking that if he had succeeded he would have been awarded the Order of the Garter? When two great nations make peace, is it reciprocally to provoke disturbances?'

Someone is knocking insistently. Napoleon stops dictating, and before Méneval has even stood up, Josephine has entered the study.

Evidently there is something she wants. Napoleon recognizes her suppliant's attitude, the imitation of a scared little girl. He is not fooled by it, but each time he feels a mixture of irritation, satisfaction and embarrassment. Let her quickly say what she wants and let him work! Has she come about her debts again? He does not want to pay any more! Or has she got another of her childish, stupid surprises for him, like the last one he had to put up with? She had put a basket in front of him covered by a scarf, and when he lifted it off, he discovered a horrible dwarf grimacing and writhing.

But Josephine is still who he spends most of his nights with. She says that then she can protect him from murderers because she is a light sleeper. To read the London press, those who want to kill him can't be short of support or money. A fine peace!

Irritably he asks Josephine what she wants.

'Madame Grand is here,' she murmurs. 'She begs you to see her.'

He knows women's obstinacy, and he knows everything about this Madame Grand, daughter of a sailor from Batavia and a dancer at a theatre in Calcutta. She has passed from bed to bed and at the moment happens to be in Talleyrand's. She wants to marry the minister who must first obtain permission from the Pope, because he was formerly a bishop and wants to revert to being a layman. Naturally Napolon has been solicited to write a letter to Pius VII supporting this request.

He hesitates. He is fond of Talleyrand, a scheming individual but one whose advice is often good. However, since Madame Grand has moved into Talleyrand's townhouse in rue du Bac, diplomats and their wives have refused to attend his receptions. The dilemma is simply put: either he marries or he resigns as minister.

Napoleon agrees to see her and watches her walk towards him. Madame Grand already has her hands clasped. She has neither grace nor beauty any more. She kneels down and starts crying and begging. What does Talleyrand see in her? This woman isn't even capable of giving him children.

The thought is painful. What about him?

He has received a letter from Roederer announcing that the results of the plebiscite are known and are going to be made public in a few days – 3,568,885 French citizens have voted in favour of Napoleon being awarded the Consulate for life and only 8,374 noes have been counted, but Roederer has added, 'You must be seen to have an heir-at-law.'

Napoleon has momentarily forgotten Madame Grand, who is still snivelling.

'Talleyrand has to marry you!' he says gruffly. 'Then everything will be resolved – but you must bear his name or no longer go to his house.'

She gets to her feet, beaming. That is her deepest desire, she says. So he will write to the Pope, won't he?

He dismisses her and Josephine thanks him with a nod of the head. He has given in to her again. He doesn't know whether the surge of anger he feels towards her is caused by this weakness or the memory of Roederer's letter.

LATER IN the evening he sees Josephine again, surrounded by a throng of guests at Malmaison. They crowd around buffets laid with every imaginable drink and food. Napoleon has a glass of Chambertin, his favourite wine. An orchestra starts to play and he leads Hortense onto the dance floor. After a few minutes the young woman asks him to stop; she is pregnant by Louis, she explains as he lets her go, laughing. Corsican women, he says, work until the day they give birth. He pinches Hortense's cheek. Does she know, he asks, that he has bought her and Louis the former house of Mademoiselle Dervieux, who was the mistress of the Comte d'Artois? Hortense flings her arms round his neck and thanks him for his regal gift. That is what it is to be first consul – there are no obstacles to one's desires; if one wants something, one can have it.

After Madame Grand left he wrote a letter to Pius VII, counselling him to grant Talleyrand his return to layman status, so that he can get married: 'This minister has rendered services to the Church and State . . . He deserves to obtain special favour.' Pius VII will accept, just as he accepted that Joseph Fesch, Napoleon's Corsican uncle, Letizia Bonaparte's half-brother, be made Archbishop of Lyon.

Why not Joseph Fesch? He is no worse than anyone else.

NAPOLEON CLAPS his hands, leads the guests to Malmaison's theatre, sits in the front row and gives the order to begin. He loves to see Hortense and one or other of his aides-de-camp or generals performing a Beaumarchais play. He forgets his day in the Tuileries and the news from San Domingo: fevers are wreaking havoc amongst the French troops; the arrest of Toussaint l'Ouverture has only stirred up the blacks even more. He forgets that he has given free rein to his entourage who have been wanting to restore slavery in Guadeloupe and Martinique, and that revolts are spreading there as well.

He applauds and laughs loudly.

He must forget, but still he thinks of Pauline and her husband, General Leclerc. He feels as if he has let his hand be forced by the sugar and coffee traders who are 'in a frenzy' to recover San Domingo, their plantations, their profits and, consequently, their slaves.

He thought of them during a discussion with Roederer about a new Constitution – which is needed since he will soon be proclaimed consul for life – when he rejected the idea that wealth should be the qualification for inscription on electoral rolls of notables. 'One cannot make a title out of wealth,' he had said. 'A rich man is so often an idler without merit . . . Anyway, who is rich? The speculator who buys up national property, the army contractor, the thief? How can one found notability on wealth acquired like that?' How is the colonist any different?

Nevertheless, he has brought back slavery.

He stands up as Hortense, who played Rosine, and General Lauriston, who was Count Almaviva, take their bow. Then Figaro, played by Prefect Didelot, comes to the front of the stage and bows in turn. Lauriston, Didelot: two ancien régime aristocrats, acting in a Beaumarchais play for him, a son of the Revolution who was a friend of Robespierre's brother and has just restored slavery.

How strange are the world and my destiny!

HE CANNOT stop thinking of it.

In a few days he is going to be thirty-three. With the consulate for life and the question of his successor – 'an heir-at-law' Roederer wrote – he sees, as never before, the finality of his existence, as if, whilst his destiny is still to be written, he knows its end. Is that why he feels irritated and nervous, with rushes of impatience, as if he wanted to act fast and run the full course as quickly as possible to that end which is going to be inserted in the Constitution? He cannot shake off these thoughts on the way to Mortefontaine, near Senlis, to visit his brother Joseph.

He is tense, on edge. All his family and relatives will be there, and Joseph will try to play the role of eldest, while Lucien makes no attempt to hide his antagonism towards Josephine. As they get closer, he grows more and more irritable, and then barely responds to the hugs of greeting. After a few minutes in Joseph's house, he decides to go rowing.

It is a stormy day and everyone seems clumsy. After a few strokes, the boat starts rocking as if it is about to capsize; General Bernière, who is sitting next to Napoleon, falls in the water. Someone screams. It seems to Napoleon that all the vague forebodings that have been dogging him now make sense. He is going to die here, stupidly, not from a cannonball or a dagger, but ignominiously in some pond. He sees the sky and the water merging into one another . . .

When he comes to again, he is lying on the bank. All the faces looking at him are contorted with curiosity. He leaps to his feet, pushes aside those huddled round him, goes into the house and demands that they start dinner.

As master of the house, Joseph takes his time, grasps Letizia Bonaparte's elbow, and explains the order of precedence: his mother will be on his right, Josephine on his left.

'The first consul's wife has priority,' says Napoleon.

Since Joseph is pretending not to have heard, Napoleon takes Josephine's arm, enters the dining room first, sits at the middle of the table and tells her to sit on his right.

What do they think, that I am already dead?

THE ENGLISH dream of that. How many of the ambassadors, gathered on 3 August for a solemn diplomatic audience, share their dream? What criminal, Georges Cadoudal or another like him, are they ready to pay so that their wish can be realized?

Napoleon passes amongst them, surrounded by his aides-de-camp and ministers and with the consuls on either side. He stops in front of each ambassador. All eyes are on him. Not a gesture he makes escapes these monarchical or imperial diplomats. None of them has accepted his country's transformation. It is not only for its conquests that they reproach it – perhaps they could come to terms with those – but France has also overturned the order of things, and no one can bring themselves to recognize the Revolution.

That is the task I must set myself – to make them admit that this country acts as it pleases, that no one can reverse the redistribution of property, and that the ancien régime will never be restored, even if the aristocrats are returning. They do so as servants of the new order – mine.

That is the challenge of peace. Will he be able to impose it? What authority should he claim – a king's? – to make the rulers of an unchanged Europe finally acknowledge the existence of the Republic?

Napoleon stops in front of Markov, the Russian ambassador. He exchanges a few words with this man who, his spies assure him, is full of bitter remarks when in society. A conversation was overheard between him and the Prussian ambassador, Lucchesini, who Napoleon turns to now. Markov was saying that if Napoleon accepted the title of consul for life, he would not be content with this distinction but would take a second step and take the title of 'Emperor of Gaul'. 'It would not be an empty title either,' Markov had gone on, 'because he has brought them all under French domination.' Lucchesini had answered, 'He wants to be another Charlemagne, enlightened by the learning of our time . . . No doubt he did not form the plan without deciding when he would put it into practice.'

He does not himself know yet what goal he is setting himself.

What will be the future, after this new Constitution is proclaimed tomorrow, 4 August 1802? It provides for him being a consul for life, as also will be the two other consuls, but *he* will nominate them. He even has the right to choose his successor. He is President of the Senate and a private council, and the two other Assemblies have been stripped of real power. He has a right of reprieve.

What am I? he wonders, as he looks at these ambassadors and ministers. A king? He is lacking only a crown and a coronation.

Would they be more ready to accept me, would they acknowledge the Revolution more willingly, if my head was girt with gold and diamonds and if God's representative had given me his blessing? Is this the price I have to pay to make them genuinely bend their knees, swallow their hatred and recognize that I, the son of the Revolution, am the equal of the greatest of the great?

Here are the members of the Senate advancing towards him; the ambassadors have taken up their positions on either side of the great hall.

Barthélémy, who was a marquis and then one of the directors in 1795, declares that the French people have appointed Napoleon Bonaparte consul for life, and the Senate has proclaimed it. A statue of Peace holding the laurel wreath of victory in its hand will be erected in his honour. He continues in a loud voice, 'The first consul is entrusted by the French with the mission of consolidating their institutions. He will never give them anything but the brilliance of glory and a sense of national greatness.'

Napoleon answers slowly, articulating every word, his gaze stopping on every face: 'Senators, a citizen's life belongs to his country. The French people wishes that mine be dedicated to France in its entirety. I obey their will.'

What am I, if not the equal of a king?

He raises his head, looks above the crowd of dignitaries and his eyes are drawn up to the slightly hazy August sky.

'Happy to have been called by the order of He from whom everything issues to restore order, justice and equality on earth, I shall hear my final hour sound without regret or anxiety about the opinion of future generations. Senators, accept my thanks . . .'

IT IS 15 AUGUST 1802. He is thirty-three.

Today his birthday and his consulate for life are being celebrated in all the churches of the Republic.

In the morning he puts on his uniform of first consul and receives the constitutional bodies in the Tuileries. Three hundred musicians play while the state councillors, senators, tribunes, deputies and ministers pay homage.

At three in the afternoon a Te Deum is sung in Notre Dame – a coronation, almost.

In the evening he dances at Malmaison and, after the ball, Hortense, despite being seven months pregnant, acts in a little play by Citizen Duval. As he applauds he thinks of the crowd in the place Vendôme who will be dancing to the music of four orchestras around an altar with eight sides, on one of which the text of the *senatus consultus* can be read. He has ordered the monuments of Paris to be illuminated and the lion, his zodiac sign, is projected onto the towers of Notre Dame.

Who could have imagined this?

Who can imagine what is still to come?

ON 21 AUGUST, he goes to the Luxembourg Palace to preside over a ceremonial session of the Senate. He is sitting in the carriage which was Louis XVI's and is drawn by eight white horses. To his left and right, he sees the officers of his staff and the troopers of his guard wheeling. Beyond them, all the way from the Tuileries to the Luxembourg, soldiers form a guard of honour. Behind them there is a dense crowd, but it is silent. He waves; they do not respond. He raises himself slightly on his seat and sees the carriage his brothers are in. They are waving as well. He personally instructed Fouché not to organize any fake enthusiasm on the route, but Fouché is devious enough to have gone to the other extreme. According to informers, posters were stuck up through Paris repeating the maxim, 'The silence of the people is the teaching of kings.'

He asks to see Fouché as soon as he gets back to the Tuileries, but the minister of police defends himself, as usual, switching from one argument to another. 'Despite the merging of the Gauls and Franks,' he says, 'we are still the same people. We are still those ancient Gauls who were known for being able to suffer neither freedom nor oppression.'

What is this gibberish? Does Fouché think he will get out of this corner with historical reflections?

'What do you mean?'

'That Parisians think the latest government measures represent a total loss of liberty and an all too obvious shift towards absolute power.'

Napoleon is gripped by a sort of rage. He has heard this

accusation of a tyrannical amount of power. It is stupid. This government, in this France, cannot be despotic because there is no feudal system, intermediate body or prejudices to support it. Fouché knows that perfectly well.

'I shall not govern even for six weeks in the void of peace,' Napoleon continues, 'if, instead of being in charge, I am only a sham authority.'

He loathes Fouché's thin smile, his calmness, his arrogance.

'Be paternal, affable, strong and just,' Fouché says, 'and you will easily win back what you seem to have lost.'

As he walks away, Napoleon calls back, 'It is an odd, capricious thing, that which is called public opinion.' He is in the doorway. 'I shall be able to improve it,' he says in a resolute voice.

PART FIVE

You can kill the French but you can't intimidate them

September 1802 to December 1803

XVIII

THEY ARE SITTING around him in the salon of the château of Mortefontaine, Joseph's home. The casement windows are open onto the Senlis forest, which is starting, in these first few days of September, to change colour.

Napoleon stands up and leaves the circle but signals to Lucien, Joseph, Talleyrand, Roederer, Lebrun and Cambacérès to carry on talking. He goes out onto the terrace. The air is mild and laden with scents of the trees. He can only hear Lucien's raised voice now. Apart from Talleyrand, who has not said anything, the others have lambasted Fouché, damning him as a minister with too much power, a hidden Jacobin, a secretive manipulator who pulls the strings of every conspiracy, an opponent to him becoming consul for life, and on obstacle to all future developments.

Joseph and Lucien have insisted on the last point and Napoleon has merely listened. He knows what they are all thinking.

What will happen after me?

Lucien has even recommended to Josephine that she go to Plombières with some of good old Doctor Corvisart's medicines. 'Come along, sister, prove to the consul he is mistaken and hurry up and give us a little Caesar,' he told her and then went on to say – Josephine had to tell Napoleon so that he could reassure her – 'Well, if you can't or won't, Napoleon will have to have a child by another woman which you adopt, because the right of inheritance must be guaranteed. It is in your interest, you must know why.'

Even Elisa, the first consul's sister, who, Fouché whispers, is 'eaten up by love and ambition', Elisa who hangs on every bombastic word of Fontanes, her poet and lover, even she has started harassing Josephine. When Josephine had said that she had had two children, Elisa had retorted in a shrill voice, 'But sister, you were young then!'

Josephine had burst into tears and Napoleon had shouted, 'Don't you know, Elisa, that just because something is true, it doesn't mean it's good to say it.'

Josephine's tears had turned to great sobs.

NAPOLEON LASHES out with his crop at a clump of flowers that spill out of an amphora standing in a corner of the terrace. Often, when he is caught in situations that he cannot or will not resolve yet, he lets his anger burst out. He will rampage through the garden or smash a porcelain vase. He has even kicked over Roustam on some mornings when he is trying to get a boot on, or has put a boot on the wrong foot.

He goes back into the salon. Roederer turns towards him.

'They are unanimous,' he says.

Napoleon merely announces he is going back to Paris. He knew before this meeting that Fouché had to be removed from his post as minister of police. He could not accept the opposition to the consulate for life which Fouché had shown without any attempt to hide it. Fouché is also convinced that the aristocratic threat still exists! Nonsense! Almost all the émigrés have returned and rushed to serve him – even Chateaubriand, who dreams of a diplomatic appointment!

The only danger is the generals, those rancid old Jacobins who have been blinded by ambition and jealousy. They do not see that, to be accepted by the monarchies and empires of Europe, 'either the form of government in neighbouring countries has to become more like ours or our political institutions have to be more in harmony with theirs. There is always a spirit of war between old monarchies and a brand new Republic'.

So, let's become king. Maybe then they will find it easier to accept the conquests and changes of the Revolution and Republic.

NAPOLEON ASKS to see Fouché at the Tuileries. He does not want to make an enemy of this man, but Fouché's calm and assurance always surprise and irritate him.

'Monsieur Fouché, you have served this government very well,' he starts. 'It is with regret that I part company with someone of your merit.'

Fouché remains imperturbable, that same unbearable little smile playing around his lips as if to say that he is not in the slightest surprised by what Napoleon is telling him. He will be a member of the Senate. The discontinuance of the Ministry of Police, now under the jurisdiction of Grand Judge Regnier, and so part of the

Ministry of Justice, has been dictated by the new international situation.

'I had to prove to Europe,' Napoleon explains, 'that I am plainly embedding myself in the arrangements of peace and relying on the love of the French people.'

But a man like him knows all that.

'Is that what you were thinking?' asks Napoleon.

Naturally Fouché agrees and asks to draw up a report on the political situation and the use of his ministry's secret funds. Napoleon listens to him talk of the perils that still exist, the 'coterie of political eunuchs who at the first sign of weakening would hand over the state to the royalists and foreign powers.' Napoleon stares at him. He is resolute, this man, he exudes an impression of strength. He is telling him now that there are two million four hundred thousand francs left in his secret account.

'Citizen Senator,' Napoleon says, 'I will be fairer and more generous than Sieyès was to that poor Roger Ducos when they were dividing up the meat of the Directory's coffers in front of me. Keep half the amount you are returning – it is not excessive – as a mark of my personal and private satisfaction. The other half will go into the coffers of my private police who, with your good counsel, will make great strides, and I hope very much that you will continue to share your thoughts on this with me as often as possible.'

One must always be on one's guard.

The new head of political police, Desmarets, has just informed him of the arrest of a priest at Calais, Abbé David, who, trembling with fear, has confessed to being an intermediary between General Moreau and General Pichegru, who is in exile in England. Desmarets saw fit to release Abbé David to have him followed, but will his spies be as efficient as Fouché's?

London is again a refuge for his most determined enemies, just as it is every time, and the English probably give them the wherewithal to act. The same question haunts Napoleon: 'Are we at peace or is this just a truce?'

HE HAS decided to give a great dinner on the 15th of each month, and invites artists, manufacturers and diplomats. In October, he introduces to Fox, the British MP, and to Lord Holland, three manufacturers, Bruguet, Montgolfier and Touney, who have just participated in the Exhibition of National Industry, winning a gold medal. Then at dinner he questions Fox, who is sitting on his right. 'What does England want?' he asks. 'Why does it let the Comte d'Artois, Louis XVI's brother, review a regiment when London no longer recognizes the monarchy by virtue of the fact it deals with the Consulate?'

Fox is evasive. He is in favour of peace, but isn't he one of the few?

Will we have to make war again when peace is dawning and, like every citizen of the country, I am starting to enjoy all its benefits?

NAPOLEON GOES by boat to the château of St Cloud with Hortense, who is going to give birth at any moment. The rumours that Napoleon is the father have not stopped, quite the opposite – but perhaps in the end he is happy for people to think it?

Napoleon takes Hortense's arm as she walks heavily along the avenues of the château. He looks at the orangerie where, less than three years ago, his fate was decided. That is where he took power – but he could have lost it all as well.

Recently he has become reacquainted with the château of St Cloud. The Tuileries are gloomy, and he is too close to Josephine there; she is used to having him sleep with her. As for Malmaison, that is her domain. St Cloud will be his home and, even if Josephine takes up residence there, as she is bound to, he will have his own private little apartment which he is having fitted out above his study.

At each stage of his life, he needs particular places. St Cloud is the residence of the first consul for life. He walks slowly through the Apollo gallery, smiling. On each side of the richly decorated gallery stand his relatives, guests, aides-de-camp and their wives. They bow and acknowledge him with a faint nod of the head. He knows that behind, a long way behind, Cambacérès and Lebrun are following. Cambacérès gives his hand to Josephine. Then come the members of the consular household followed by the valets in green livery with gold braid.

There must be an etiquette to display power and its hierarchy.

Everyone must know that the first consul is sovereign in his country, just like any other sovereign in theirs. Napoleon, moreover, has approved of Talleyrand's asking the Prussian government to sound out Louis XVIII to see if the Bourbons would agree to abdicate their rights in favour of Napoleon Bonaparte. That way the political rupture of the Revolution would be closed, but the essentials would remain: the transfer of property, the new institutions, the Civil Code, the chambers of commerce and the lycées.

It is Sunday. Napoleon takes his seat in the chapel in what used to be Louis XVI's place. Josephine sits next to him, in front of the two consuls, like a queen.

HORTENSE'S SON, Napoleon-Charles, born 10 October 1802, is baptized in this same chapel. Napoleon himself is a godfather – perhaps that will give even more fuel to the rumours? So much the worse for Louis. He looks at the child. Actually, it could be a legitimate heir, if that's what public opinion needs.

Isn't this how kings act, and mustn't he be more and more regal so that everyone finally knows that the Revolution is over?

He wants to know what the people think of this change. He dismisses with a shrug of the shoulders and a show of scorn those like Lebrun who advise him against going to Normandy, a monarchist area that could give him a bad reception and where he might be at risk. That's exactly why he should go there.

ON 29 OCTOBER 1802 at six in the morning, he leaves St Cloud in his travelling berline with Josephine. It is drizzling. He can barely make out in front of the carriages the figure of Moustache, his courier who goes with him whenever he travels.

He wants to take his time. They are at peace. If war resumed, the drivers would have to spur their horses on, but now he can stop where he wants. He jumps out of the carriage shortly after Mantes and walks along the Eure under a sky that is now blue. He wants to see the battlefield of Ivry. He will sleep this evening in the prefecture of Evreux. Tomorrow he will be in Louviers. Then Rouen, Honfleur, Le Havre, Dieppe and Beauvais.

At Rouen, he suddenly mounts his horse and, followed by a

few of his escort, he rides until five in the afternoon. He needs these races. He stops on the heights overlooking the Seine and breathes deeply; he feels free, happy.

When he gets off his horse, he is surrounded by a crowd. He is the sovereign. In the study that is prepared for him at each stage, he dictates a letter to Cambacérès so that the newspapers should know. 'I have travelled through huge crowds and been forced to halt at every step,' he says. 'In all the villages, at the door of the church, on a dais outside, the priests have sung canticles and scattered incense, surrounded by great throngs.'

Those political eunuchs Fouché talked about may criticize the Concordat – Fouché was one of them himself – but do they know that the Archbishop of Tours has just declared that 'the Consulate is the legitimate government, national and Catholic, without which we would have neither right of worship nor our country.'

The Norman curés do: they welcome me and give me their blessing.

When they reach Le Havre the city is lit up. Napoleon walks into the middle of the crowd with Josephine on his arm. They are like a king and queen. That evening, in the great hall of the prefecture, he opens the ball.

At Dieppe he sees an old man coming towards him whose face seems familiar. It is Domairon, one of his teachers at the military school of Brienne. So that time of childhood and isolation did exist! The memory makes him feel stronger, invincible. He asks one of his aides-de-camp to find out Domairon's situation, to help him if necessary. Having power means rewarding whoever one wants, however one wants.

He visits the hospitals and factories. On the country roads, peasants stop to greet him. He gets out and talks to them. When the carriages drive off again, the peasants run after them, shouting, 'Long live Napoleon Bonaparte! Long live the first consul!'

What could jeopardize this?

He listens distractedly to Beugnot, the prefect of the Lower Seine, who speaks of England's claims and the threat of war. He stiffens, then begins pacing about, a resolute look on his face, his voice hard as he takes snuff.

'I still have my doubts whether it will,' he starts, 'but if England attacks me, it has no idea what it is laying itself open to, no idea at all.' He stops and bows his head, his eyes half-closed. 'You shall see what this war will be like,' he continues. 'I shall do everything to avoid it, but if I am forced I shall overthrow everything I find in my path. I shall make a descent on England and go to London, and if that enterprise does not succeed, then I shall turn the continent upside down. I shall subjugate Holland, Spain, Portugal and Italy, and I shall attack Austria and go to Vienna itself to destroy every support that odious power enjoys.'

He starts pacing back and forth, closer to the crowd of guests who are bunched together, not daring to approach him. 'We will see what I can do and what I will do. I shudder in anticipation, but the world will know me.'

He raises his voice and seems to address them all, rather than just the prefect. 'Moreover, I shall continue to work just as hard to assure the prosperity of France, to allow its commerce, agriculture and industry to flourish.' He stops in front of the guests. 'And we will be happy, in spite of our rivals!' he exclaims.

HE IS HAPPY. He has the feeling that nothing can resist him. He is never tired. It is as if the applause and cheering and signs of admiration that meet him wherever he goes give him renewed strength.

At six o'clock almost every morning he is on his horse. He jumps ditches and streams and hedges. His escort lags behind, his horse collapses with exhaustion. He changes mount and sets off again; the surprise in the notables' eyes at his exact knowledge and his energy stimulates him even more.

Sometimes he glimpses in the crowd a woman's face and breasts and body and he feels a glimmer of bitterness. He stares at this young woman and sees acceptance, submission, even invitation in her eyes. He would like to be able to walk straight ahead, scattering the crowd, because he is sure she would follow.

He cannot bear the invisible barrier that prevents him acting as he wishes, and when he finds Josephine, smiling and gracious as a sovereign, he treats her harshly.

But she *is* the wife of the first consul. Shortly after his return from Normandy on a November evening he agrees to go to the Théâtre Français with her. She is wearing a straight, pink muslin shift which leaves her neck and arms bare, on the model of classical antiquity. She is no longer beautiful, but she is graceful. The play is *Iphigenia on Aulis*, a tragedy he loves, as he also loves the atmosphere in theatres, the tremor that goes through the auditorium as he enters his box, the way he can sense the actors are unsettled because he is there, a special member of the audience.

Now here is Clytemnestra, appearing out of the darkness:

> My daughter we must leave, letting nothing hold us back
> And in flight shield your glory and mine from attack

She is statuesque, broad shouldered, with rounded arms and heavy breasts, and she declaims in a sultry voice. She moves with the vivaciousness of youth. Her skin has the whiteness of marble.

He cannot take his eyes off this body, the movement of her shift which reveals her strong thighs. He is turned to stone. He wants this woman.

He returns to the Tuileries at the end of the performance, without lingering as he sometimes does. He sends for Constant. His valet is to find out who she is and tell her to come to St Cloud tomorrow evening. Napoleon does not even conceive of the possibility of her refusing. Actresses are like that, and they are not the only ones. Since he has become surrounded with glory and holds power, he knows that women, all women, can be conquered.

WHEN MADEMOISELLE George enters his private apartments in St Cloud next day, in the early evening, Napoleon knows that she has been Lucien's mistress, and now is given money and homage by Prince Sapieha, a Pole – but that is how things are; the past is of no concern to him.

He goes to her. There always have to be a few passages of arms before a surrender, and this one must be complete.

'You must have nothing except what I give you,' he says. He tears the veil from her head, which he senses is a gift of Prince Sapieha, and tramples one of her rings and a medallion underfoot.

'Except what I give you,' he repeats.

He tucks a large bundle of banknotes into her cleavage and laughs.

He feels peaceful with her, for a moment. He loves her youthfulness. He sings with her, falls asleep, his head on her breasts. Can she really only be sixteen? She seems ten years older. And he seems ten years younger, she murmurs. He laughs again. She must come back.

She becomes Georgina. He sees her two or three times a week at St Cloud, where he spends more and more time, and at the Tuileries. It is no matter if Josephine is jealous, sometimes venturing up his private staircase and then retreating when she sees Roustam mounting guard. He has won the right to experience the pleasure of being with the woman he wants. The time of tearful love affairs is over.

One evening he dines at St Cloud with Josephine, Roederer and Cambacérès. Georgina is going to meet him in the middle of the night. He looks intently at Josephine. 'The more I read Voltaire, the better I like him. Up to the age of sixteen, I would have stood up for Rousseau against all Voltaire's friends, but now it is the opposite . . .'

He nods his head. Perhaps no one understands what he thinks? That life imposes the hard laws of reality, and that Voltaire teaches that better than the dreamer Rousseau. 'I read *The New Heloise* when I was nine. Rousseau turned my head.'

He gets up and Josephine does not even try to stop him. He sleeps with her only when he chooses. It is more and more rare.

He goes to wait for Georgina in his apartments, reading in front of the fire. When she arrives, he will sweep the files aside and find peace in caressing that milk-white skin.

It is winter. He loves these nights, this time that feels secret, as if he was in a cave, a sort of childhood. He sings, recites poetry, plays. Then Georgina goes and he puts on his First Consul's uniform.

He stays at St Cloud for all of December. It is his palace. He only goes to the Tuileries for a handful of audiences. On 5 December, he sees Hawkesbury, the English minister, accompanied by the ambassador, Whitworth. He observes the Englishmen.

He would like to shake them, but instead he simply repeats that 'the relations of France with England are the Treaty of Amiens, the whole Treaty of Amiens and nothing but the Treaty of Amiens'. He cannot, however, refrain from asking angrily why England has not evacuated Malta in compliance with the treaty.

Hawkesbury remains impassive, and then says that London has taken due note of France's annexation of Piedmont and the island of Elba, and the fact that Holland has not been evacuated.

'These are questions the Treaty of Amiens did not address,' Napoleon roars. Then he collects himself and shows the minister and ambassador out.

Peace, full peace to consolidate Europe?

WHEN HE IS returning to St Cloud in the greyness of that December 1802, Napoleon feels doubts. Perhaps war is knocking again. London is delighted by General Leclerc's death in San Domingo, the failure of the plan to re-establish influence in the French West Indies and the impossibility of building a colonial empire in America. Soon France will have to give up Louisiana, which will only be averted if war breaks out again.

Napoleon slowly walks through the galleries of the palace of St Cloud. He has ordered a period of ten days mourning, court mourning, in acknowledgement of Leclerc's death. His aides-de-camp wear mourning bands round their arms and on their swords

He shuts himself away in his study and writes to Pauline, who is about to come back from San Domingo with her husband's remains. 'Everything passes swiftly on earth apart from the opinion we leave imprinted on history.'

He sends for Méneval and dictates an order putting Toussaint l'Ouverture, who is locked up in Fort Joux in the Jura, under closer surveillance. He gives instructions for the black man to be stripped of all signs of the rank of general which he awarded himself. This man is probably going to die a long way from his home, in the freezing damp of a fortress. Life is implacable, and one must yield to its course.

He feels no hatred for Toussaint l'Ouverture, nor does he despise him because he is black. He is simply an enemy and perhaps Napoleon, or General Leclerc, were wrong not to come to terms with him. He could have been France's black ally against England, but it is too late.

Napoleon leaves his study and goes through to his private apartments where Georgina is waiting for him. Does she know, he asks her, what the English call him? 'The Mediterranean mulatto'! He laughs as he strokes Mademoiselle George's white skin.

XIX

Josephine is crying. He cannot stand it, but she has got into his study again. She whines and moans. She is deceived, betrayed. Then she loses her temper in a jealous fit.

He does not really believe she is sincere, and he loathes these scenes she feels obliged to make. Coldly he says, 'Imitate Livia and you will find me another Augustus.'

She does not know Roman history. He stares at her and says, 'Ah, that wretched way of wearing your hair!'

He could remind her of her infidelities, when he was just an absent husband made to look ridiculous, but it is so long ago, even if the memory of that humiliation and his dependence has not faded. The grievances pile up, the misunderstandings multiply, and each calculates what he or she has to gain or lose by staying together.

Josephine fears divorce more than anything else. She goes to Plombières to try to recover her fertility: isn't a child the only way to hold onto Napoleon?

'Who gave you that scarecrow's hair?' he adds, since she is still plaguing him.

She leaves his study.

Relations between people are like those between nations: a balance of strength and interest, honour and glory, obstinacy and imagination.

He sits at his desk. He has before him a copy of the *Moniteur* newspaper, which, on his instructions, contains Colonel Sébastiani's report after a long journey in the Orient. Sébastiani claims that it would be easy to reconquer Egypt with a corps of six thousand. This has made the English furious.

Napoleon brutally shoves the table away. The English nation has no memory! It is like Josephine. Why doesn't it evacuate Malta, why doesn't it respect the Treaty of Amiens, why does it pretend to be offended when it has been the first one at fault?

Hypocrisy!

He wants to know what these English really want. He brushes aside Talleyrand's prudent manoeuvring. Enough of diplomacy – he wants to speak directly and openly to the English ambassador, Lord Whitworth. He sends word for him to present himself at the Tuileries, on 18 February 1803, in the evening.

HE WATCHES Lord Whitworth walk towards him and signals to him to sit at the end of the large writing-table that occupies the middle of his study. The ambassador sits stiff-backed, his face inexpressive.

Can this man understand what I want to say to him? What is the use of all this if London is bent on war? He must be reminded of every injury England does to France, to me. A pension for Georges Cadoudal! Insults, slanders in the newspapers! The welcome they give to French émigré princes!

As he is running through his grievances, Napoleon loses his temper. 'Every wind that blows from England brings me nothing but hatred and insults,' he exclaims. 'Now we have come to a situation from which we absolutely must extricate ourselves. Will you or will you not execute the treaty of Amiens?'

He stands up. 'If you are for war, only say so and we will wage it unrelentingly. If you are for peace, you must evacuate Alexandria and Malta!' He paces round the table. 'What would the world say if we were to allow a solemn treaty signed with us to be violated? It would doubt our credibility and resolve.'

He stops and rests both hands on the table.

'For my part, my resolution is fixed. I had rather see you in possession of the heights of Montmartre than of Malta!'

Lord Whitworth remains silent for a long time, and then he starts to expound his arguments.

This man does not understand me!

Napoleon interrupts him. He has respected the treaty point by point. Piedmont, Holland, Switzerland, where he has become the mediator – none of these are in the treaty. He is orchestrating a process of reorganization in Germany, certainly, but he is entitled to.

Whitworth murmurs, 'The report of Colonel Sébastiani . . .'

Napoleon rejects any such suggestion; it is not worthy of the relations of two great nations. Besides, he can reassure Whitworth. Whitworth must listen carefully now. He leans towards the ambassador.

'I am not contemplating any aggression,' he says. 'My power is not great enough to allow me to venture with impunity upon aggression without adequate motive. All the faults must be yours.'

He straightens up.

Does this man see what I am saying?

'Though yet very young, I have attained a power, a renown to which it would be difficult to add,' Napoleon continues. 'Do you think I am keen to risk this power, this renown in a desperate struggle?'

He seems to forget Whitworth's presence. He enumerates the difficulties of crossing the Channel for an invasion of England. 'It is a temerity, an awful temerity, my lord, but I am determined to hazard it if you force me . . . I have crossed the Alps in winter.' He strikes the table. 'Posterity will weep tears of blood over the resolution you have forced me to take.'

He sits back down. Has he convinced Whitworth?

'Act cordially with me, and I promise you an equal cordiality on my part. See what power we could exercise over the world if we could bring our two nations together . . . You have a navy and I have a hundred thousand men . . . Everything is possible in the interests of humanity and our double power, France and England united.'

WHAT IS the use of frankness? The English won't accept a strong France.

Napoleon calls Talleyrand the prudent, the cautious, because he wants to continue negotiations.

Isn't this the same rivalry that began under Louis XIV? Exacerbated by the fact that I am the culmination of the Revolution? Which the English refuse. They probably would not make peace with a Bourbon, but with me they definitely never will!

The Bourbon is on the lookout. Naturally, he has rejected the proposal to abdicate in Napoleon's favour.

On 11 March, Talleyrand asks to be seen and hands a dispatch to Napoleon, explaining that the speech it reports is of no consequence – Lord Whitworth told him about it, didn't he?

Napoleon reads in a few seconds the text of a message addressed to Parliament by George III, the King of England. George claims credit for adopting precautionary measures.

'War!' exclaims Napoleon.

Talleyrand rejects this interpretation. Lord Whitworth insisted that this wasn't in any way a preparation for hostilities.

Napoleon wants to remain calm but his rage is mounting. Can one tolerate such a slap in the face?

For two nights he cannot get out of his mind the thought that London is playing with him, that eventually there will be war, and that that is what England wants after a year's truce.

He dismisses Mademoiselle George, almost cruelly, and then has Constant call her back, but he is not in the mood to sing or laugh or love.

THE NEXT DAY but one is a Sunday, 13 March, the day on which he receives the diplomatic body. He calmly passes the time before the audience begins by playing with Napoleon-Charles, Hortense's son.

One of the prefects of the palace, de Rémusat, comes in to announce that the circle of diplomats has formed and they are waiting for the first consul. Everyone is there, he says, including Lord Whitworth.

That name sounds like the lash of a whip. Napoleon puts the child down, strides into the reception room and, ignoring the other ambassadors, makes straight for Lord Whitworth.

'You are bent on war then!' Napoleon exclaims. 'We have fought for ten years; do you desire that we should fight for ten years longer? How dare you say that France is arming?' He speaks vehemently, enumerating the contents of the treaties.

'I cannot suppose, either, that by your armaments you design to intimidate the French people. One may kill them my lord, but intimidate them, never!'

He vaguely hears the ambassador protesting England's desire for peace.

'Then it must respect treaties!' cries Napoleon. 'Woe betide those who do not respect treaties!'

He walks away, then stops in front of the Spanish and Russian ambassadors and complains that the English refuse to abide by their commitments; treaties should be covered in black crêpe from now on.

He knows his behaviour has gone beyond what is considered acceptable; he has let himself be carried away by his anger, so that his whole body was shaking with rage, and he was gesticulating violently. He returns and says a few amiable words to Whitworth and then leaves the room.

He does not regret the sensation this affair produces. On the contrary, he feels a stronger resolve than ever. He is consumed by the desire to act, to forge ahead, and to be finished with the uncertainty of a peace which the other party has absolutely no wish to uphold.

He dictates orders to his generals almost daily. Europe's coastline must be closed to English merchandise. Men are also needed: a law envisages levying sixty thousand conscripts aged twenty. He has timber purchased everywhere for the construction of a war flotilla.

He meets Fouché, who is concerned.

'You are yourself a product of the Revolution,' Fouché says. 'War will throw everything into doubt again.'

Napoleon is furious. How can Fouché fail to see that they cannot yield on this without yielding on everything?

'It would be dishonourable. If we gave in on Malta, the English would demand Dunkirk. We shall never be English vassals, it is just too bad for them!'

The dice are rolling now. Napoleon again spends peaceful nights with Mademoiselle George.

One morning he is shown the first one-franc coin, moments after it has been struck. He weighs it in his hand. Nine tenths of its five grams are fine silver. Here is a weapon and one of the reasons for war. The English don't want a rich, commercially active France with a stable currency. They are breaching the peace to stifle a mercantile rival.

He turns the coin over. Under the words 'French Republic', he sees his effigy.

He stays like that for a long time, playing with the coin, which is another of his marks on history.

He decides to go hunting in the woods which surround the palace of St Cloud. He rides through the forest. He feels a sense of physical wellbeing. War can come, he is ready.

ON 1 MAY, he sees Talleyrand, who presents him with a letter from Whitworth.

He barely looks at it. The die is cast.

'If the note contains the word ultimatum, make him feel that this word implies war. If it does not contain this word, make him insert it, remarking to him that we must know where we are!'

No more time for hesitation! He listens to Talleyrand's arguments for further negotiations. He shrugs his shoulders and calmly takes several pinches of snuff. He accepts Talleyrand's idea to propose to the English that they should either transfer Malta to Russia or agree to the French establishing themselves in the Gulf of Taranto in compensation for Malta, but he is convinced they will refuse.

'Besides, since we have to fight sooner or later against a people who cannot tolerate France's greatness, today is better than tomorrow.'

He opens the window. This first day of May 1803 is brilliantly clear. Soldiers are drilling in the walks of the park around the château.

The nation's energy has not been dulled by a long peace. I am young, the English are in the wrong, more so than they have ever been, and I would prefer to have done with it.

THERE ARE only a few more days to wait, a few last measures to decide on. He likes this sort of moment, when the horizon reveals itself and lines become clear. He sends for Monsieur de Barbé-Marbois, minister of the treasury.

'My resolution is taken. I will give Louisiana to the United States.' It cannot be defended against the English. 'I will demand a sum of money from them to pay for the extraordinary armament I am planning against England.'

Now he has to wait for London's responses to his last offers.

He seeks to distract himself in amusements and invites Josephine, Hortense, Caroline and Cambacérès to ride in a caleche which he will drive himself in St Cloud park. He whips the six horses, which bolt, there is a collision and the carriage tips over. He is thrown to the ground and bruised.

People rush up, but he stays for a moment, stretched out on the ground, thinking of war, of the succession of unforeseeable events that can change the course of things. He gets back to his feet, refusing to be helped. The passengers get out of the carriage unharmed.

It grows dark. He hears Josephine suggesting to Hortense that she stay at St Cloud and her daughter replying that Louis, her husband, has forbidden it. Napoleon rails against his brother in an explosion of anger, and perhaps against everything that evades his will, against the future that at every moment is full of uncertainty.

NAPOLEON IS AT Malmaison on 12 May. He has got up earlier than usual, and has gone for a walk in the park. He hears the gallop of a courier, then an aide-de-camp gives him an envelope. It is a message from Talleyrand, announcing that Lord Whitworth has applied for passports and left Paris. He is going to stop at Chantilly and then travel slowly, by stages, to Calais. General Andréossy, France's ambassador, has already left London and is heading to Dover. Paris is calm, but a great crowd of silent onlookers gathered to watch Lord Whitworth's departure.

War is here.

Napoleon gives an order. He wants to set off immediately for Paris.

AT THE Tuileries he confers with Talleyrand and then dictates a final proposal for Whitworth, which will be communicated to him at Chantilly.

History shall not say that he did not try everything up to the last moment to avoid this war, even though he knows it is inevitable.

LORD WHITWORTH has not replied.

Napoleon gives orders. General Mortier is to march to Le Havre and take control of the coast. He reviews the six hundred pupils of the Prytanée on the Champ de Mars. That evening he goes to a performance of *Polyeuctes* at the Theatre of the Republic.

The atmosphere is grave and Corneille's verse is listened to with a sort of meditative contemplation. It seems as if he is hearing for the first time lines such as:

> The truly virtuous seek to avoid unnecessary danger
> They who choose a perilous path wish to fall.

He suppresses a mounting anxiety.

> I have ambition, but a nobler, more beautiful kind
> These glories perish, I want one death cannot bind.

Each verse soon seems to talk to him personally:

> Dying gloriously, I shall die content
> I would do it again were it my duty.

When he is in his study at the Tuileries on 20 May, the first couriers arrive as the dispatches from the telegraph pile up. They announce that England has authorized the seizure of French and Dutch merchantmen and their cargoes from 16 May onwards, without declaring war. Word is already coming of the inspection of numerous vessels. There may be hundreds of them captured in this fashion, in what is still peace.

Napoleon orders government spokesmen to proclaim the rupture of the Peace of Amiens to the three Assemblies at three o'clock in the afternoon. In response to the act of English piracy, he orders the arrest of all British subjects.

He walks slowly up and down his study and goes into the adjoining room where the maps are laid out. After ten years of war, the Peace of Amiens will only have lasted a year.

How long will this war last?

He leans over the map in the region of Boulogne and traces with his finger the French and English coasts. 'Since the English want us to jump the ditch, we will jump it,' he says.

He returns to his study. 'In three days, foggy weather and

slightly favourable circumstances could see me master of London, Parliament and the Bank. The English will shed tears of blood at the end of this war.'

IN THE EVENING of 25 May, he goes to the Théâtre Français where *Tartuffe* is being performed.

Afterwards he sees Mademoiselle George.

The order has gone out for all soldiers on leave to report for duty.

XX

Napoleon settles himself into his carriage, which speeds away, clattering over the cobbled courtyard of the château of St Cloud. He barely gives Méneval time to take out his quills and inkstands and prepare his sheets of paper before beginning dictation.

'Decision. Duhamel, former soldier, has requested to keep a uniform and greatcoat which he has been told to hand in. Referred to Colonel Bessières to ensure justice is done for this old soldier.'

He does not look at his secretary. He sits perfectly still, his eyes wide open, as if the letters he has to answer, the proclamations he has to make and the orders he has to give are all unscrolling before his eyes. He loves pouring out the contents of his brimming mind. He feels physical pleasure when he dictates. His memory breaks free. His voice is tense, as if he is reading what he is saying, and his tone rarely changes.

> To Josephine at Plombières.
>
> Your letter, my dear wife, informed me of your discomfort. Corvisart said it was a good sign, that the baths were having the desired effect and that you would be in good shape when you'd finished. But knowing you are suffering grieves my heart acutely.
>
> Yesterday I went to see the Sèvres factory and St Cloud.
>
> A thousand amiable things to you all.
>
> For life.
>
> Bonaparte.

He is silent for a few minutes. Méneval's quill makes a scratching sound as he writes.

Josephine is desperate to cure her sterility. Corvisart claims that he can restore her menstrual cycle. Has he? And even if he has, will she have a child? A son and heir?

Napoleon returns to his dictation. 'General Sébastiani should remind the hussars that a soldier must be horseman, foot-soldier, artilleryman; that he must be competent for anything.'

He thinks of the war as he continues to dictate.

There are only two ways to conquer England; cross the Channel and march on London or dominate Europe and close it to English goods through a continental blockade. He has already chosen the first way. Now it is only a question of organization, willpower and obstinacy. He must rouse the people's energies and bind them together.

He writes to each of the admirals, Bruix, Ganteaume and Latouche-Tréville, and the naval minister, Decrès. He must convince them that, despite the disparity in strength, which is three to one in England's favour – they can line up a hundred thousand sailors and more than a hundred and twenty ships – it will be possible to get across the Channel the tens of thousands of men who are already on the march for Boulogne where camps are being prepared for them.

He gives further instructions for shipbuilding to begin in Le Havre, Cherbourg, Toulon, Brest, Genoa and even Paris, on the quai de la Rapée, where pinnaces and flat-bottomed boats are to be launched.

He has had the idea, while questioning the engineer of the navy, Sganzin, and Forfait, an expert in naval construction, of a flotilla of small craft. These brigs, gunboats and pinnaces will each carry a hundred soldiers and a number of cannon. They will be propelled with oars as well as sail, since fine weather can becalm the bigger ships.

He has stopped dictating. He sees these thousands of craft harrying the English ships of the line.

They will need more than two thousand vessels. They will have to cross on those two or three days that occur in every season when the sea is calm. Even if they should have to sacrifice a hundred of these craft, the operation would still be possible. An army of one hundred and sixty thousand men could be assembled, a hundred and twenty thousand of them at Boulogne.

If one added to that complement, already sufficient for success, a fleet of rated ships from Toulon, Brest, Ferrol and Texel that could control the Channel, even if just for three days, and pin down the English squadron, then success would be certain.

He will only make his move when he has all these cards in his hand. 'One gains nothing in war except by calculation. Anything which has not been profoundly thought through in its every detail produces no result.'

He leans back into his seat.

'And then there are the unexpected circumstances that scuttle good plans of battle and sometimes crown bad ones with success.'

When his carriage crosses the place Vendôme he has it slow down, then drive round the square and stop for a few moments.

He imagines the monument he has been thinking about for a long time, perhaps since when Fontanes, Elisa's lover, started comparing him incessantly to Charlemagne. He gets out of the carriage and walks to the middle of the square. Perhaps he is one of that race of empire builders?

Passers-by have stopped and they start cheering him. He gets back in his carriage and begins dictating: 'There shall be raised in Paris, in the centre of the place Vendôme, a column similar to that erected in Rome in honour of Trajan. The column will be topped by a pedestal finished in a semi-circle, adorned with olive leaves and bearing an unmounted statue of Charlemagne.'

HE RETURNS to his study and continues dictating. All the foundries in the Republic must be at work day and night.

He walks about the room, hands behind his back, taking pinches of snuff.

Preparations must be made to man four hundred field cannon, quite apart from the siege artillery.

What stage has been reached in the construction of the brigs?

He harries the foremen of the shipyards with brief dispatches which are taken by courier to quai de la Rapée and quai de Bercy.

The troops must drill in all weathers, the ships must put out to sea and take on the English frigates. They must build forts at the entrance to Boulogne. They must, they must, they must . . .

He wants to see everything himself.

He gets into a pinnace at the quai des Invalides and directs the drill as a crowd gathers on the banks, recognizes him and starts to applaud. He takes the oars downriver from the pont de la Concorde.

He would like to be able to row to London.

Soon he will be at the head of the 'Grand Army of England', and the time will come to invade.

HE RECEIVES Philippe de Cobenzl, cousin of the chancellor of Austria. He senses that Cobenzl is on the lookout for information. Like Berlin, all Vienna can think of is this war that is beginning. The Austrians have seen their influence reduced in Germany since the French-inspired reorganization of the German principalities. The Emperor of Austria will never be the Emperor of Germany again.

That is my work.

'Wars that are inevitable are always just,' Napoleon begins. Then, in an even voice, as if it had no importance, he adds, 'This war will inevitably lead to another war on the continent. In which case . . .'

He observes Cobenzl. The man will make his report to Vienna and in this way matters will be clear. 'In this case, I should have Austria or Prussia on my side. It will always be easy for me to win over Prussia by giving them a bone to gnaw on. In Europe, Austria is all I have to fear.'

Now it is up to Vienna to choose their camp. He scrutinizes Cobenzl's face.

Austria will make its decision by virtue of my strength or weakness. Is there any other law? So I must be strong, invincible.

And for that he must supervise every detail in person. He is therefore going to inspect the camp of Boulogne and choose permanent residences which he can return to on each visit. He will take part in drilling the troops. He wants to see them embark and then disembark.

He tells Duroc, 'A general's presence is indispensable: he is the head and the whole army.' He will set off for Boulogne on 24 June.

HE HAS decided on the size of the entourage that will first visit the cities of the north. He wants a detachment of the Consular Guard, aides-de-camp, Decrès the naval minister, Chaptal the minister of the interior, Admiral Bruix and Generals Soult, Marmont, Duroc, Moncey and Lauriston.

On the morning of their departure, he carefully chooses his uniform. Commanding means being seen. He will wear the uniform of the Chasseurs of the Guides: green coat, orange trim, and the little black felt hat without galloon but with a tricolour cockade.

He goes into Josephine's apartments. He wants her to come too, as a consort accompanies a king.

He goes up to her, touches the folds of her Indian muslin tunic and shakes his head. He would prefer her to wear colourful clothes in taffeta or the silk satin they make in Lyon, rather than these tunics of English material. He does not listen as she throws herself on her sofa, hides her face behind a handkerchief and starts to cry. She cannot forgo her muslin clothes, these tunics that every woman in Paris is wearing.

They'll give them up, he tells her brutally. Can't she stop her whimpering? 'Remember, you're not fifteen any more, or even thirty. You can't carry on behaving like a child.'

He gives her a few moments to change.

Does she know they are at war with England and that he has decided to ban all English goods? She is the wife of the first consul. She must set an example.

SHE HAS obeyed and chosen a blue, flowing taffeta dress. He smiles at her and then goes to his travelling berline whose four horses are pawing the ground. He will be able to continue working. Méneval has already prepared the files in the drawers which have been put in the berline for this purpose.

Napoleon gives the signal to leave. The convoy is led by the service carriage which contains the quartermaster sergeants who are in charge of the stages. Behind is his berline, and a third coach conveys the First Consul's suite. With a wave, he invites Josephine to get in next to him. She will not be going as far as Boulogne; she is to leave him at Amiens.

HE WANTS to know if the end of peace has caused a change of opinion in the northern cities of Compiègne, Montdidier, Amiens and Abbeville. He is soon reassured; he is enthusiastically welcomed everywhere.

He is happy to be alone again after Amiens. Early in the morning at Abbeville he rides along the coast on horseback for almost six hours. The wind is fresh, the day a beautiful one and the sea calm. In the distance, he sees the sails of an English cruiser. He stops. On the horizon, veiled in fog, he thinks he can see the cliffs of the English coast.

In Boulogne the people have come onto the streets to hail him, even though he arrives at ten o'clock in the evening on 29 June. He walks rapidly through the rooms of the house on the place Godefroy-de Bouillon which has been prepared for him, but he is impatient. He goes up onto the terrace from which one can see the port and roadstead lit up by the moon.

He stays there a long time. Beyond the jetties, it seems as if he sees a front line, there on the horizon. He would like to leap forward and join battle. He goes back downstairs, sends for the naval minister Decrès, dictates orders, draws up plans of the camps and ports that he wishes to see built or enlarged.

He sleeps barely two hours and, at a quarter past three, he is already on the ramparts. The labourers are at work and he wants to see everything with his own eyes: the coast, the basins and the foundations of the three forts he has chosen to have built. Vast posts are being gathered which will be driven into the sand in the middle of the mooring line and serve as foundations for a redoubt armed with several cannon.

He goes to Odre cliff. There barrack-huts will be built for him and Admiral Bruix, who will take command of the fleet, and another for the generals and naval minister. He does not feel any tiredness, only a great sense of peace. He is acting. Ideas are becoming actions, soldiers, workers, sailors.

At ten o'clock, when the sun is already high, he has the gunboats and gunbrigs put out so that they can manoeuvre before him. At that moment two English frigates appear and the gunboats open fire. When the English withdraw, there is an eruption of cheering. This is what soldiers need: combat and victory. There is no better way to instil courage.

When he returns to Boulogne at eleven o'clock the local dignitaries are there to welcome him. He sees the Bishop of Arras, Monsignor de la Tour d'Auvergne, coming towards him. He listens to the clergyman's speech.

'In this diocese,' Monsignor d'Auvergne says in a voice thick with emotion, 'the Bishop of Arras glories in his mission to increase the number of Napoleon's friends. He knows the true worth of the restoration of the religion of his fathers . . .'

This country is Napoleon's, he is sure of it. The Grand Army is his.

'Supported by justice and God, however disastrous the war may be, it will never force the French people to bow before this arrogant race which makes a mockery of everything that is sacred on earth . . .'

He knows they will follow him where he wants to go: the other side of the sea, and further still.

He goes from one town to the next: Dunkirk, Lille, Nieuport, Ostend, Bruges, Gand, Anvers, Brussels, Maastricht, Liège, Namur, Mézières, Sedan, Reims. He doesn't tire of the receptions, the rides on horseback. He gallops ahead of a small escort, he visits the ports, fortifications, churches and factories.

He feels at home in these regions which are now part of France – but is it France or his empire? The word often comes to mind when he receives the delegations from Brussels or discusses the situation of the Church in Belgium with Cardinal Caprara, who has agreed to accompany him as if he were a monarch – and isn't he?

He loves this headlong life, when he physically feels he is outrunning time and launching himself into his future. At every stop he works, writes, and dictates. On 12 July, he completes the overall plan of the descent on England. He hunches over the maps, checks the number of flat-bottomed boats which he has ordered to be built, summons the admirals, ministers and generals. If he needed proof that he is their leader, he finds it in seeing them exhausted and sleepy. He has to infuse them with his energy, rouse them, like the state councillors who used to fall asleep during the discussion of articles when they were preparing the Civil Code.

Where does this strength of his come from? This inability to stay still? This obligation to forge forward, fast, to the end?

Which end?

HE WILL be thirty-four in a few days. It is almost a month since he left Paris and when his berline turns onto the road leading to the château of St Cloud in the late afternoon on 11 August 1803, he thinks of all the landscapes he has devoured day after day and the 'transports of admiration' that have accompanied him throughout the journey.

He passes through the château's galleries and salons, regains his study and immediately begins reading the latest dispatches.

HE THROWS down the papers he has just read, clenches his fists and takes a pinch of snuff, muttering to himself. The energy boiling up in him can no longer find a way to express itself. He grows indignant. Admiral Truguet writes that any thought of a descent on England must be abandoned because the navy is not ready, but England has just decreed a mass levy of all men between seventeen and fifty-five! The English know an invasion is possible, and they are prepared to defend themselves in any way they can.

Which assassins have they paid now? Georges Cadoudal again? He reads a letter, his face contorted with fury, in which a spy reports that the Comte d'Artois, with Generals Pichegru and Dumouriez, has reviewed troops in England, and that Georges Cadoudal is most probably in France by now.

Brigands! It is not just him as First Consul they want to kill, but him as the son of the Revolution. Pichegru and Dumouriez, who the Revolution made, are side by side with a Chouan!

He remembers. He is going to celebrate the Festival of the Republic and, better still, give a pension to Charlotte Robespierre, Maximilien's sister, in memory of his time in Nice, and because, after all, Robespierre in his way had tried to check the Revolution's progress and had been made into a convenient scapegoat.

Brigands!

Perhaps Fouché is right and the danger does not lie among the old Jacobins but amongst those brigands in the pay of England and the Bourbons.

Hasn't Desmarets, who runs the secret police, just announced the arrest of two of Georges Cadoudal's men, Quérelle and Sol de Grisolle, whose purpose can only have been to assassinate me? But should I assign importance to these brigands when I am preparing for the greatest of wars?

He thinks of those lines in *Cinna*, his favourite play by Corneille, the long speeches of which he often recites in a deep voice,

If there are souls so vile as to betray me
At least my courage will never forsake me

Repeating these lines, he walks through the salons of St Cloud, where Josephine is entertaining. Madame de Rémusat, one of her lady companions, seems to have heard. '*Cinna*?' she murmurs.

She is beautiful, in blue and red taffeta. He feels like talking. He says, 'Tragedy should be put above history; it fires the soul and elevates the heart. Tragedy can and should create heroes . . .'

He does not reply to Cambacérès, who is talking about the Grand Army and the fear it is causing in England. Instead he recites,

If it is the destiny of royal grandeur
That their best favours win them naught but hate
They have no security; he who can do all must needs fear all
What! Wouldst thou be spared who sparest none!

He looks at Madame de Rémusat. 'I only understood the ending of *Cinna* quite recently,' he says. 'Clemency is such a poor and trifling virtue when it does not rely on politics that the clemency of Augustus, who suddenly has become a mild-mannered prince, never seemed a fitting way to end that fine tragedy. But then I saw the actor Monvel saying 'Let us be friends, Cinna,' in such a clever, sly way that I realized that this was only a tyrant's feint, and I admired as a piece of calculation what I had thought puerile as an expression of feeling.'

He steps back a few paces, observes Josephine's guests one after the other and then, looking intently at Madame de Rémusat, he adds, 'One must always say those lines so that of all the people who are listening, Cinna is the only one who is deceived.'

He leaves the salon.

That evening he has decided to go to the Théâtre Français on his own where Talma is performing *Cinna* with Mademoiselle George.

XXI

NAPOLEON IS SITTING on the carpet, in front of the fireplace, staring into the crackling fire. He doesn't look at Mademoiselle George, who has sat down near him, with her back to the blaze. She has wrapped her naked body in a large yellow silk shawl.

It is the middle of the night.

He feels a mixture of resentment and fury. He keeps repeating to himself what he told Josephine before he went to his private apartments where he knew Georgina was waiting for him, 'I have to cut myself off from everybody, I must only rely on myself.'

It is what he has always thought, since Autun college when his father left him alone, since Brienne school when he was the butt of his schoolmates' jibes – always, always. So he shouldn't be surprised. Yet he would like it to be different, because he continues to believe that his relatives, his family, for whom he has done so much, should help him by understanding what he wants and submitting, as he has done, to the higher laws of destiny and ambition.

But every time he is disappointed.

He repeats, Madame Jouberthon! Mademoiselle Paterson!

Georgina moves closer and strokes his shoulder, then stops immediately. He cannot even stand her touching him. Alone. That is what he is.

Madame Jouberthon, a divorcée, a stockbroker's widow and, so they say, a loose woman, has become Madame Bonaparte by marrying Lucien!

Mademoiselle Paterson, a young American from Baltimore, is, according to the French consul in the United States, the object of Jérôme Bonaparte's passionate love; he has abandoned ship and is planning to marry her at any moment.

Oh this fine, great Bonaparte family! He had other plans, other dreams for his brothers.

Ah well, he will be alone, he will manage his destiny alone, without help, since his family refuses to support his plans. Does Lucien hope that a child of Madame Jouberthon's will one day be his successor? Can one give Jérôme, who is not yet twenty, a position when he will be the husband of a Miss Paterson? Of Baltimore!

Don't they understand that to be accepted by ruling dynasties as one is – that is, risen up through the Revolution – one must at least do something to throw them off the scent? Josephine wasn't a virgin, it is true, but she was a Tascher de La Pagerie de Beauharnais! And her husband, the general, had been guillotined!

I understood that.

He is almost a king and his brothers still have not grasped it. How is one to found a dynasty with such resistance and blindness amongst one's own? Pauline, luckily, has not mourned General Leclerc for long. She has been given a dowry of five hundred thousand francs and has married Prince Camillo Borghese: a name, diamonds, a fortune – perhaps not a husband in her bed, but the title of princess.

He turns round and tells Georgina he would like to hear her act *Phèdre*. He gets up on the library ladder which he asks her to wheel along to look for Racine's works. He recites,

What savage ways, what bitter enmity
Would not in seeing you know ease?

Then he climbs back down before finding the book, and says that he is leaving for Boulogne tomorrow. He takes a handful of notes from a drawer of one of the chests and slips them, as is his habit, between Georgina's breasts. He strokes her back as she slowly leaves the room.

He needs the sea breeze, the sight of the boats in Boulogne's roadstead, the cheering of the soldiers and sailors when he goes aboard the ships, and the sixty-gun salute fired in his honour by Admiral Bruix's ship for the bitterness to fade, and to stop him thinking of Lucien or Jérôme, or some brigand of the press, pamphlet scribbler, salon gossip, or one of those turbaned shrews who spread their rumours, such as that 'bird of ill omen', Madame de Staël, who insists on staying in France.

Before leaving Paris for Boulogne, he has dictated two letters to the Grand Judge Regnier to prevent Monsieur Necker's daughter, 'that foreign intriguer', from staying in France, 'where her family has done enough harm'. Her arrival, yes, exactly like a bird of ill omen, 'has always been the signal for some trouble'.

Chase her off, and imprison this Charles Nodier who is writing more and more pamphlets attacking me, and if, in the corridors of St Pélagie, he meets the Marquis de Sade – who I have had locked up since March 1801 because it was intolerable he mock Josephine under the name of Zoloé, one of his dissolute characters – then let them talk about me, but only behind bars.

Let us have a change of air and forget all this.

HE LIKES the château of Pont-de-Briques, four kilometres from Boulogne, which he has made his headquarters near the Grand Army's camps.

He sleeps only a few hours, so impatient is he to rejoin the troops'. He breakfasts alone and goes often to the seventy-metre-long barrack huts which have been built on the Odre cliffs. From there he sees the sea, the English frigates prowling around, the gunbrigs.

He goes aboard one of them, then from ship to ship, greeted each time by thrice-repeated cries of 'Long live the first consul! Long live Napoleon Bonaparte!' During the day he also rides along the cliffs, despite the November and then December rain.

At night, he puts the troops through manoeuvres. He takes part in boardings and landings in rough seas and darkness. When he returns to the barrack hut he writes to Cambacérès out of a need to relive his experience, but also because he must communicate the energy of the camp of Boulogne to the people who have stayed behind in Paris.

'I am lodged in the middle of the camp and on the edge of the ocean,' he dictates. 'I see the coast of England as one sees Calvary from the Tuileries. One can make out the houses and the movement. The Channel is a ditch which will be crossed when one has the audacity to attempt it. I have reason to hope that in a reasonable amount of time I shall attain the end which Europe awaits. We have six centuries of insults to avenge.'

ONE NIGHT, in heavy weather, he strides towards a moored brig. There is a strong wind and it is raining. He looks at the officers around him bowing their heads, and says he wants to sail out and visit the anchorage. He jumps into the brig and takes up a position in the middle. Once it has cast off, it pitches, starts to drift and in a few minutes founders on a bar a few dozen metres from the shore. The waves flood over it.

Sheets of water hit him full in the face as he struggles to stay on his feet. The sailors throw themselves into the sea and, forming a close group, try to withstand the waves. Then they carry Napoleon on their shoulders through the spray to the shore.

They cheer and his aides-de-camp, who have stayed on land, look at him with a sort of fearful admiration.

It is essential that he is the man who amazes, who sets the examples, who defies death. Later that night he dictates a few more lines to Cambacérès. 'I spent the whole day in port, on horseback and in boats, which is the same as telling you that I was constantly drenched. In such a season as this one would do nothing if one cared about rain. Luckily it does me no harm and I was never so well in my life.'

THE OTHERS are sick: for instance, Monsieur de Rémusat, the Prefect of the Palace, who has come to Boulogne and cannot stand the wet. How can these men let themselves be laid low like this?

He asks for Madame de Rémusat, who has come to her husband's bedside, to be shown into the salon of the château of Pont-de-Briques. He commiserates with her. Does she remember their conversation about the tragedy *Cinna*?

'Here I have been as well as I always am,' he says. 'The sea is terrible and the rain never stops, but . . .'

With a change of tone, he declaims,

> I am earth's master and mine own as well
> I am and I wish to be so . . .

Cinna, no?

He wants to be with her, while she is in the camp of Boulogne. He likes to see her after his rides and his trips out to sea. He summons her to his barrack-hut. He confides in her and senses her fascination. He tells stories of his campaigns. She is only twenty-two.

'The time I spent in Egypt was the most beautiful of my life because it was the most ideal,' he says.

She listens and sometimes challenges his ideas.

'Style barely registers with me, I am only aware of the strength of the thought. I love the poetry of Ossian because I love the wind and the waves.'

He moves close to her. Hasn't she, like him, a passion for life?

NATURALLY JOSEPHINE is jealous but, after all, isn't it his turn? Isn't this the natural movement of life which causes things to be overthrown in a perpetual revolution, as in the celestial mechanics so beloved of Laplace? He rereads the letter Josephine has sent him: 'This is my desire and my wishes which all boil down to wanting to please you and to make you happy. Yes, my will and pleasure is also to please you and to love, or rather, adore you.' Before, in Italy, he was the one who used to write that sort of letter.

HE SEES Josephine and Madame de Rémusat side by side in the room at the Tuileries where, on 15 January 1804, Josephine gives what she calls a 'little ball'. He smiles at each of them but refuses to dance, talking instead to Portalis, Lebrun and Girardin. He can make them change opinion in a few moments' conversation. He bowls them over like a battalion of young recruits. They are not strong enough. Portalis is defending the freedom of the press – that would bring back anarchy soon enough, Napoleon replies. 'If the newspapers could say anything they wanted, Portalis, wouldn't they say that Portalis was a Bourbon supporter whom I should be wary of? That he has supported their cause in this or that situation?'

Portalis coughs and looks down.

'But all is forgotten, Portalis.'

He takes a few paces and looks at the couples dancing. Here the old and the new rub shoulders, the aristocrat and the regicide. Cambacérès is standing next to Monsieur de Rémusat.

'The ingredients for anarchy are still present in this country.

The number of people with nothing is swelled by those who have a great deal. There is no post in the clergy, the civil service, the army or the treasury which has not had two holders, an old and a new. Think what a ferment of revolution that provokes.'

He acknowledges Madame de Rémusat with another smile.

That is why he has introduced workers' records, he explains, to contain these ferments; they will enable the employer to know everything about the man he is employing and so remain in charge. 'But the different parties are plotting,' he goes on. 'They know that a coup cannot succeed while I am alive.'

He takes a pinch of snuff and then crosses his hands behind his back.

'The target of their plots is me,' he says. 'Me alone. Bourbon supporters, terrorists – they all join together to stab me.'

He glances round the room and adds, as he goes over to Cambacérès, 'To defend me I have my luck, my genius and my guards.' He walks quickly across the room and invites Cambacérès to follow him into his study.

He picks up a letter from Desmarets off the table. The head of the political police has written to remind him that five Bourbon 'brigands' are imprisoned in the Temple and ask what should be the fate of these individuals – Picot, Lebourgeois, Ploger, and particularly Desol de Grisolles and Quérelle, who have been linked to Georges Cadoudal.

Napoleon reads the letter. He wants these men urgently brought before a military commission, tried and sentenced to death. 'They will talk rather than be shot,' he concludes. Then he adds, 'The air is full of daggers.'

PART SIX

I am the French Revolution and I shall defend it

JANUARY TO 28 JUNE 1804

XXII

NAPOLEON WALKS SLOWLY along the ranks, less than a metre away from the first row of soldiers. He stops at every third or fourth step. He looks the man facing him in the eyes. He recognizes this one, questions that one. Egypt? Italy? He says a few words. He takes his time.

He feels invulnerable – and yet it would only take one of these men for everything to come to a halt. He imagines the dagger thrust of a soldier, the officer breaking out of the ranks and rushing at him, arm raised. They would strike here, in the throat. Or else they would fire from a window of the palace. He makes a fine target here in the Tuileries courtyard.

At one of the palace windows near his study, he sees a councillor of state, Réal. Réal is afraid, and earlier advised him not to take part in reviews. Napoleon did not even reply. Even before Réal began relaying the confession which the royalist Quérelle made before being shot – men being what they are – Napoleon knew that the dogs had been loosed on him. How many brigands have been sent to hunt him down? How much money has been spent to kill the first consul?

All the reports that have arrived from England in the last few weeks have made him think these thoughts. Georges Cadoudal, the spies say, is living in style in London and rallying the Chouans. All the talk around the Comte d'Artois and the Duc de Berry is of expeditions to France. Messieurs de Polignac, Armand and Jules go around everywhere declaring that they will defy this First Consul Buonaparte.

It is so easy for England to pay assassins, whereas defeating the Grand Army would be impossible for them and they dread being invaded.

What would remain of my work if I die? Without me everything could collapse. Without me England is victorious. So they are going to have to kill me. This is the battle I must fight before turning to my armies.

Napoleon has stopped again. The wind blows in gusts; it is freezing. The soldiers' faces are red. The cold seeps in under his greatcoat; his fingers are stiff, despite his gloves; yet he must stay longer and expose himself to death.

The royalist Quérelle talked because he was afraid of dying, because he trembled at the thought of facing the muskets of the firing squad.

All I fear is defeat. Am I going to tremble at a handful of brigands?

He leaves the Tuileries courtyard slowly.

RÉAL COMES forward to meet him. His face is covered in sweat. As he is walking, Napoleon announces that from today, 29 January 1804, Réal is entrusted 'under the direction of the Grand Judge Regnier with the investigation and implementation of all matters concerning the peace of the Republic'.

With his forearm Napoleon brushes aside the papers piled on the table standing in the centre of his study. Nothing matters from now on apart from this battle. It is not to protect his life – destiny will provide for that, and he feels so much strength and energy that he is not worried; they will not succeed in killing him. However, evil must be eradicated, all evil. Use the knife, because conspiracies are a gangrene.

So Cadoudal, according to Quérelle, has landed in France and is bound for Paris with a band of Chouans. Then what is his plan – kidnap me, kill me in an ambush?

Quérelle must tell all he knows. Working their way back from Biville cliff between Dieppe and Le Tréport where the Chouans landed, they must find all the lodgings which gave them shelter and the accomplices who have given them help.

'I want everything: places, names, all the branches of the conspiracy. Everything.'

Réal was Fouché's man before. Even if Fouché is no longer a minister, he is still a precious ally. He was the one, a while ago, who was talking of 'the air full of daggers'. The situation demands he rely on Fouché.

I can count on him. But who else? Murat, military governor of Paris since 15 January? General Savary, commandant of the elite gendarmerie?

'I must be informed at every moment,' Napoleon tells Réal.

The hunt is on. They wanted to make him the prey. Well, they will find out who the mort is blown for.

IT IS AN icy February. Napoleon gets up even earlier than usual and immediately goes to his study in the Tuileries.

The fire in there is never allowed to go out. Sometimes he stays motionless for a long time, his hands stretched out in front of the flames, his eyes locked in a fixed stare.

Réal's reports pile up. Savary's messages multiply. The general has gone to the place known as Biville cliff, where he and his gendarmes have disguised themselves as peasants or smugglers. There is a cleft in the rock that forms a passage up the cliff, which the smugglers take, pulling themselves up by a cable, and climbing two or three hundred feet. The precipice corresponds exactly to that described by Quérelle in his cell in the Temple. A certain Troche, a watchmaker at Eu, has been arrested. He was present at, and lent a hand to, three disembarkations. He also acted as guide. He does not know the names of the persons who entered France, but they were people of quality, perhaps even generals. He can testify to Cadoudal having landed.

So Cadoudal has been in France for weeks, hiding in Paris.

Suddenly Napoleon flies into a rage. Can he not be found?

He remembers their meeting, here in the Tuileries: Chouan with the body like an ox and the huge face. He remembers the man's brutality, his hatred.

He sends for Réal. What more is known? He wants to be notified of every arrest and every confession.

He grows calm.

RÉAL, MURAT and Savary only see one aspect of this war. On a battlefield, they are good and loyal underlings, but he, the general in chief, is the one who has to imagine and anticipate what may happen. This conspiracy is of huge significance, immense, since London, which pays the conspirators and transports them to France, is aiming to win the war before it has hardly begun.

By killing me and breaking my country's energy.

Who can the English count on here? His old opponents, the jealous generals? He thinks of Moreau who has retired to his estate at Grosbois, where police spies report that he mocks the 'pious charades' of the Concordat, the légion d'honneur, the first consul as another king. At one dinner he decorated his cook with the Order of the Casserole. His wife is a creole from a rival family to that of Josephine's. She refused to wear mourning after General Leclerc's death. Moreau, whose ambition and jealousy have been simmering for years, may be the one they have chosen in London to succeed the first consul.

Moreau! Other generals as well, probably – Pichegru, who is in exile in London, Augereau, Bernadotte? They must be waiting for a signal – and with them, those Bourbons who parade about, dreaming of vengeance and the restoration of the monarchy.

Napoleon pokes the fire.

This is the last test before the true battle.

PICOT, A SERVANT of Cadoudal's, has been arrested, announces Réal. They have also arrested Bouvet de Lozier, who was adjutant-general of the Royal Army and Cadoudal's principal lieutenant.

He has tried to commit suicide, Réal says, but he has been brought round and now he wants to talk. This is what he has started writing: 'A man just escaped from the gates of the tomb and still covered with the shadows of death, calls for vengeance on those whose treachery has plunged him and his party into ruin.'

It is as if the enemy line has suddenly collapsed at one point. That is where he must throw all his forces. Réal is to interrogate Bouvet de Lozier until he has said everything. Everything. A man who has seen death is no longer the same.

I am waiting.

AT SEVEN o'clock in the morning, on 13 February, Réal appears.

Napoleon is in his dressing room with Constant, shaving. He looks questioningly at Réal, whose voice shows the signs of a sleepless night.

Réal impatiently glances at Constant, but Napoleon seems to pay no attention to his valet's presence.

'Bouvet de Lozier . . .' begins Réal, and then breaks off. 'Generals Moreau and Pichegru,' he resumes in a high-pitched, exhilarated voice.

Two names that ring out, confirming what I sensed.

Napoleon rushes forward, puts his hand over Réal's mouth and leads him to his room, away from Constant. He listens to the report. He has been imagining it, and yet deep down he could not believe Moreau would betray him. However, Bouvet de Lozier's testimony is overwhelming: Moreau has met General Pichegru, who has come back into France via Biville cliff. He has conferred with him several times, and Pichegru organized a meeting between Moreau and Cadoudal on the boulevard Madeleine. The three men spoke together for several minutes and then, according to Bouvet de Lozier, Cadoudal left, furious. Moreau and Pichegru wanted to topple the first consul, but only for their benefit, with Moreau replacing Napoleon but refusing to make Georges Cadoudal the third consul. 'You are working for yourselves and not for the king at all!' Cadoudal had said. 'If we must needs have any usurper, I would rather the one who is already in place.'

This is the real battle. Napoleon grows indignant.

The attempt to unify all the people who want to bring me down has begun, and already they are tearing themselves apart. Yet nothing is secure. Moreau is a popular and victorious general whose soldiers love him, and the people think of him as a Republican. How many allies has he got? Who on the Tribunate and the Legislative Corps may follow him? To accuse him when Cadoudal and Pichegru are still at large would make it look as if I were committing an injustice and behaving in the eyes of the public as a jealous tyrant.

Napoleon must think and weigh every argument.

Pichegru must be caught, since he is in Paris, he says. Then he murmurs, 'Ah Réal, I understand things now. I have told you before that you have not grasped a quarter of this affair.'

Must I explain, if he hasn't understood it for himself already, that this conspiracy makes February 1804 the most dangerous juncture since 18 Brumaire: the moment when the largest commercial power on earth, England, floods France with its gold to induce all my opponents to attack and kill me?

'Ah well, Réal. For the moment you don't know everything, but you will know more eventually.'

He must remain alone.

It is a war. He must exploit his opponent's flaws. Moreau has exposed himself this time. He is no longer just the jealous general, the ironical member of the Fronde and loyal husband of an envious wife, but also a conspirator who has entered into preliminary discussions with the assassin Cadoudal, the princes' agent, organizer of the conspiracy of the Infernal Machine, and with the proscribed Pichegru, a mercenary in the pay of London.

By doing so, Moreau has damned himself.

If I want, I can crush him. He is in my grasp. He either kneels or falls.

He summons a secret council in the middle of the night on 14 February 1804, and waits until they are sitting in an arc in the council chamber in the Tuileries. Cambacérès and Lebrun, the two consuls, are next to each other. Regnier, the grand judge, is a little to one side and Fouché has gone right to the end, far from everyone else. He is smiling.

He must already know through Réal. Perhaps he even knew before me.

He must be brief. Napoleon speaks in a staccato manner: the conspiracy is obvious; Pichegru and Cadoudal are being looked for; they will be taken dead or alive. That leaves the band of henchmen who wanted to kidnap and kill him. And Moreau.

He falls silent and waits. He knows the prudence of all these men and the cowardice of some.

'If we do not arrest Moreau . . .' he begins in a calm voice, then he stands up. 'People will say that I am afraid of Moreau,' he exclaims. 'That shall not be permitted. I have been the most clement of men, but I shall be the most terrible if I have to be and I shall strike Moreau as I would anyone else, since he has entered into a conspiracy which is odious both in its aims and in the connections it presumes.'

They agree. He will have Moreau arrested.

He detains Regnier. Moreau will be tried by the criminal court of the Seine and not by a court martial: 'Otherwise people will say that I wanted to get rid of Moreau, that I had him murdered, under the guise of law, by my own partisans.'

There is a bitter line at the corners of his mouth. Either way, he will be accused of being afraid of Moreau as a rival.

He sleeps little, and on the morning of 15 February he goes into Josephine's room and starts playing with Napoleon-Charles, Louis and Hortense's son. He strokes the child. He has that slightly exhausted lucidity that follows a succession of sleepless nights.

'Do you know what I have just done?' he asks. 'I have just given the order to arrest Moreau. That's going to make a great to-do, isn't it? People will not fail to say that I am jealous of Moreau, that it's vengeance and other such poor nonsense. Me jealous of Moreau! He owes the greater part of his glory to me . . . I stopped him compromising himself a thousand times; I warned him that people would try to cause trouble between us. He sensed it, just like me, but he is weak and arrogant and women control him.'

A sneer of derision crosses Napoleon's face.

'The parties have got to him.'

THE AIDE-DE-CAMP brings a dispatch. Moreau has been arrested on the road not far from his estate at Grosbois, and has been taken to the Temple. The general has remained calm throughout.

Napoleon crumples up the dispatch.

Moreau has no idea of the charges levelled against him, or the evidence I have. I must warn the army and pre-empt any calumny.

He dictates.

To General Soult

Moreau has been arrested and fifteen or sixteen brigands with him. The others are on the run. The police have seized fifteen horses and uniforms which were to be used in attacking me on the road between Paris and Malmaison, or between Malmaison and St Cloud, with my picket which, as you know, consists of twenty men.

He sends for Murat.

He must guide the hand of this brave but guileless fellow. He flatters Murat, asks him for news of his wife Caroline and congratulates him on the turnout of the troops in Paris, of which Murat is governor.

Murat swells with pride and Napoleon continues: Paris must be covered with posters explaining the conspiracy and announcing the brigands' and Moreau's arrest. 'I want Paris closed,' he adds.

Taking pinches of snuff and glancing at Murat every now and then, Napoleon lists the measures to be taken. Anyone can enter Paris, but no one can leave. Detachments of infantry are to be placed at the gates of the capital, the horseguard will patrol the walls constantly, and the sailors of the Guard will row watch on the Seine day and night. Anyone who shelters Georges Cadoudal or Pichegru will face the death penalty.

This is war. He must be implacable. To win, he must see everything, know everything, not be fooled by anything.

He sits down and opens the file containing the police reports of 18 February 1804. He forces himself to remain calm as he reads the contents of a poster that was stuck up overnight.

Innocent Moreau, the friend of the people and the soldier's father in chains!
Bonaparte a foreigner, a Corsican turned usurper and tyrant!
People of France, you must judge!

AN ANAGRAM of Buonaparte, his Corsican surname, is also written on walls:

NABOT A PEUR (The dwarf is afraid)

He sits up. Afraid? He feels a surge of fury. Afraid of Moreau? Of those brigands? Of Cadoudal and Pichegru?

He leaves his study. There is a diplomatic reception today. In the reports made by the police, he has learnt that amongst those arrested is a Swiss gentleman attached to the Russian embassy, and that Monsieur de Markov has asked for him to be handed over.

He goes up to the ambassador and challenges him: 'Does Russia suppose it is so superior to us that she can act in this manner?' He takes a step back and raises his voice even more. 'Does she think we have so utterly laid aside the sword for the distaff that we must tolerate such conduct? She is much deceived.'

As he walks away, he calls out, 'I will suffer no affront from any prince on the face of the earth.' Then he leaves the salon, goes back to his study and resumes reading the reports.

People say that he is recreating the Committee of Public Safety, and that the times of the Terror have returned. He shrugs his shoulders. If that is what is needed to resist the princes, then why not?

'Everyone is talking of the arrest of General Moreau,' notes one of the reports. 'All the soldiers who have served under him say that he is incapable of entering a conspiracy, and that he is as much an honest, affable, popular, benevolent soul as he is a good general. They think of him as their father and would shed their last drop of blood for him. In short, they say his arrest is a matter of party politics rather than justice . . .'

He pushes away the report. His anger has faded.

Reason must always be uppermost. Moreau is still a force in public opinion. If he accepted my clemency, I could say like Augustus, 'Let us be friends, Cinna.'

He sends for the Grand Judge Regnier. Is he the right man for this? If Fouché were still minister of police, everything would have been handled more efficiently. Perhaps Pichegru and Cadoudal would have been captured already?

'Go to his prison and question him,' Napoleon tells Regnier, 'then bring him in your carriage to the Tuileries. He can settle everything with me and I will forget the aberrations caused by a jealousy which was perhaps more that of his entourage than his.'

Regnier seems flustered. 'You understand me?' Napoleon repeats several times over. Then he waits.

What matters is to break Moreau; it is irrelevant whether he is sentenced to death or submits.

The hours pass.

Here is the grand judge back again. Moreau does not wish to see the first consul, he explains.

Napoleon turns away. Moreau is an imbecile. He will yield when Pichegru and Cadoudal are caught.

He has given orders that he be notified immediately of any arrest, and during the night of 25–26 February, he is woken up. Pichegru has been overpowered in his bed, bound and wrapped in his blankets, taken to Réal and immediately locked up in the Temple.

Is there time to remember when General Pichegru was a glorious figure at the height of his powers, President of the Council of the Five Hundred, former teacher of mathematics at Brienne College, proscribed in 1797 when I sent Augereau to serve Barras in Fructidor? No, there is no time to think of Pichegru's destiny. Cadoudal is still free.

IN THE HOURS that follow, Messieurs Armand and Jules de Polignac and Monsieur de Rivière are arrested.

So here they are, captured, these representatives of the aristocracy who I tried to win over. The Chouans who have been captured all say in their confessions that a prince is expected who will rally the country after my death. A prince? A Bourbon? The Comte d'Artois? The Duc de Berry? Who else?

Napoleon exclaims to Talleyrand, 'These Bourbons fancy they can shed my blood like that of some vile animal. My blood is worth as much as theirs. I will repay them with the terror they wish to inspire in me. I forgive Moreau his weakness and the errors to which he has been led by a stupid jealousy,' his voice grows louder – curt, trenchant, 'but I will pitilessly shoot the first of these princes who falls into my hands. I will teach them what sort of man they are dealing with.'

XXIII

DAY BREAKS ON 1 MARCH 1804. Napoleon is cold, and he has slept so little. He stands in front of the fireplace for a moment and then goes from his study to the room where the maps and plans are laid out. He looks at them, but then turns away almost immediately. He doesn't want to think about the 'descent' on England – or rather he can't. He has stopped reading the messages Admiral Bruix sends him. Later, when the conspiracy has been crushed and all its roots torn up, he will be able to think about the invasion and the Grand Army again, but the time for that has not come yet. Cadoudal is still on the loose with his henchmen, his 'desperadoes'; Moreau is keeping quiet or saying he doesn't know anything; Pichegru is rampaging round his cell in the Temple like a maddened dog; and public opinion is still unsure, not yet convinced of the reality of the plot, despite the arrests.

Napoleon goes back to his desk. He has had brought up from the Ministry of Police's archives the documents concerning the conspiracy of Rennes, including the libels composed and circulated by officers close to General Bernadotte.

He finds the police reports which reproduce the posters, sometimes handwritten, they had used:

Long live the Republic! Death to its enemies!
Long live Moreau!
Death to the first consul and his supporters!

Moreau! So the conspiracy is deep rooted and old. He has not yet managed to win over those officers who, for several years, have been clandestinely and cautiously opposing him.

He remembers how, in 1797, during the time of 18 Fructidor, Moreau had seized papers in the baggage of the Austrian general Klinglin which revealed that Pichegru was already in league with the princes and the enemy. Moreau had only passed on these papers when the royalists' defeat in Paris was certain.

There is the old link. It must be stopped.

He sends for Roederer.

He watches him coming towards him. Roederer is one of the men who have bound their destinies to his. Napoleon pushes the documents seized by Moreau over to Roederer, telling him to examine them.

Roederer does so and grows indignant. How can public opinion allow Moreau still to have any credit?

Napoleon goes to the window.

'People do not know me yet,' he says in a muffled voice. 'I have not done enough to be properly known.'

Roederer shakes his head in surprise.

'I respect the Parisians for their defiance,' Napoleon continues. 'It is proof they will not give themselves up as slaves to anybody.'

He looks out of the window again. 'I have always told you that I need ten years to carry out my plan,' he says in a clipped voice. 'I have only just begun.'

He remains alone. He feels strong. He is made for presiding over the country's highest destiny. He alone is able to respond to the French nation's expectations. He does not want to expose France to the hatred of emigrants such as Cadoudal, Polignac, the princes, the Bourbons, nor abandon it to their opponents. 'He is the man to stabilize everything,' and for that a monarchy must be reorganized around him, through him and in him. Perhaps this conspiracy will create the moment when he can act: crush the conspirators and found his dynasty.

Méneval brings in the latest reports. One of them announces the arrest of Major Rusillon. This royalist has confirmed that Cadoudal is still in Paris and has met Moreau and Pichegru. Rusillon has confessed everything he knows 'with a naivety bordering on idiocy'. And these are the men who want to lead this nation, although they are only clumsy, blind, incompetent intriguers!

Napoleon quickly opens another dossier and finds Méhée de la Touche's report.

He knows everything about this secret agent, a master spy who has switched from one camp to the other. He leafs through the few pages of the dispatch. The man is on best terms with the English who have recruited him, after he has successively served Louis XVI and Danton, participated in the September massacres, and been an informant of the Directory's police and then Fouché.

A name keeps coming up in the report: Louis Antoine Henry de Bourbon, the Duc d'Enghien, a prince of the blood, cousin to Louis XVIII, a Condé and a Bourbon. He is is living in Baden, at Ettenheim near the French border, and has close relations with the royalists in Alsace and the circle of émigrés at Offenburg.

Perhaps this is the prince they are waiting for, who can enter France easily if I am killed.

Napoleon wants to see Réal immediately. They must find out everything about the Duc d'Enghien and send a member of General Moncey's gendarmerie to confirm the prince of the blood's presence at Ettenheim. Perhaps the mystery has finally been breached and this is the moment to strike a great blow.

Napoleon asks Desmarets for information about the Duc d'Enghien, and a few hours later the reports are there for him to read. The duke served as a general in the Royal Army and then in that of the enemy. He was one of the most determined and courageous generals. The police have had him under surveillance for several months already. He has broadened his contacts with the émigrés, the leaders of the royalist faction and especially with his former comrades in arms who have returned to France. His grandfather, the Prince de Condé, brokered Pichegru's treason.

Napoleon clenches his fists.

So now the threads are being drawn together. The conspiracy is coming to a head. On several occasions, the police remark, the Duc d'Enghien has praised the military merits of General Moreau. A loyal and valorous adversary, he has called him in writing.

A prince of the blood; General Pichegru; General Moreau; and Cadoudal, the executioner – there is the conspiracy laid bare.

Napoleon is feverish with impatience. He would like to take action himself – but perhaps the Duc d'Enghien has already left Ettenheim.

Napoleon badgers Réal every day. Have they got General

Moncey's report? Have his gendarmes seen the Duc d'Enghien in Ettenheim?

ON 8 MARCH 1804 Napoleon gets up, as he does every day during those weeks, at dawn. He brushes past Constant and Roustam and goes down to Josephine's apartments, but then cannot stay there. He goes up to his study. Why are they waiting to bring him the day's first dispatches?

Méneval puts down a letter from General Moreau, and Napoleon glances through it with a frown of contempt. Moreau has neither the courage to confess, nor the audacity to claim his acts as his own, nor the intelligence to ask for Napoleon's mercy. Instead he argues, acknowledging his contact with the conspirators but claiming that 'whatever proposal was put to me I rejected out of hand, and considered it as the most arrant of follies'.

'This is for the judge,' Napoleon exclaims, handing the letter to Méneval. Moreau has said enough to show that he has lied, and has been approached to join a conspiracy whose existence he hid. It's over, Moreau!

MÉNEVAL PASSES him a letter from Talleyrand.

The Minister of Foreign Affairs must already know that I am having the Duc d'Enghien investigated.

'If justice obliges punishment to be rigorous, politics demands that punishment should know no exceptions,' it says.

Clever Talleyrand. Loyal through self-interest. Like Fouché. Two men whom I can count on so long as Fortune favours me.

It does.

Réal enters the study, brandishing the report of Senior Sergeant Lamothe of the national gendarmerie who went to Ettenheim on 4 March.

'I have learnt that the *ci-devant* Duc d'Enghien is still in Ettenheim with the former general Dumouriez—'

Napoleon lets out a roar and rushes at Réal, threatening him with his fist.

Dumouriez as well? Dumouriez who went over to the enemy in 1793! They are all there, the traitors, engaged in this far-reaching conspiracy to kill me.

Senior Sergeant Lamothe also mentions the presence of an Englishman in Ettenheim, probably that Spencer Smith ordered by George III to recruit spies and traitors, paying them however much he needs to buy their services.

'Why?' shouts Napoleon. 'Why didn't you tell me before that the Duc d'Enghien is four leagues from my border organizing military plots?'

He marches furiously from one side of the room to the other.

'Am I then a dog who can be cut down in the street while my murderers are sacred?' He turns back on Réal. 'I am being attacked bodily!' he yells. 'I will meet war with war; I will punish these conspiracies; the heads of the guilty will give me redress!'

On 9 March at seven in the evening, Cadoudal is captured after a chase from the place Maubert to the rue des Quatre-Vents in the Odéon. He puts up a fight, kills a policeman and wounds another, but the crowd helps collar him.

He is imprisoned in the Temple.

'I was not the one who dethroned the Bourbons,' Napoleon says to Caulaincourt. 'In all truth they can only bear a grudge against themselves. Instead of hunting them and maltreating their friends, I have offered them pensions and welcomed their servants.'

He shows Caulaincourt the first report from Georges Cadoudal's interrogation. He reads out, 'Cadoudal has acknowledged as English a dagger found on him. He coolly admits he murdered the policeman.'

'The Bourbons,' Napoleon continues, 'have responded to my overtures by arming assassins.'

Then, in a resolute voice, he adds, 'Blood calls for blood.'

XXIV

NAPOLEON HEARS THEM entering his study. He raises his head for a moment and signals to the consuls Cambacérès and Lebrun, Grand Judge Regnier, Murat, Réal, Talleyrand and Fouché to sit down. Then he bends over his desk again.

The reports since Cadoudal's arrest yesterday evening have piled up on it. He has been sent a further instalment of the Chouan leader's interrogation. Napoleon feels no contempt for this fighter who insolently admits 'that he came to Paris to attack the First Consul and that that attack was to be open, by main force'. Evidently Cadoudal is revolted by the thought of being called an assassin! He wants to erase the memory of the Infernal Machine. He claims that his intention was never to 'assassinate'. Sophistries!

Napoleon continues reading. What matters today is the short sentence in which Georges also declares 'that he was waiting for a French prince to come to Paris before acting, and that the prince had not arrived there yet'.

Another prisoner, Léridant, who was driving the cabriolet in which Cadoudal tried to escape, gives a more detailed confession. 'I have often heard that we were waiting for a young prince. I have sometimes seen a visitor to Georges at Chaillot, a young man of around thirty, very well dressed, interesting face, distinguished manners, and I have thought that this could be the prince I had heard about.'

Napoleon pushes aside the papers and scrutinizes the faces of the men sitting in an arc round the table.

Who could this prince be apart from the Duc d'Enghien?

His decision is made. He is going to have him kidnapped in Ettenheim in Baden – on foreign territory, in other words – but if the enterprise is successful, the Duke of Baden will have to put up with it. The Duc d'Enghien will be tried and sentenced. This is war and the duke has made his choice. Dumouriez is with him. To hesitate would be to show weakness and perhaps lose everything.

NAPOLEON WANTS everyone to express their opinion. This will also allow him to know each of them at this crucial moment and, even though his choice is made, to confront the arguments of those who disagree.

Cambacérès, his face purple, is the only one to raise his voice: 'I think that if a figure such as a member of the Bourbon family were in your power, you should not show this degree of severity . . .'

'I do not wish to show especial consideration to people who send assassins against me,' Napoleon interrupts him.

He approaches Cambacérès.

'No doubt,' replies the consul, 'but if one were to take the Duc d'Enghien, I think it would be enough just to keep him in prison as a hostage.'

Napoleon looks hard at Cambacérès. 'You have become very miserly of Bourbon blood,' he says curtly.

Who are these men who are afraid of the things they have done, and think that by denying them they will be forgiven?

Napoleon enters the map room. Now that he has obtained approval for his decision, he wants immediately to dictate the precise orders necessary. He summons General Berthier, minister of war. Then he turns round. Cambacérès has followed him, and Napoleon, with a nod of his head, shows that he respects the consul's stubbornness.

'You have avoided the crimes of the Revolution thus far, but now you will be implicated,' says Cambacérès.

How can this man fail to understand that this has nothing to do with crimes? History is not a succession of private matters.

'The death of the Duc d'Enghien,' Napoleon replies, 'will, in the eyes of the world, be merely a well-deserved reprisal for the attempts made on me. The Bourbon house must be taught that the blows it aims against others can also fall on itself.'

He does not feel any rancour. Does Cambacérès not realize that a war has begun?

'It is between me and the Bourbons – it is not a clash of two families, as in a vendetta, but of two Frances – and I must defend the Revolution of which I am the product.' He looks at Cambacérès whose face has crumpled. 'Death is the only way to compel the house of Bourbon to abandon its abominable enterprises . . . When one has gone so far, it is impossible to pull back.'

HE BEGINS searching through the maps and calls Méneval over. 'Help me find a map of the Rhine, won't you,' he says with an impatient wave.

It is the middle of the night already. He follows the banks of the river with his finger, stopping at the villages and bridges. When General Berthier and then General Caulaincourt are announced he has them shown in. Asking Berthier to take the quill, he starts dictating in a strained voice, so fast that sometimes he has to go over it again so Berthier can catch it all: 'You will be pleased, Citizen General, to give this order to General Ordener, who I put for this purpose at your disposal. He is to start tonight for Strasbourg, travelling post. He will travel under a false name and report to the general of division. The object of his mission is to repair to Ettenheim, surround the town, and to carry off the Duc d'Enghien, Dumouriez and all other persons attached to them. The men will take rations for four days and furnish themselves with cartridges. The two generals will take care to ensure the greatest possible discipline, and in order that the men demand nothing of the inhabitants you will give them twelve thousand francs. You will order the arrest of Kehl's postmaster and other individuals who could give information.'

For the first time since this conspiracy was discovered – for weeks now – dictation gives him a joyous sense of relief. It is as if he has finally given the order to open fire on the principal redoubt, or charged at the head of his men like he did at Toulon, so long ago. He is in action and he is sure he has chosen the best strategy.

When Berthier gives him the order to sign, he glances over the plan he has dictated. He has allowed for everything. He knows one must never stint on manpower, even for an operation of this sort, so one thousand and sixty-five men in all, a small army, are to take part in the action. One must always be able to crush the enemy by superiority of numbers, and when one has embarked on the action, one must risk everything to succeed. Berthier hurries out of the room. A good general, Berthier, loyal and meticulous. Napoleon hears him giving his instructions to General Ordener, who has just arrived at the palace. Now they must wait.

HE CHAIRS the daily council meeting and senses the tension of Cambacérès, Lebrun, Talleyrand and the other ministers. He, by contrast, is calm. He has confidence in the machine he has set in motion and equipped with all its component parts. The rest is only a matter of good luck.

He writes to a number of officers, including Soult and Marmont. Men need to share, or believe they are sharing, the secrets of whoever commands them. This is how one creates the little group of the faithful around oneself, without which there is no power.

'Paris is still surrounded,' he explains to Soult on 12 March, 'and will be until these brigands are apprehended. I tell you in confidence that I entertain hopes of taking Dumouriez. That wretch is near our borders.'

HE TAKES UP residence at Malmaison. The park is beginning to turn green and he goes for long walks, thereby avoiding speaking to Josephine. She is very watchful; perhaps someone has told her? He imagines her feelings and those of her entourage, such as Madame de Rémusat. He wanted her companions to belong to the nobility, because he wanted to bring about the fusion of all the French, but he is well aware that the kidnap of the Duc d'Enghien will reopen wounds and that he will have to cauterize them immediately by going further and higher himself very quickly, so that the instability does not spread.

He goes from his study to the small bridge and walks along the avenues. Sometimes he goes walking despite the wind and rain, and he goes on long rides too.

Can he found a dynasty on a Bourbon corpse? If the death of a prince gives birth to a monarch, and one family succeeds another, then perhaps the wound will be closed.

A dynasty – that would be the crowning moment of the Revolution, almost its sanctification. He stops under the trees which are shaking in the wind. A dynasty – but he is neither a king nor the son of a king. He has given birth to himself. Like an emperor.

On 15 March at eight o'clock, he is chatting in Malmaison's salon with the women when he hears a galloping horse, then the voice of a courier who jumps down onto the cobbles of the courtyard while the servants bustle around him. Napoleon goes outside. The courier is exhausted and spattered with mud. He left Strasbourg on the 14th at one thirty in the afternoon and he only stopped to change horses.

Napoleon has taken the letter, but before opening it he asks the courier his name. Thibaud? He congratulates the man.

Then, he reads the dispatch as he is walking to his study. It says that the troops have started off to Ettenheim under the command of General Ordener.

More waiting.

A night, a day, a night, a day.

He plays with Hortense's son. If he adopted this child, the boy could be his legitimate successor, the first in the dynastic line; if he is to become emperor, he must plan his succession.

At five o'clock in the afternoon on 17 March the second courier arrives.

While holding out his dispatches, thick ones, the gendarme, Amadour Clermont, says that he left Strasbourg on the 15th at nine thirty in the evening.

'See that he takes something to eat,' says Napoleon.

He enters his study. He has no doubt of the success of the operation.

He opens the envelope and sees first of all a list of names.

1. Louis Antoine Henri de Bourbon, Duc d'Enghien.
2. General Marquis de Thumery.
3. Colonel Baron de Grienstein.
4. Lieutenant Schmidt.

He leafs through the report and finds the name of its signatory, 'Head of the 38th Squadron of the National Gendarmerie Charlot'.

He resumes reading. 'General Dumouriez, who was said to be lodging with Colonel Grienstein, is in reality none other than the Marquis de Thumery . . . I enquired as to whether Dumouriez had appeared in Ettenheim and I was assured that he had not. I presume he was only supposed to be there because of confusion between the sound of his name and that of General Thumery . . .'

Neither Dumouriez nor Spencer Smith were in Ettenheim, only Thumery and Schmidt. Napoleon rereads the report line by line.

He lets his mind wander. Would he have given the order to have the Duc d'Enghien kidnappped if he had not been convinced that Dumouriez was there and was part of the conspiracy, thus confirming the scale of it?

'The Duc d'Enghien has assured me that Dumouriez has not come to Ettenheim,' Charlot writes. 'It may have been possible that he was charged to bring him instructions from England, but it was beneath his status to have dealings with such persons.'

Is he innocent, the Duc d'Enghien?

What is innocence, when one is a prince of the blood? When one has served a foreign power against one's country?

Napoleon reads the last lines of Charlot's message: 'The Duc d'Enghien respects Bonaparte as a great man, but as a prince of the Bourbon family, he has vowed implacable enmity both to him and to the French, against whom he would wage war on all occasions . . . He says that he is sorry not to have fired on me, thus ensuring that his fate was decided by arms.'

NAPOLEON DOES not return to the salon where everyone is chatting. It has grown dark. The die is cast; the Duc d'Enghien is on his way to Paris under a heavy escort. He will be imprisoned in the fort of Vincennes.

What shall be this man's lot? The law, the whole law, will decide that, just as it would for any émigré who had borne arms against France. The duke has done that and so he will be tried by a military commission with seven members.

Napoleon opens the French window; it is cold that night. He hears laughter coming from the salon; musicians are playing.

If the duke appears before the military commission, the law of 23 March 1793, 25 Brumaire Year III, says 'Death'.

IN THE carriage taking him to the Tuileries on Sunday, 18 March 1804, Napoleon turns to Josephine. Her chin is resting on her chest and she seems overwhelmed. Since telling her that morning of the Duc d'Enghien's arrest and his intention to have him tried, she has said nothing, only sighed.

He had to tell her. She will talk to all those around her, he is sure, for she cannot keep a secret, and it will be useful if the news spreads. By thousands of channels of confidences, people will know the results of his action. He needs to move fast: strike hard and be feared.

He takes Josephine's arm. She must attend mass at the Tuileries with him. It is Palm Sunday. She mustn't be morose and sad and preoccupied. Does she understand? She forces a smile.

ON 19 MARCH, early in the morning at Malmaison, he is walking in the park when he sees a courier going into the house, carrying two satchels. These are the papers seized from the Duc d'Enghien's house in Ettenheim.

He secludes himself in order to examine them on his own. A man is revealed in these pages, these intimate letters to Charlotte de Rohan. The duke describes his hunts or replies to the Prince de Condé.

Napoleon does not feel any hatred for this man, but it is an enemy who writes, 'Monsieur le Duc d'Enghien begs Monsieur Stuart to convey to his sovereign and to his government the state of extreme impatience in which he finds himself in his desire to prove to His British Majesty the extent and sincerity of his feelings, his devotion and his gratitude . . . and the happiness he will experience when he is finally in a position that will place him within reach of acquiring the esteem of his sovereign benefactor and of his energetic and estimable nation.'

A Bourbon in England's service!

He declares that he wants to remain 'close to the frontiers because, as I said a moment ago, a man's death can, as things stand, bring about a complete change.'

Napoleon stops reading and goes out to walk in the park.

A man's death, the duke wrote. It is my *death he is talking about, that is what he is waiting for. This truly is war. It is them or me. Them or us.*

He returns to his study and resumes reading.

The duke flatters himself on his ability to rally deserters. 'There would be a large number of these at the moment amongst the armies of the Republic,' he writes. 'The Duc d'Enghien has been prompted to convince himself of this in a positive fashion.'

An enemy who wishes to destroy the nation's army – the law must be turned on him, the whole law. Napoleon feels pitiless.

He looks up. Josephine is there, red-eyed. She stammers something, coming towards him and throwing herself on her knees.

She does not surprise him as she whispers, 'He is a Bourbon.'

He pushes her away roughly. Why does she fail to grasp what is happening? 'Women should have nothing to do with these sorts of affairs,' he says.

He takes several pinches of snuff and talks without looking at her, as if to himself. 'Politics demands this coup d'état. Through it I will acquire the right to be merciful later. Leniency now would encourage the parties and so I would be obliged to persecute, exile and put to death constantly, revoking everything I have done for the émigrés and putting myself into the Jacobins' hands. The royalists have already compromised me more than once in relation to the revolutionaries. The execution of the Duc d'Enghien will free me with regard to everybody.'

She has got to her feet and is insisting.

'Go away, you're just a child,' he snaps.

She sobs and says in a shrill voice, 'Well Bonaparte, if you have your prisoner killed, you will be guillotined yourself, like my first husband, and this time I will accompany you.'

They are afraid, all of them. My mother sends me a letter urging me to show mercy, Caroline my sister, Hortense and Madame de Rémusat are crying too. Are they blind?

He crosses the salon. They are huddled up next to each other, these mourners. He calls out, 'The Duc d'Enghien is a conspirator like any other! He must be treated like one.'

Before going out he turns back. 'I am the French Revolution,' he cries.

He sends for General Savary so he can pass on orders for Murat: the governor of Paris will assemble a military commission of seven people. It will be chaired by General Hulin, who participated in the fighting on 14 July 1789, following the storming of the Bastille. It will convene immediately at the château of Vincennes, where the Duc d'Enghien will be held prisoner when he arrives from Strasbourg. It will try the accused forthwith and without intermission. He tells Savary, 'Everything must be settled in the course of the night.'

It is 20 March. He walks alone in the park. The prisoner must be executed as soon as sentence is passed. No shilly-shallying. Public opinion must be gripped, stunned, petrified. Thunderstruck, he says to himself.

He hears the clatter of a coach on the cobbles and turns round just as Fouché jumps out. Cunning Fouché – he supported the abduction and now he is coming to counsel prudence. Or is he too cunning? He will understand.

'I know what brings you,' Napoleon says. 'I am striking a great blow today, a necessary one.'

'You will set France and Europe against you if you do not provide irrefutable proof that the duke was conspiring against your person at Ettenheim,' answers Fouché.

Napoleon is obviously startled. Fouché's saying that! Fouché who poured grapeshot into Lyon under the Terror. Fouché!

'What need is there of proof? Isn't he a Bourbon, and the most dangerous of them all?' He walks away and Fouché follows, still arguing.

'Haven't you and your like said a hundred times that I would end up being the Monk of France and restore the Bourbons?' Napoleon says scornfully. 'Well, there would be no way back after this. What stronger guarantee can I give the Revolution, which you yourself have cemented with the blood of kings? In any case, we must put an end to this. I am surrounded by conspiracies. We must impose terror or perish.'

Napoleon is walking back when the coaches of Talleyrand, Cambacérès, Lebrun and then Joseph Bonaparte arrive.

Whatever they may say, all of them, I shall never go back on my decision.

IT IS THE night of 20–21 March. He is alone. General Hulin must be opening the trial against the Duc d'Enghien. Napoleon sits down and writes a brief message for Réal; he is to go to Vincennes immediately and question the prisoner again. On the edge of the grave, people speak.

Perhaps it will mean a reprieve for the Duc d'Enghien. If destiny wills it, I will give it to him.

HE WAITS. At eight o'clock on 21 March 1804, General Savary enters the salon at Malmaison. On his face, Napoleon sees the death of the Duc d'Enghien.

'Why did they try him without waiting for Réal?' Napoleon asks.

Réal appears. He is pale. He was given the letter too late. He was asleep.

'That is fine,' Napoleon says in a muffled voice. He turns his back on them.

Josephine follows him, repeating, 'The Duc d'Enghien is dead. Oh, what have you done?'

He says loudly, 'At least they will see what we are capable of. From now on, I hope they will leave us in peace.' He faces up to them all. 'I have shed blood,' he continues. 'I had to, and perhaps I shall shed more – but not in anger and simply because blood-letting is part of political medicine.'

Their eyes express horror.

Why do they refuse to see what is happening? 'They want to destroy the Revolution by attacking my person,' he adds. 'I am the man of state, I am the French Revolution and I will defend it.'

XXV

NAPOLEON IS STANDING with his back to the fireplace. He loves this heat, the smell of burning wood. Since he has come into the salon at Malmaison and taken up his position like this in front of the fireplace, no one has dared approach him.

Josephine and Madame de Rémusat are crying. Eugene de Beauharnais has the grave face of someone grieving over the loss of a relative. Sometimes Josephine says in a loud voice, 'It is an atrocious act,' and she turns towards Napoleon.

They had wanted Savary to tell them about the Duc d'Enghien's last moments. He showed them a ring, a lock of hair which the prince cut off in front of the firing squad, and a letter he wrote in the moat of the castle of Vincennes on bended knee, all of which are for Princess de Rohan-Rochefort.

My mother has promised to deliver these mementos. She is also in mourning for the Duc d'Enghien.

They had better keep away from him, these weepers who are behaving like children.

Various generals arrive, accompanied by ministers and the consuls, and they hold forth vehemently, surrounding Napoleon and congratulating him on what he has done. They report what the tribune Curée, a regicide, said this morning: 'I am delighted, Bonaparte has made the Convention!' Senators and state councillors have already started thinking about what to do next: 'Some people want to kill Napoleon, do they? They should make him immortal.'

Napoleon takes Le Coulteux de Canteleu, the vice-president of the Senate, to one side. He must make his move quickly now, he thinks.

'The circumstances in which we found ourselves,' Napoleon says, 'were not at all the sort we could treat with chivalry. That attitude in affairs of state . . .' He looks over at the sofa where Josephine is sitting with Madame de Rémusat. '. . . would be puerile.'

He sees Josephine stand up. She has stopped crying already. No doubt the sight of all the generals, who seem happy at the news, has made her doubt the validity of her tears. He hears her saying to different people, as if apologizing, 'I am a woman and I confess it did make me want to cry.'

Napoleon goes to her, takes her by the arm and says so that everyone can hear, 'We must put this behind us at all costs.' Then he announces that this evening he will go to the Opera as planned.

Josephine whispers that she is afraid how the spectators will react; they may show their disapproval of the 'atrocious act'. He should wait.

He grips her arm. 'This evening,' he repeats, 'I shall be going to the Opera.'

THE AUDIENCE applauded, as usual, and now the first communications from the soldiers of the Grand Army at Boulogne reach his study. They approve of the Duc d'Enghien's execution and ask Napoleon to proclaim himself Emperor.

The moment has come to take things further.

He goes to the State Council. When an action has been carried out, it is stupid not to claim it as one's own. 'Let France be under no illusions,' he says. 'It will have neither peace nor rest until the last member of the Bourbon race shall be wiped out. I had one seized at Ettenheim . . . What right of nations can be appealed to by people who have plotted assassination, ordered it and paid agents to commit it? And now people talk to me about asylum and violation of territory! What strange and puerile absurdities!'

He stops for a moment and his eyes travel round the assembly.

'They do not know me well,' he thunders. 'I do not have water in my veins, I have blood.'

HE MUST frighten, but he must also reassure. He sweeps Roederer along, speaking in a calm voice. 'I am far from returning to mass proscriptions, and those who affect to fear that I will don't believe it in the slightest.'

There will be no terror; he will conform to the maxims of government. 'I only judge individual actions; I don't want to condemn a whole crowd of people. I will seize and strike the guilty ones, but I will not take any general measures.'

Then he is overcome by a wave of anger. 'The Duc d'Enghien bore arms against us. He waged war against us. By his death he will have repaid some of the blood of the two million French citizens who have perished in this war.'

Scowling with contempt, he says, 'The Bourbons will never get further than the antechamber of the Great Hall in Versailles; they are destined to perpetual illusions. Oh, it would have been different if they had been seen on a battlefield like Henri IV, all covered in blood and dust. You don't recapture a kingdom with a letter dated from London and signed Louis.'

He laughs mockingly. 'I have on my side the will of the nation and an army of five hundred thousand men. I have shed blood.' Hasn't he the right to be a king, an emperor?

'Fouché says so constantly,' Roederer murmurs.

Fouché?

Fouché explains, Roederer continues, that it would be absurd for men of the Revolution to compromise everything for the sake of principles, when they need only enjoy the present. Bonaparte is the only man in a position to keep them in our properties, ranks and positions.

Fouché has drafted a report which he has submitted to the Senate. 'The government of France should be entrusted to a single man who should enjoy the right of hereditary succession . . .' he has written. The Senate should invite the first consul to 'complete his work by making him as immortal as his glory'.

Emperor.

Napoleon repeats the word. He has been thinking about it for a long time, perhaps for ever, and now here it is, within arm's reach.

HE SEES the members of the Senate on 28 March, listens to what they have to say, and asks for time to reflect. He has decided, but, as before going into battle, he wants to deliberate further. He goes to Malmaison and walks in the park alone.

Hereditary? So who should succeed me?

He sees Joseph, who refuses to relinquish the rights favouring his descendants, and protests when he finds out that Napoleon is considering adopting Napoleon-Charles. In any case, Hortense is refusing to let her son be adopted because Louis is madly jealous.

The rumours that Napoleon is the child's father are wounding and make him furious, so adoption, which he thinks would seem to confirm them, is out of the question.

This, my family!

He will give them a warning. 'I am going to pass a law that will at least make me master of my own family!' he bursts out in front of Joseph.

It is beautiful, cool weather. He starts going to St Cloud again and concerning himself with the Grand Army and the planned descent on England. On certain nights, Mademoiselle George, brought by Constant, slips up the stairs leading to his private apartments.

He waits for her, but she diverts him less now. He knows she has told others about their nights together, and so he makes their meetings fewer and further between, seeing other actresses instead.

Sometimes he sees Madame de Rémusat. She is part of Malmaison's circle; he can talk to her. He mentions the motion moved by the tribune Curée and voted for by the Tribunate on 30 April, which proclaims 'Napoleon Bonaparte Emperor, and his successor to be chosen from within his family'.

'We are no longer in a position to move slowly,' Curée has said. 'Time is hurrying apace; Bonaparte's century is in its fourth year and the nation wants just such an illustrious leader to watch over its destiny.'

Can Madame de Rémusat imagine that? Without waiting for an answer, he adds, 'You like the monarchy, don't you? It is the only form of government that appeals to the French.' He smiles. 'Calling me sire, people will feel a hundred times more at ease than they do today.'

He goes up to her. He could tell her that he saw Cardinal Caprara this afternoon, to inform him of his wish to be crowned Emperor by Pope Pius VII. He had the idea only recently. Crowned by the sovereign pontiff he would truly be a legitimate emperor. Who could then invoke against him the kings who make religion the cornerstone of their power?

'I was intending to keep the consulate for another two years,' is all he decides to say to Madame de Rémusat, 'but this conspiracy aimed to throw all Europe into upheaval; it therefore became necessary to enlighten Europe and the royalists. I had to choose between small, individual targets and a decisive blow.'

Could she imagine a choice other than the one he made? He struck a decisive blow – that is what the execution of the Duc d'Enghien was.

Now I have imposed silence on the royalists and Jacobins for good.

THEY TRY to heap opprobrium on him again when Pichegru is found dead in his cell in the Temple on 6 April, strangled. A Mameluke did it, some say, a murder designed to silence an awkward witness who could have revealed certain aspects of the First Consul's past. However, the rumour doesn't find many willing to spread it across the nation.

'There was a court to try Pichegru, soldiers to shoot him,' Napoleon says, 'and he was the most conclusive evidence against Moreau. So why would I have him killed?' He frowns contemptuously. 'I have never done anything pointless in my life.'

Pichegru has committed suicide! His body must be put on display and a public inquiry set up. Let the dogs bark as much as they like. The trial of Moreau and the other brigands will still take place. 'God will punish in the next world, but Caesar must reign in this one,' he says.

'What about Monsieur de Polignac and Monsieur de Rivière?' asks Madame de Rémusat. 'Are they to be sentenced to death and executed as well?' She begs for them to be pardoned.

'Let them stand trial first,' Napoleon declares. The man who deliberates their appeal will not be the First Consul anymore, but the Emperor.

ON 18 MAY 1804, Napoleon waits in uniform in the large study in the palace of St Cloud. He is standing in the centre of a circle of his state councillors and generals. Behind him the ministers and the consul Lebrun are standing in a line.

This is the moment.

He watches Cambacérès walking towards him and listens to him announcing that, by a *senatus consultus*, 'General Napoleon Bonaparte has been proclaimed Emperor of the French under the name Napoleon the First.'

'Sire . . .' begins Cambacérès in a ringing voice.

Sire!

So, it is done; he is Emperor. Is this the happiest moment in his life? he wonders as Cambacérès concludes his speech: 'For the glory as well as the happiness of the Republic, at this very instant the Senate proclaims Napoleon Emperor of the French.'

Napoleon hears the booming of the cannon announcing the news in Paris, their echo reaching as far as St Cloud.

Happy?

What does that word mean? He has accomplished what was born within him, what had to be put into practice because it was the expression of that energy which has brought him all this way, to these words: *Emperor*, *sire*. It feels to him as if everything in his life has been necessary and ineluctable.

He takes a step forward and says in a loud, firm voice, 'Everything which can contribute to the good of the country is essentially connected with my happiness.' He nods his head slightly. These men and women around him form a circle of which he is the centre. 'I accept the title which you believe to be useful to the glory of the nation. I submit to the people's sanction, the law of hereditary succession.'

He looks at the assembled dignitaries. 'I hope that France will never repent of the honours with which she will invest my family. At all events, my spirit will no longer accompany my posterity the day they cease to deserve the love and confidence of this great nation.'

He is clapped and cheered; the whole thing only took fifteen minutes.

He catches sight of Josephine's gaunt, strained face; she looks afraid.

He receives Duroc, the governor of the palace. He wants protocol to be strict. Everyone should address each other by their correct title. Joseph is grand elector, Louis is constable and both are Imperial Highnesses. Cambacérès is arch-chancellor and Ségur is grand master of ceremonies. Eighteen generals have been made marshals.

'Duroc, you will be the grand marshal of the palace.'

IN THE EARLY evening Napoleon enters the salon. Everyone is there for dinner, and he walks forward and allocates everyone present their titles in an impersonal voice, as if his brothers and mother and sisters were as remote from him as Murat or Cambacérès. This is the game of power and life. Baubles? Who doesn't play?

He catches sight of Caroline Murat who is biting her lips and crying. Elisa Bacciocchi is also showing her jealousy. Moments after the meal ends, Caroline faints. She is not a princess, she sobs. Napoleon goes to her and addresses both her and Elisa. 'Truly, seeing your pretentions, Mesdames, one would think that we have received the crown from our late father, the king!'

It is he, and he alone, who is the initiator.

He repeats this to his mother, who is known as Madame Mère from now on. 'I intend to exclude two of my brothers, Lucien and Jérôme, from my political succession for the moment – one because, despite all his brains, he has embarked on a grotesque marriage, and the other because he has seen fit to marry without my consent an American woman. I will restore their rights if they renounce their wives.'

He slowly crosses the salon. As he passes by, his intimates fall silent and bow their heads. He is the Emperor. He looks hard at Joseph and then Louis.

Both of them must already be thinking about my death. I am without descendants, and if I don't adopt their children or grandchildren Joseph or Louis will succeed me. But what can I be sure of? Will all this last after me?

NEXT MORNING, 19 May, he hears Constant opening his bedroom door.

'What time is it? What's the weather like?' he asks as he does every morning.

'Seven o'clock, fine weather, sire.'

Sire. The first morning.

He pinches Constant's ear. 'Monsieur is witty,' he murmurs.

XXVI

NAPOLEON WAITS IMPATIENTLY for the end of the last act. One never knows how a play will turn out until the curtain has fallen on the last exchange. It is 25 May 1804, and the trial of General Moreau, Cadoudal and his accomplices has just begun. Can the judges be trusted? He reads the police reports. Thuriot, the examining magistrate, is dependable – he was a member of the Committee of Public Safety – but what is one to think of Lecourbe, whose brother, a general, has always been close to Moreau? And what support does Moreau still command in the army?

EVERY EVENING Napoleon receives an account of the day's sitting. He does not like the atmosphere in the court, as described by the police informers. Numerous army officers attend in plain clothes to give Moreau support, ignoring the instructions confining them to barracks. The front rows are filled with aristocrats from the salons of the faubourgs, who go into raptures when Cadoudal or Armand de Polignac reply arrogantly or ironically to questions, or fulminate when, for instance, Picot, Cadoudal's servant, says that he was tortured, his fingers crushed in the hammer of a musket.

Napoleon flies into a fury. What is this farce?

When he goes down into the salon, he is met by the sighs of Josephine and Madame de Rémusat. They plead with their mimes and tears, one for Polignac and one for Bouvet de Lozier. He feels like shouting, 'I'm the one they want to kill!'

One evening he is overwhelmed with fury. General Lecourbe, in plain clothes, held up Moreau's son in the middle of the court and cried, 'Soldiers, this is your general's son!' and the soldiers stood to attention. If Moreau had had a little nerve the whole court could have been swept aside and the prisoners freed.

Is it possible that the play will end like this?

FOUCHÉ PRESENTS himself at St Cloud, where Napoleon is waiting for the verdict. Which side does Fouché favour? Napoleon hands him a dispatch. It is a declaration by Louis XVIII, denouncing 'the usurper Bonaparte', but that's not all. Go on, read it, Fouché. Louis XVIII condemns all illegal acts committed since the Estates General of 1789. If one is to believe Louis XVI's brother, these are what have plunged France and Europe into an appalling state of crisis.

Fouché is as impassive as ever. He says what Napoleon feels: that many generals, even those who have become marshals, want Moreau acquitted; Moncey even says that he is not sure of the gendarmerie. 'An act of mercy would inspire more respect than the scaffold,' he sums up.

'Let them be sentenced to death and then the right of reprieve can be exercised,' Napoleon replies.

On 10 June in the evening, the verdict is delivered. Cadoudal, Armand de Polignac and Rivière are sentenced to death, and Moreau to two years in prison.

Two years!

Napoleon gesticulates wildly, cursing the judge Lecourbe. 'Prevaricator!' he cries.

By law Moreau deserved the death penalty, but the judges were afraid.

'These animals have been saying there was no way General Moreau would be able to escape the death penalty, that his complicity was obvious – and now they've sentenced him as if he were a handkerchief thief!'

He carries on shouting and kicking the chairs. 'What do you expect me to do? Spare him? He would be a rallying point.'

He masters himself and remembers the line from *Cinna* which he has so often recited: 'I am earth's master and mine own as well.'

'Let him sell his property and leave France. What should I do with him in the Temple? I have enough to occupy me as it is without him.'

Next morning, he is working in his study with Talleyrand, listening to the minister describing the reactions of the European powers to the execution of the Duc d'Enghien. The Tsar's court went into mourning when they heard the news.

'Mourning!'

Napoleon shoves his desk away with a violent push.

Does Alexander, who had his father strangled with the help of the English ambassador, Lord Whitworth – who then in turn started intriguing in Paris, for which I personally reproached him on the eve of the breach of the Peace of Amiens – does Alexander claim the right to teach me lessons? Is this what the world is? Is this the world of Russia and England? If they form a coalition with Prussia, where they are also mourning a prince of the blood, then we will break them.

La Valette enters and Napoleon hears women's voices and sighs. 'What are they doing in my wife's apartments?' he asks.

'Everyone is crying, sire . . .'

Before he can finish, Josephine comes into the study, accompanied by several people she seems to be shielding with her open arms. A pretty woman in tears throws herself at Napoleon's feet, begging and sobbing until she faints. Madame de Rémusat whispers that it is Madame de Polignac.

The old Madame de Montesson, who Napoleon knew when he was a pupil at Brienne School, also appeals for mercy. 'What is your interest in these people?' Napoleon grumbles.

He leads Madame de Rémusat off to a corner of the room as the others bustle around Madame de Polignac, who is pleading for clemency for her husband.

'The royalist party is full of young hotheads who won't stop if we don't teach them a strong lesson.'

Madame de Polignac approaches, supported by Talleyrand. She is affecting and beautiful.

'They are deeply culpable, those princes who compromise the lives of their most loyal servants without facing the same perils,' says Napoleon.

He paces up and down. His study is now full of women, including Hortense and his sisters Caroline and Elisa. They are pleading for the lives of one or other of the prisoners, Lajolais and Bouvet de Lozier. Napoleon hesitates. He does not want to show any weakness. Then suddenly he calls to Madame de Polignac, 'Madame, your husband plotted against my person, but I can pardon him.'

This is what it means to be Napoleon the First, Emperor – not a Bourbon but a man who has risked his life himself.

Later Napoleon grants other pardons, gives Moreau permission to leave France, and with police funds has his property purchased, including the estate at Grosbois and the town house in Paris. He confers the town house on Bernadotte and Grosbois on Berthier. Showing oneself generous is also a political act. Perhaps these generals will be grateful.

The curtain is slowly falling. Only Georges Cadoudal is left. He remembers the big head; it will roll into the basket. The scaffolding for the guillotine has already been erected on the place de Grève – but this Chouan has risked his life too . . . He was courageous . . . Napoleon sends for Réal and instructs him to explain to Georges that if he asks for pardon it will be granted.

In the evening of 25 June, Réal brings the reply. Georges refuses.

It is better this way.

On 26 June, Samson, whose father executed Louis XVI, decapitates Cadoudal and twelve of his accomplices.

Napoleon walks alone in St Cloud park. He has just read an account of the Chouan's execution: Georges shouted 'Long live the king' on the scaffold, a smile on his lips.

What a man! And he will serve as an example to the others who will always rise up against me.

Napoleon heads slowly back to the château. He is going to send for Fouché. He needs a minister of his calibre at the head of the imperial police.

PART SEVEN

What is the word 'Emperor'? A word like any other!

JULY 1804 TO DECEMBER 1804

XXVII

NAPOLEON LISTENS FOR any sound. He has opened the windows of his private apartments above his study. On this July night the air is cool and damp from the forest surrounding the château of St Cloud. Napoleon goes to the little door that gives onto the hidden staircase that leads from his study to his apartments. The staircase is forbidden to anyone without his formal authorization.

He listens and grows impatient.

Why must he hide like this? He resents Josephine for forcing him to stoop to these shabby pretences which are unworthy of him, his title and above all his nature. He has brushed aside all hierarchies, carried kings before him – even the Pope, who he is convinced will come and crown him here in Paris – and tonight, in this apartment he is just a husband waiting for his mistress and hiding to avoid the thunderbolts and jealous furies of his wife.

Intolerable!

At times such as this he wishes he had given in to his family's entreaties. Since he has been proclaimed Emperor, his brothers and sisters have not stopped urging him to get a divorce. He has asked them to be quiet a hundred times, showered them with Carolingian titles and allowances – 700,000 francs for Elisa – but it makes no difference; his brothers and sisters have not stopped saying that he must abandon Josephine before the coronation because it would be scandalous for her to play any part in it when she is not even capable of giving her husband a child!

He opens the door. No furtive rustle of feet, no shadows on the stairs. He goes to the window again. Perhaps Marie-Antoinette Duchâtel will come by the gardens. She must be staying in Josephine's salon to throw her off the scent, and waiting for a moment of inattention to get away. Josephine is not easy to trick, she is always on the lookout. He can't bear her suffering – but at the same time, by what right should he renounce the pleasure of a night with a young woman? And why must he not contemplate divorce?

He may have given this dynasty he is founding all the necessary appearances and forms, but it will remain precarious and threatened as long as he has no heir in the direct line, a son of his own – which Josephine cannot give him.

He knows this.

And then there's the fact that he needs other women. This Marie-Antoinette Duchâtel he is waiting for is only just twenty. She is married to an old fogey, a distinguished count who was imprisoned under the Terror and is a good director of the register, but unable to satisfy his wife's desires.

Josephine can't give me what I expect anymore, either.

Marie-Antoinette has all the passion of her age. She does not have Georgina's 'hideous feet', but on the contrary, a very delicate, elegant figure.

He opens the door to the stairs again.

Constant must rent a house, on the Champs-Élysées perhaps, where I can go when I please and not be afraid of being caught like here, or have a servant or, even worse, Josephine come in and discover Madame Duchâtel.

Suddenly he is tempted to break off with her, brutally, before the coronation. Then he collects himself. He hears the swish of a dress, a shoulder brushing against the wall, footsteps on the stairs. He takes a step forward and sees Marie-Antoinette Duchâtel's blonde hair. He grabs her by the wrists and pulls her to him. She is out of breath and apologizes profusely, 'Sire . . .' she begins.

He does not listen to her. They have so little time. Soon, she must go back to Josephine, because Napoleon has made her one of her ladies of honour.

He laughs. At least he has the power to do that. He feels so powerful, so young. He is barely thirty-five years old, and he is Emperor of the French.

EMPEROR?

He wants everything the title entails – coats of arms, regalia, pomp. He assembles the members of the State Council. Turning towards Cambacérès, he says, 'Arch-chancellor,' and Cambacérès bows and murmurs, 'Sire.'

Every matter must be meticulously regulated and decided upon after reflection. He lets each of the councillors speak. Cambacérès advocates keeping the bee as the symbol of empire. Another speaks of the lion. Why not the cockerel? says a third. The elephant is a symbol of power, murmurs Portalis.

The decree concerning the great seal of empire has already been drafted: 'Lion at rest on a field of azure.' Napoleon crosses out the word 'Lion' and replaces it with 'Eagle displayed'. The eagle is Rome and Charlemagne – that is his ancestry – and the armies will have eagles like the Roman legions and cohorts.

What about the bee? Cambacérès reminds him in his soft voice that one finds gold bees on the tomb of Childeric the First, and in the coats of arms of several of the first dynasty of the kings of France. When Louis XII entered Genoa in 1507, he wore a robe covered with gold bees. The eagle displayed and the bee, then?

Napoleon gives his consent, thereby taking his place in the lineage of kings and gathering them into his dynasty. Every ceremony, every costume and every gesture have their own importance, he says.

ON 13 JULY, by decree, he fixes the order of 'honours and precedence'. He wants no more of that 'little etiquette war', he tells the Arch-chancellor.

He makes decisions, establishing the precedence of major-generals over prefects, and creating guards of honour which will be drawn from the younger generations of the best families.

Quill in hand, he himself indicates that the Imperial Guard will have more than 9,000 men, of which 2,800 will be cavalry-men. He tells Berthier, 'Tall men, at least 1 metre 70, who have five years' service and have fought in two campaigns will form the guard.'

The Minister of War bows.

Then Napoleon murmurs dreamily, looking at the general, 'What is the word "Emperor"? A word like any other! If I had no title apart from this one with which to present myself to posterity, they would laugh in my face.'

He smiles at Berthier's bewildered expression.

'Men need a favourable light, like pictures,' he continues, and then asks Berthier what he thinks. Berthier stammers something.

Men need simple words, strong, clear ideas and dazzling ceremonies.

He is going to play his role. He is the Emperor.

ON 15 JULY 1804, a Sunday, the annual celebration of the storming of the Bastille, he leaves the Carrousel at midday.

He sees the rows of soldiers lining the route and the four coaches of Josephine, her ladies, her princesses and their officers, which are already on their way to the Invalides.

That morning, in her pink tulle dress spangled with silver stars, Josephine had looked beautiful and dignified, and it had cheered him up, made him happy. It would all be so simple if she was what she should be: a young wife, crowned with her title and her beauty, faithful, attentive and fertile – and a virgin bride. But she has never been that!

Constant and Roustam have helped Napoleon into his colonel of the Guard uniform. He has put on his black hat and now he is at the head of the procession, caracoling on a white horse. Behind him come the officers of the Guard, the leading officials of the crown, the aides-de-camp and, bringing up the rear, the mounted grenadiers.

At the Invalides the marshal governor presents him with the keys and then, following the clergy, he walks to the throne which has been set up for him to the left of the altar. He remains standing at first, bareheaded, looking at the vast nave, the galleries, the uniformed crowd arranged by categories – here the pupils of the École Polytechnique, there the invalids, here the ambassadors and leading officials, and there the military men. Then he sits down. The world is in order and he is at its centre.

The cardinal legate reads the Gospel and then, after the address of the grand chancellor of the Légion d'honneur, Lacépède, Napoleon gets to his feet. He has put his hat back on. He wanted the awarding of the Légion d'honneur ceremony to be exactly like this, framed by the rituals of religion and in church. After the distribution of the stars of the Légion d'honneur, the Te Deum will begin, and this ceremony celebrating the Fourteenth of July will represent the fusion he is searching for and express the meaning he gives to his Empire.

He starts speaking in a loud voice which echoes though the vast building. 'Commanders, officers, legionaries, citizens and soldiers, you will swear on your honour to devote yourself to the service of the Empire, to the preservation of the integrity of its territory, and to the defence of the Emperor, the laws of the Republic and the property it has sanctioned; to fight, by all the means permitted by justice, reason and the laws, all enterprises which might seek to restore the feudal regime . . .'

He falls silent, because everyone must understand what he is saying. He is the Emperor of a new order. He is restoring the old codes so as to preserve what is new and what came into being on 14 July 1789.

He raises his voice still further.

'Finally you will swear to devote all your power to maintaining liberty and equality, the essential foundations of our institutions. This you will swear!'

Then the cheers erupt and reverberate under the vaulted roof. The Te Deum rings out.

He feels transformed, and when he gives each of the grand officers and dignitaries their decorations, his movements seem slower, more deliberate. He is the one who sanctifies and confers glory and honour. The cannon boom.

At three o'clock, he returns by carriage to the Tuileries. His carriage goes through the gardens. It is the Emperor's privilege.

HE SPENDS another two nights at St Cloud and Madame Duchâtel comes to him again. He saw her in the Invalides, all dressed up as a lady of honour, not far from Josephine. He had been surprised by his wife's grace when she left the Tuileries, but how could Josephine match Marie-Antoinette Duchâtel? Time is a morass which sucks you down, and despite her make-up, the rouge on her lips and her cheeks, Josephine looked grey next to the young woman.

He desires her. He has never felt so sure of himself. He is the eagle with outspread wings. He wants to put his hand with splayed fingers like claws on Madame Duchâtel's young body.

She comes into his room. He pulls her to him and picks her up. No one must stop him being who he is or doing what he wants.

He reaches Boulogne on 19 July 1804 and processses through the town. Batteries fire nine hundred rounds in his honour, young girls throw flowers as he passes under the triumphal arches that have been erected in every street. On the port a fifteen-metre-high wooden column has been raised, carrying notices threatening England that it will soon face 'avenging thunderbolts'.

Napoleon salutes the dignitaries but wastes no time before embarking in a dinghy and visiting the line of anchorage. It is a beautiful day. He gives the order to certain boats to put out.

There's quite a stiff wind, but even so the sea isn't too heavy and Napoleon stands at the front of the dinghy. Suddenly, as they pass a headland, he catches sight of the English squadron which instantly opens fire. He loves this tension of battle which seizes hold of men, changing their voices and attitudes, pinching their faces.

They return to harbour, and he takes up residence in his barrack-hut on Odre cliff. From its glass circular hall, he looks at the port and the sea. Then he sets to work, writing to Fouché and telling him to get General Lecourbe, who was in league with Moreau, out of Paris. There are still too many spies, too many enemies. He must not let himself be intoxicated by success.

In Boulogne itself, transformed into a vast military camp flooded with wine and money, to which the girls have flocked like flies to a lump of sugar, almost every day English spies are arrested. Often they are émigrés. They are sentenced to death and shot. It is war. Fouché must remember that.

Napoleon rages in his barrack-hut. One would think he was the only one who understands that they have to act constantly and remain like a taut bow, not slacken off or fall asleep or take their time.

He dictates a second letter to Fouché: 'I have just read Citizen Fulton's proposal which you have sent me – far too late, seeing as it could change the face of the world.' For a moment he imagines the inventions of this American, Fulton: ships that function without sails, by means of a furnace creating steam, and other craft that go underwater. 'I want you to set up a commission of members of the different branches of the Institute to test them . . . Try to ensure this is no more than a week's work . . .'

He spends the night consulting maps and writing to Vice-Admiral Latouche Tréville, who is the commander in Toulon. He wants to convey his resolve, enthusiasm and energy: 'Between Etaples, Boulogne, Wimereux and Ambleteuse we have one thousand eight hundred sloops, gunboats and pinnaces, carrying one hundred and twenty thousand men and ten thousand horses. Let us be masters of the Channel for six hours and we are masters of the world!'

This certainty is like a weight on him. He sleeps poorly and at dawn is already on the cliffs or in the port or at the coastal batteries. There is a violent, gusting wind and one has to hunch over if one is walking into it. Lightning rends the sky on the horizon; the sea heaves with high waves crested with foam.

He walks forward into the wind. This too must be conquered. He orders Admiral Bruix, who has come to join him on the cliff, to send out the ships for a review of the flotilla. Bruix says there's a terrible storm brewing; he does not want to expose the men needlessly to danger.

'I have given the order,' Napoleon says.

Bruix refuses.

Can one make war or command an army if one's orders are not carried out? Bruix is defying him.

Napoleon clenches his whip and then hurls it to the ground and turns to Rear-Admiral Magon, who is already running off to see that the flotilla puts out.

Shortly afterwards the storm breaks and Napoleon watches the brigs being driven onto the rocks. Some are shattered, others capsized. Men drown.

Napoleon leaps into a boat to go and help them. The struggle isn't over until dawn. When he gets back, soaked to his skin, he goes to his barrack-hut, where Soult announces that around fifty men have died.

I command an army, an Empire; I am waging war. The death of men is in the nature of military matters. Admiral Bruix was right to refuse to organize the review, just as I was to impose it, since I had wished it to take place.

He considers making Bruix a member of the Order of the Légion d'honneur.

The admiral stood up to me. When I threatened him with my whip, he even put his hand to the pommel of his sword. I need men like him.

NAPOLEON HAS had a fire lit to get dry. He sleeps for half an hour or so, but he needs to confide in someone. He starts a letter, grinding his quill into the paper, and he writes so fast that it often catches and big blots of ink obscure parts of words.

Madam and Dear Wife,

For the last few day I have been absent from you, I have constantly been on horseback and on the move, without such exercise in any way impairing my health.

The wind freshened during the night and one of the gunboats that was in the roads dragged her anchors and went ashore a league from Boulogne. I thought boat and crew were lost, but we managed to save everything.

The spectacle was grand; the alarm guns, the coast in a blaze of fire, the sea in a fury and roaring as we passed all night anxious whether we would save these unfortunates or see them perish.

The soul was suspended between eternity, the ocean and the night.

At five o'clock in the morning it cleared up, everything was saved and I went to bed with the sensation of having lived through a romantic and epic dream, a situation which might have made me reflect that I was all alone if fatigue and my soaked body had left me with any needs other than sleep.

Napoleon.

It is not everything that happened, but what he has written did take place, and it is what he wants to remember.

A FEW DAYS later, a courier from Paris brings Napoleon translations of the English newspapers. All of them talk of four hundred sailors and soldiers dying as a result of orders given by 'the Ogre Buonaparte'.

So he still has around him that swarm of spies and chatterers ready to commit any betrayal, tell any lies to bring him down, and earn their pay. Pitt has just persuaded Parliament to vote for an extraordinary credit of two and a half million pounds sterling 'for continental purposes' – enough to pay thousands of men and buy their eyes and their minds.

That's what Nelson's fleet is worth! How should I respond?
Unite men around me.

ON 16 AUGUST 1804, Napoleon reviews the troops in a little valley half a league from Boulogne, not far from the sea, between the Hubert mill and Terlincthun.

He stops in front of the new square flags with the eagles on top of their staffs. There is a cracking sound as they billow in the wind. Strings of white clouds slip over the green hills, momentarily obscuring the brilliant blue sky. He stands with his legs apart, to counter the gale. He is going to distribute the decorations of the Légion d'honneur to the army of Boulogne. He calls each of the names in a loud voice; it is as if he is dubbing them knights. He takes each cross out of Bayard's helmet which an aide-de-camp holds for him.

These men must be as loyal to him as knights. If called upon to choose between honour and English money, between loyalty and fear, they must not hesitate. This is how it must be from one end of the Empire to the other, across the whole of Europe, if England is to be defeated.

THAT DAY Napoleon decides to visit the towns on the left bank of the Rhine where Charlemagne ruled.

XXVIII

HE LETS HIMSELF RELAX and for a few moments his body jolts along to the rhythm of the coach. He crumples up the letter he has been given by Méneval, who is sitting opposite him. He catches his eye and his secretary immediately looks down.

Napoleon looks out of the window. They are driving through undulating country and the rain is slashing down. It has been raining since they left Boulogne. It rained at St Omer during the review of the reserve cavalry divisions and it rained at Arras during the march-past of the troops which lasted several hours.

Napoleon stayed out in the downpour, congratulating General Junot on the fine turnout of his men. He saw Laure Junot again, but only exchanged a few words with her. He had to give an audience to the officers, the prefect, the local dignitaries and the bishop. He performed his obligations because he is the Emperor and a leader must not feel fatigue, he must forget his body. He barely slept and then set off along the road from Arras to Mons and Brussels. He is going to stay at Laeken castle and then carry on to Aix-la-Chapelle, Charlemagne's city, where Josephine is waiting for him.

He feels the paper between his fingers and he crushes it furiously. So, Admiral Latouche Tréville has died at Toulon of an illness. The news disturbs him. This was one of the few admirals he had any confidence in. A few days ago he had sent him a letter, every sentence of which he can remember: 'If you give Nelson the slip, he will go to Sicily, Egypt or Ferrol . . . Moreover, to clarify my ideas on this operation which has some chance of success and promises such enormous rewards, I await details of the plan you mentioned.'

But now Latouche Tréville is dead.

And I could die too.

He shuts his eyes; he doesn't want to dwell on that thought, but the letter announcing the admiral's decease is crumpled in his fist. One can die of an illness, even when one is a soldier, or an emperor. He shrugs off the thought. He is confident in his body, he doesn't need to listen to Corvisart. What can a doctor do? But sometimes he feels his body is changing. A pain will shoot through his stomach or his guts. He must eat even less, just fried eggs, a salad and a little Parmesan, or at certain meals, on campaign, roast chicken, soup, or broth.

He points out to Méneval one of the cupboards in the berline which contains a bottle of his Chambertin. He wants a glass of wine. He watches Méneval as he uncorks the bottle, stops him with a gesture and asks him to pour a little water in the glass. He only wants to drink his Chambertin diluted. He throws the letter down on the seat, takes the glass and drains it in one.

Can an emperor slow himself down, by listening to what is happening inside the machine that is his body?

He begins dictating a letter to Portalis, who is the temporary minister of the interior. 'You should have today,' he pronounces in a clipped voice, 'the sum of votes for the hereditary crown.'

He stops for a moment. There will only be a few thousand votes against in this plebiscite for the Empire, but he must neglect nothing that will make the number of yes-votes overwhelming. 'Add those of the army and navy to it and let me know the total result. There should be more than three million votes.'

Let the prefects take the appropriate action. First and foremost he is the Emperor of the French. Approval must be universal. Perhaps then those governments whom England is trying to league with will hesitate.

He starts to speak faster, addressing a letter to the minister of foreign affairs. Let Talleyrand inform Vienna of Napoleon's satisfaction at Austria's recognition of the French Empire. Napoleon the First will in turn recognize the King of Austria's new, self-allocated title of hereditary Emperor. Talleyrand shall, however, signify to the Tsar his regret – Napoleon hesitates, says 'his anger' then retracts it – his *regret* that the Russian chargé d'affaires has asked for his passports and left Paris.

Might Russia line up at England's side?

Will I one day have to wage war against all of Europe to be accepted and recognized?

He shuts his eyes again.

It is peace that I want – but can one impose it any other way than by the sword?

He arrives in Aix-la-Chapelle on 3 September. The weather is beautiful again, the city is covered in flowers and young women bring him bouquets. Crowds throng the streets as he goes by, and in the evening, when he goes to a fête given in a hall in the redoubt in his honour, all the façades are lit up. Portraits of Charlemagne have been put here and there. As he enters the hall he is cheered. Princes surround him. He sees Josephine in the midst of her ladies of honour, but he has learnt a few moments ago that Madame Duchâtel has not been invited on this trip. Josephine probably already has her suspicions. This irritates and hurts him. Is she trying to imprison him in a fidelity he does not want?

Furious, he goes up to her and meets the eye of a young woman who looks back with a mixture of submissiveness and invitation. She is tall and wearing a blue silk dress which leaves her shoulders bare and shows the tops of her breasts. He nods brusquely to Josephine and stops in front of the young woman. Let someone so much as dare to stop him talking to, and seeing, who he wants, how he wants!

Who is she? Madame de Vaudey, replies the young woman, curtseying elegantly. He will expect her, he says quietly; he will send her his orders this evening. He moves on even before he has finished speaking, already filled with a sense of beneficence.

He joins the German princes, who quiz him on his plans. He tells them that he will go to the cathedral to kneel in front of the tomb of Carolus Magnus and meditate over his relics. He wants to see the sword of Charlemagne, with which he pacified Europe.

Can one renounce the sword if one is seeking peace? He wants his coronation in Paris to evoke the grandeur of Charlemagne, because his greatest wish is to make Europe a land of peace and good administration. He wants Charlemagne to be his 'august predecessor'.

He leaves the hall, returns to his residence and orders Constant to find Madame de Vaudey, lady of honour, and bring her to him tonight. He cannot imagine her refusing. In her eyes there was that flame which he sees in the eyes of almost all the women he meets:

the desire to be chosen, an appeal and an offering. He is the Emperor.

SHE COMES, as he expected. Beautiful, young, curious and gay, she also has a hint of impertinence which makes their encounters very lively but which he does not completely trust. He also senses on that first evening that she is greedy and concerned about her future, already starting to think about her situation when she returns to Paris.

A woman should receive without demanding. This one, he guesses, offers her charms as a lure – but she is amusing, it is true, and when he sends her away at dawn, he pledges to see her again at St Cloud or the Tuileries.

Then he goes walking through the streets of the old town. So this is where Charlemagne ruled. He goes into the cathedral and there is the Emperor's tomb and relics, but he is disappointed by the sword, and most of the rarest pieces – the sceptre, the gown, the orb – are in Nuremberg. Nevertheless he is still convinced that his coronation must have the magnificence of a Carolingian ceremony.

He walks down the nave, and hears his footstep echoing under the vaulting of the roof. Is there any greater enterprise than to undertake to recreate the Empire of Charlemagne and impose one's mark on Europe, as he is doing?

Haven't I already shown that nothing is impossible for me? That I just have to want something stubbornly and passionately to be able to achieve it? And that Fortune, when one trusts her, disposes her pieces favourably on the great chessboard of the world?

HE SETS OFF again for Krefeld, Juliers, Cologne, Koblenz and Mayence, to inspect the fortifications of these towns. He has his carriage stop on the road running alongside the Rhine and he walks for a long time alone, contemplating the river.

He now has a precise idea of what form his coronation ceremony should take. It will take place at Notre Dame rather than the Invalides, and he will order his architect Fontaine to clear the surrounds of the cathedral so that it is free-standing, in open space. The houses clustered round it should be demolished and the rue de Rivoli, the place du Carrousel and the quai de la Seine paved. The work must be done at night, by torchlight if necessary. The approach must be a broad flat expanse like a Roman road, not streets that could be turned into a muddy quagmire by rain, because it will be November, the anniversary of Brumaire. The work must therefore be hurried along as much as possible.

He gets back into his carriage. He imagines the ceremony; Notre Dame full of twenty thousand people. He thinks of the costumes, the cloak he wants to wear, the sword and crown. He orders new ones to be made since, although he may be the continuation of Charlemagne, he is also the inventor of his own Empire, the son of a revolution without parallel.

He should – this is his task – knot together the threads that link him and Charlemagne, and that is why he is so keen for the Pope to be present at Notre Dame.

AT COLOGNE, on 15 September, in the imperial palace which he has made his residence, he listens to the crowd's cheers. There hasn't been a town he has passed through which hasn't given him a triumphal welcome. He stands at his window for a few moments – the square has not emptied since he entered the palace – but it serves no purpose, looking out at this enthusiastic crowd. He must prepare for the future, and this will be shaped by his coronation. He calls in Méneval and starts to dictate.

> Most Holy Father.
>
> The happy effect which the re-establishment of the Christian religion has had on the morality and character of my people induces me to ask Your Holiness to give a new proof of the interest you take in my destiny and in that of this great nation in one of the most important circumstances offered by the annals of the world.

He goes to the window again. The crowd is still there in front of the imperial palace. If he continues his work, he will take his place in the line of Charlemagne's descendants. Hasn't he already inscribed himself in the 'annals of the world'? He continues:

> I beg Your Holiness to come and give a religious character to the anointing and coronation of the first Emperor of the French. This ceremony will acquire a new lustre if performed by Your Holiness yourself.

Then he sends for General Caffarelli, one of his aides-de-camp. He has a high opinion of this officer whose elder brother died at St Jean d'Acre. He is going to take the letter to the Pope. He is not a bishop, as is traditional, but his brother is Bishop of St Brieuc, isn't he?

Napoleon smiles and then, suddenly grave, says to Caffarelli, 'Treat the Pope as if he has two hundred thousand men.' He has already said this before, but he wants to say it again. The Pope is an authority who disciplines souls far better than a division with its bayonets.

Napoleon walks to and fro in the large room without looking at Caffarelli or Méneval. He is not speaking for them but for himself, it seems, as if he wants to clarify his ideas.

'What must be considered here is whether this approach to the Pope is useful for the mass of the nation.'

He thinks it is.

'It is a way of attaching the new countries to us.'

What will they be able to reproach me for when I have been anointed by the Pope?

'It is only by involving all the authorities that I shall guarantee my own.'

He walks back towards General Caffarelli and takes several pinches of snuff.

'By my own, I mean the authority of the Revolution that we want to consolidate,' he sums up.

BUT WHO understands his system? And will the mechanism he has set in motion since 18 Brumaire work? Will the other powers accept this French Empire whose revolutionary origins he is trying to hide beneath the gold of his coronation and the pontifical unction?

HE SETS OFF again and reaches Mayence. Is this fatigue he is suffering from? His face is gaunt. He learns that England has seized some Spanish ships without declaring war, and that Louis XVI's brothers have once again, from the depths of their exile in Calmar in Sweden, condemned the Usurper.

So, I am wished in hell, despite all the Te Deums I have participated in and all the blessings bishops of every town have bestowed on me since the Concordat! I am the one they can't accept, the one whom the kings band together against.

He looks with a scowl of contempt at the German princes who have flocked round him in the great, brilliantly lit hall of the Elector's palace. He does not reply to their questions about his intentions, but simply says, 'There has been nothing left to do in Europe for the last two hundred years. The Orient is the only place where one can work on a grand scale.' He grimaces, as if to convince them he is only saying this to hide his plans, but as he leaves he thinks of Egypt and the road he once dreamt of opening to India, like Alexander.

The next day, Sunday 30 September, he orders that the garrison's four regiments of cavalry be assembled outside Mayence's walls. It is cool already, but he likes the wind and rain that lash his face and for several hours he drills the men like an ordinary general, giving orders in a ringing voice. Here on the drill ground, as on the battlefield, action bears within itself the answers to the questions one asks.

Forward march – there is no other law than that. Forward march to victory.

HE STARTS out again.

Frankenthal, Kaiserlautern, Simmern. Trèves, Luxembourg, Stenay: he passes through these towns, receiving the homage of their authorities, reviewing their troops, examining their fortifications and then finally he turns onto the Paris road. He reaches the château of St Cloud shortly after eleven o'clock on Friday 12 October 1804.

XXIX

IT HAS BEEN MORE than two months since Napoleon left St Cloud and now, as he walks through its deserted galleries, it seems to him as if he has returned to Sleeping Beauty's castle! He flies into a rage. What are his aides-de-camp doing? He berates Constant and Roustam, telling them to bring him a uniform so he can get out of his dusty clothes. They can serve him here, in his study; he will have two fried eggs, some Parmesan and a glass of Chambertin for his lunch.

He bolts down the eggs. Do they think one governs by lazing around? He often feels that he is the only motor of this government and all this power.

THE FIRST of the dispatches fills him with indignation. What? Pius VII has not yet officially replied to the invitation sent to him? So, the Pope will not set off before the end of the month and the coronation will not be able to coincide with the anniversary of Brumaire. The Pope must be chivvied along – time is always short, one must devour it before it can devour you. One must act as if the enemy is about to fall on you.

He quickly reads the reports from Fouché and the police spies. In his usual sarcastic tone, Fouché details the activities of the English chargé d'affaires in Hamburg, an individual named Rumbold who receives émigrés and maintains a royalist network, paying all and sundry. And this is tolerated! It would be enough to snatch Rumbold, bring him to Paris and make him talk; he'd give up all his agents.

They're not courageous, these sort of men, and we are at war. We must exert more influence on the Russians and this Tsar who is growing closer to England and whose advisers and entourage are all paid by London. What are we waiting for? We must intervene.

HERE IS Fouché, questioning me as if I have just come back from a holiday!

Fouché listens with his usual, slightly disdainful and superior air. He is not in favour of a brutal action against Rumbold, who is accredited to the King of Prussia's court – the king would protest – and as for the Tsar, he will be extremely indignant at attempts to influence his court and his inner circle.

Napoleon leaps to his feet, not at all fatigued by his long journey. What is the matter with these sleepers, these prudent souls?

'What?' he exclaims. 'Is a veteran of the Revolution like you so pusillanimous?'

He takes a pinch of snuff and walks about to calm himself down.

'Ah sir,' he continues. 'Is it really for you to say that something is impossible? For you . . .' He goes up to Fouché, looks him up and down and forces him to avert his eyes. 'For you who for the last fifteen years have seen things happen which could quite reasonably be judged impossible?'

He points his finger at Fouché.

'The man who has seen Louis XVI bow his head under the executioner's blade, who has seen the Archduchess of Austria and Queen of France darning her stockings and patching her shoes before she went to the scaffold, and who finally sees himself a minister when I am Emperor of the French, such a man should never have the word "impossible" in his mouth!'

He stares at Fouché, who is not the sort to be put out. In fact there is an impertinent note in the minister's voice when he replies, 'You are right, I should have remembered that Your Majesty has taught us that the word "impossible" is not in the language.'

Let him carry out my orders then.

NAPOLEON GROWS calmer. This October day is a mild one, the sky dotted with elongated clouds that perhaps herald rain.

What else is in store tonight?

He leaves his study and walks briskly to Josephine's apartments. The ladies of honour are there. He sees Madame Duchâtel and Madame de Vaudey, who brazenly signals to him. He catches Josephine watching.

Perhaps she knows already? She has the intuition of a jealous, anxious woman. Well, she must accept what I am.

He smiles at Madame de Vaudey in reply and then returns to his study without having said a word.

'Tonight,' he tells Constant, as he sits down at his desk, 'Madame de Vaudey.'

HE QUICKLY reads the report into the results of the plebiscite that Portalis has sent him, exclaiming at every figure he reads. The total is 2,962,458 votes, of which 120,302 are from the army and 16,224 from the navy. What is this?

He takes his quill, crosses out the last results, puts 400,000 and 50,000 instead, redoes the other sum and puts 3,400,000 as the total. He does not change the 2,567 noes. Hasn't Portalis understood that numbers only have a visual importance? Can one let the English think there are only 120,000 yeaes in the army? Don't these senators and ministers and state councillors, who only exist because of him, understand that power is, first and foremost, a question of appearances?

These are my results which the Senate will proclaim with all due solemnity on 6 November. Who will think of contesting them? I am the Emperor; the plebiscite only took place to confirm what already exists, however dazzling the confirmation may be.

The truth? What is the truth? Aren't I the Emperor of the French?

HE THINKS of the days to come.

People in the remotest villages and the most distant valleys must know that I am the Emperor and tell stories at each other's houses in the evenings about my anointing, just as they used to say that the king cured any sick he touched when he came out of the cathedral at Reims.

He wants to see everything: the route and composition of the procession, the seating plan in Notre Dame, the dignitaries' costumes. He draws up the list of personages attending the ceremony, and that of the delegations coming from all over Europe. Once the Pope accepts, he grows impatient at the time he is taking to join him in Paris.

After all the Pope is only a man like any other, and he must give in to my demands, since he will find it to his interest.

He writes to Cardinal Fesch, his great-uncle, the plenipotentiary in Rome who is going to travel from Rome to Paris in the company of Pius VII: 'It is imperative that the Pope hastens his march. I am willing to defer further, until 2 December, to allow for travelling time, but if the Pope has not arrived by then, the coronation will take place and the anointing will have to be postponed. It would be impracticable to detain the assembled troops and departmental delegations, 50,000 people in all, any longer in Paris.'

He would like to have to rely only on himself – then he would remove all obstacles – but there are other people, with their nonchalance, their blindness, their jealousies, their hatreds even. And their greed.

Often he flees them and gallops alone, buffeted by the wind, squeezing his horse between his knees and spurring it on. He tries not to think of them while he goes hunting in the woods of St Cloud, or rides ahead of his suite and runs down the game the dogs have driven from cover. He loves these headlong pursuits; for a few hours, he forgets his files, even the coronation, and devotes everything to this war between him and the game. The tiredness he feels is healthy; it liberates and calms him and leaves him invigorated.

When he gets back, he calls for Roustam, asks for a hot bath to be drawn and then waits for the woman who has been summoned. If it is Madame de Vaudey who enters, she simpers coquettishly and is tender and solicitous, but only so as to give him a list of her debts and the names of her creditors. He pays her. A police report has warned him that Madame de Vaudey is playing for high stakes. 'Why should I have to pay large amounts of money for what one can find so cheap?' he asks Duroc.

ONE DAY an aide-de-camp brings him a letter which he reads, and is moved and worried. Madame de Vaudey is on the verge of killing herself because the Emperor won't see her any more. He sends Rapp to the woman. He finds her having a high old time around the gaming table, joyous and carefree!

No one makes fun of me! Let her be removed from her post and forbidden to be seen again at St Cloud or the Tuileries.

Why must I flounder about in these degrading, shabby situations just because I want to live by my laws whilst trying to be fair?

He sees Marie-Antoinette Duchâtel, who is so different from

Madame de Vaudey, so loving. He showers her with presents because she is not a schemer. He heaps honours on Baron Duchâtel because he is a good director of the Registry, an efficient civil servant and a courtly husband, who obligingly turns a blind eye.

On one occasion, when he is spending the night with Madame Duchâtel, there is a noise at the door which gives onto the little staircase. Napoleon gets up and Marie-Antoinette covers herself, hides her face, and bursts into tears as Josephine starts to hammer on the door.

What is this farce he is being forced to play?

He throws the door open. Josephine is insulting him and hurling abuse at Madame Duchâtel. He shouts. What right does she have to intrude like this? Then it's Josephine's turn to burst into tears and run away. He chases after her. He cannot abide being made to look ridiculous like this, he cannot abide her trying to shackle him.

'Divorce!' he shouts in Josephine's apartments as she sobs. He will show no pity, since she subjects him to the yoke of her jealousy. If he is attacked, he defends himself. From now on he will listen to the voices that advise him to take a wife able to give him children.

He leaves, still fuming. Does Josephine think that she is going to subject him to her law of the old spouse, of the jealous wife.

He meets Eugene de Beauharnais. He loves Josephine's son, an upright, courageous man, and finds it hard as he utters the words 'divorce' and 'compensation' in front of him.

'At such a moment, if such a great misfortune befell my mother, I would not accept anything for myself,' Eugene says with scornful dignity.

Napoleon turns his back on him.

Is a divorce fair?

He stalks off, jerkily and repetitively taking pinches of snuff.

HE THINKS about it constantly. At the christening of Napoleon-Louis, the second son of Hortense and Louis, he hears Joseph and his sisters making fun of Josephine. Why is he wounded by this, as if it was him they were insulting?

He is told that Joseph is going round Paris proclaiming himself Napoleon's successor designate, and telling people that Josephine won't be playing a part in the coronation but is about to be repudiated. Why is he, the Emperor, forced to flounder in this swamp?

So what does Joseph think? That he has claims on me? What has my brother done, what can he point to as justifying that? Why does Roederer give Joseph such a prominent place in his report on the results of the plebiscite which he has prepared for the Senate? What does my elder brother want? To dominate me? Replace me? Does he think that the title Grand Master of the Grand Orient of France gives him the power to decide the future? I must know what he is hiding.

On 4 November, Napoleon summons Roederer to St Cloud.

IT IS ELEVEN o'clock and Napoleon watches Roederer come into the room. He thought he could trust this man who is said to be part of Joseph's entourage. If he isn't, why would he have promised Joseph such a great destiny?

'Well then, what about this report?' Napoleon asks him. 'Tell me the truth, are you for me or against me?'

Roederer protests his loyalty.

'So what is the reason for putting Joseph in the same line of succession as me? My brothers are nothing except by my doing. They are only important because I have made them important.' After walking about for a moment, Napoleon adds, 'I cannot allow my brothers to be put on the same line as me.'

He sighs. The words demand to be said and finally he says them: 'I am fair, and I have been so ever since I started to rule. It is out of fairness that I have not sought a divorce. My interest, and perhaps that of the system itself, demanded that I remarry, but I said, "How can I send this good woman away, just because I have become greater? If I had been thrown into prison or sent into exile, she would have shared my lot and yet, because I become powerful I should send her away? No, that is too much for me. I have a man's heart; I was not born to a tigress. When she dies I will remarry, and then I can have children. I do not want to make her unhappy." '

He bows his head and is silent for a few minutes. Then he says, 'I have treated Joseph with the same fairness.' He carries on walking round his study. 'I was born in poverty. Joseph was born like me in the most undistinguished of circumstances. I raised myself by my actions; he stayed where nature put him.'

He goes up to the window and points to the courtyard of the château.

'To reign in France, one must either be born in grandeur and be seen from birth living in palaces with guards, or else one must be a man capable of distinguishing oneself by one's own enterprise from all the rest.'

He never suspected he felt such a sense of grievance towards Joseph, this fine fellow who refuses every title he gives him.

'He doesn't want to be a prince? Does he claim that the State gives him two million just to walk about the streets in a brown dress coat and a round hat!'

Napoleon's voice changes, becomes querulous. 'Titles are part of the system and that is why they are necessary.'

He walks back towards Roederer.

'Don't you have the grace to concede me a little intellect and good sense?' he asks.

Why has he awarded all these marshals' titles? Because the generals were attached to Republican principles but they had to accept the Empire: 'It was impossible for them to refuse it or accept it with grace when they saw that they were themselves being awarded a considerable title.'

He walks away from Roederer.

'What does Joseph want? Does he claim to challenge my power? I am built on rock.'

He listens to Roederer searching for excuses for Joseph. He may not be well. Napoleon shrugs his shoulders. 'Power does not make me ill, I thrive on it. I have never felt better . . . My mistress is power, I have done too much to win it to let it be taken from me or even suffer someone to covet it . . .'

He grimaces bitterly. 'Joseph has screwed my mistress,' he murmurs. Then he flies into a rage.

'The Senate and Council of State could be in opposition to me and that would still not make me a tyrant. All it takes to make me a tyrant is the behaviour of my family. They are jealous of my wife, of Eugene, of Hortense, of everything that surrounds me. My wife is a good woman who has done them no harm. She is happy to play the Empress a little, to have her diamonds and beautiful dresses, the trials of her age . . .'

He falls silent for a moment, as if surprised by what he is saying.

'She is always the butt of their persecution. If I make her Empress, it is out of fairness. I am a fair man above all. It is only fair that she share in my grandeur . . . Yes, she *shall* be crowned, even if it costs me two hundred thousand men,' he roars.

'It is very easy for Monsieur Joseph to make scenes. When he has finished, he only has to go to hunting at Mortefontaine and enjoy himself. When I leave him, I have all of Europe as an enemy facing me.' He raises his arms wide.

'And then everybody is always talking to me about my death. My death! It's always my death! It is a sad thought to be always thrusting in my face . . . But if I died tomorrow, my whole house would be against Joseph straight away . . .'

He grows calm for a moment.

'I can overturn this system, whether I have children or not. The thing must work. Caesar and Frederick did not have any children . . .'

He gives Roederer a friendly cuff on the ear. 'You should be for me, march for me . . .'

He has put his hands under his coat-tails. An aide-de-camp enters. It is one o'clock. Mass is about to be said; they are waiting for the Emperor.

Napoleon smiles.

'The system,' he repeats.

So he has decided that Josephine will be crowned with him. They are jealous of her. They hate her too much for him not to feel wounded by their attacks. He defends her to defend himself, to respect himself.

At dinner in the large dining room at St Cloud, he listens to his sisters and Joseph's wife whining because they have to carry Josephine's train at the coronation in Notre Dame.

They will do it, they will yield to me.

I am the Emperor. I want this.

XXX

HE GOES HUNTING. Sometimes he digs his spurs into the sides of his horse so fiercely that it rears up, whinnying and bucking. Napoleon pulls on the reins, brings his mount under control and starts towards that dark wood, not far from the road to Nemours, in which he has gone stag hunting almost every day since taking up residence at Fontainebleau. For three days he has been waiting for the Pope. He urges his horse into a gallop, and lying forward on the neck, passes under the lowest branches. He wants to scream.

Every morning he curses as he reads the messages from the prefects, announcing the progress of the four pontifical convoys. This Pope is doing just what he pleases, with his suite of 108 people, his ten coaches and seventy-four horses just for his entourage. Napoleon is angry with Cardinal Fesch for failing to press the Pope to start off sooner.

He has made up his mind: he will not wait after 2 December. Paris is crowded with delegations, the tension between members of his family is mounting; they argue every time they see each other. Enough!

That is another reason he left St Cloud and moved to Fontainebleau on 22 November.

He goes for walks in the park despite the rain or drizzle, roaming in the fog, and visits the constable's apartments which Vivant Denon, who is in charge of the Louvre and went on the Egyptian expedition, has got ready for the Pope.

Napoleon stops in front of a huge painting representing *The Daughters of Bethulia going to meet David*. He turns towards Denon.

'A religiously inspired work, sire,' Denon murmurs with a smile.

Napoleon leaves the apartments. He cannot stand this waiting. He sends for the painter Isabey and asks him to represent the different stages of the coronation ceremony in a series of drawings, because they cannot rehearse in Notre Dame. The workers have not yet finished the improvements. He wants a detailed plan, as for a battle. Which is what this ceremony is.

DURING THE morning of 25 November, an aide-de-camp announces that the Pope is approaching and will be coming in on the Nemours road. At last.

'It will be a meeting by chance,' Napoleon says.

He leaves the château at midday, in hunting clothes, on horseback. It is cold and grey. He stops at the obelisk and then the firing range of the military school. The guns salute him with a salvo. At the cross of St Hérem, the master of the hunt gives him his report, since, ostensibly, he is here to hunt. He is the Emperor, he doesn't want to seem to submit to the Holy Father. The Pope and he are 'the two halves of God'.

And now here he is! Napoleon gets off his horse and walks towards the Pope's carriage as he gets out.

He is just a tired old man.

Napoleon scrutinizes him for a few seconds, then embraces him and waves his Emperor's carriage forward. He gets in first, on the left-hand side, leaving the right to the Pope.

He sees Talleyrand on the steps of the château, coming forward to greet the Pope.

My minister. A former bishop who joined the Revolution, has had his priestly status annulled, and has married. Nothing is impossible in this age.

HE FEELS calm now. The coronation will take place on its appointed date of 2 December.

In one of the drawing rooms Isabey has set up a model of Notre Dame and filled it with little figures in wood with paper clothes painted by him. Napoleon walks round the table, moving them about. This is how one should be able to govern men: submit them to a higher necessity, which is why he likes the discipline of armies. Soldiers obey the logic of the thoughts of the man who commands them.

He examines the details of the ceremony one by one, goes over the costumes, the places of all participants at every moment of the day in the procession and the cathedral.

David undertakes to capture the scene for posterity. It must be a picture that appeals to the imagination, a magnified representation of what will take place.

Suddenly Napoleon becomes sad. He tells David that he wants Madame Mère to be in the picture, and then he walks away, his hands behind his back. Letizia Bonaparte has stubbornly refused to attend the ceremony. She has chosen instead to join Lucien in exile in Rome. He feels her absence like an ache, proof that it is not always possible to bend people to his will, even those closest to him.

The thought irritates him.

AT THE GREAT dinner given on 26 November in the largest of the halls in Fontainebleau, he remains silent. The Pope, who sits opposite him, is a small man, deathly pale but with quick, bright eyes which he does not lower. Napoleon is surprised after dinner when he refuses to attend the arranged concert, and as he is leaving the room, he catches a complicit look between Pius VII and Josephine. Suddenly he has an intuition that he is missing something, that Josephine and the Pope have formed an alliance against him.

He tries to dismiss the thought from his mind, examining yet again the order of the procession which will travel from the Tuileries to Notre Dame.

Cardinal Fesch comes up and starts whispering. His Holiness has learnt that the marriage of Napoleon Bonaparte and Josephine has not received the nuptial benediction and so they are not married in the eyes of the Church. Pius VII will not be able to participate in the ceremony of consecration in these conditions unless the religious marriage is celebrated before 2 December. Fesch has received permission from the Pope to perform it.

The trap has closed on Napoleon.

He is flooded with rage. This is what this woman is like, she whom he has refused to leave, whom he has defended against his brothers and sisters. He clenches his fists. He has always been careful not have their marriage blessed, thereby leaving the possibility open for their ties to be dissolved. A civil marriage is ended by a piece of paper.

He pushes aside Constant and Roustam when they help to undress him. He insults Josephine. Then suddenly he grows calm. What can he do except give in?

ON 28 NOVEMBER he is sitting next to the Pope in a carriage that at six twenty-five in the evening passes through the Gobelins gate. The crowd is vast, orderly; some kneel when the Sovereign Pontiff passes. Napoleon observes these displays of piety by the crowd; this is what men are like, ready to submit.

They cross the esplanade of the Invalides, the pont de la Concorde and then drive along the quai des Tuileries. Everywhere the crowds are dense.

Out of the corner of his eye he often looks at the Pope, who is responding to the acclaim by bestowing his benediction. This man is a force and he knows it.

When the carriage stops in the courtyard of the Tuileries, under the peristyle formed by the stairs of the Pavilion of Flora, Napoleon has resolved to bow to circumstances. He will have his marriage to Josephine blessed by Cardinal Fesch. It is what the moment demands and he must submit to it.

THEREFORE, two days later, while the Pope is seeing representatives of the state bodies, Napoleon goes to Josephine's apartments. She is surrounded by her ladies of honour, and the clothes for the ceremony, including her white satin court coat trimmed with gold and silver, are laid out on chairs and sofas.

Napoleon says in a level voice that Cardinal Fesch will conduct their religious marriage at four o'clock the next day, in the private apartments of the Tuileries.

She takes a step forward to kiss him, but he slips away. He will not be the prisoner of this trap she has set for him. This marriage will be without witnesses and thus easier to dissolve. The door to the future will remain ajar.

He is not a man who can be kept confined.

XXXI

AT LAST IT IS BEGINNING!

Napoleon is sitting in the throne room of the Tuileries. It is eleven o'clock on the morning of 1 December 1804. The doors open; the senators enter and then stop a few metres from the throne.

This is the first ceremony, the one which makes him an Emperor unlike any other. The Senate has just given the results of the plebiscite which, according to François de Neufchâteau, the president of the Senate, 'reclaims for Republicans, whose patriotism has been the most fervent and suspicious, the right to be the staunchest of supporters of the throne'.

His speech is a long one. 'Sire, you are bringing the vessel of the Republic into harbour, yes, sire, the vessel of the Republic,' are his final words.

Napoleon gets to his feet. It will be the coronation tomorrow. Every moment of the ceremony has been negotiated with the Pope. Napoleon will kneel and receive the pontifical unction, but he will crown himself and Josephine. The Pope has agreed.

In this way all the signs of power, anointing with holy oil and coronation are united in me. Just as today, on the first day of December, it is the vote of the people that consecrates me.

'I shall ascend the throne, whither I have been called by the unanimous wishes of the Senate, the people and the army, my heart full of the great destinies of this people whom I was the first, long ago, while in the camps, to recognize and hail by the name of "Great",' Napoleon begins.

Never has he felt so sure of himself. He has finally attained this goal.

'Since my adolescence, all my thoughts have been devoted to it and I must say here that all my thoughts and suffering are taken up with the happiness and hardships of my people.'

All these faces turned towards him are like a great, blurred wave.

'My descendants will keep this throne for a long time. In the camps, they will be the first soldiers of the army to sacrifice their lives for the defence of the country . . .'

He says more but 'my descendants' are the words that stick in his throat. Will he be able to bequeath what he has conquered and built up to a son?

This is all he thinks of in his private apartments in the afternoon of 1 December when he listens to Cardinal Fesch performing his marriage to Josephine.

When the ceremony is over, he hears Josephine whispering to Fesch that she wants a certificate confirming she has received this sacrament.

She is afraid, then. She has understood why there were no witnesses. At this confession of weakness, he feels a surge of tenderness towards her.

Let us share these days. Fortune will decide the future.

ON THE NIGHT of 1–2 December he cannot sleep. From six in the evening to midnight, artillery salvoes are fired every hour. Between the explosions he hears the military bands that are all over Paris, and when he goes up to the window he sees the workers who by torchlight are covering the courtyard and terrace of the palace with sand. It is snowing and freezing cold.

ON THE MORNING of 2 December, he lets himself be dressed by Roustam and Constant. His white and crimson velvet coat with gold embroidery glitters with diamonds. Then he goes to Josephine's apartments. She is beautiful, young. He knows it's cosmetics, powder and rouge, at which she is an expert, but in her dress and white satin coat, she looks barely twenty-five.

They walk to the carriage and its team of eight richly caparisoned horses. The pages are waiting to jump up behind the coachman's seat and at the back of the carriage. Louis and Joseph come and take their places opposite Napoleon and Josephine and the procession swings into motion.

The intense cold seems to paralyse the crowd that presses against the three rows of soldiers lining the route. Napoleon tries to see individual faces, most of them silent, but the colonels of the

Guard wheel back and forth in front of the doors and when the horses race ahead all he sees are soldiers.

When he enters the cathedral he is stung by the cold which catches the back of his neck, numbing it. On either side of the nave and of his throne he sees the guests in rows in the stands. It makes him think of the little figures Isabey used in the model.

I have constructed this orderly, hierarchical France in less than four years. Here it all is, from its prefects to the members of its Institute, from the councillors of state to the delegations from the armies. It is a pyramid and I am at the top.

He advances, holding the sceptre and the wand of justice. His train is carried by the two princes, Joseph and Louis, and Josephine's by Elisa and Caroline. As he climbs the steps he feels the weight pulling him backwards and he totters slightly before straightening up. He sees that Josephine is hesitant and off-balance as well, until at last she gets control.

The Pope comes up and embraces him. '*Vivat Imperator in aeternum*,' he says.

Napoleon has barely knelt down, before, as agreed, he crowns himself and Josephine while the Pope contemplates the scene.

I am the actor, the only actor, at my coronation.

Napoleon leans towards his older brother. 'If only our father could see us now, Joseph,' he murmurs.

He must hear mass, and feels the cold again. Then, once mass has been said, the Pope withdraws and the grand almoner collects the New Testament from the altar and holds it open in front of Napoleon.

The presidents of the Assemblies present him with the form of the oath. He is going to read the text he has written himself; it will echo under the vaulted roof of the cathedral, like an utterance of the Revolution.

It is what he wanted; it is what he is.

'I swear,' he begins in a loud voice, 'to maintain the integrity of the territory of the Republic, to respect and to cause to be respected the laws of the Concordat, and of the liberty of worship; to respect and to cause to be respected the equality of rights, political and civil liberty and the irrevocability of national property.'

He catches his breath.

He is saying this with the crown on his head, standing in front of the altar with his hand on the open Gospels. It is the Revolution which is hereby being crowned and the people who have bought feudal and Church property who are hereby being protected.

I am the one who has brought this to be.

'I swear to raise no impost and to establish no tax except by virtue of the law; to maintain the institution of the Légion d'honneur and to govern solely with an eye to the interest, the happiness and the glory of the French people.'

As a herald at arms proclaims, 'The most glorious and august Emperor Napoleon, Emperor of the French, crowned and enthroned,' the cheering erupts and fills Notre Dame.

No one will ever be able to undo the France I have sanctified here.

He walks out into the square. The sky is grey, snowflakes are beginning to fall, and it will soon be dark on this short day.

It is barely three o'clock. The streets are lit up. The crowds are enthusiastic. Napoleon smiles and takes Josephine's hand.

HE DECIDES to dine with her tonight *à deux*. He wants her to keep her crown on. He is enjoying himself, laughing; he goes over to the ladies in waiting and calls out, 'I am the one you have to be so charming to, Mesdames.' His gaze glides over the faces of these young women.

He is spending tonight with Josephine.

He owes her that. He has not forgotten what she has done for him, even if the wounds she has inflicted are still present in his memory.

Tomorrow . . .

Who knows what tomorrow will hold?

His only thought is that he needs descendants.

ON 3 AND 4 DECEMBER, he hears the salvoes of artillery and sees the balloons rising up above the place de la Concorde. In the evening, fireworks light up the low, dark sky. There are fêtes all over the city and he is working. Spain is going to declare war on England, which has itself acquired a new ally in the form of Sweden. In the midst of all these celebrations he must think of the war that is brewing. Shall he put Admiral Villeneuve in charge of the fleet at Toulon? Will he be able to match Latouche Tréville, who died so stupidly?

When, on 5 December, he goes in driving rain to the Champ-de-Mars to distribute the eagles, he knows the troops filing past in the mud, snow and rain will soon be marching under grapeshot. Where? In England or on the soil of continental Europe? The future will tell, but whatever the place of battle, these men will have to confront danger before long.

He goes into the military school where he was once a pupil. It was in the days of Phélyppeaux, his adversary and the defender of St Jean d'Acre – a valiant man but one who had chosen the other camp.

The officers he gives the flags to, which are now crowned with eagles with outspread wings, must not only be heroic but also loyal – attached to him personally.

He receives them in the Tuileries in his study. After calling out each of their names in turn in a stentorian voice, Thiard, the chamberlain, shows in the generals, admirals and colonels who have to swear a personal oath to the Emperor.

He wants this direct connection.

He looks for a long time at each of these men whose deeds of valour, strengths and weaknesses he knows. He says a few words to each of them after they take the oath. Ruling means creating the feeling that the Emperor is speaking and acting for each person individually and that he is expecting an exceptional performance from each of them.

He says to General Lauriston, 'Always remember three things: concentration of one's forces, constant activity, and the firm resolve to perish with glory.' He gets up from his desk. 'These are the three great principles of the military art, which have always made Fortune favourable in all my operations.'

He looks outside and adds in a brusque voice, 'Death is nothing, but to live defeated and without glory is to suffer death every day.'

It snows and freezes during December. Normally so susceptible to the cold, Napoleon barely notices the glacial wind and the gusting snowfalls. The reviews of the national guards from all over the Empire, the army corps that march past, and the representatives of every institution who come to swear allegiance allow him to forget the harshness of the winter.

On Sunday 16 December he goes out onto the balcony of the Hôtel de Ville for the fête offered him by the city of Paris. He lights the huge fireworks; the rockets shoot up; and silhouetted against the sky is a model of Mount St Bernard which belches flames like a volcano as the figure of Bonaparte appears at the top, leading the army across the pass.

I did that.

He remembers it. So many challenges taken up – and perhaps they are not that many, compared to the ones that still await him. When they present themselves he will be stronger, because he is the Emperor of this nation gathered together around him.

A FEW DAYS later, he enters the auditorium of the Opera. Assembled there are all the marshals who have organized a celebration in his honour with their own money. He no longer fears rebellion from some of them. They are marshals, and so they accept him being Emperor. His 'system', as he put it to Roederer, is working.

But what would these men do if one day he was defeated, on the ground?

Is it the time to think of that?

He opens the ball with Josephine amid cheering, in the golden light of a hundred chandeliers.

Why shouldn't he triumph tomorrow as he was victorious yesterday?

He dances in the admiring gaze of the couples who crowd round the dance floor. He still feels so young. He is in his thirty-fifth year.

PART EIGHT

The crowned heads understand nothing: I am not afraid of old Europe

JANUARY 1805 TO AUGUST 1805

XXXII

Napoleon glances at Marie-Antoinette Duchâtel, who is walking with him, leaning on his arm, in the avenues of Malmaison's park. For more than an hour they have been strolling side by side like this in the early afternoon of an icy but sunny January day in 1805. Madame Duchâtel's cheeks are pink with cold and she sometimes shivers, but he has not suggested that they go back. Josephine's guests fill the drawing room. As they chatter away, they must be looking out at the park and then lowering their eyes and voices and acting as if they hadn't seen Napoleon in the company of this young woman. They know all to well what her relations with the Emperor are.

I do what I like.

Josephine must be sighing and grumbling. Hasn't she got everything she wanted? Her religious marriage, the coronation, the glory? Well then, she must accept Madame Duchâtel.

He squeezes her arm. Is she cold? The house is chillier than the park, he says, but he wants to spend a few days here to get away from Paris, go hunting, walk under the trees with her, and talk as well.

Does she know that he never forgets anything? Can she imagine what he was like twenty-five years ago, or even only ten years ago? Sometimes he is amazed himself. In 1795, only ten years ago, he was a half-starved brigadier general who had been in prison a few months before for Robespierrism. Does the name Robespierre make Marie-Antoinette Duchâtel shudder? She is too young to have experienced the Terror.

Ten years ago, too, he was in love with a young woman from Marseille who today is Madame Bernadotte, the marshal's wife – can she believe it?

What shall I be ten years from now, in 1815?

He leads her out of the woods and into the walks where the sunshine provides a little warmth. The light is so bright it is dazzling.

He often comes across people he knew back then, ten or twenty years ago, he continues telling her. Recently he received with full military honours the Marshal de Ségur, who signed his gentleman cadet's certificate twenty-one years ago, in 1784; the old man was so moved by the experience that he almost fainted as he was shown out. He has also seen his landlady at Valence, one or other of his teachers at Brienne and, naturally, the great Laplace, his examiner at the Military School.

I haven't forgotten anything. The participants in the siege of Toulon have been rewarded. Friends or rivals, time has smoothed the differences and all that remains are the memories of those years. Marmont is a marshal and General du Teil, who was in command at Auxonne, has been appointed commandant of Metz fortress.

'I never forget anybody who has helped me . . . or loved me,' he murmurs.

She doesn't ask for anything, but he is not fooled. He recognizes from her voice, as she is passing on one or other of the petty intrigues occupying the salons, that she wants Murat and his wife, whose friend she is, to get ahead. He says he will make Murat a prince and grand admiral. Is she satisfied? She simply smiles. He will also appoint Eugene de Beauharnais arch-chancellor, and make him a French prince. He must maintain a balance between the clans and root his power in all the different self-interests. He has no illusions, even about Marie-Antoinette Duchâtel. He must give, that is what is expected of him, and he needs to so that people remain loyal.

As he listens to her prattling away, in his mind he finishes the list of those he is going to make high dignitaries – there will be six – the civilian grand officers on whom he will bestow the grand sash of the Légion d'honneur amidst the pomp of the throne room. Forty-eight – he remembers the names of them all – will receive the Grand Eagles.

'Do you know,' he says as they head back towards Malmaison's buildings, 'that it is with honour that one achieves everything with men.'

BEFORE THEY go into the drawing room, he whispers to Madame Duchâtel that he will see her in the little house in the allée des

Veuves, off the Champs-Élysées, which he has rented for her so that they can see each other without worrying about a visit from Josephine or one of her unbearable scenes.

JOSEPHINE'S FACE is gaunt and the thick powder on her chin is flaking as her face quivers with rage and bitterness. He smiles at her and leads her to one side. How can she fail to understand that love is not for him? Love is for other people. She knows it is politics that absorbs him completely.

She does not stop frowning. Hasn't he just spent several hours with Madame Duchâtel in the park in the sight of everybody? That hurt her.

She is the Empress, he replies impatiently. He cannot bear the inquisition she subjects him to; she humiliates him with her constant spying; she is just giving his enemies a rod for his back. He will not accept it any longer.

She should set her mind at rest on one thing: 'I do not want in any way to see my court fall under the sway of women. They did Henri IV and Louis XIV harm and my calling is a great deal more serious than that of those princes. Besides the French people have become too solemn to forgive their sovereign having open affairs and acknowledged mistresses.'

Josephine has recovered her equanimity somewhat. She will not complain any more, she whispers.

When the day comes, and it cannot be far off, he says in a cheerful voice, he will ask her 'to help him break off a liaison which barely gives him any satisfaction.'

He must reassure Josephine. Besides, isn't it true that he cannot love any more?

HE RETURNS to the Tuileries and then sets off for St Cloud. Sometimes he forgets where he is: he performs the same gestures so often, accomplishes the same tasks, sees the same faces.

'I am a creature of habit,' he tells Méneval before starting to read the reports of Desmarets, who is in charge of the High Police, the branch of the secret services which is responsible for spying on foreigners. He is just as passionately interested in the memoranda of Fouché's spies and of the *cabinets noirs*, the departments of the post office which open private correspondence. How can he govern without knowing people's opinions and the conspiracies that are being hatched?

His enemies have not disbanded.

He reads an anagram which is going round Paris:

NAPOLEON EMPEREUR DES FRANCAIS

OR

CE FOL EMPIRE NE DURERA PAS SON AN

(This crazy Empire won't last a year)

He looks at the epigrams the spies have picked up in cafés, which people tell each other in low voices,

The prefect's zeal demands admiration, nay awe,
But though he sweep and put down sand at every chance
The Court will still put in an appearance
And everywhere strew muck and filth galore

Napoleon crumples up the sheets of paper, throws them on the ground, and then picks them up again. He finds the text of a poster which was stuck up at the Carrousel, a stone's throw from the Tuileries.

The Imperial Players today present

THE EXCLUSIVE PREMIERE

OF

THE EMPEROR IN SPITE OF THE WHOLE WORLD

followed by

FORCED CONSENT

A charity benefit performance for a poverty-stricken family

People make fun of Pope Pius VII too; *Pistachio*, the lemonade sellers shout to the great hilarity of the idlers on the street, the spies report.

What is Fouché doing? What is the prefect of police doing? These rumours, gibes and pamphlets are a gangrene rotting the country. Can one allow the Pope to be mocked while he is still in Paris?

'I want the prefect of police,' Napoleon dictates, 'to monitor all the masquerades at Carnival in February and prevent people running about the streets in ecclesiastical costume. Furthermore, I want a police department set up to monitor newspapers, theatres, printers and booksellers, and it is to be illegal for anyone to reproduce articles from English newspapers.'

They are our enemies.

AS THE YEAR 1805 gets under way, he has a sense that the time of fêtes is over. He kicks away the police reports which are still strewn all over the floor of his study. These attacks have woken him up, not that he was ever really lost in a dream world – but for a few days in December he did put to the back of his mind the cares that now assail him.

'This is no longer a time for pleasant, frivolous matters,' he says. 'Everything now must be of a grave and serious complexion.'

He stays briefly at Boulogne, reviewing the troops and going aboard several sloops. It is the depths of winter, cold winds and storms. He listens to Admiral Bruix and remembers their dispute, but he is not stubborn this time. The invasion of England will be put off until spring.

Perhaps he should make more effort to avoid war.

He dictates a letter to George III, the King of England: 'I see no dishonour in taking the first step.' He looks hard at Berthier, who is standing next to the desk at which Méneval is writing. The minister of war's surprise is pleasing.

Does he imagine I think the King of England will accept my suggestions? But I must make them nonetheless. If there is a chance to be seized, just one, I will try to seize it, but if there isn't, then the public will know that I wanted peace.

'I have shown sufficient proof that I do not fear any likelihood of war. The world is large enough that our two nations can live in it.'

The world may be, but is Europe?

He spreads out the maps, kneels down and sticks pins with different-coloured heads on the vast expanses of the oceans. Here, at Toulon, is Villeneuve's squadron; there, at Cadiz, that of our Spanish ally, Admiral Gravina; at Brest, Ganteaume's fleet, and at Rochefort, another squadron commanded by Missiessy.

He straightens up, takes a pinch of snuff and walks about, one hand behind his back under his coat-tails.

'It would be enough . . .' he says.

Then he starts dictating. Sometimes he stops, eyes staring as if he sees the squadrons passing in front of him.

Villeneuve, Gravina and Missiessy's fleets are to make for the West Indies, drawing the English fleet after them, and then head back to Europe at full sail. At that moment, Ganteaume is to set out from Brest and blockade the Channel, which will only contain a few English warships, the rest having been sent in pursuit of the French squadrons in the Caribbean: 'Hold out for just two days, Ganteaume. Do not lose sight of the great destinies you will hold in your hands. If you do not lack daring, success is certain.'

Then the Grand Army of Boulogne will cross over to England on gunbrigs and pinnaces.

Villeneuve will leave Toulon on 31 March, Ganteaume will leave Brest on 1 June.

And I shall cross the Channel before 15 June.

'SO, THAT IS the naval plan,' he says.

If only I could command the squadrons, as if they were cavalry and grenadiers.

He is talking to General Lauriston, who has entered his study.

'Our admirals need to be bold, but they must not mistake coasters for warships or merchantmen for fleets.' He grits his teeth. 'There must be decisiveness in their deliberations, and once the squadron has left port, it must go straight to its destination, and not put into harbour or return.'

Except that he is not master of the fleets. The oceans, with their sudden gales and tidal waves, don't obey any logic.

ONE LATE afternoon, Méneval comes in with a new dispatch sent by visual signalling from Boulogne. He looks distressed; Napoleon tears the letter out of his hands.

Admiral Bruix is dead.

Napoleon leaves his study; doors slam. Illness and death, like the ocean, are unpredictable.

He cannot tolerate being beholden to something like this that he has no control over. This is the second admiral who has died, as if there were a curse hanging over all his maritime projects. He puts the thought out of his mind and tells himself that it will take two days to cross the Channel, just two days.

He sits down and has his dinner served on the small mahogany pedestal table in the drawing room next to his study, where he mainly dines alone. It is sautéed chicken with tomatoes, but he only picks at it.

'You do realize that you give me too much to eat, don't you?' he asks his major-domo, Dunan. 'I don't like it, it doesn't agree with me.'

He touches his stomach. He is putting on weight. Dunan brings him his usual cup of coffee, which Napoleon drinks quickly and, as often happens when he bolts his food and drink, he feels as if he is suffocating.

He walks up and down, trying to get his breath back, and asks to be driven to one of the woods on the outskirts of Paris where he will able to feel freer, out in the March wind and rain; the spring of 1805 is a bitter one.

On Thursday 14 March, therefore, he is galloping through the forest of Rambouillet; he wants to see the château where François the First died. He walks through dozens of rooms, which are barely furnished since no one knew he was coming. He opens the windows himself and breathes in the smells of the forest. He is going to spend the night there, like an officer on active service. The staff bustle around him as he warms himself in front of the vast fireplace in which two enormous logs are blazing.

He loves the solitude of such a night, amidst the scurrying activity of quartermaster sergeants and aides-de-camp. He can think deeply. He takes a pinch of snuff and walks up and down a little.

In three days he is going to receive the Italian deputies. Through informers and Melzi, the vice-president of the Italian Republic, he knows that Lombardy's delegates are going to offer him the title of King of Italy.

A new step.

At first he did not want to take it. He has been seeing Joseph since January and has offered him the Italian crown, which Joseph accepted, with certain reservations.

Once again he thought of my death; he said he wanted to keep his rights of succession in France. But how can it fail to concern the European powers if the King of Italy is also the Emperor of the French?

In the end, however, Joseph backed out; he will not be the King of Italy.

Napoleon feels a wave of bitterness. He has since seen Louis and Hortense to propose again that he adopt their son and make him the King of Italy. The scene of Louis's jealousy is a painful memory

'I am that child's father,' Louis shouted before I sent him away.

As for Lucien, he doesn't want to divorce, preferring that woman to the crown.

This is what my brothers are! And so I am going to become King of Italy.

Emperor of the French, King of Italy. Fortune wishes it so. If I don't do something, no one will do it for me.

I used to dream of a dynasty. I wanted to see my brothers around me like sovereigns. Yet I can only bestow one principality, Piombino, on my sister Elisa. As for my descendants . . .

With a brutal kick with the heel of his boot, he shoves one of the logs into the middle of the fire and a huge shower of sparks fans into the air.

ON 17 MARCH, as anticipated, the Italian delegates proclaim him King of Italy, and on the 24th he goes to the Council of State. He listens impassively to the senators' paeans of praise as they hail his new crown.

How many of them think, as Fouché does, and as he has actually dared tell me, that this Italian crown will provoke a war on the continent? As if the kings needed this pretext to try to stifle me and wipe the Revolution off the map!

'The sea may be failing me, but the land won't,' Napoleon had answered Fouché.

He is surrounded by respectful ministers and councillors of

state, and yet he sees expectation in their eyes, he is sure: the belief he will be defeated and fall. Sometimes he wonders if these men don't actually want it, even if it is contrary to all their interests.

They cannot bear my success.

'Old fogies don't understand anything, and the kings haven't got any energy or grit.' He looks intently at each of his councillors and ministers in turn. Apart from Fouché, they all bow their heads.

'I am not afraid of old Europe,' he says.

XXXIII

Napoleon first hears a vague murmur which is obscured by the rattling of the wheels on the rutted road, but gradually voices emerge clear and distinct: 'Long live the Emperor!' His berline slows down and he leans out of the window. The quartermaster's carriage in front has been reduced to walking pace, the crowd of peasants at the side of the road is so dense.

'Long live the Emperor!'

Women and children run alongside and he waves at them. This is the first time since he left Fontainebleau, where he slept the night of 1 April, that there has been such enthusiasm. A few hours before, at Troyes, the crowd was curious more than anything else, and it seemed slightly intimidated. He explained to the town's authorities that he is going to Milan to accept the King of Italy's iron crown, and that he is going to visit the principal cities of that kingdom which he has created out of nothing. He will also return to the battlefields of Castiglione and Marengo.

The moment the berline had moved off and driven out of the courtyard of Fontainebleau, he was certain that this journey to Italy would also be a sort of pilgrimage to the sites of his first years of glory – and if Josephine had insisted on going with him so vehemently, it was also because of her memories of Italy, of the start of his success and a time when a young general felt a great passion for her.

The time of my jealousy.

He had not thought their route would take them so close to Brienne, to those years of often bitter loneliness, twenty-five years ago. It is two o'clock in the afternoon on Wednesday 3 April 1805 and he says that he is going to go to Brienne, and that Josephine can carry on with the greater part of the convoy towards Lyon. This is how, in the early evening, his berline comes to be moving through this crowd of peasants shouting 'Long live the Emperor!'

Couriers had to be sent on from Troyes to prepare the stop. He looks about and sees Brienne château, where he was a guest once, when he was only a taciturn child who dreamt of his native island. Women and children are crowded together, waving scarves, standing on carts from which the oxen have been unharnessed, and in the middle of the groups fires are burning, because it is cold and the sky is low.

It seems to him as if he recognizes these woods and hedges from the time of his first marches and manoeuvres. He remembers every detail, and familiar faces spring out at him.

Here are some coming towards him in the main hall of the château. The school is just waste ground now, he is told. The Revolution passed like a tornado, they sigh; the buildings were pillaged, sold, abandoned and then destroyed. He sits in a window recess while he waits for Madame de Brienne to show him to his room, which was once occupied by the Duc d'Orléans. He tries to make out the ruins of the school in the gathering darkness. He will go there tomorrow.

Then he says, 'The time of the Revolution is over, there is only one party in France now.'

IT IS STILL dark, but as a child in winter he was up at this time in his school dormitory. He was cold, always cold, and perhaps this cold has never really left him.

He walks among the ruins of the school, picking his way through the rubble, with his equerry Luis de Canisy, Madame de Brienne's nephew. The dormitory might have been here. There, next to that hedge, he made his hermitage where he used to read on his own. Once a firework had gone off and chests of firecrackers, or ammunition, had exploded and, as they stampeded, the terrified schoolboys had destroyed that refuge he had taken months to build.

Suddenly he falls silent and mounts his horse, and before his suite can follow he rides off down the Bar-sur-Aube road on his own.

He follows the promptings of his memory, making for a clump of trees he remembers or a remote house, leaping hedges and streams in the bright sunshine and feeling intoxicated by the smell of the earth. Riding through the past like this both troubles and exhilarates him. Some peasants straighten up when he flies past. In their fearful, surprised attitude, he sees how astonished they are by this rider going hell for leather over the fields and disappearing into the woods.

He is free. Free. Nothing and no one can constrain him. He alone chooses his route.

He hears a gunshot: his aides-de-camp are looking for him and calling him back. He rides on, but then slowly reins in his horse and returns at a trot to Brienne château, where Caulaincourt, Canisy and the officers of his suite rush forward to meet him.

He jumps off his horse.

He will not have Brienne school rebuilt. The past will only be used to invent the future.

He returns to Troyes and then, on 5 April, sets off for Semur, Chalon, Mâcon and Bourg. It is years since he has driven through this country that he has seen so many times in his life. He is enthusiastically cheered; the workers at Creusot fire cannon in salute.

He recognizes an old woman who comes up to him in Chalon. He had enjoyed her hospitality when he was a second lieutenant in the La Fère regiment. For a moment he is shocked. She is so old that it feels as if he sees in front of him all the time that has passed. How many years are left for him to see his destiny through, and accomplish what is in him and what he has as yet only sketched out?

He murmurs to Caulaincourt who is standing near him, a few paces back, 'Believe me Caulaincourt, I am a man. Whatever some people may say, I feel compassion, I have a heart.' He pays no attention to what the local dignitaries are saying as they come up, one after the other, to present themselves to him. 'But it is a sovereign's heart,' he goes on. 'I don't feel pity at a duchess's tears, but I am touched by the sufferings of the people. I want them to be happy, and the French will be. Everyone will be comfortable if I live for another ten years. Do you think I don't like giving pleasure too. It does me good to see a happy face, but I am forced to be wary of this natural tendency because people otherwise would take advantage of it.'

He shakes his head as if he wants to shake off these thoughts and put an end to this soliloquy.

HE GETS INTO the berline and resumes reading all the dispatches concerning the movements of the fleets since he has left Fontainebleau. Villeneuve has, according to plan, run out of Toulon on 30 March, given Nelson the slip and, after passing Cadiz and linking up with Admiral Gravina's Spanish squadron, reached Martinique.

'I am almost starting not to feel any anxiety,' he writes to Vice-Admiral Decrès, minister of the marine.

If he was one of these admirals and commanded at sea, nothing could withstand him; but he must make do with writing to Vice-Admiral Ganteaume, whose squadron is still in Brest: 'I hope you will set off from the rendezvous point with more than fifty ships. You have the destiny of the world in your hands.'

Will Ganteaume understand? Will these admirals be equal to their roles?

He lets his gaze wander over the banks of the Saône. He recognizes the outskirts of Lyon where he is going to see Josephine again. From there they will set off for Turin, where he is to meet up with the Pope, who left Paris a few days before him, and then on to Milan and the coronation.

He dictates his instructions for Vice-Admiral Verheull, who is in command of the Dutch fleet, and then, as if talking to himself, he adds, 'The hour of glory is perhaps not far away. Now it depends on a few strokes of luck and some events.'

It is Fortune who holds the reins.

He carries on and Méneval writes: 'We need only be masters of the sea for six hours for England to cease to exist.'

HE STOPS dictating as the berline crosses place Bellecour. He remembers how three years ago, the people of Lyon had written asking permission to give this square, on which he had reviewed the troops back from Egypt, the name of place Bonaparte. It seems as if he can hear his voice dictating to Bourrienne, 'No place Bonaparte. Names should never be used if the owner is alive.'

But now he is the Emperor. He has founded a dynasty. He is the one they cheer on the quays of the Saône and in the archiepiscopal palace. He is the one the crowds want to touch when he is walking to the foundations of a new bridge which is going to be thrown across the river, and everybody is waiting for him to light the first firework marking the start of the building. He has therefore agreed to two cities in the west, La Roche-sur-Yon and Pontivy, being renamed Napoleon-Vendée and Napoleon-Ville, in what used to be the heart of rebel, Chouan country.

HE TALKS to the notables who flock around him after the banquet given by the city, who listen to him as if to an oracle. He looks past these grave men's faces to Josephine, surrounded by her readers and ladies of honour who have made the journey. He speaks quickly, in clipped sentences, because he wants to go over to these young women – Madame Gazzini, perhaps, a beautiful young woman from Genoa who he noticed at Fontainebleau when they were leaving, or that Mademoiselle Guillebaud who lowers her eyes every time he looks fixedly at her.

'A state must have fixed principles,' he says. 'As long as one does not learn from childhood whether one should be republican or monarchist, Catholic or non-religious, the State will not form a nation. It will rest on unsteady and blurred foundations and will be constantly exposed to disorder and change.'

I am the one who incarnates these fixed principles now; I represent the nation's only party.

'Semi-intellectuals, who have no basis for their morality and no fixed ideas, must be made to hold their peace,' he adds. It is no longer the time to encourage people to read Rousseau or strive as philosophers to win the prize of the Lyon academy.

He has done that in the past.

'I would rather see the children of a village in the hands of a monk who doesn't know any of his catechism but whose principles I know, than in the clutches of one of those semi-intellectuals . . .' He looks defiantly round at the circle of people about him, but they agree noisily with what he is saying. 'States never prosper through ideology,' he adds.

He starts off towards the group of women and, looking back, adds, 'Force of arms is their primary support.' *These cloth and silk merchants, these financiers, have to know that we are at war and that it is the sword that decides*. He goes back over to them. 'States need to trust,' he sums up.

For the past few days the bankers have been very reluctant to lend the necessary sums.

Do they think one wins wars just with soldiers? Barbé-Marbois, the treasury minister, has been gulled by Ouvrard, that bullion dealer who is in touch with this or that banker in Holland, who himself is in contact with the City of London, and so Barings Bank – Pitt, in other words – will be the one deciding my finances if I don't do anything about it.

He talks about money for a few minutes. 'While I live I will not issue any paper.'

He remembers the assignats, that currency that ran through your fingers. Both Louis XVI and Robespierre, at either ends of the spectrum, had their heads cut off for financial reasons. The bankers are the ones who, from the shadows, control the workings of the guillotine.

'I wish to establish and make ready for my successors resources which will take the place of the extraordinary methods I have been able to create.'

He doesn't wait for them to agree before making his way over to the Empress, those young women and the officers who surround them.

But who will my successors be if I die without descendants?

HE IS SURROUNDED by women. Beside Madame Gazzini and Mademoiselle Guillebaud are Caroline's ladies in waiting.

One would think that my sister has chosen these young women especially for me. What is she hoping? That I will leave Josephine for one of them? Or is it just to wound and humiliate the Empress, and take their revenge for not being first, that my sisters – Elisa and Pauline are just the same – act like this?

A little off to one side stands a young woman, or, rather, a young girl. Her bearing is so discreet that she must be a Lyonnaise, because she doesn't have that impertinence of Parisian women, whether they belong to his Court or the Palais Royal.

He goes up to her and questions her brusquely. She is awkward, stammering her name – François-Émilie Marie Leroy. He likes those names, he tells her. She is the first woman that he knows of to have them. He leads her away.

Neither in war nor in love – but aren't they the same thing? – is he a man of sieges; he is a man of attacks.

JOSEPHINE ACCEPTS it. She knows that I don't want to see her face distorted with jealousy any more. She is the Empress, isn't that enough? She enters Milan Cathedral at my side, receiving her full share of glory, even if this Italian royalty is mine alone.

Napoleon puts the iron crown of the King of Italy on his own head. The Piazza del Duomo is full of an excited crowd who cheer him heartily.

'God gives this to me,' he says as he takes hold of the crown. 'Woe to him who touches it.' Then, in a lower voice, he adds, 'I hope this will be prophetic.'

A few days later he decides to annex Genoa and Liguria to France. He makes the Republic of Lucca a principality and entrusts it to his sister Princess Elisa, who already governs Piombino.

Things are simple as soon as one has the strength and the determination.

Besides, who could stop me? The Pope? In Turin Pius VII has been perfectly agreeable in return for several concessions which will establish a religious system in the Kingdom of Italy identical to that of the Concordat.

Will England have the means to wage war against me here?

'A nation is mad indeed when it has no fortifications and no land army,' he remarks to Caulaincourt. If they get the six hours they need, England will see 'a seasoned, elite army of a hundred thousand men landing in the heart of their country'.

What will it be able to do to resist me? Form an alliance with Russia?

The King of England and the Tsar of Russia have concluded a treaty to drive France back to its 1789 frontiers, instal a government in Paris that suits them and erase the Revolution.

Who could do that?

'There are people who think I lack bile or claws. Write to them in heaven's name that they shouldn't bank on it,' he tells Talleyrand.

Let them come up against me if they dare!

He is sure of himself. He visits the battlefields from the early days of his glory: Marengo, Castiglione. Cheers ring out as he enters the cities he once conquered, such as Mantua and Verona, and of which he is now the King. He visits Bologna, Modena, Piacenza and Genoa. He drills thirty thousand troops on the battlefield of Marengo, and Milan's garrison marches past on the Foro Bonaparte.

He loves this countryside, these towns and these bridges which he once crossed at the head of his troops. He loves this Italian spring. He goes for long rides and sometimes wears out five horses in a day.

Occasionally a painful memory surfaces. One day he goes up on the fortifications of Verona and is looking at the city with its tile roofs like a red lake.

'My poor brother Louis,' he says. 'This is where he had the most terrible accident, in this same city, during our first campaign. A woman he barely knew broke into his house. Since then he has been prone to nervous attacks that vary according to the atmosphere, and of which he has never been able to cure himself.'

Look, the shadows are drawing in again: Louis, sick, hostile, refusing to let his eldest son be adopted. And what about Lucien?

Napoleon unburdens himself to Caulaincourt; his voice is hard and he gestures agitatedly as he says, 'Lucien prefers a disgraced woman who gave him a child before they were married to the honour of his name and his family.'

These thoughts wound him in the last hot days of June, which he spends in Genoa. He looks at the bed which, according to the Genoese who show him the room, is the one Charles V slept in.

So, he is a man who people compare to the greatest rulers of history, and at the same time one whose brothers refuse to help him. He is the Emperor without sons.

He carries on in a bitter voice. 'All he can do is moan,' he says of Lucien's aberrant behaviour. 'A man whom nature caused to be born with every talent and whom a matchless egotism has deprived of a host of admirable fates and led far from the path of duty and honour.' He goes towards the window of his room in the palace which looks over the port of Genoa. Three frigates and two brigs are manoeuvring under full sail. He watches them for a long time.

A few hours ago he had to alter his plan for the descent on

England. Villeneuve has not been able to join up with Missiessy in the Caribbean and so all the planned manoeuvres have fallen behind. The invasion of England will take place between 8 and 18 August and not this month, June.

He leans his elbows on the window and contemplates the boats. Jérôme is in command of them – Jérôme, who has agreed to give up his American wife and listen to reason.

Perhaps he is the only one of my brothers who will obey me? Perhaps I won't find any support in my family? And if I don't have any sons, who can I rely on?

PERHAPS ON Eugene de Beauharnais, who he has just appointed viceroy of Italy. He tells Roederer, 'If a cannon fires, Eugene is the one who will go and see what is happening. If I have a ditch to cross, he is the one who gives me his hand.'

He has confidence in this dignified, courageous, young twenty-three-year-old. He would like to help him in the extremely difficult job of governing men. 'Our subjects in Italy are naturally more dissembling than the citizens of France,' he writes to Eugene. 'Do not accord your entire confidence to anyone . . . Speak as little as possible, for your education has not been sufficiently thorough to allow you to indulge in discussions. Learn how to listen. Show such esteem for the nation you govern as is appropriate, particularly as you accumulate reasons for esteeming it less. A time will come when you realize that there is very little difference between one people and another.'

What of the people? He observes and listens to them throughout his return journey to France at the start of July.

On the outskirts of Lyon he has his berline stop on a short cut and the crowds in the fields head towards the road to cheer and catch a glimpse of him. He alights from his carriage and begins to walk towards the steep hill of Tarare, having got rid of those of his entourage who want to follow him. He wants to mingle with the crowd on his own and see the people.

NOW HE IS alone, no one recognizes him. He slowly climbs the hill and questions an old woman he comes across. What is she doing there?

'The Emperor is going to pass this way,' she says.

He chats with her, studying her every gesture. She is of the people who live far from palaces.

'You have the tyrant Capet and then you have the tyrant Napoleon. What the devil have you gained from the likes of them?' He bends down towards her and sees confusion on her wrinkled face.

'Forgive me sir, but there is a great difference between them.' She nods and smiles mischievously. 'We chose this one and got the other one by chance.' She raises her voice. 'One was the nobility's king and the other is the people's king, he is ours.'

Napoleon strides briskly back down the hill, whistling and taking pinches of snuff. 'I like the basic good sense you find on the streets,' he tells Méneval and then gets into his berline.

XXXIV

IS IT THE HEAVY HEAT of these final days of July 1805, or having to wait for news of the fleets? Whatever the reason, Napoleon cannot stop himself losing his temper several times a day. He sends for Murat, who arrives resplendent in his uniform of grand admiral, prince, grand eagle and chief of the 12th cohort of the Légion d'honneur. Before he has been asked anything, he begins talking about the collection of paintings he has assembled in the Élysée Palace.

A fine time and place to talk about paintings! What stage are the troops at? Are they drilling? Are supplies secured?

Murat stutters.

Napoleon flies into a fury in Fontainebleau park, walking by its lakes. The weather is stormy, but the rain won't fall and the heat builds up under a low sky which is shattered by long bolts of lightning.

It feels as if the electricity is crawling over my skin.

Napoleon shivers and goes back inside.

What news? Where are the admirals? What is Ganteaume doing? What is Villeneuve doing? Do they know where Nelson is?

He writes to Ganteaume, 'Great events are taking place or about to take place; do not render your forces useless . . . Be prudent, but bold too.'

He writes to Villeneuve, 'For the great aim of enabling a descent on England, that power which has oppressed France for six centuries, we could all die without regret. These are the feelings with which all my soldiers should be inspired.'

Bent over his desk, he examines the state of the different fleets: seventy-four ships for the French and Spanish, barely fifty-four for the English.

But why are the admirals waiting to take action? He feels ensnared, bound hand and foot. The sticky heat clings to his skin. The couriers set off with instructions to ride their horses into the ground if need be, but to reach Brest, Vigo or Cadiz without stopping once.

How can he decide if he doesn't know where the squadrons are or what they are doing?

In the meantime, Talleyrand confirms, England is urging Austria to join the conflict, and Russia is already in league with London. If Vienna dares . . .

He receives Cambacérès and the treasury minister, Barbé-Marbois. He stands in front of the open window. Not a breath of wind. If the weather is the same on the ocean, the fleets will never reach Boulogne.

He turns to Cambacérès. The arch-chancellor is concerned, Barbé-Marbois even more so. The financiers are baulking, he explains. They've got us by the throat; they're afraid of the hazards of an invasion of England.

Napoleon starts walking up and down, his hands behind his back.

'Reassure the money-grubbers,' he says in a muffled voice.

What can he do to control them? What can he do without them?

'Make them understand that no risks will be taken that haven't been provided for.'

What do these fellows think – that one wages war on an impulse? Nothing is more carefully analysed than one of my campaigns.

'My affairs are in such good order that I am not going to risk anything that will jeopardize the happiness and prosperity of my people. Most likely I will land with my army, everyone should see the necessity of that, but . . .' He raises his hand. 'I and my army will only land when everything possible is in our favour.' As for Austria, if it does not disarm, 'I shall go with two hundred thousand men and pay it a good visit which it will remember for a long time.'

He turns to Cambacérès. 'Tell them you don't think it's going to be war. One would have to be very deluded to go to war against me.' He smiles. 'There is no finer army in Europe than the one I have today.'

HE LEAVES Fontainebleau for the château of St Cloud.

He must calm himself, but the heat is just as oppressive there. He sleeps badly. He hits Roustam and Constant and demands

Méneval's presence at every moment of the day. He has to write so that his words will affect men like spurs. 'Enter the Channel,' he dictates for Villeneuve, 'and England is ours. Be there for twenty-four hours and all is ended.'

When dusk comes, the heat loosens its grip a little and he goes out to make a start on what will be too long a night. Often he goes to the opera or theatre and sometimes he brings the actors to St Cloud. But will he be able to laugh at *The Wise Women*?

The questions still seethe inside him. Will he be able to cross this sound or not? Will he plant the tricolour on the Tower of London?

He goes up to the actors. He likes the theatre world, these provocative, often beautiful and always experienced women who are so easy to conquer.

They succeed in distracting him. Talma is speaking with that storyteller's skill which transforms a little story of an affair between a lady and a dignitary into a great moment of comedy or tragedy. For a few minutes everything disappears and only Talma remains.

Napoleon likes to watch the the actor, listen to him and then talk to him. 'You use your arm too much,' he says on one July evening after a performance of *The Death of Pompey*. 'Leaders of an empire are less flamboyant in their movements; they know a gesture is an order, and that a look can mean death, so they are sparing with them . . . Don't make Caesar talk like Brutus – when one says he abhors kings we must believe him, but not the other. Mark the difference.'

Madame de Rémusat comes over. Why is she surprised he is talking to Talma like this? He is only an actor, she says, and the Emperor seems to have more regard for him than an ambassador or even a general.

He laughs. 'You know full well that a talent, in whatever field, is a genuine source of power, and that I never receive Talma, as you have seen, without taking off my hat.' Then he adds in a whisper, 'There are also some women of great talent.'

Madame de Rémusat slips away. Has she turned faithful? But still, there is Madame Duchâtel – and Madame Gazzini – and Émilie Leroy who has just arrived from Lyons at his request and who he has married to a Monsieur Pellapra, a very understanding financier who will be made receiver of finances in Caen to allay his scruples, if he has any.

That way the July nights grow ever shorter, and then dawn comes and the spies' reports are laid out prominently on his desk.

They are what Napoleon always reads first.

In certain cafés, the informers report, people are amazed the Fourteenth of July wasn't marked by any fête, and criticize the announcement of ceremonies and balls on the 15 August, the 'Feast of St Napoleon'. They make ill-natured fun of him, and worry about the rumours of war and a new coalition that is going to ruin France. Some claim that the times of the assignats are going to return; people are hiding their gold.

He throws these reports on the floor. Does he want this war?

One spy alleges that, far from going to the United States, as he had pledged to do after his trial, General Moreau is living in Spain and telling everyone that he is going to fight for the Tsar, lead a royal army, and put an end to Bonaparte and the Revolution.

Wouldn't it have been better if the judges had sentenced him to death?

Who pardoned him? I did. Who is he betraying? Me and France, his country. Can one seriously contemplate not responding?

On Friday 2 August, at three o'clock in the morning, when it is still pitch black, he sets off in his large berline for Boulogne to join the army.

AT EVERY STOP he jumps down from the carriage before the footboard has even been unfolded and, with his hands behind his back, his face expressionless, indifferent to the cheers of the little crowd which gathers each time, he paces up and down outside the buildings of the relay, in the courtyard. He begins to show signs of impatience after a matter of minutes and an aide-de-camp comes running up to tell him that the horses have been harnessed.

In the berline he dictates orders to the Highways Department to begin urgent repairs on the roads leading south and east from Paris, towards Turin and Cologne. If he has to give up the idea of invading England, then he will have to march to Germany to crush Austria, as well as the Russians, if they have had time to reach the battlefields.

He must consider this hypothesis seriously, and it irritates him so much he grows furious and gives the order to bypass the final stages and work the horses to death if need be. He wants to be at the château of Pont-de-Briques as soon as possible.

Sometimes, as he is driving through a village, he sees a triumphal arch with the inscription 'The Road to England' and these words fan his anger. It still has him in its grip when he enters the courtyard of the château of Pont-de-Briques at four o'clock in the morning on Saturday 3 August. His boiling hot bath is ready and Roustam is standing in the door, but Napoleon wants to give his orders first: general review, all troops, tomorrow, Sunday, from ten o'clock onwards.

THIS IS HOW he calms himself and this is how he waits: every day a review. On Sunday 4 August he is on horseback from ten in the morning to five in the afternoon, and from Cap d'Alprech to Cap Gris-Nez he gallops along the divisions.

There isn't a single day until 13 August when he doesn't inspect the men and the ships. He boards the sloops and goes out to the anchorage line. He looks over the maps again: the main landing of eighty thousand men will be at Deal, thirteen kilometres from Dover. London will be only two or three days march away.

He gives a great dinner for the officers in his quarters in the Odre lighthouse. He says little, letting the generals talk about the crossing, the English countryside, the beauties of London, the English whores and the émigrés' fears, how they will take flight.

They will be rid of the broker of coalitions. Peace will finally be established when the English fox is crushed in his earth.

He says nothing, but when the dinner is over he questions Méneval and then Monge and then Daru, who is the general administrator of the army and has organized the camp at Boulogne since 1803.

'Where is Villeneuve?' he keeps asking, barking the question in an infuriated voice.

He goes out of the barrack-huts. The wind is strong but the sky is clear. One can hear the breakers. The sea is there, a few dozen metres below. It would just need a handful of hours to cross it. Sometimes, as on this evening, there is a moment when he longs to give the order to embark and set sail without waiting for the fleets to arrive, trusting to Fortune instead, but he puts it out of his mind. War is not a game of chance. He cannot risk this army which, if he decides to turn about, will allow him to crush Austria and Russia, he is sure of it. Then he will become master of all Europe and England can rot in its hole.

He stays standing on the edge of the cliff for a long time. When he goes back inside, he says to Daru, 'In war as in politics, wasted opportunities never present themselves a second time.'

IT IS DAWN on 13 August.

He is in the château of Pont-de-Briques, looking at the maps of Germany. He hears the gallop of a horse and then the voices of the grenadiers of the Guard and one of his aides-de-camp. A courier has arrived from Admiral Villeneuve.

He tears it out of the officer's hands.

Villeneuve has put into Ferrol instead of making for the Channel at full sail where I am waiting for him!

Napoleon throws the dispatch on the floor.

'Get me Daru!' he shouts.

He takes pinches of snuff as he waits, and dictates a brief letter to Talleyrand: 'My decision is made. I want to attack Austria and be in Vienna before this coming November to confront the Russians if they present themselves. Or else I want . . .' He stays silent for a long while. Perhaps everything has not yet been decided. Perhaps the Austrians will not commit themselves to the war. Perhaps Admiral Villeneuve will overcome his fear and reach here before the end of summer. 'Or else I want, and that is the *mot juste*, there to be not a single Austrian regiment left in the Tyrol. I wish to be left to wage war on England in peace.'

Then he dictates dispatches to the minister of the marine for Villeneuve: if he still can, he must force him to act. Then he throws himself, more than sits, on a chair facing the desk which is covered with maps.

He glances over them, stands up, takes a pinch of snuff, and then with a wave signals to Daru that he is about to start dictating.

His voice is calm, his steps measured and the words unerringly precise. He gives the places, the days, the strengths; his eyes seem to follow the troops' marches in Germany. He will unleash seven torrents under the commands of Marmont, Bernadotte, Soult, Lannes, Ney and Augereau. Wurtzburg, Frankfurt, Mannheim, Spire, Karslruhe and Strasbourg are the destinations of the seven armies. He decides on the halting places, the number of kilometres to be covered at 3.9 kilometres per hour, and where the supply and ammunition depots will be established.

He talks for several hours as if, for months already, an exact disposition had been taking shape under all the waiting and uncertainty, so it could burst out now on this thirteenth day of August. He is going to pivot the army, and send it by forced marches deep into the heart of Germany.

He has finished. Only then does he seem to realize Daru is there, still writing, surrounded by dozens of pieces of paper covered in his notes.

Is everything decided?

He does not want to throw the dice yet. Everything is ready for either of the two games.

'If Admiral Villeneuve appears in the Channel, there is still time. I will be master of England,' he writes to Talleyrand. 'If, on the other hand, my admirals waver, manoeuvre badly and do not accomplish their goals, I will have no alternative but to wait for winter to cross with the flotilla and the operation would be dangerous. In those circumstances, I shall attend to the most urgent matters first. I shall find myself with 200,000 men in Germany and 25,000 in the Kingdom of Naples. I shall march on Vienna and not lay down arms until I have Naples and Venice, and have so added to the states of the Elector of Bavaria that I shall never have anything to fear from Austria again. Austria will certainly be pacified this way during winter. I shall not be coming back to Paris except to pass through. My intention is to gain two weeks. I want to be in the heart of Germany with 200,000 before anyone suspects a thing.'

He waits. It rains every day, but the wind is weak and the sea calm. On the night of 20–21 August, he goes out on the cliff and calls for his aides-de-camp. Let the drums beat and the bugles sound: all troops are to head for the port and embark.

After a few minutes he hears the first shouts coming from the port, mingled with the drumming and bugle calls, and then soon the rumble of troops on the march.

He stays standing on the cliff until dawn.

He could try to act without the fleet.

He could.

In war daring is the finest tactic that genius can use – but will this be daring, or one of the worst faults a military leader can have: a frenzied imagination, the sort that loses battles?

He goes back into his hut, with his head bowed, and gives the order for the troops to disembark.

Now the decision is taken. It is as if he had to follow one hypothesis through to its conclusion to put himself to the test.

He reads Villeneuve's dispatch, which Decrès, the minister of the marine, sends on to him on 22 August, and crushes the letter in his fist. Villeneuve has put into harbour and is staying there.

It's no surprise and yet still his anger explodes and he bellows the thoughts that has been welling up in him for days: 'Villeneuve doesn't have enough character to command a frigate! He is a man with neither firmness nor moral courage!' He shakes his head, his hands clasped behind his back, his body almost tipping over as if he is going to run at someone. 'Two Spanish ships have been boarded, a few men have fallen ill, an enemy warship has come to observe him, there's a wind and rumours that Nelson is about – and this is enough to make Villeneuve change his plans! He is a poor fellow who sees double and has greater powers of delusion than he does strength of character.'

Napoleon takes a pinch of snuff and then spits contemptuously on the floor.

'He is a man who has no familiarity with war and no knowledge of how to wage it.'

Everything has become clear; the gangrene of waiting is over.

Daru has written up the different dispatches for each of the army leaders and now they go off.

'I am changing my dispositions,' Napoleon writes to Masséna. 'The coalition is not expecting the speed with which I will cause my 200,000 men to pivot. My movement has begun. The aim is to gain twenty days and prevent the Austrians crossing the Inn while I bear down on the Rhine.'

He consults the maps almost blithely. He has never fought in Germany. He is going to show that Emperor Napoleon is superior even to General Bonaparte. He has just entrusted command of the Army of Italy to Masséna. He thinks of Lodi, Arcola, Marengo. How young he was then, still inexperienced. Now he knows; he has seen so many battlefields, commanded so many men.

He dictates the order of the day:

> Brave soldiers of the Camp of Boulogne! You shall not be going to England. English gold has seduced the Emperor of Austria who has just declared war on France. His army has broken the line it should have held and Bavaria has been invaded. Soldiers, fresh laurels await you on the other side of the Rhine! Let us fly to defeat enemies whom we have already defeated before!

He goes to the edge of the Odre cliff. It is a clear day. The pinnaces moored in rows bob up and down in the harbour. Dust is rising past Boulogne, inland.

The troops are already on the march.

PART NINE

Soldiers, I am satisfied with you

September 1805 to December 1805

XXXV

HE WOULD LIKE to be at the head of his troops in Germany already, but he wants to throw the coalition of England, Austria and Russia off the scent and so he forces himself to resume his routine at Malmaison and St Cloud. He chats away in Josephine's drawing room, and then smiles at one of the young women who come and find him in the evening after receiving word from Constant, but he is hardly in the mood for these diversions. The troops are on the march; he imagines them on the side of the road. They set off at dawn to cover a stage of thirty to forty kilometres every day. They stop five minutes every hour and halt halfway. The drums lead the columns and bring up the rear. He would like to be amongst them because he knows that just by his presence he gives fresh energy to those staggering and sometimes dropping with fatigue. He learnt that in the deserts of Egypt and Palestine.

The men have to advance by forced marches to take the enemy by surprise. Speed is my weapon.

HE IS SITTING in front of the fireplace where a fire is burning because the woods of St Cloud are cool again. Carlotta Gazzini is flirting and chattering away. He isn't listening, but her voice is calming. He mulls over the procedures he has fine-tuned, the details of which he has clarified in the dispatches he has sent to the marshals. Daru has put into practice the plan he dictated on 13 August. The armies of Ney, Lannes and Marmont will fall on the right flank of General Mack, who has advanced into Bavaria with sixty thousand or so Austrians. Murat's cavalry will lead Mack to expect a frontal attack while he is being cut off from his rear and his flanks are then routed.

But everything depends on the legs and feet of the infantry, just as in Italy or Egypt, and the challenge is greater than at Marengo or Aboukir because, if he is beaten, the losses will be enormous. Everything he has erected, the new institutions like blocks of granite, will be overthrown. It is what London, Vienna and St

Petersburg want. As for Prussia, still playing a cautious game, it will waste no time falling into the same camp.

The kings and emperors are against me. And the 'money men' are watching me. Every morning police reports tell of banks crowded with people wanting to exchange notes or bills for gold. The treasury is empty.

Winning the war will fill it.

THE PLAN must be kept secret for twenty days or thereabouts, enough time for the armies to spread through Germany like 'seven torrents', and so he must stay here at Malmaison or St Cloud, or go to the State Council and see Roederer.

'There are two different men in me; the man of the head and the man of the heart. Don't think that I don't have a sensitive heart like other men, I am even fairly kind-hearted, but from a very young age I took pains to mute this chord which now no longer makes any sound for me,' he says.

Does Roederer believe him?

Or does he understand that I must be thought to be severe and hard and unfeeling? And that that sometimes spares me the need to be so?

However!

He seizes a dispatch which he has just received from the Minister of Marine. That incompetent Villeneuve has sequestered himself in Cadiz! Doesn't that deserve an exemplary punishment?

Napoleon's anger explodes as if all the tension that has been building in him for weeks provokes these words that shoot forth like lightning. 'Villeneuve has gone too far now,' he cries out. 'There is no longer a name for his behaviour. He is a villain who should be ignominiously discharged. Without tactical ability, without courage, without thinking of others, he would sacrifice everything so long as he could save his own skin!'

HE SHUTS himself away with the maps of Germany. He marks the most advanced positions of troops on the march, but since the arrival of the couriers they must have covered dozens more kilometres. It is here that the game will be decided, and this is where he must devote all his forces, even if it is difficult to forget

Villeneuve and the missed opportunities that have left England unconquered.

He feels a surge of weariness that lasts for a few minutes at most in which he thinks of the unforeseeable obstacles that could rear up and prevent him realizing the grand designs he has dreamed of.

His road to Asia was blocked at St Jean d'Acre because an Englishman was there. Now the conquest of England is impossible. He *must* be victorious in Germany, then. There is no other choice. Tomorrow he will have the Senate decree a levy of sixty thousand conscripts and he will set off to join the Grand Army. This is what he is going to call the divisions marching to Germany, because has there ever been as large an army? There are 186,000 men, almost thirty thousand of whom are foreigners: Italians, Belgians, Dutch, Swiss, Syrians, Irish and others – mercenaries and those who have rallied to France's cause.

It is the army of my Empire.

HE WANTED Josephine to accompany him as far as Strasbourg. He looks at her sitting in the berline, facing him, as the countryside goes past the window. It is shrouded by the persistent rain of these last days of September.

It is damp and cold. Josephine is swathed in a large shawl, but as soon as they draw near to a town, she straightens up, powders herself, gets her hair back in order, and at places like La Ferté-sous-Jouarre, Bar-le-Duc and Nancy, she smiles at the authorities who come and pay homage.

He was right to want her close to him. Her presence is reassuring. This war can't be that ferocious or long, people will think, since she has come too. Men need hopes and illusions.

ON THURSDAY 26 September, at five o'clock in the afternoon, the berline stops at the Saverne Gate in Strasbourg. He gives Josephine his hand and they walk amidst the guards of honour towards the mayor, who offers him the keys of the city. The crowd pushes forward, applauding, and follows the procession that passes through streets hung with flags and garlands of flowers.

He walks ahead, through the Rohan palace, as Josephine falls behind. He listens to her answering graciously, congratulating the mayor on receiving them in such a luxuriously furnished building. He takes his leave. Let her take care of the good people of Strasbourg and flatter and fête them. He has the Austrians to think about, and a war to wage and win.

HE DOES NOT sleep. He hears the rain falling and thinks of the troops in the fields, waiting to set off again at dawn to cross the Rhine.

He has ordered his generals to be on the bridge of Kehl at six o'clock today, Friday 27 September, but he is already up at four and Roustam has run his hot bath. At five o'clock, when it is still dark, surrounded by twenty-two light cavalry of the Guard, a trumpeter and their commanding officer, he waits on horseback at the head of the bridge.

At last he is here, among his soldiers. It is pouring with rain, the drummers can't set a marching rhythm, but the troops pass and occasionally shout 'Long live the Emperor!' The Guard appear in their tall bearskins, and they break step as they cross the bridge. The water runs off their moustaches and their curling side whiskers, obligatory marks of membership of this elite, highly paid troop.

Napoleon sits straight on his horse. He doesn't feel the rain rolling down his badly soaked, misshapen hat and his sodden, heavy greatcoat. This is how one commands men who are going to die, by remaining at their side. He stays motionless at the head of the bridge for several hours.

He must be seen; every soldier must know that the Emperor was there, and that he is going to lead the campaign.

LATER HE returns to the mirrors, carpets and pictures of the Rohan palace. In one of the drawing rooms, lit by dozens of candles, he sees Talleyrand, whose presence in Strasbourg he has demanded, Josephine in a long taffeta dress, and the Prince Electors of Baden and Württemberg whom he wants to make his allies, like Bavaria, in order to create a barrier of states dominated by him between Austria and France.

He starts towards these gentlemen in their court attire and

catches sight of himself in the mirrors, splattered with mud, his greatcoat dripping with rain. He feels a sense of pride. He is the Soldier Emperor. He belongs to another type of men. Of course he can sleep in this palace with its walls hung with Gobelin tapestries, he can be called Majesty or sire, but he knows he will never be like these princes. He dominates them, but he is not one of them. He has the singular destiny of being a founder of empire, close to the soldiers he reviews every day on either side of the Rhine, at Kehl, the arsenal or the citadel, and to their comrades he is in a hurry to rejoin in Germany.

'SOLDIERS,' he proclaims on 30 September, 'the war of the third coalition has begun . . . You have had to proceed by forced marches to the defence of our borders. Never again shall we make peace without guarantees. Our generosity will never again mislay our politics. Soldiers, your Emperor is in the midst of you . . .'

Later, he goes into Josephine's room.

'I am leaving tonight. Woe betide the Austrians if I can steal a march on them.'

XXXVI

HE FEELS COLD ON that 1 October 1805 when he crosses the Rhine. He pulls his greatcoat closer around him. The bridge shudders and reverberates under the hooves of the horses of the chasseurs of the Guard escorting his berline. Napoleon shivers and has trouble breathing, as if there was a weight pressing down on his chest. He makes an effort to relax, so as not to have another painful attack, as he did the previous evening, a few hours before they set off.

He had collapsed in his room in the Rohan palace in front of Talleyrand and Monsieur de Rémusat, who had gone up with him. For a few minutes he felt as if the walls were coming down and crushing him, and as if the floor was falling away and taking him with it. A veil came down over his eyes.

When he regained consciousness, Talleyrand and Rémusat were rubbing him with eau de Cologne and he was half-naked. He had dismissed them, demanding complete silence on this episode, which was most probably a fit of exhaustion, but, despite the scalding baths he soaked in all night, the cold stays inside him. If he relaxes his teeth start chattering.

He has to master this body of his, just as one tames a restive horse that bucks. The mount must walk steadily for as long as it is needed.

HE REACHES Ludwigsburg, establishes himself in the palace of the Elector of Württemberg, and scribbles a few lines to Josephine to reassure her. Talleyrand is bound to have told her of his indisposition last night, in order to increase his influence over her by taking her into his confidence.

'I am at Louisbourg and I am in good health,' he writes. 'I faithfully hope that you enjoy good health too. There is a very fine court here, an extremely beautiful new bride, and in general extremely agreeable people, even our Electress, who appears most amiable despite being the daughter of the King of England.'

He imagines Josephine showing the letter around, and her ladies of honour repeating its reassurances. War is that too – not letting disquieting rumours spread.

Besides, I'm better, I'm well.

AT LAST THE weather lets up and 4 October dawns a beautiful day. Napoleon goes out in his berline on the roads, which are crowded with troops on the march who cheer him when they recognize his escort of chasseurs of the Guard.

In the evening in Stuttgart, when he enters the court theatre, the Elector of Württemberg deferentially shows him to his seat and, as the curtain rises, predicts that this *Don Giovanni* of Mozart will be enchanting.

He listens, and then, in the berline on the way back to Ludwigsburg, by the light of an oil lamp, he dictates a letter to the new minister of the interior, Champagny: 'I am here at the court of Württemberg and, although waging war, I have heard some very good music. German singing, however, seems to me rather baroque. Is the reserve on the march? Where are you with the conscription for 1806?'

For war is voracious and one can only win if one can thrust more regiments into its maw.

THE FIRST fighting has taken place on the right bank of the Danube at Wertingen. Murat's cavalry charged, but only after, as a consequence of an altercation between him and Ney, a division was almost crushed by over thirty thousand Austrians.

These are my marshals, brave, often narrow-minded, and jealous of one another.

He goes onto the battlefield. The rain has started again, and the troops are lined up in the freezing downpour, but he is with his soldiers. He is watching as men, those who he has been told by their colonels were the best fighters, step out of the ranks. This dragoon, Marcate of the 4th Regiment, had saved his captain who, a few days before, had stripped him of his NCO stripes and reduced him to the ranks. Napoleon tugs his ear and pins the eagle of the Légion d'honneur on his chest.

THE RAIN does not stop. The countryside disappears under the deluge. Napoleon rides with his escort, the carriages of his suite haven't followed, and they enter the village of Ober-Falheim. The houses have been ransacked and pillaged, the walls torn open by soldiers searching for hidden gold.

Napoleon instals himself in the presbytery. An aide-de-camp prepares an omelette, another a bed. He stretches his legs out in front of the fire and tries to dry his clothes. He feels good here; the news from the battle is promising.

The Danube has been crossed at Donauwerth; Davout and Soult have entered Augsburg; Bernadotte and Marmont are in Munich; the Austrians under General Mack have fallen back on Elchingen and Ulm. They are going to wait for the Russians there, so they must be crushed, fast.

He jokes with the handful of officers standing around him. He hasn't even got his Chambertin here, in Europe, whereas he never went without it once in the sands of Egypt. He is brought a glass of beer. Is it really possible that in such fertile country beer can be so bad?

The next night he sleeps at Burgau, not far from Augsburg.

Victory is within his grasp. He feels it, as he does every time it approaches. He is advancing in tandem with the vanguard along the Danube until they cross it at Elchingen.

IT IS DAWN on 14 October and engineers are building a footbridge under a hail of grapeshot. Napoleon is down among the first soldiers that dart forward. He has been under fire so many times already that it seems as if he cannot be hit.

Eventually the grenadiers take Elchingen abbey, which dominates the river, and Napoleon establishes himself there. The wounded are brought in, in their hundreds, but the Austrians have been cut to pieces and driven back and General Mack, harried by the cavalry charges of Ney and Bessières, has concentrated himself in Ulm.

He is caught in a trap.

Napoleon goes back out. An enemy battery fires on his escort and the horses shy and skitter, but Napoleon remains impassive, galloping on up to the Michelsberg heights where he has cannon positioned which then open fire on Ulm.

They mustn't slacken their grip, so that Mack will surrender.

Then, that evening in Elchingen abbey he writes a note to Josephine:

> The enemy is defeated and has lost its head, and everything suggests this will be the most successful, the shortest and the most brilliant campaign I have ever conducted.
>
> I am in good health, the weather is atrocious though. I change clothes twice a day, it rains so much.
>
> I love and kiss you,
>
> Napoleon.

HE LEAVES the abbey. The freezing rain is still falling so heavily that the walls of Ulm, where General Mack is, have disappeared behind a grey curtain. Napoleon's horse proceeds gingerly along the paths on the heights where he has deployed the cannon. He dismounts, aims a cannon himself, and gives the order to fire. Mack must be kept under constant pressure and driven out of cover, so that he is forced to surrender before the Russian armies come to his aid.

When he returns to Elchingen abbey, Napoleon is shivering, despite the logs burning in the tall fireplaces. The officers report the troops' exhaustion. Rain and hunger are causing the Grand Army to disintegrate; they need shelter, bread, wine; their uniforms are in tatters.

Napoleon listens without seeming to take in what he is hearing.

Commanding men also means not revealing one's anxiety, whilst responding to that of one's subordinates by expressing only complete certainty.

Mack will surrender in a matter of hours, he says. They will enter Vienna, the Austrians will be defeated. It will only take a few days to crush the Russians, and then they will be finished with the third coalition.

He calls in General Ségur, who is going to demand a parley with General Mack. He must terrify the Austrian general, obtain his surrender, subject him to a merciless barrage.

ON 20 OCTOBER the Austrian troops finally lay down their arms, without even having fought.

Napoleon watches thirty thousand men filing past him, throwing their weapons and flags at his feet, like a Roman triumph.

The rain has stopped, but he is soaked and covered in mud. He feels the weight of his hat and grey greatcoat which are dripping with water. He stands with his army, on an elevated slope, dominating the scene. He is the conquering Emperor, his troops gathered behind him, and from time to time he turns round to them.

Victory, as it does every time, has transformed exhaustion and doubt into a sort of joyous pride. It has put new life into every soldier; he is going to decorate a number of them.

'Soldiers!' he cries. 'This success is due to your unbounded confidence in your Emperor, to your patience in enduring fatigue and privations of every kind, and to your intrepidity.' The sixty Austrian cannon pass in front of him, and he exchanges a few words with the twenty captured Austrian generals standing around him. Some of them have traces of wounds which testify to their campaigns against the Turks.

They are brave and experienced but I have defeated them. Who couldn't I defeat?

THAT EVENING, when the rain has started again, he finishes dictating his proclamation to the Grand Army: 'We shall not stop here; you are impatient to commence a second campaign. That Russian army which the gold of England has brought from the ends of the earth shall share the same fate.'

Each time he stops talking he hears the groans of the wounded who have been brought to the abbey. The battle of Elchingen was won at a relatively low price. But tomorrow?

'All my care will be to obtain victory with the least possible bloodshed on our part. My soldiers are my children.'

This proclamation is to be read out, printed and posted, he orders, and then published in the *Bulletin of the Grand Army*, which is designed to inform the soldiers both of the Emperor's intentions and of their exploits.

He sits down by the fireplace and takes some paper. He is going to write a letter himself, with the paper resting on his knees and lit by the flames.

My good Josephine,

I have fatigued myself more than I should. Being all day long for a whole week wet to the skin and with cold feet has made me rather unwell . . .

I have carried out my designs. I have destroyed the Austrian army by simple marches . . . I am satisfied with my army; I have lost only 1,500 men, two-thirds of whom are but slightly wounded.

Prince Charles is covering Vienna. I think by now Masséna should be at Verona.

Adieu my Josephine, a thousand kind things to everyone.

Napoleon.

XXXVII

IT IS SNOWING NOW. Napoleon gets into his berline; the escort of light cavalry of the Guard are already in the saddle in front of Elchingen abbey. The afternoon is just beginning and the sky is low. On the road that passes Ulm, and pushes on into the hills towards Munich and, beyond that, Vienna, that black trail is the Grand Army on the march. Sometimes shots ring out – officers ordering men to open fire on looters, or the men themselves shooting pigs or oxen. The men are hungry and they are cold.

Napoleon gives the order to start off for Munich, and the berline struggles onto the road, its wheels sinking into the snow. He leans forward and tells his aide-de-camp they have to go faster. Everything depends on speed, once more.

He must take Kutuzov – the Russian general who he has been told is a good tactician – and the Austrians he has linked up with, by surprise. At the same time, he mustn't let himself be drawn too far forward.

On the sides of the road, Napoleon sees the soldiers of the infantry of the line marching forward in the snow, their heads bowed. The intoxication of victory has worn off; only tiredness remains. They have been marching since Boulogne and, even if they have not seen much combat, they are exhausted.

We must make an end of it. Force the enemy to fight in the conditions and at the time I have chosen – like a chess player who calculates several moves ahead and lures his enemy into the trap he has set for him.

In the berline driving to Munich, with a map spread out on the seat, despite the feeble light of an oil lamp and the bumpy road, Napoleon tries to picture this trap. It is still too soon. The game with the Russians has not truly begun; Vienna must be taken first.

But I must see beyond that.

He wants the next battlefield to be as familiar to him as all the battlefields of Italy. He begins to dictate a letter to Cambacérès:

'I am manoeuvring today against the Russian army, which is in position on the other side of the Inn. Within two weeks I shall face 100,000 Russians and 60,000 Austrians who have come from Italy, or other corps which were in reserve in the monarchy. I shall defeat them, but it will probably cost me some losses.'

The windows of the berline are steamed up, but he can still see the soldiers' hunched silhouettes. How many of them will fall? He closes his eyes.

The Ogre – that's what the newspapers in the pay of the English call me.

As if he wanted men to die, as if he lived off it! But he doesn't have any illusions either. He murmurs as Méneval looks at him, not knowing if he should note it down: 'Whoever does not look at a battlefield dry-eyed will pointlessly send a lot of men to their death.'

HE IS IN Munich. In the huge rooms of the royal palace, which runs the length of the northern side of Residenz Platz, he is received by the Bavarian court.

He feels, as he does every time he finds himself among foreign royalty, a sort of fearful curiosity, almost dread. He is invited to hunt, which he does, and then he goes to the theatre. He has asked for a concert to be given in his honour in the courtyard. Talleyrand, who has just arrived, sits next to him and whispers throughout the performance, explaining that they shouldn't crush Austria outright, but form an alliance against the true enemy powers: England, Russia and Prussia.

Talleyrand also brings the latest news from France. The financiers are still anxious, and the Récamier and Hervas banks have gone bankrupt. It is feared it will be a long war, and the outcome is thought uncertain.

To the victors, the gold, Napoleon says. So this war must finish in victory.

Talleyrand agrees and then speaks about Josephine, who is very concerned because she has had no letters from the Emperor, and is so perfect that she has won over all Strasbourg, where she is awaiting the Emperor's good will.

Napoleon writes to her that evening:

I have been given details which prove all the tenderness you feel for me, but you must have more strength and confidence. In any case, I had told you that I would not write for six days.

My health is fairly good. I am advancing against the Russian army. You must be cheerful, amuse yourself, and hope that we shall see each other again before the end of the month.

I gave a concert for the ladies of the court here yesterday. The choirmaster is a man of merit. I shot on a pheasantry of the Elector's; as you see, I am not too fatigued. Talleyrand has arrived.

THE NEXT day Napoleon again leaves the palace. It is time to forget hot baths and concerts and resume his journey.

Sometimes in the berline, or even on horseback when he has decided to advance like this with the men, he thinks that he likes this life, roving, perilous, hard. He sleeps in the presbyteries with their rudimentary furnishings. In Lembach he stays in a convent; the cell he spends the night in is freezing and he feels even colder than on the road in the squalling snowstorm. He writes to Josephine:

I am on the march. It is cold and the ground is covered with a foot of snow. Rather severe conditions, but luckily there is no shortage of wood; we are still marching through forests. I am in pretty good health. My affairs are satisfactory; my enemies must be more anxious than me.

I want your news and to hear that you are not worried.

Farewell, my friend, I am going to bed.

But how can one sleep? He picks up the report General Savary has sent him. He rereads it and remembers the strange man Savary has already talked to him about, a citizen of Baden, son of a pastor, an ironmonger, grocer and tobacconist by turns, but also an excellent spy who served the Austrians for a long time. A few days ago this Schulmeister was still in Ulm with General Mack. Now he has changed camp, approaching Murat and Savary and giving information about the Russian troop movements. Kutuzov is planning to draw the French a long way east. Savary must have infiltrated the joint Austrian and Russian headquarters, passing himself off as an officer. He has included Schumeister's notes, signed Charles-Frédéric, with his own notes.

Spies are indispensable.

Napoleon deciphers the minuscule writing for the third time. The details Schulmeister gives confirm Napoleon's intuitions. The enemy must be prevented from withdrawing further east. It is not enough to fight them and thereby enter Salzburg and Innsbruck, as Bernadotte and Ney have done, or take the bridges over the Danube that will allow Lannes and Murat to encircle Vienna and occupy the third city of Europe.

We must fight but above all we must destroy the enemy as I did at Ulm.

FROM THE large room he has chosen as his quarters in the Palace of the States in Linz, Napoleon looks out onto the square and the tall column of the Trinity, which was erected in 1723 in memory of the city's deliverance from the plague and the Turks.

Napoleon stands in front of the window and remembers his plan to go to Constantinople.

He thinks of the destiny that has brought him here to Linz, so close to Vienna which he is sure he will enter, unlike the Turks who could only besiege the capital in vain. He thinks of all the towns he has conquered already, the fifty battles he has fought. Where will his destiny lead him?

'I am manoeuvring today against the Russian army,' he dictates for his brother Joseph, 'and in these circumstances I have had cause to be less than satisfied with Bernadotte.' Joseph must know that Bernadotte, his brother-in-law, is not the stainless marshal he imagines. 'Bernadotte has made me lose a day, and on a day depends the fate of the world.'

It often seems that I am the only one to understand and feel this. Other people, even the best of them, take their time, imagining that the future is in their hands. I am the only one who is entitled to believe that, and I don't believe it. Everything is uncertain, the future just as much as war.

'Everything can change from one moment to the next; a battalion decides a whole day.'

HE REFUSES to receive Prince Giulay, the envoy of the Austrian Emperor, who has come to propose an armistice.

What do these Austrians think? That I can fooled by that feint? Two weeks! Just the time needed for Kutuzov's troops to get in position and for their reinforcements to arrive. Why should I give them time, when the waste of time is irreparable in war and operations can be undone by delay?

Giulay was disappointed, the chamberlain Thiard reports, and has been speaking in an unguarded fashion. The chamberlain falters, but Napoleon encourages him to continue, so Thiard explains that Giulay was amazed that the Emperor, not having a child, does not get a divorce. Why doesn't he think of marrying the Archduchess of Austria, Marie-Louise, the Emperor's daughter? Such a marriage could be arranged, Giulay is sure.

Napoleon goes to the fireplace and stretches out his hands to the flames.

It would be an alliance between the two houses, as Talleyrand wishes, and as used to be customary under the monarchy. Louis XVI married Marie-Antoinette. Have I reached such a point in my destiny? Do I have to take up history at the place where it stopped?

Napoleon turns round to Thiard.

'That cannot be,' he says. He strides up and down the vast room, often stopping in front of the window. The snow has started falling in large flakes again.

'Archduchesses have always been fatal for France,' he continues. 'The Austrian name has always caused displeasure, and Marie-Antoinette did not do anything to soften this estrangement.'

He stands in front of the fireplace again.

'Her memory is too recent.'

WHEN HE enters the park of the palace of Schönbrunn in the late afternoon of 13 November, he walks for a long time alone in the avenues of its French-style gardens.

Vienna is over there, less than half an hour's drive away, and Bernadotte and General Clarke's men have already entered it without meeting resistance; the capital of the Empire has been declared an open city.

Napoleon stops in front of several of the thirty-two statues standing in the flowerbeds, shrouded with snow. The main fountain is frozen and the statues of Neptune, horses and tritons are covered with ice. As he goes back up the main walk, he heads towards an obelisk and comes across Roman ruins. The four chasseurs from his escort, whose job it is to follow him every time he leaves the berline, follow a few paces behind. He finds himself at the top of a sort of hill which is reached by a portico and looks out over the entire landscape; in the distance, in dark fog, he sees Vienna.

Before, when he commanded the Army of Italy, he had dreamt of getting here. Now, by unexpected paths, his life has brought him here, to Schönbrunn, the Versailles of the Hapsburgs – and one of the Austrian Emperor's intimates has proposed he marry the Archduchess, just like a Capet!

Who could have imagined that? And why, after everything else, should this marriage be impossible? Hasn't his life been a succession of events that would be unbelievable if they had not actually happened?

Isn't he the Emperor?

HE ESTABLISHES himself in one of the large rooms of the palace, and through the window he watches the Imperial Guard, who are taking up their quarters. He gives the order to the grenadiers to prepare their parade uniforms and then, when it is dark, he sets off for Vienna, with just his escort.

The city is quiet, but the infantrymen he sees look like a conquered army. They are wearing mismatched uniforms and have bottles, bread and poultry hanging from their belts. The Grand Army is worn out by the hundreds of kilometres it has travelled; he will have to take it in hand before the battle is joined.

Returning to Schönbrunn, he sends for General Bessières to organize a march-past of the Imperial Guard in Vienna as soon as the Guard is ready. The Viennese must be electrified by the army's power and discipline, and so forget the image of soldiers in rags.

He remains lost in thought for a long time as Roustam bustles about in his room, and then he writes a few lines to Josephine:

> I have been in Vienna for the last two days; I have walked around it at night. Tomorrow I receive the city's authorities and corporations. Almost all my troops have crossed the Danube in pursuit of the Russians.

> Farewell my Josephine. The moment it is possible I will send for you. A thousand loving things to you.

He jams the quill so hard into the paper for his signature that the line under 'Napoleon' is a long crooked blot of ink.

He studies the maps of the region around Brünn and north of Vienna. A succession of plateaux, ponds and narrow valleys, the space it affords is restricted, but none the less enough for a decisive battle. But he must act fast. The Prussian troops are on the march. Frederick William III, the King of Prussia, and Queen Louise have received Tsar Alexander with great ceremony; spies tell Napoleon that, on 3 November, the two sovereigns travelled to Potsdam by night, went down to Frederick II's burial vault, and in torchlight swore eternal friendship on his coffin.

Ridiculous. What are sovereigns' oaths worth? Frederick II and the Russians fought against each other for seven years! How long would this friendship last if the Russian armies were decimated? I must be victorious.

On 16 November, Napoleon leaves Schönbrunn. Before getting into his berline he writes another letter to Josephine. The Empress must leave Strasbourg and cross the Rhine:

> Bring what you will need to give presents to the ladies and officers who will be of service to you. Do nothing that is not seemly, but receive the homage paid to you; you are owed everything and you owe only what is seemly.
>
> I will be very glad to see you when my affairs allow me. I am leaving to join my advance guard. The weather is terrible, it is snowing a great deal; otherwise my affairs are in good shape.
>
> Farewell my good friend.

In the morning of 17 November he is in Znaym. He goes for a walk in the snow and looks at the countryside stretching out below the town, which is built on a hill.

The Comte de Thiard comes running up, out of breath and stuttering. Some Austrian officers, taken prisoner, have reported that the English have sunk Admiral Villeneuve's fleet at Trafalgar, close to Cadiz. The battle took place on 21 October and the fleet lost thirteen out of its eighteen ships of the line. The English lost none of the vessels that were engaged in the battle. The French navy is no more. Admiral Villeneuve has been taken prisoner. Nelson was killed during the battle on his ship, the *Victory*.

Napoleon doesn't ask any questions. On 21 October, the day after the victory of Ulm, he had issued a proclamation to the army. It is as if destiny wanted on the same day to show that it was only giving him power on land, not domination of the sea. England will therefore only be defeated on land.

I must win here.

He does not want to dwell on this defeat, which catches up with him just as he is preparing for battle. It has already been buried under so many days, swamped by the ocean of time that has elapsed since 21 October.

Let us forget it. We have to.

HE REACHES Pohrlitz, where he sleeps in the presbytery. The next day he travels the local roads by berline and then on horseback. He dismounts and sees a cavalry engagement not far from the village of Lattein. He knows this feeling that has taken him over, a mixture of tension and calm. He looks at the hills, plains, plateaux and valleys; he sees villages, and imagines the troops moving here and there. In the evening, at Brünn, he climbs up to the citadel of Spielberg, which looks down on the whole area. Clouds hang on the hills; to the south-west the horizon is hemmed by a band of brighter sky.

CANNON AND musketfire can be heard: the Russians have stopped retreating. Kutuzov must accept battle; they must draw him here, to the Pratzen plateau. Napoleon spreads out his maps.

On 20 November in the morning, he dictates a brief order. 'Marshal Davout is ordered to go to Austerlitz.' With his fingernail, Napoleon draws a line under the name of this town, situated below the Pratzen plateau at its southern tip.

THE NEXT morning, Thursday 21 November, he gets up before dawn. He is rested and calm. He mounts his white horse and gallops forward, surrounded by his escort and aides-de-camp, riding along the Goldbach valley, through the villages of Kobelnitz and Bosenitz and up onto the plateaux. He dismounts frequently.

This is where he wants the battle to take place, on these plateaux and in these valleys dotted with ponds. He decides to walk for a while, so Roustam holds his horse by the reins. He turns to his aides-de-camp and orderly officers.

'Young men, study this terrain well, we will fight here.'

XXXVIII

On the morning of Wednesday 27 November 1805, Napoleon is waiting for dawn at the top of the citadel of Spielberg. The chasseurs of his Guard are at the foot of its walls. He wants to look at this countryside alone as it slowly emerges from the darkness and fog. The weather has changed in the last few days: the cold is more intense, but the snow and rain have stopped. There have been heavy frosts, good for cavalry charges which will echo on the hard, dry ground. When the fog thins, the sky is overcast but bright and the sun looms like a red host in the east.

He knows every square metre of this country, this vast triangle where the battle which he has been waiting for, which he devised, will take place like giant manoeuvres on a chessboard. He remembers the games of chess he used to play in the Café de la Régence in the Palais-Royal, at the time when he roamed about Paris, destitute, his ambitions unsatisfied, a general without command and recently struck off the army roll. He would always win, with that burning sense of intense joy when, in the decisive move, he would reach for the seemingly unimportant pawn which would decide the game.

He looks around him.

Brünn is the apex of a triangle, two sides of which are formed by tree-lined roads which join the foot of the citadel of Spielberg at right angles to one another. One of the roads runs eastward to Olmutz. He follows it as far as he can, until it disappears into the mist. Olmutz is where the two Emperors, Austrian and Russian, Francis II and Alexander, have set up their headquarters. Talentless players, they are going to fall into the trap he is setting for them. For a few days now, he has been ordering the cavalry to flee whenever the enemy appears, and Soult's men, who still occupy Austerlitz, are under orders to be ready to withdraw, to leave today, to make sure the Austrian and Russian forces keep advancing.

Napoleon turns and looks at the second road which forms the

right angle at Brünn. Vienna lies at the end of it, and the Pratzen plateau is the hypotenuse of the triangle linking these two roads.

The greatest chess games are always simple. You must imagine what your adversary wants, and then make him think that what he wants, what he dreams of, is possible – that what he thinks is right and what he sees is right. Then he loses his reason.

The two Emperors want to seal off the road to Vienna. He must persuade them that nothing can withstand their will. He is going to pull his troops out of Austerlitz and withdraw. The enemy divisions will advance, spread out at the foot of the Pratzen plateau and attack the right wing, which, after having pulled back, will put up a fight. Meanwhile, the centre and left wing will advance, take the Pratzen plateau, and fall on the exposed enemy flank.

THE SUN has risen. Napoleon goes out onto the Olmutz road with a scanty escort. The light is blinding and he is forced to stop every now and then. The axis will be here, on this rise crowned by a chapel. He climbs it. The left wing will charge from here, rolling up the base of the triangle and, like a door slamming, cornering the Russian troops who will be concentrating on advance. With their exposed flank, they will be like someone standing with their arm in a half-open door, not even bothering to find out if it might slam at any moment.

He gives the order to fortify this knoll, and he hears the chasseurs of the Guard saying it reminds them of the 'santon', the marabout's tomb which they had occupied during the battle of the Pyramids.

He jumps onto his horse and races off down the Olmutz road. A low building slowly emerges from the mist: Posorsitz's coaching inn; a narrower road runs southwards to the town of Austerlitz.

Everything is ready for the battle.

He returns to Brünn.

HE SEES THE horses first, then the Austrian officers holding them. Two of the envoys from the Emperor Francis II, Stadion and Giulay, are there waiting for him. He listens to them, his head bowed. He must play the anxious, irresolute man, tempted by negotiation, unsure of his troops, ready to accept an ultimatum but at the same concerned, through pride, not to be seen to give in.

Look, here now is the envoy of Frederick William III, the King of Prussia, Monsieur d'Haugwitz, who also, under the guise of mediation, demands his surrender. He is so sure of himself!

Napoleon listens to him patiently, and then asks that he go and see Monsieur de Talleyrand, the minister of foreign affairs, in Vienna; he will be able to make a start on negotiations with him. Haugwitz joyfully accepts his request. In the envoy's eyes Napoleon sees the certainty that they will only have to wait a few days for the Grand Army to be a conquered rabble in full flight, and then they will dictate whatever conditions they want to this Bonaparte.

Napoleon gives an aide-de-camp the task of escorting Monsieur d'Haugwitz to Vienna, via the battlefield of Holabrünn where the two cavalries faced each other. 'It is good that this Prussian learns with his own eyes the way we wage war,' he murmurs.

Now, I still have to convince the Russians of my weakness and the fear gnawing at me.

He sends General Savary to Alexander, so that the Tsar can communicate his demands and send a plenipotentiary.

IT IS 28 NOVEMBER, in the evening. Napoleon is galloping in the darkness and mist, and his escort are finding it difficult to keep up. He returns to the inn at Posorsitz. Behind him he hears Lannes and Soult cursing and threatening each other and throwing down challenges. He turns to them and watches. What sort of men are they to quarrel like this? A fight is only worthwhile if it absorbs your whole being; everything else is risible.

He rides through the small valleys and over the hills and skirts the ponds. He is now going to move the pawn everything depends on. He calls an aide-de-camp over: he is to take to the 4th Division occupying Austerlitz the order to abandon the town and fall back towards the Vienna road.

The mouth of the trap is about to open.

He gets into his berline. Wrapped up in his coat, he eats a drumstick and drinks a glass of Chambertin and water. Then he goes to sleep.

AT DAWN ON the 29th he is on horseback. He races towards the advance posts, rides past them, and then returns to his bivouac, which has been set up a little way from the plateau in the direction of Schaplanitz. He is impatient. Will the Russians have played it as he anticipates, advancing to occupy the abandoned positions, and withdrawing their troops from the plateau? Hands clasped behind his back, he hurries towards Savary, who has come back from the Russian camp and announces that Kutuzov's divisions are on the march and have entered Austerlitz.

There! The game has begun in the way he expected. He can go and meet this Prince Dolgorouki who Alexander has consented to send him.

Napoleon pushes his horse into a canter. He feels so sure of himself that what is happening seems completely unsurprising. Then he baulks – what is this confidence? One must *never* be sure of oneself. One can miss out on everything like that.

Suddenly he thinks of Trafalgar. The battle he is about to fight will erase that moral defeat.

HE DISMOUNTS and climbs a small slope, trampling the wet grass underfoot. Facing him, full of contempt, is Prince Dolgorouki.

An impertinent whippersnapper who imagines he has me in his power.

The prince demands Italy, Holland and Belgium – surrender, in short.

I must listen to him anxiously, almost humbly, to convince him that I fear this battle, and that my troops will fall back, or run away, if it becomes more of a threat. This prince speaks to me like 'a boyar who is going to be sent to Siberia'. Let him hold forth! Let him report to the two Emperors that Napoleon trembled with fear before him!

Napoleon returns to his bivouac. The sappers of the Guard have made him a table and benches, like those you see at village fêtes, out of the remnants of doors and shutters. Napoleon sits down. He has some carefree, joyful conversations and then gets into his carriage and falls asleep.

ON 30 NOVEMBER, after having ridden along all the roads and assured himself that the Russians and Austrians are continuing to advance, he retires at four thirty in the afternoon to his berline.

To win this battle every soldier must know what is at stake. I am the Emperor of the French, and not one of those sovereigns who push their men around as if they were pieces of wood.

He begins dictating the order of the day for the Grand Army.

Soldiers, the Russian army appears before you to avenge the Austrian army of Ulm. The positions that we occupy are formidable, and while they are marching to turn my right, they will present their flank to me.

He stops. He wants each soldier to understand the manoeuvre he is playing a part in. If that happens, the Grand Army will be invincible.

Soldiers, I shall myself direct your battalions. I shall keep out of the fire if you, with your customary bravery, throw disorder and confusion into the enemy's ranks – but if the victory should for a moment be uncertain, you will see your Emperor the first to expose himself to danger, for victory must not hang doubtful on this day, most particularly when the honour of the French infantry, which so deeply concerns the honour of the whole nation, is at stake.

He opens the door of the berline. Night is falling. Winter days are short; there won't be much time for the battle. Every minute will count.

Let not the ranks be thinned upon pretext of carrying away the wounded, and let everyone be thoroughly impressed with this thought: that it behoves us to conquer these hirelings of England, which is driven by such a bitter hatred for our nation.

This victory will put an end to the campaign . . . and then the peace I shall make will be worthy of my people, of you and of myself.

He jumps down from the carriage and settles at the table with his aides-de-camp. He talks of the Egyptian campaign; he feels calm. Nevertheless the weather has changed, there are long, raging storms of hail and rain.

But the bad weather applies to everybody.

HE SLEEPS a few hours, at most, in the berline and then, because it is still dark on this first day of December, he goes without an escort to the front of several regiments. The rain has stopped but the sky is overcast, except to the east, where clear patches possibly promise good weather tomorrow. As he is passing the 28th Regiment of the line, a voice calls out, 'We promise that tomorrow the only fighting you will have to do will be with your eyes.'

He shivers; these men have understood his order of the day.

'In a French army,' he tells his aides-de-camp, 'the worst punishment is shame.'

Reaching General Ferny's brigade, he speaks to the men and asks them if they have checked their cartridges. Some shout that they have got their bayonets too; others cry, 'Sire, you will not need to put yourself in danger.'

In the evening, as he is galloping beside the ponds, escorted by his twenty light cavalry of the Guard, a Cossack patrol bursts out. The Russians launch a furious charge, bellowing, their swords drawn; his aides-de-camp get him away, and he rides off across the fields as his escort confronts them.

He dismounts and walks on alone. Tomorrow will be the day of the battle. He walks through the cantonments to his bivouac; suddenly a soldier lights a torch to check who is passing through the line. He recognizes Napoleon and shouts, 'Long live the Emperor.' Other voices join in from other bivouacs. They grab handfuls of straw and set fire to them. 'It's the anniversary of the coronation,' they shout.

He hadn't thought of that. Just a year ago he was walking into Notre Dame.

He carries on back to his bivouac, and when he looks round the whole battlefield is spangled with dots of light, as many torches as there are soldiers, and the shouts ring out, 'Long live the Emperor!'

Savary returns from a reconnaissance. He is out of breath and dripping with sweat. The Austrian and Russian troops have continued their march; they are advancing without even protecting their left flank. Davoult and the right wing are going to be attacked head-on by them tomorrow. At that moment Bernadotte, the Guard, Soult and the entire centre of the French disposition will storm the undefended Pratzen plateau, take the ridge and fall on the advancing enemy armies, while on the left wing Lannes and Murat will turn the whole Russian disposition.

Listening to Savary, Napoleon has played out the whole game once again. Victory cannot elude him.

'This is the finest night of my life,' he says, 'but I regret the thought that I will lose a good number of these brave fellows.' He bows his head. 'They really are my children,' he whispers.

Constant gives him a cup of tea which he drinks slowly, asking that Savary, Berthier and Roustam be given one too. He loves this feeling of fraternity on the eve of a battle, when everyone knows the next day may be the last of their lives. He could have been killed by the Cossacks less than an hour ago.

Tomorrow, if he keeps well away from the front line, a cannonball might still carry him off. He is the Emperor, but he subjects himself to the same risks as everybody else at war.

He gets into his carriage. He is going to sleep.

WHEN HE GETS up on 2 December he sees the fog. That means it won't rain. He is immediately on horseback with his escort at his side, riding along the troops who haven't moved off yet.

At eight o'clock the sun comes up and dispels the fog. The great red disc climbs slowly as the men led by Soult, Davout and Bernadotte begin to take the Pratzen plateau by storm.

He goes to the right wing, puts himself at the head of the reserve and follows the movements of the troops through his field glass. He sees the towering cavalrymen of the Russian Imperial Guard in their white and green uniforms being cut to pieces. He sees the bodies piling up by their thousands. The Russians counter-attack a number of times, and he sends in the horse chasseurs of the Guard. After a few minutes General Rapp returns, wounded, followed by a prisoner, Prince Repnin, the colonel of the Russian guards.

The Pratzen plateau has been taken. The Austrians and Russians have no choice but to die or surrender. Checkmate in a handful of moves.

Napoleon watches the Russians who have ventured onto the frozen ponds to the south of the right wing. He gives the order to fire at the ice, which then opens up. The water is not very deep, there won't be many drowned, but the Russian guns are swallowed up and the artillerymen either surrender or die of cold.

NIGHT HAS fallen so quickly! There's rain and hail as he rides over the battlefield. He has to see this, the dead, the wounded in agony, the dark masses of horses tangled together, disembowelled by cannonballs.

Everybody be quiet! They must hear the moans of the wounded; they've got to help them.

He returns to his bivouac, but he can't sleep. At six o'clock in the morning he is on horseback again in total darkness. He rides along the road to Olmutz; dead and wounded are strewn either side of it; this is where Lannes and Murat crushed the Russian General Bagration.

He takes the side road that leads to Austerlitz. Corpses and Russian guns are everywhere. In the town he instals himself in Prince de Kaunitz's castle.

The victory is just as he anticipated, but he is not at all jubilant. The events have unfolded as he imagined, but he is frozen. He sits down in front of the fireplace in the banqueting hall and writes to Josephine, his back to the fire.

> I have beaten the Russian and Austrian army commanded by the two Emperors. I am a little tired; I bivouacked outdoors for eight days on fairly cold nights. I am spending tonight in Prince de Kaunitz's castle, where I shall sleep two or three hours. The Russian army is not only beaten, it is destroyed.
>
> With love.

Gradually the heat seeps into his body and his tiredness drains away but like hundreds of the other soldiers, his eyes feel as if they are burning. The wind and cold and the rides have inflamed them.

He stands up, immerses his face in hot water and then, while his eyes are still hurting, he begins to dictate. His words must provide a conclusion to this great victory.

He walks about the vast room. He thinks of those soldiers who shouted as he passed that he need only watch the battle from afar. He thinks of the torches on the night of 1 December, of the shouts of 'Long live the Emperor!'

> Soldiers, I am satisfied with you. In the battle of Austerlitz you have justified all that I expected from your intrepidity. You have decorated your eagles with immortal glory ... Those who escaped your weapons are drowned in the lakes ... 40 colours, the standards of the Imperial Guard of Russia, 120 pieces of cannon, twenty generals, more than 30,000 prisoners are the result of this ever-to-be-celebrated battle ... Soldiers, my people will see you again with joy and it will be sufficient to say, 'I was at the battle of Austerlitz' for them to reply, 'There is a brave man.'

On 4 December in the morning, Napoleon leaves Austerlitz castle with his staff and escort. At the Paleny mill, halfway to the Austrian and Russian outposts, he dismounts and goes up to the big fire the grenadiers have made and stretches his hands out to the flames. Here he is going to receive the Emperor Francis II, descendant of the Hapsburgs, who is coming to solicit an armistice after suffering defeat.

He ought to be astonished, but this event seems just as natural as the victory of Austerlitz. The Austrian Emperor's carriage arrives, escorted by his officers, and Napoleon steps forward, embraces him and leads him off a little way from their respective staffs who he can feel looking at them.

He points to the fire and the mill. 'Such are the palaces which Your Majesty has obliged me to inhabit for these three months,' he says with a smile.

'Staying in them makes you thrive so much,' Francis II replies, 'that you have no right to be angry with me.'

Napoleon tries to convince him that Austria must separate its cause from that of Russia. As he walks at Francis's side, he remembers what Talleyrand, who wants an Austrian alliance, said – and Giulay, the Austrian envoy, when he spoke of the possibility of marriage to the Archduchess Marie-Louise. Since he is the victor, everything is possible. He has broken down the door.

He accompanies Francis back to his carriage, embraces him again, and calls him 'my brother'.

Isn't he, Napoleon, the founder of a dynasty that has defeated two Emperors?

Alexander will sign an armistice as well, and the King of Prussia will congratulate himself on not having had time to enter the battle.

Everything is so simple when one is strong and victorious.

HE RIDES back to Austerlitz and the soldiers he passes shout, 'Long live the Emperor!'

Prisoners are stacking corpses in carts, taking them from the piles they've formed beside the road in the sodden fields. He must adopt the children of any soldier or officer who has fallen at Austerlitz and assure their futures. He closes his eyes, which are still irritated.

At the castle of Prince Kaunitz, he writes to Josephine himself.

> I have concluded an armistice; peace will be sealed within a week. The Russians are leaving. The battle of Austerlitz is the finest of all the battles I have fought: 45 colours, more than 150 cannon, the standards of the Russian Guard, 20 generals, 30,000 prisoners, more than 20,000 dead: a terrible spectacle. The Emperor Alexander is leaving in despair for Russia. I saw the Emperor Francis II in my bivouac: we talked for two hours and we agreed to conclude peace quickly.
>
> I have 3,000 wounded and 7–8,000 dead.
>
> There's something a little wrong with my eyes. It is a very common ailment and nothing serious.
>
> Farewell my friend, I want to see you again very much.
>
> I am going to sleep in Vienna tonight.
>
> Napoleon.

On 26 December Napoleon signs the treaty of Presburg with Austria.

ON 30 DECEMBER 1805, the Tribunate meets in a state of wild enthusiasm. Paris is covered in snow, but not a single tribune is absent from this session at which it is unanimously proposed – and accepted – that the Emperor should henceforth be called *Napoleon the Great.*

NAPOLEON: THE EMPEROR OF KINGS

Continuing the adventures of Napoleon Bonaparte, *The Emperor of Kings* magnificently recreates the most thrilling and turbulent years of the Little Corporal's reign. From triumphs on the battlefields of Jena and Wagram through to his divorce and remarriage, it takes us from 1806 to 1812.

Turn the page to read the first chapter . . .

I

HE IS THE MASTER.

Since 2 December 1805, since the Austerlitz sun rose over the frozen ponds where so many Russian soldiers were to drown, useless allies of the already conquered Austrians, Napoleon has been thinking the same thought: he is the master.

Now it is Saturday, 28 December 1805 and he has just left Schönbrunn Palace in Vienna to go to Munich. In the berline taking him to Melk Abbey, where he will stay the night, he has wrapped his legs in a fur rug, but he is wide awake.

He is the master.

From time to time, he sees the silhouettes of the troopers of his escort through the carriage windows, and the words of the proclamation he issued on the day of victory come back to him, rhythmed by every turn of the wheel, 'Soldiers, I am satisfied with you. In the Battle of Austerlitz you have justified all that I expected of your intrepidity. You have decorated your eagles with immortal glory . . . My people will see you again with joy and it will be sufficient to say, "I was at the Battle of Austerlitz," for them to reply, "There is a brave man."'

He is the master.

He can do anything, it seems. As he told his soldiers, he has cut to pieces or dispersed an army of one hundred thousand men jointly commanded by the Emperors of Russia and Austria; and the King of Prussia only escaped a thrashing because France's victory at Austerlitz convinced him that he had better submit without a fight.

Napoleon is the master.

AFTER THE BATTLE Talleyrand came to see him in Schönbrunn Palace. The minister of foreign affairs brought the terms of the Treaty of Pressburg which would drive Austria out of Germany and penalize it for its defeat.

'Sire,' Talleyrand began in his shrill voice, 'everything that conquest has given you belongs to you, but your nature is a generous one.'

Examining the clauses of the treaty, Napoleon saw that, acting on his own initiative, Talleyrand had reduced the financial contributions he had himself imposed on Vienna.

'Monsieur de Talleyrand, you have contrived a treaty at Pressburg which makes things very awkward for me!' Napoleon cried, throwing the copy of the treaty to the floor.

He is the master – Talleyrand should have realized this – but as so often, the minister instead took refuge in politeness and cunning, flattery and argument.

'I rejoice at the thought,' Talleyrand enthused, 'that this latest victory of Your Majesty should put him in a position to assure the peace of Europe and guarantee the civilized world against invasion by the barbarians.'

Napoleon listened, watching the fires in Schönbrunn's vast fireplaces that lit up the panelling and giant tapestries.

'Your Majesty can now either crush the Austrian monarchy,' Talleyrand continued, 'or set it back on its feet. Once broken, it will no longer be in Your Majesty's power to reassemble the scattered remnants and restore them to a single mass. However, the existence of this mass is necessary: it is indispensable to the future safety of all civilized nations. It is a sufficient bulwark against the barbarians, as it is a necessary one.'

Napoleon did not reply. He is the master.

NOW, IN HIS BERLINE, he thinks that it is years since he has had such a feeling of sovereignty, such a sense of control over his destiny, of dominion over the lives of men and the fate of empires. He tells himself that Austerlitz is his true imperial coronation, just as five years ago, on 14 June 1800, he was convinced that victory at Marengo had assured his position as first consul. Everything would have been compromised back then if he had been defeated in the Italian plains; and what would his Emperor's crown be worth now if the Austrians and Russians had defeated the Grand Army at Austerlitz?

His crown would be lying in the dirt.

But he has carried the day. He is the master and now, like

another Charlemagne, he can model a Europe to suit his specifications.

He dreams and imagines as the carriage takes him closer to Munich.

HE ARRIVES IN the Bavarian capital on 31 December 1805. It is cold and wet. The berline drives alongside the royal palace's austere facade, which only has a statue of the Virgin for decoration. Soldiers of the Guard open the bronze gates and, at one forty-five, the carriage enters the palace. It passes slowly through the four courtyards, skirts the fountains and draws to a measured halt at the foot of the great steps that lead to the apartments.

Officers rush forward; the Empress's ladies in waiting hover at the top of the stairs.

Napoleon gets out and looks around. He remembers the last letter he wrote to Josephine. He was still at Schönbrunn, on 20 December. Everything still hung in the balance. Austria was debating the clauses of the treaty. Napoleon had written a few lines in his jerky handwriting,

> I do not know what I shall do: I depend on events; I have no will; I await the outcome of everything. Remain in Munich, amuse yourself; this is not difficult when one has so many amiable companions and when one is in such a beautiful country. I am myself fairly busy. In a few days I shall have decided.
>
> Farewell, my friend. A thousand amiable and tender things.

Now events have decided. The treaty has been signed. He is the master. He climbs the stairs; everyone bows to him; in their eyes he glimpses a mixture of admiration and servility, and perhaps, for the first time, a sort of dread as well, as if such a devastating victory over the coalition between Vienna and St Petersburg has revealed him to be part of a sacred dynasty, whom nothing can resist.

He passes rapidly through the antechambers and reception rooms, walks along the gallery decorated with Italian and dark Flemish paintings, then enters the bedroom. There, leaning against the great gilt bed, stands Josephine.

It is weeks since he has seen her. She has not even written to him. He had reprimanded her in a letter: had the festivities at Baden, Stuttgart and Munich 'made her forget the poor soldiers who live covered in mud, blood and rain? Mighty Empress, not one letter from you . . . Deign from the height of your splendours to take a little notice of your slaves.'

Now here she is, alluring, older, smiling with her lips pressed together so as not to show her blackened and decayed teeth. She makes a shallow, slightly ironic bow, but a bow none the less.

He is the master.

EVERYONE MUST KNOW this and accept it. He makes the decisions; their duty is to obey. He feels powerful, capable of prodigious feats which will make him the founder of a new dynasty, the fourth after Charlemagne. For this he must rally the different nations around his person and his family, make kings of his brothers and relatives.

Now, if he had a son . . .

But he has no son.

At the Munich opera on 6 January, during a performance of *The Clemency of Titus*, he does not let himself be swept up by Mozart's music. Instead, he furtively watches Josephine. She has not been able to give him the descendant he hopes for, the son who is so essential to founding the imperial dynasty without which all his work will crumble the day he dies.

Why must it always be like this? Why must new challenges present themselves just when he has climbed a summit?

He leans over to Josephine.

He has decided, he says, to waste no time and organize the marriage of Eugène, Josephine's son, and Augusta, the King of Bavaria's daughter. It will be the first strand in the web he plans, like Charlemagne, to spin from one end of Europe to the other. He will adopt Eugène, although without right of succession to the French throne. Then he will choose which of his brothers are to occupy the various European thrones. In Naples, why not Joseph? He must be rid of those Bourbons, the King and Queen of Naples, who are in compact with the English. Isn't the Queen of Naples, Marie Caroline, Marie-Antoinette's sister? Hasn't she declared to the French ambassador her wish that the kingdom of

Naples be the match sparking the conflagration that will destroy the French Empire? Marie Caroline of Naples is going to find out that one's fingers can get burnt if one plays with fire.

Napoleon stands up. He does not wait for the end of the opera, but returns to the royal palace. He must act fast. Time is short.

He writes to Eugène de Beauharnais, ordering him to start post-haste for Munich. He extracts the King of Bavaria's consent. He gives his daughter a magnificent dowry. Augusta of Bavaria will receive fifty thousand florins the day after her marriage, one hundred thousand francs a year for her personal expenses and an estate worth half a million francs on the death of her husband.

And now here is Eugène, Viceroy of Italy, with his long, turned-up moustache of a colonel of the chasseurs of the guard. Napoleon pinches his ear and gives him a little pat on the neck – his usual marks of affection. He must trim that moustache, says the Emperor, it's far too long to be to Augusta's liking. That too is an order.

He is the master.

He tells Cambacérès that he is delaying his return to Paris for a few days in order to arrange Eugène and Augusta's marriage. 'These days shall seem long to my heart,' he says, 'but after having been constantly absorbed by the duties of a soldier, I feel a sense of tender release at occupying myself with the details and duties of the father of a family.'

ON 13 JANUARY 1806, at one in the afternoon, in the great gallery of the royal palace, Napoleon witnesses the official signing of the marriage contract. And on the 14th, at seven in the evening in the royal chapel, he presides over the religious ceremony followed by a Te Deum and a banquet. On the King of Bavaria's arm, Empress Josephine is radiant. Still beautiful. Napoleon escorts Augusta.

'I love you like a father,' he tells her. 'And I count on you having all the affection of a daughter for me.'

The newly-weds are to return to Italy.

'Take care of yourself on the journey, and in the new climate when you arrive, take plenty of rest,' murmurs Napoleon. 'Remember that I don't want to have you falling ill.'

After the banquet, Napoleon retires to his study.

The still of night envelops him after the noisy brilliance of the festivities, the shimmer of dresses and uniforms, the allure of the beautiful women, the grace of Augusta and the joy of Eugène de Beauharnais. He loves this stepson of his, who is now his adoptive son. By this marriage a first link has been established with the ruling families of Europe. Max-Joseph, the King of Bavaria and father of Augusta, is a Wittelsbach, whose ancestors appear in all the dynasties.

How can I assure the future of my dynasty that sprang from the Revolution, other than by forcibly, on the battlefield, introducing it into those royal houses whose legitimacy derives from the passage of centuries?

But some people do not understand this plan.

On his desk, Napoleon finds a letter from Murat, probably dictated by Caroline, his wife and Napoleon's sister.

'When France raised you to the throne, she thought she would find you a popular leader, adorned with a title which would lift him above all other European sovereigns. Today you pay homage to great titles which are not yours, which are in opposition to ours, and you are only going to show Europe how much you value what we all lack, illustriousness of birth.'

So, the valorous Murat and the ambitious and jealous Caroline challenge my strategy – out of attachment to revolutionary principles, anxiety or spite? What matter? I am the master.

'Prince Murat, sir,' Napoleon replies, 'I always see you with confidence at the head of my cavalry. But this is not a military operation we are dealing with here, it is a political action and I have thought it through at length. This marriage of Eugène and Augusta displeases you. It is agreeable to me and I consider it a great success, a success equal to the victory at Austerlitz.'

HE IS THE MASTER.

And this marriage is only the first pawn, the first move. He is thinking of combining Holland, Switzerland and Italy into a single entity. 'My Federal States,' he murmurs, 'or the true French Empire.'

He decrees that the Civil Code will apply in the kingdom of

Italy. Hasn't he been crowned King of Italy in Milan? And isn't Eugène Viceroy of Italy?

On 19 January 1806, he offers the kingdom of Naples' crown to Joseph, his elder brother, and orders its occupation by French troops. The Bourbons have fled to Sicily under the protection of the English fleet.

Now the only hostile sovereign left in Italy is the Pope, Pius VII. His Holiness protests, writing to Napoleon to express his indignation at the French occupation of Ancona, papal land.

'I have always considered myself,' Napoleon replies, 'the protector of the Holy See . . . I have considered myself, like my predecessors of the third and fourth generations, as the eldest son of the Church, as the sole possessor of the sword with which to protect it and shelter it from defilement by Greeks and Moslems.'

Why doesn't the Pope understand that?

Napoleon's indignation mounts. He says to Cardinal Fesch, his great-uncle who represents him in Rome, 'I'm religious, but I am no bigot. The Pope has written me the most ridiculous, the most lunatic letter . . .' There is no question, Napoleon rages: Pius VII must submit to his authority.

'As far as the Pope is concerned, I am Charlemagne, because like Charlemagne I join the crown of France to the crown of Lombardy and my empire touches the East. I therefore expect the Pope to accommodate his conduct to my requirements. I shall make no outward changes if he behaves well. Otherwise, I will reduce the Pope to a mere Bishop of Rome . . . Truly, there is nothing more unreasonable than the Court of Rome.'

I am the master.

BUT TO RULE, one must be implacable. One must show no pity, no hesitation.

When he appoints General Junot as Governor General of the States of Parma and Piacenza, he says, 'You don't maintain peace in Italy with words. Do as I did at Binasco [during the campaign of Italy]: order a large village to be burned; have a dozen insurgents shot and form mobile columns to seize the brigands wherever you find them and set an example to the people of these countries.'

But will Joseph, the scheming, hesitant Joseph, be able to display the necessary firmness? Napoleon summons Miot de Mélito, who is leaving with the new King of Naples.

In a curt voice, Napoleon says, 'You will tell my brother Joseph that I am making him the King of Naples, but that the slightest hesitation, the least uncertainty, will ruin him entirely . . . No half measures, no weakness. I want my blood to reign in Naples as long as in France. The kingdom of Naples is necessary to me . . .'

Napoleon remembers his brother's reservations at the time of the coronation, his refusal to accept the viceroyalty of Italy, his older brother's jealousy at a younger brother's glory.

Napoleon draws closer to Miot de Mélito.

'At present all feelings of affection yield to state reasons,' he says. 'I recognize as my relatives only those who serve me . . . It is with my fingers and my pen that I create children . . . I can have no relations in obscurity. Those who do not rise with me shall no longer form part of my family. I am creating a family of kings, or rather of viceroys . . .'

A few days later, Napoleon receives a letter from Joseph, King of Naples.

'Once and for all,' Joseph writes, 'I can assure Your Majesty that I shall approve of everything you may choose to do . . . Do everything for the best and dispose of me as you judge most fitting for you and for the state.'

Napoleon is indeed the master.

VALERIO MASSIMO MANFREDI

Alexander: Child of a Dream

PAN BOOKS

A huge international bestseller, *Alexander: Child of a Dream* is the first in Valerio Massimo Manfredi's outstanding trilogy of brutal passion and grand adventure in ancient Greece.

Who could have been born to conquer the world other than a god? A boy, born to a great king – Philip of Macedon – and his sensuous queen, Olympias. Alexander became a young man of immense, unfathomable potential. Under the tutelage of the great Aristotle and with the friendship of Ptolemy and Hephaiston, he became the mightiest and most charismatic warrior, capable of subjugating the known world to his power.

A marvellous novel of one of history's greatest characters and his quest to conquer the civilized world.

VALERIO MASSIMO MANFREDI

Alexander: The Sands of Ammon

PAN BOOKS

Continuing the epic saga of Alexander the Great, *The Sands of Ammon* brilliantly describes Alexander's quest to conquer Asia, the limitless domain ruled by the Great King of the Persians.

In a seemingly impossible venture, Alexander and his men storm Persian fortresses and harbours, crippling King Darius's domination of land and sea. Even the legendary Halicarnassus is defeated by the Macedonian army.

But the Island City of Tyre and the Towers of Gaza prove to be formidable obstacles. Undeterred, Alexander surges forth over land and sea to the mysterious land of Egypt.

And there, in the sands, lies the Oracle of Ammon, waiting to reveal an amazing truth to Alexander. One that will change his already amazing life.

VALERIO MASSIMO MANFREDI

Alexander: The Ends of the Earth

PAN BOOKS

Alexander's epic quest continues into the heart of Asia and on towards the mystery of India.

The Macedonian Army marches ever onward, crushing resistance at every turn. The beauty of Babylon is quickly ravaged and the Palace of Persepolis burnt to ashes. An empire is destroyed and a new and bloody era begins.

But there are other things on Alexander's mind. An ambitious project to unite the peoples of the empire in one homeland begins to obsess him until the curious beauty of Queen Roxanna gives him the strength to fulfil his destiny . . .

This is a truly compelling, exciting and romantic book and a breathtaking conclusion to the bestselling 'Alexander' trilogy.

VALERIO MASSIMO MANFREDI

Spartan

PAN BOOKS

An epic story of passion, courage and adventure in ancient Sparta

Herodotus tells us that not all of the three hundred Spartan warriors died at the hands of Xerxes, King of the Persians, in the battle of the Thermopylae: two were saved bringing a life-saving message back to the city . . .

This is the saga of a Spartan family, torn apart by a cruel law that forces them to abandon one of their two sons – born lame – to the elements. The elder son, Brithos, is raised in the caste of the warriors, while the other, Talos, is spared a cruel death and is raised by a Helot shepherd, among the peasants.

They live out their story in a world dominated by the clash between the Persian empire and the city-states of Greece – a ferocious, relentless conflict – until the voice of their blood and of human solidarity unites them in a thrilling, singular enterprise.

Full of passion, courage and magic, *Spartan* is an enthralling novel of the ancient world.

MARGARET GEORGE

The Autobiography of Henry VIII

PAN BOOKS

This is a monumental novel, showing us Henry the man more vividly than he has ever been seen before and brilliantly combining magnificent storytelling with an extraordinary grasp of the pleasures and perils of power.

Margaret George approaches her subject from a new and original perspective: writing from the King's point of view, but injecting irreverent comments from Will Somers – Henry VIII's confidant and jester.

In a triumphant blend of historical fact and imagination the author brings to life this most colourful of kings . . . from the young man who married six times, longed for a son and neglected his daughters, to the disease-ridden and fat degenerate he later became. This towering novel will delight all lovers of historical fiction.

'Magnificently researched and admirably written'
Mary Stewart

'The saga of Henry's six wives is, as ever, compelling. Ms George contributes intriguing material to the popular mythology . . .'
New York Times